THE
*DARING DRAKE
SISTERS*
SERIES

A DEAL WITH
A *DUKE*

The Daring Drake Sisters Series Book 2

CHRISTIE KELLEY

A DEAL WITH A DUKE
Published by Christie Kelley

Copyright © 2019 by Christie Kelley

This is a work of fiction. Names, characters, places and incidents are either the product of the author's imagination or are used fictitiously, and any resemblance to actual persons, living or dead, business establishments, events or locales is entirely coincidental.

Edited by Peter Senftleben
Cover Design by Kim Killion

OTHER BOOKS BY CHRISTIE KELLEY

THE DARING DRAKE SISTERS SERIES

THE CURSED COUNTESS

THE WISE WOMAN SERIES

BEWITCHING THE DUKE
ENTICING THE EARL
VEXING THE VISCOUNT

THE SPINSTER CLUB SERIES

EVERY NIGHT I'M YOURS
EVERY TIME WE KISS
SOMETHING SCANDALOUS
SCANDAL OF THE SEASON
ONE NIGHT SCANDAL

CHRISTIE KELLEY

Prologue

Kent 1814

"Hasten your step, Harry, before someone discovers us," Louisa Drake said with a giggle.

Harry, Marquess of Langport, smiled as he trailed the chestnut-haired beauty. Walking into Lord Huntley's study, he locked the door, giving them privacy as the rest of the party played along with Lady Huntley's treasure hunt. While ladies and gentlemen were not encouraged to work together, many of the guests had joined up to win the unknown prize.

Thankfully, Louisa had been standing near him when the announcement of the treasure hunt was made, allowing him to claim her before any unmarried ladies tried to accompany him. Lady Huntley's country parties were typically strictly orchestrated, but after days of rain, she seemed to be running out of ideas to entertain everyone.

"Did you lock us in?" Louisa asked, her blue eyes twinkling with mischief.

"I did."

"You are terribly wicked, Harry."

"Thank you."

"And now we are finally alone," Louisa said with a sigh as she collapsed onto the sofa. "It has been far too long."

Harry walked to the corner table where decanters sat, waiting for the attention they deserved. He picked one and lifted the top, only to determine it was port—not a favorite of either of them. The next bottle was precisely what he was looking for. With one whiff, his nose filled with various scents from figs to spicy vanilla.

"Stop smelling and pour."

Glancing back, he smiled. Louisa lounged with her feet stretched across the pale green sofa as if she lived here. His heart pounded. He wanted to see her in that exact position on his sofa in Northwood Park. After pouring two snifters of brandy, he handed her a glass and then lifted her lower limbs to sit on the opposite end of the sofa with her. Lowering her feet to his lap, he released a long sigh.

"Harry, you are a rascal." She tried to move into a more lady-like position, but he held her ankles in place.

"Yes, I am. Don't forget wicked." His thumb rubbed against the delicate bone of her stocking-covered ankle. No one need tell him how inappropriate it was to have his hand on her limbs, but he'd tried so many times to make her understand how he felt. Perhaps this would help her see him as something other than a friend.

"Did you read the article I slipped under your door?"

Harry smiled down into his brandy. "Yes, I did. Not the usual type of note I receive from a lady."

A low giggle erupted from her. "I don't believe I want to know what kind of missives you normally receive under your bedchamber door. But wasn't the article fascinating? The military believes they will have this little war with the United States over in no time at all now that we have finished with Napoleon."

"It would be lovely to be at peace for a while," Harry responded, wishing she had asked him more about the letters he normally received from ladies. If only to spark a bit of jealousy in her. But that wasn't what she wanted from him. "I heard they have forces heading toward Washington and the fleet up the Chesapeake toward Baltimore."

"The capital? Oh, my," she replied before sipping her brandy.

Harry wondered, not for the first time, how she always steered the conversation toward some news of the day or invention. He wanted to discuss something far more serious than wars and innovations. "I happened to notice you dancing with Blakely last night."

Her giggle raised gooseflesh on his arms.

"I did. I will give you threes guesses what he spoke of most of the dance."

"Having never danced with Blakely, I cannot fathom a guess."

Louisa laughed as she shook her head. "Horses." She sipped her brandy. "It is all he ever speaks of with me."

"Hmm." While Louisa could ride a horse tolerably well, she had no real interest in the animals. "Does that mean, should he ever get the idea to propose, you would reject him?"

She sipped her brandy again before replying, "Of course I would. Could you imagine me as Viscountess Blakely?"

"No, you might even have to give up drinking brandy."

"Exactly." She drained her snifter and held it out to him. "Think of what a hardship that would be for me."

He shifted her limbs off his lap and rose to refill her glass. Hearing footsteps outside the door, he put a finger up to his lips.

The door rattled as a disembodied voice said, "Lord Huntley must not wish anyone to enter his study. Come along, Lady Langley."

Once the footsteps moved away, Louisa brows furrowed. "I think that was my sister and Lord Dereham. Thank God, she didn't find us in here alone."

"Oh yes, that would be dreadful indeed," he said sardonically. After pouring her another brandy, he returned to his seat.

Louisa had shifted her slender legs under her as if to avoid his touch again. She reached for the brandy he held out to her. "I am far too young to marry anyone."

At nineteen, she was the exact age most men wanted for a wife. Young enough to mold to their likes. Not that Louisa would ever conform to anyone or anything. It was her indomitable spirit that drew him to her. She would never let a man control her completely.

"I suppose we both are a bit young for marriage," he mused.

"Of course you are, Harry. No man should marry before..." she paused, tapping her finger against her lips. "Thirty."

"Thirty?" That was almost six years from now. It seemed like a lifetime from the present. "And what is the appropriate age for a lady to marry?"

"For most ladies or me? There is a vast difference." She giggled again as she tended to when drinking.

His thumb caressed her ankle again. "For you, then."

"Hmm. At least twenty-three, maybe twenty-four."

"Why so late? You would be considered a spinster by then."

Someone else shook the door handle, silencing them. "I heard a voice in there," a lady said softly. "A man's voice."

"Come along, Clarissa," a man urged the woman. "If the door is locked, we are not wanted in there."

Harry shook his head while Louisa cocked hers.

"Who was that?" she whispered with a grin.

"Sutcliff."

"Ainsley's younger son? And Clarissa Carter?" She pressed her lips together as if suppressing another giggle, but it finally escaped.

"Her father will never tolerate that match. He expects a title for his precious daughter and not a second son with no prospects."

"You are right." But Harry doubted his friend would listen to reason with Miss Carter. Finishing his first brandy, he noticed she'd already emptied her second snifter. It wasn't that unusual for her to drink two glasses, but rarely this early in the afternoon and never so quickly. "What is wrong, Louisa?"

She shrugged as she stared at the bottom of her empty snifter, twisting the glass in her hand. Rising, she snatched his snifter before moving to the corner cabinet. "My mother believes Tessa should accept Dereham."

"And you're not happy about that."

"No," she replied, returning to her seat. She curled her legs under her again. "There is no need for her to marry so soon. It's only been a year since Langley passed. Tessa should be able to enjoy the benefits of widowhood before tying herself down with another man."

"It is up to her, is it not?" he asked, noticing how quickly she had already taken two sips of the brandy. Clearly, the idea of her sister marrying another older man affected her.

"Your father is encouraging the match."

"Why would my father help Tessa find another husband?"

She shrugged. "I can only guess Mamma asked him for assistance in the matter. He did help with Langley. But Tessa deserves some happiness after her previous marriage. Langley was thirty years her senior."

"What would you have me do?"

Her blue eyes beseeched with him. "Speak to your father. Tell him Tessa deserves a better man than Dereham…a younger man. Mamma listens to him. She respects his opinions…she always has."

He supposed he could do that. In truth, his father would not care for his opinion on the matter. Mrs. Drake wanted a good match or rather a wealthy match. If not Tessa, then Mrs. Drake would insist Louisa make a good match. His stomach clenched with the idea of her marrying anyone. But perhaps that was what should happen.

"There is another option," he started slowly, praying she'd had enough brandy to accept him without overthinking the idea as she usually did everything.

"Oh?" Her brows furrowed in thought. "I've spent hours thinking of an acceptable solution."

"Me."

"You?" Her blue eyes widened. "You want to marry Tessa?"

"No." He drained his brandy for the strength needed to propose. "We could marry. Our marriage would keep Tessa from having to wed Dereham."

She stared over at him. Her eyes were wide with surprise as shock etched her face. "You think we should marry? Have you lost your mind?"

"Always a possibility." His heart sank. There had to be a way to convince her that they would suit.

"I doubt our union would help Tessa," she continued. "Mamma wants all her girls wed and out of the house. Besides, you're a rake. Not that most would deny your right to sow your oats while you are young, but there is no guarantee you will reform when the time is right."

"And that time, according to you, is thirty."

She rose to pace the room. "Yes. At least." She turned and faced him. "Besides, I am far too young to marry."

And yet, she hadn't completely dismissed the idea. Her only apparent objection focused on their age. "You are correct on our youth. However, I believe our friendship would make a marriage most tolerable, don't you?"

Her dark brows furrowed in contemplation. "Perhaps. But we do not love each other the way a husband and wife should."

Don't we? "We would come to love each other in that manner, Louisa."

She scowled at him. "There is no guarantee of that. My parents thought they loved each other, but my mother certainly did not properly love my father."

"I never took you as the romantic sort, Louisa."

She turned away but not before he noticed the blush staining her cheeks. "I have no romantic tendencies, Harry. But when I wed, I want to be certain the man I marry won't keep a mistress."

"And you think I would?" Anger lined his voice.

"Don't be annoyed. You are young still. I doubt you're ready to settle down with a wife and children."

So, they were back to their ages. Louisa wanted him to mature. And perhaps she was right. The difficulty would be to keep her from forming an attachment during that time. "Well, I believe I have a solution."

"You do?"

"Yes." He walked to Lord Huntley's desk and then pulled out a piece of paper. "You say our main impediment is our age. But what if we do not find another person to marry? You don't want to marry for another four to five years. By then, many men will consider you too old, or believe something is wrong with you for not marrying. And there is always the chance that your mother will attempt to match you as she has Tessa."

Her face drew pallid. "I hadn't thought of that. But I would never allow such a thing."

"Your mother can be most persuasive." He waited for her nod of acknowledgment before continuing, "I say we make a deal."

"A deal?" she asked, stepping closer to the desk to see what he was writing.

"Yes."

"What sort of deal?"

"If you are still unmarried by the time you are…twenty-five and I'm unmarried by thirty, we marry each other."

She laughed. "You cannot be serious, Harry."

He laughed to make her think he was not serious. "But of course I am," he added with another laugh. "Do you agree?"

He signed the piece of paper and then handed the quill to her. Seeing her hesitation, he added, "You can use this as an engagement contract if you feel you are being forced to marry by your mother. She could scarcely say no to a marquess."

"We truly have had too much to drink this afternoon," she said, taking the quill from him. "I will agree to this madness. After all, there is little chance either of us still being unattached by that time."

He watched her sign the paper as his smile slowly faded. There was no way of stopping her should she decide to marry someone else. Six years. How would he manage?

Some distance might help his cause and help change her mind. Perhaps he should pay a visit to the estate in India as he'd planned two years ago before he met Louisa. Harry needed to make the trip once before he inherited to have a firsthand account of the estate.

He knew she would miss him, but she also might realize how much she loved him. She was far too logical to accept another man without conferring with him. She would want to verify that she had looked at every angle for a flaw in the man.

And if she did decide on a man, she would be forced to delay any wedding to write to him for advice. He could then return and sweep her off her feet.

India was so dreadfully far away. He would be gone for well over a year, maybe two. Harry swallowed back the bitter taste of trepidation. It was time to leave England.

Leave Louisa.

But only in preparation for a victorious return.

Chapter 1

Northumbria 1819

"Do not stop now! You're almost there. There will be a fire and tea waiting for you."

Louisa Drake knew no one would hear her, just as she knew no tea would be waiting for an uninvited guest. But she needed to say the words aloud as an affirmation to herself that she would make it to Northwood Park without collapsing into a snowdrift.

Lifting her head slightly, she noticed the estate coming into view, not that she could see much detail as the wind whipped the snow sideways. The house couldn't be more than a quarter of a mile down the long drive. She continued to trudge through the snow determined to reach the house before sundown.

Or before she froze to death.

At this point, she wasn't certain which might happen first.

"This is all your fault," she yelled toward the house.

As expected, the house did not reply.

Everything, from her spinsterhood to her current predicament plodding through a blizzard alone was all his fault. Well, she supposed she couldn't entirely blame her unmarried state on the occupant of the manor ahead. That had to do with her stubbornness and pickiness. But her reputation as one of the Daring Drake Sisters had at least a little to do with his family.

His father to be precise.

The rest she could blame on her mother and older sister, Tessa.

And she supposed she should take a small portion of culpability. Not that she'd done much, other than rejecting a viscount, and lately, a gentleman's proposal. Most people just thought of her as the plain Drake sister who tended to stumble at inopportune times and who preferred books to people. Few knew of her friendship with the marquess, which would be considered unacceptable for an unmarried woman. These same small-minded people would never comprehend how a man and woman could be simply friends.

As the drive curved, she faced the arctic wind again. Her teeth chattered. "Damn you, Harry!"

She was truly ready to kill Harry for choosing to mourn his wife at his estate in Northumbria. The ducal estate in Worth was far closer to London and much easier to reach in winter.

After spending two days in a bumpy, cramped, and cold stagecoach, she arrived in the small village of Kirknewton two hours ago only to be told it was over two miles to the estate. Since the snow had just started, she assumed she would have plenty of time to reach Northwood Park before the storm worsened. Immediately after she left the village, the snow began to fall heavier, and the wind increased. Several inches had now reached the ground, making her trek miserable.

She should have stayed at the inn while she visited to prevent any scandalous talk should someone discover them. But the price of the coach, bribing a woman to pretend to be her aunt, and the meals on the journey had only left her enough money for the return trip. Surely Harry wouldn't mind her staying with him. It was the end of December. Who would be traveling this far north?

Concentrating on the approaching manor, she tripped over something, landing face first in the cold, wet snow. She released a scream of frustration as she rose and brushed the frigid flakes off her face, hair, and cloak. This day could not get any worse. Her clothes were damp, her hair half out of her coiffure, and there was the ever-increasing possibility that she would freeze to death.

Maybe storming out of her sister's house on Christmas Day without a solid plan in mind hadn't been her best course of action. She should have considered every detail, especially the cost involved, the weather in the north, and the possible damage to her reputation.

But did she do that?

Of course not! That would have been far too sensible. No wonder she hadn't found a husband yet. She was foolish and impulsive and...and...almost frozen for it.

With weak legs, she took her final steps to the large wooden door and lifted the knocker. The brass handle fell out of her icy hand and banged against the door. An eternity passed before an imposing older man opened the door and stared down his large straight nose at her.

"Deliveries should be taken to the side door," he said in a voice as cold as the blowing snow. "And no, we have no need for extra servants at this time."

"I am here to see Lord Lang...excuse me, the...His Grace." She would never feel comfortable using that honorific.

"For what purpose, madam?"

Tears welled in her eyes, but she brushed them away in fear they would freeze her eyelids shut. "Please just let me in," she begged.

"Oh, very well," he replied, opening the door further for her. "Please do not drip all over the floors. The maids just finished in here."

She wanted to ask him where she should drip but didn't wish to antagonize the man, afraid he would boot her out. "Could you please let His Grace know that Miss Louisa Drake is here?"

"Alone?" he questioned.

"Yes, alone!" Was the man blind as well as arrogant?

"Of course, Miss Drake."

He walked away, leaving her sodden and cold in the hall. How dare that man not even bring her to a salon! She hugged herself to warm up, but the cold had invaded her entire body. Her teeth started to chatter again, and she wondered how long her legs would hold her. Intent on finding a fire, she walked down the hall until she found a small salon with a cheery fire burning.

"Thank God," she whispered as she entered the room.

That dratted butler hadn't even taken her wet wool cloak from her. She let the cloak drop to the floor. Her only thought was to get as close to the fire as possible. The heat beckoned her like a moth to candlelight.

She shifted a large, burgundy wingback chair closer to the blaze and then sat to wait for Harry. Finally, warmth seeped into her, making her sleepy. She rested her head in the crook of the chair as her eyelids became heavy. Her head jerked back as she realized she'd been nodding off. She couldn't let that happen.

Forcing herself to rise, she walked closer to the fire. But the chair summoned her to return to its soft comfort. Louisa lightly slapped her face to keep awake. What was taking the blasted butler so long? He should have offered her tea. Or brandy. Something to pass the time while she waited for Harry.

Her nerves tingled with anticipation. Harry would be so happy to see her again.

"Miss Drake?" Harry asked in confusion. "Miss Louisa Drake?"

He repeated his butler's announcement for clarification. Jenkins must have told him the wrong name since Harry was quite certain Louisa could not be here. In his home. In Northumbria. Her being here made no sense at all.

"Yes, Your Grace. The young woman is dreadfully disheveled and arrived on foot with no companion or chaperone. She does not look like a lady at all. Shall I send her on?"

"No." What the bloody hell was Louisa doing out here alone? Something dreadful must have happened, but with her family, that was hardly unusual. "Did she say why she had arrived unannounced and without a chaperone?"

"No, Your Grace."

Louisa had always been a brash young woman, but this must be important if she so boldly defied convention to visit him. The last time he'd seen her was at the small dinner party his father had held in Harry's honor. The night his wife died. The night he should have been paying attention to his father's actions, not stealing glances at Louisa.

The wind howled around the corners of the house, reminding him of the raging storm. He clutched the arms of the chair, his knuckles turning white. She would have to stay here for at least the night.

Louisa Drake in his home.

Alone.

Rubbing his temples against the painful guilt, he sighed. Louisa had changed him and made him a better man. How could he face her after what he'd done? After what his father had done to her sister?

He would never have left England if not for her. He would never have been forced to marry. She might not know what happened in India, but in many respects, he blamed her.

It always came back to Louisa.

Guilt turned to resentment. Irritation that she had the nerve to show up at his home. Anger that she'd been naïve not to see how he felt about her six years ago. Fury that she turned his life upside down.

"I will see her," he said in a low tone.

"Yes, Your Grace."

"Get a bedchamber readied for her. This storm is getting worse."

"Yes, sir."

"Is she in the receiving salon?"

A blotchy red color saturated the cheeks of Jenkins' pale face. "She was dripping from the snow. I left her in the hall until I knew if you would see her."

No more than she deserved. Harry clenched his fists. His conscience railed at him to do the right thing. "Put her in the salon and get a fire started. I shall be down presently."

As his butler left, Harry shook his head. The man looked down on anyone below the rank of viscount, assuming they were not good enough to speak with the duke. He rose from the chair in his bedchamber and went to the mirror.

Seeing how badly Charlotte had mangled his cravat this afternoon made his lips turn downward. Bloody hell, how would he keep Louisa from discovering Charlotte? It was only for the night. By morning, Louisa—and the memories of the past—would be gone.

He stroked the short beard covering his face and wondered if he should wait to greet Louisa after shaving. He shrugged. She had interrupted his holidays, so she could bear to see him in his disheveled state.

Walking down the black marble stairs, he again thought that her being here would bring back memories he'd tried so hard to suppress. As he reached the last step, he noticed Jenkins looking around as if he'd lost something, or perhaps someone. "Did you misplace her, Jenkins?"

"I left her right here, Your Grace," he said, pointing to a particularly wet spot. "Her bag is still here."

"Did you check the receiving salon?"

"I was about to, sir."

"I will check myself. Make certain Miss Drake did not leave due to your lack of hospitality."

Perhaps she'd realized her mistake in coming here and hastily departed. As if to remind Harry of his unwelcoming thoughts, the wind howled outside. Striding down the hall, his anger at her returned. No matter how important, she should have written to him. There was no reason for her to put her health at risk by traveling during a blizzard.

He walked into the silent receiving room and thought it empty until he heard a soft sigh. Then he spied the black wool cloak on the floor. Stepping toward the wingback chair by the fire, relief washed over him.

Louisa Drake sat in his favorite chair with her eyes closed and her full pink lips slightly parted. Her chestnut hair had fallen out of its chignon, and dark brown tendrils clung to her lightly freckled cheeks.

When they first met, she'd only been seventeen and still had a slight fullness to her face. That roundness had disappeared over the years, exposing high cheekbones on a heart-shaped face. He'd always been fascinated by the soft angles of her face, and even now, he couldn't look away.

"What have you done now, Louisa?" The enormity of her actions caused him to drop into the chair next to her. Any other woman of her station would know how improper it might appear if someone discovered her at his home without a chaperone.

"Did you find her, sir?" Jenkins asked in a hopeful tone from the threshold.

"Yes," he whispered. "Have the maids open the rose room and ask Mrs. Raney for a maid to assist her. And tea, Jenkins. She will need tea to warm up."

"Of course."

For a few moments, Harry just stared at her. What could be so damned important that she would risk her reputation to see him? Of course, she'd never been overly concerned with her name. There were numerous times they had almost been caught on the terrace of someone's house instead of being in the ballroom. Not that they'd been doing anything but talking.

That was all she'd ever wanted from him.

A long sigh escaped his lips. Everything was different now. He was the Duke of Worthington. The responsibility of the estates, Charlotte, the tenants, and so much more, all fell on him. He could no longer be the irresponsible young man she knew so many years ago.

And as a responsible adult, he needed to see to her safety and comfort. No matter how annoyed he may be with her foolish actions. He rose and glared down at her.

"Louisa, you need to awaken," he snapped.

She slowly opened her eyes and then frowned. "Harry? Is that you?"

"Yes."

She smiled up at him. "You look so different."

"It's been two years," he replied with a frown tugging his lips. "And we barely saw each other then. Why are you here, Louisa?"

"Must we do this now? I would like to change into something dry."

The poor girl was cold and wet, and he was demanding answers that could wait until she had changed. "As you wish. Do you need me to carry you?"

She brushed away his hands. "If I can walk two miles in a snowstorm, I can manage a few steps to a bedchamber."

"Of course you can." Always the independent one.

"I am so sorry to intrude." She stared up at him with bright blue eyes. "I hadn't counted on a storm...or the costs at the inns," she mumbled the last bit.

Perhaps she hadn't thought to stay more than the night. But where was she off to then? His mind swirled with questions, all of which would now have to wait until later.

She rose to her full height, which at just over five and a half feet was tall compared to most women, but he still towered over her. While always slender, she appeared even thinner than he recollected. Perhaps it was her bedraggled state, but he never remembered her looking so fragile.

"Come along, I had a room made up for you."

"And a bath?" she asked with a glimmer of hope in her eyes.

"Of course."

"Your Grace, you have more callers," Jenkins said, entering the room. Remembering his duties, he retrieved Louisa's cloak from the floor. "Lord and Lady Gringham, sir. They don't believe they can make the two miles to Kirknewton."

"Bloody hell, when did I start running an inn?" Harry glanced down at Louisa, who had the sense to look dismayed.

"Lady Gringham is a dreadful gossip," she whispered.

"I suppose you should have thought about that before arriving at my home unchaperoned."

Her eyes widened in apparent shock at his tone. What did she expect? He clenched his fists in frustration. "Jenkins, show them into the main salon while I see to Miss Drake."

"Yes, Your Grace."

Before Jenkins could bow to him, the heavy footsteps of the Gringhams approached.

"There you are, Your Grace." Lady Gringham entered the room like a whirlwind. She stopped short at the sight of Louisa. "Miss

Drake, what are you doing here?"

"The storm, of course, Lady Gringham. I assume you had the same difficulty. Like you, I only just arrived."

Lady Gringham pursed her lips as she scrutinized Louisa's attire. "Yes, we did have the same problem."

Harry glanced over at Jenkins. "Ready a room in the east wing for the Gringhams, Jenkins."

"I did as soon as they arrived, sir."

"Excellent." Harry clenched his fists in frustration. Having already seen Louisa, there was no telling what the countess might decide to say to people. He had to think of a way to prevent the linking of their names.

"Your Grace, I do believe I shall retire to my rooms for a bath and rest before supper," Louisa said.

"As you wish, Miss Drake. We shall dine at six." He gave a quick nod to Jenkins.

"Follow me, Miss Drake," Jenkins said before turning toward the Gringhams. "I shall see if your rooms are prepared. Would you also like a bath readied?"

"No, thank you," Lord Gringham replied. "Just warm water in the basin will be enough."

"Of course, sir."

Once Louisa was out of earshot, Lady Gringham spoke out. "How dare that little upstart arrive here unannounced. And unescorted?"

Unescorted? Lady Gringham could not know about that. "She has a companion."

Lady Gringham seemed a bit deflated with that news. "Oh."

"Your rooms are ready, my lord," Jenkins announced from the threshold. "Please follow me."

Bloody hell, Lady Gringham might make his life miserable. A

companion? What made him blurt out that lie? Now he would need to invent a chaperone for her. He had to speak with Louisa before she contradicted him to Lady Gringham.

As soon as the footmen settled the Gringhams into their rooms, he walked up the stairs. He glanced down the east wing hall. Seeing no one lurking about, he turned left toward the west wing. He rapped on the door.

"Lou…Miss Drake, I must speak with you at once."

The door opened, and a petite maid stood there with a slight frown. "Your Grace, Miss Drake is still in her bath. She's had an exhausting day."

"You are?"

"Lily, Your Grace," she said with a quick curtsy. "Mrs. Raney asked me to assist the lady with her bath. As the lady is bathing, you must return later."

This was one of the few times Harry wished he had a better ducal glare to put the brash maid in her place. "Put the screen in front of the tub and leave us," he said in a firm tone. "*If* you wish to keep your position here."

Lily swallowed and nodded as she slowly closed the door. "Of course, Your Grace. Give me one moment."

The sound of angry whispers behind the door intrigued him. "Louisa, I am coming in whether you wish to speak with me or not."

With that, he opened the door just as Lily placed the screen in front of her.

"Leave us," he commanded.

Lily glanced at the screen and then him before saying, "Yes, sir."

"Why did you dismiss Lily? I need her to dress for supper." Louisa's husky voice sounded from behind the screen.

"Lady Gringham noticed you seemed to have no chaperone or companion with you."

"Oh, dear, I was afraid of that."

He sat down on the edge of the bed, staring at the peacock design on the oriental silkscreen. For a moment, he wondered what Louisa looked like naked. Her breasts would be full but barely a handful for him. Her nipples would be the color of a pale rose in bloom. *Damnation!* He could not think of her in this manner. She wasn't supposed to be here.

Frustration crept over him again. She had finally come to him, but now it was too late.

"I told her you had a companion."

A dark silence stretched across the room. Even the occasional splash of water from the tub had quieted. "Why would you do such a thing?"

"What would you have had me say?" he asked harshly.

"Nothing without conferring with me first," she replied sharply. "Now she will be suspicious of every move I make."

"Which is why you must dine here tonight. I will inform the Gringhams you were tired from the trip and took a tray in your room."

"You obviously do not know Lady Gringham all that well. If I do not attend supper, that will only make matters worse. Lady Gringham will believe we are trying to hide something from her."

"We are."

A long sigh emanated from the tub. "And if you sequester me away, she will believe the worst."

He wasn't sure it could get much worse than one of London's biggest gossips at his home while Louisa soaked in tub down the hall from them. Harry rubbed his temples. "Do you realize what you have done?"

Chapter 2

hat she had done!

She was bloody well tired of taking the blame for what others had done in the name of family, reputation, and love. "I have done nothing, *Your Grace*."

"You arrived in the middle of a blizzard alone," he said in a harsh tone so unlike the Harry she'd known for years.

"Of course, I'm alone. I'm perfectly capable of taking care of myself."

Hearing a bark of laughter from him, she yanked the towel from the chair and then rose from the tub, water dripping down her body. Gooseflesh covered her as she wrapped the large linen cloth around her. She strode from behind the screen. "So what else have I done, Harry? Nothing that happened between our families was my doing."

"Christ, Louisa! You are only draped in a towel."

"You are the one who interrupted *my* bath." Louisa sighed. She, of course, knew better than to walk around all but naked. Heat crossed her cheeks as she stepped back behind the screen where she pulled on a shift and then her dressing gown before returning to confront him. "Better?"

"No." His steely gray eyes stared at her until she felt a flush of embarrassment across her entire body.

Her dressing gown covered her from neck to ankles. How could this be inappropriate? "Why are you here...in my bedchamber,

Harry? And what have I purportedly done this time?"

"I told you." His exasperated voice hardened even more as he added, "And what you did was arrive at the home of an unmarried man alone. Even *you* should have better sense than that."

It could not have been prevented. She was done waiting to fall in love. It was time for action. "And yet you could not wait for me to finish my bath to order me about."

His cheeks flushed with the reminder of his transgression.

"And if the Gringhams cannot leave tomorrow? Am I a prisoner in this bedchamber all day and night until the storm passes?"

He let out a heavy sigh as if grasping the complexity of this situation. Rubbing his temples, he said, "I suppose not. But you must act as if you have a chaperone with you."

"As you wish, Your Grace." Louisa knew that there would be no satisfying Lady Gringham. But Louisa could pretend to have a companion with her, which might ease the older lady's suspicious mind.

"Please stop calling me that," he said, irritation lining his voice.

Louisa wondered why it felt good to get under his skin just a little. They were supposed to be friends, not adversaries. While they had teased each other over the years, it had always been in amusement. Not at all like this odd desire to madden him. But she couldn't stop herself.

"Do you not think they will consider it more suspicious if I don't dine with them?" Her lips twitched. "In fact, they might even believe I am your mistress, Your Grace."

His eyes looked like clouds just before a storm. "Why did you come here, Louisa?"

"This is not something we can discuss quickly, and you have guests to entertain."

Glancing over at the clock, he gave nodded. "Very well,

tomorrow in my study at nine."

"Are you always so commanding now? You were never so severe."

"I wasn't a duke then." He rose and gave her a stiff bow before leaving the room.

Louisa dropped into a chair as he left. A lot had happened to them both in the past few years, but he couldn't have changed that drastically. He'd been her friend. Her confidante. They had even written each other several times while he was in India. In secret, of course. At least they had until a year after he arrived when her letters went unanswered.

It wasn't until he returned to London that she learned the truth.

They were no longer confidantes.

He had never told her about his wife. Not one letter to inform her.

Not one word.

She paced the extensive room. She would go mad if she were stuck here all night. Besides, she did not doubt that her absence at supper would only aggravate Lady Gringham's penchant for gossip. At least if Louisa was present, she could make up a tale Lady Gringham would believe. A story so convincing that Harry's name would only be a passing footnote.

There was one man who could aid her. A gentleman who would not be bothered with his name on the gossips' lips, as it was a commonplace occurrence. Being friends with Harry, the earl would keep their secret safe.

And thankfully, she hadn't agreed to stay in her room tonight.

A light rap announced Lily's return. Her maid entered and then glanced over at her. "Is everything all right, miss?"

Louisa contemplated her actions again. Harry might be angry with her, but this was her reputation at stake, not his. "Please pull out my burgundy velvet."

Lily cocked her head and stared at her. "Jenkins told me you would be taking a tray in your room tonight."

She waved a hand at her maid. "The duke thought me too tired to dine with the others, but I find I am not weary at all. The bath invigorated me, so I have decided to join him...and his guests."

"Yes, miss."

At least she had remembered to pack one decent gown. Once Lily had helped her dress, the maid set forth to do something with Louisa's hair. She had always envied her sisters' hair. While Tessa had beautiful auburn locks with just the perfect amount of curls, and Emma's wavy golden tresses took to any style her maid could imagine, Louisa's brown hair had no wave, no curl, and usually fell out of even the simplest of chignons.

While her sisters had the beauty, Louisa had the brains. And the smart mouth that went along with knowing too much, as she'd been told numerous times. Mostly by Harry.

"Take a look, miss," Lily said, holding up a hand mirror. "You look so beautiful."

Louisa laughed until she looked in the mirror. Her mouth gaped, seeing the elegant upswept coiffure. "How did you get my hair dressed in that manner? My maid has about given up on it."

Lily winked at her. "I can't give away all my secrets, miss."

"I love it, Lily."

With a deep breath for strength, she walked out of the room and to the steps. Realizing she had no idea where the dining room was, she followed the delicious aromas as her stomach rumbled. When she found the room, the Gringhams were already seated, as was Harry. She straightened her back and strolled into the room with a smile.

"Good evening," she said in a light tone. "Please excuse my

tardiness."

Lord Gringham and Harry rose as she entered the room. Lord Gringham smiled at her while Harry's face darkened into a deep scowl.

"Miss Drake, it has been months since we have seen you," Lord Gringham gushed. "I do hope you are well. You appear much more refreshed since your rest."

"Good evening, Miss Drake," Harry bit out. "I thought you had requested a tray in your room tonight."

Louisa smiled at him as he glared at her. "Indeed? You must be mistaken. How could I not dine with the Gringhams? They are always a wonderful diversion."

"Wherever is your companion, Miss Drake?" Lady Gringham asked.

"Oh Lady Gringham, did the duke not tell you?" Not waiting for a reply, Louisa continued with her tall tale, "Poor Mrs. Fitzhugh has taken dreadfully ill. That is why I thought it best we stop here for a night or two and not continue with the storm bearing down on us."

Louisa took her seat, and the gentlemen followed suit. A footman placed a plate of roast beef, potatoes, and beans before her. She silently applauded Harry's basic supper. It was just what she needed tonight.

"Indeed, the duke's home would be far more comfortable than an inn. I'm certain your sister would understand."

Louisa clenched the stem of her wineglass as Lady Gringham's barb hit its mark. Would Tessa understand? Her sister had never talked about Harry after the accusations two years ago. And Louisa had never asked. Perhaps she'd feared Tessa would blame Harry for his father's actions.

Lady Gringham sipped her wine before continuing, "We were returning from our estate near Hownam where we'd spent

Christmas. And where were you off to?"

"Yes, Miss Drake, you did not have the chance to tell me to where you were traveling before being waylaid," Harry challenged with one brown brow arched.

"I suppose you haven't heard the news," she answered as she cut her beef. "Lord Ainsley asked me to join him and his mother in Scotland through Twelfth Night." She deliberately paused her fork in midair as if she had just realized this critical thought. "I fear he will worry when I don't arrive on time."

Harry choked on his beef and then reached for his wine. "Lord Ainsley you say?" he asked as he placed his wineglass on the table.

"Oh, my," Lady Gringham said with wide eyes. "I had not heard that bit of news. When did this all occur?"

"It was rather sudden," Louisa admitted with a secret smile to make everyone trust her…save Harry. With a glance at his angry face, she knew he did not believe a word she uttered. "I must admit, even I was surprised since he'd given me no special notice this Season. But since late August, he has called on me several times a week. He asked me to join them before he left to spend Christmas with his mother."

Lady Gringham tilted her head with a slight smile. "Well that explains Emerson," she said so softly Louisa barely heard her.

Louisa looked wistfully toward her glass of wine. "Ainsley seems to understand me in a way no other man has managed."

Harry coughed as if still choking on something.

"Oh," Lady Gringham said with a sigh. "It is past time for that rake to reform."

"Yes, it is," Louisa replied. "I suppose after that dreadful accident that took his dear father and brother, he has to find a lady who will be his countess."

"Your mother must be so pleased," Lady Gringham added as she picked up her wineglass. "She most likely had given up on you ever catching a man."

Louisa clutched her knife, trying to ignore the urge to hurl it at the countess. "Yes, she had thought me to be a hopeless spinster. But time will tell, I believe."

Harry leveled her a questioning look. "I hadn't heard such news either, Miss Drake. I must admit, I am a bit surprised."

She smiled sweetly at him. "How would you have heard anything this far from town, Your Grace?"

"News does tend to reach out here."

While he likely knew about Blakely, Harry couldn't possibly know about Emerson. It had only been four months since that debacle. She put it out of her mind, determined to enjoy her first real meal in days. For a few moments, the men chatted about politics, allowing her time to eat in peace.

"How is your sister, Miss Drake?" Lady Gringham inquired before receiving a cold glare from her husband.

"Emma is recently engaged to Lord Bolton." Louisa gripped her wineglass tightly before taking a large swallow. *Do not ask about Tessa.*

"And your older sister?" Lady Gringham continued as if unaware of how both Harry and her husband gawked at her.

"She is quite well, too. She is expecting her first child in early summer."

"It certainly is about time," Lady Gringham commented before taking a bite of meat. "She has been married for two years. My daughter was barely wed four months when she informed us she was with child."

There must be something utterly wrong with Lady Gringham not to notice how uncomfortable poor Harry looked with this conversation. Louisa had to change the topic and what better than the weather. "Your Grace, do you believe the storm will be over soon, so we might be able to continue our journeys tomorrow?"

He gave her a brief look of relief with the change in conversation. "We will have to see in the morning. It appears to be over a half foot of snow and still falling and blowing."

"Oh no," Lady Gringham said with a sigh. "My eldest, Sarah, is nearing delivery of our first grandchild. I must get to Suffolk."

"We will find a way," Lord Gringham replied, patting his wife's plump hand.

"You may take my sleigh," Harry added. "Once you get out of the heavy snow, leave it with an inn. I will have a man return your carriage when the roads clear."

"Oh, thank you, Your Grace," Lady Gringham exclaimed.

Louisa smiled, thankful that the couple would be gone come morning. Then she could tell Harry the real reason she arrived. She could only hope he would listen to her idea with an open mind.

Harry scowled as the realization struck that he was now stuck with Louisa until the coaches could get through. She couldn't return with the Gringhams after telling them she was off to see Ainsley in Scotland. A story certainly made up to throw them off her real motive for arriving unannounced and unchaperoned.

He and Ainsley had been friends since Eaton. Ainsley would have spoken of the matter when he arrived in early December before heading on to Scotland.

"Shall we all move to the sitting room and have tea and brandy together? I wouldn't think we should stand on convention with only four of us." Lady Gringham wiped the corners of her mouth with her napkin. She placed it on the table as she scraped back her chair before anyone could answer.

"I suppose we should," Harry said as he rose from his chair. "Miss Drake, allow me to escort you in."

He gave her his arm, and her warmth wrapped around him. A light scent of lilac floated around her, kindling his senses. He'd forgotten how beautiful she was when she smiled fully. Her entire face lit with emotion and her blue eyes twinkled. He pushed the thoughts away with force. There would be no thinking of her in such a manner.

"I do not appreciate having my request ignored," he said quietly so the Gringhams would not hear.

"I refused to be locked in my bedchamber like a lunatic."

"Any lady who arrives at a gentleman's estate alone should be locked in a bedroom." *But not alone.*

She broke away from him and moved to the chair by the fireplace.

He took the seat opposite her while the Gringhams sat at opposite ends of the settee. "Tea?" he asked, looking at the ladies.

"Yes, thank you," Lady Gringham replied.

"Brandy, please," Louisa said sweetly.

"Miss Drake, do you think that is wise?" Lady Gringham said with a slight frown. "The taking of such strong spirits is not a ladylike quality."

"True," she said, turning away from Harry's smirk. "But I have taken quite a chill today, and I do believe brandy is the best course to warm me."

Before Lady Gringham could retort, Harry said, "Very good."

He rose and asked the footman to bring in the tea while he poured three snifters of brandy. It had taken all his control not to laugh at Lady Gringham's comment. Louisa had been known to match him drink for drink. After handing the glass to Lord Gringham, he brought Louisa her brandy.

"Thank you, Your Grace," she said before lifting the snifter to her full rosy lips.

Damnation, he had to stop thinking about her in that way. Every time he thought about her, his guilt came tumbling back to him. He would never forgive himself for what he'd done in India.

Lady Gringham chatted about various people in the *ton* whom Harry hadn't seen in years. His mind drifted back to that night years ago at the Marchtons' ball on a warm May night. Louisa had been wearing a light pink gown covered in pearls and small bows. Oh, how she'd hated that dress.

Still, after a few drinks, he couldn't help but notice her standing alone across the room. He couldn't explain what caused him to stare at her. Perhaps it was her height. Perhaps it was the dreadful pink gown. Perhaps it was the defiant look in her eye that told him she would rather be anywhere but in that ballroom.

Once she left the room for some air, he stalked her. When she made it quite clear that she was not interested in marriage or Society, they struck up a conversation.

He should have walked away, but he couldn't. Instead, they talked at length about the tea plantation in India. No other woman had ever been interested enough to ask about it. Every ball after that, they made it a point to sneak away and converse at length about topics far and wide.

She was, without a doubt, the most fascinating woman he'd ever met. Even today, while angry with her for bringing back memories that he'd done his best to bury, he couldn't look away from her.

"Your Grace?"

Harry blinked and smiled at Lady Gringham, who had just placed her teacup down. He hadn't even noticed the footman bring in the tea. "Excuse me, I was woolgathering."

"I asked if you knew of Miss Jane Bigby?"

"I have not had the pleasure."

Lady Gringham smiled. "She is a lovely young lady from a fine family. She is related to the Earl of Bingham if I remember correctly.

This will be her second Season out. You must meet her when you come to town."

"I am not certain I will be in town for the Season this year," he replied flatly. He was done with the Season and Society. Now more than ever.

She waved a hand at him. "Of course you will. You have far exceeded the normal mourning period. You must come to town and find a wife."

"I do not believe there is such a thing as a normal mourning period," Louisa interjected. "After all, I think it should depend on the love you felt for your husband or wife."

"Nonsense," Lady Gringham said with a shake of her head. "Society says one year for a husband or wife is plenty."

Harry glanced over at Louisa as she rolled her eyes before sipping her brandy. "I must say, I agree with Miss Drake."

Louisa smiled over at him. "Thank you, Your Grace. Mourning should be based on the feeling and not what Society dictates."

Lady Gringham gave the room a loud *harrumph*. "I suppose you take no issue with a woman who comes out of mourning early?"

Harry cringed, knowing that jab was directed at Louisa's sister for doing precisely that after the passing of her third husband.

"I do not. If a woman is compelled into a marriage without love, then why should she mourn the man for more than a few months? Likewise, if a man loved his wife deeply, why should Society decree only a year of mourning?"

Except he hadn't loved his wife. He closed his eyes against the shame flooding him. She had been a good woman. He'd come to care for her, but he'd never been in love with her. His choice was to hide away from the memories of what his father had done to Louisa's sister and Harry's wife. Escape the gossip.

"I believe your mother should have taught you that as an

unmarried lady, you must keep your opinions to yourself, Miss Drake. Perhaps if she had, you would not be unmarried at your age." Lady Gringham pursed her lips in blatant disapproval. "We should retire now. Come along, my lord."

Lord Gringham gulped the rest of his brandy and then said, "Goodnight."

They started across the room when Lady Gringham stopped and looked back at Louisa. "Miss Drake, you must also retire."

"I must?" Louisa said in a surprised voice.

"You cannot be left alone with His Grace. It is highly improper." Louisa looked askance over at him.

"Goodnight, Miss Drake," he said, grateful to not be left alone with her. She would want to talk when he only wished to be left alone.

"Come along now, Miss Drake," Lady Gringham said sternly. "Your chaperone is upstairs, so I must see to your reputation."

"Goodnight, Your Grace," Louisa said tightly.

Harry watched her walk away and sighed. Having her here wreaked havoc on his senses. The sooner she left, the better, before she, or the Gringhams, discovered Charlotte. That would only cause more difficulties.

Chapter 3

Louisa dressed the next morning slowly, hoping by the time she arrived downstairs the Gringhams would have departed. Facing Harry required every ounce of courage with no distractions. Even after days in the coach, she had no idea what she would do if he rejected her request.

His wife's death had changed him from the light-hearted rascal she'd known to someone much more solemn. She didn't know this man, and that frightened her. Before he had married, Harry would have teased Louisa's plan out of her instead of demanding a reason for her presence.

She missed that Harry.

With a breath for courage, she proceeded down the stairs. As she reached the last step, the Gringhams walked out of the salon, followed by Harry. Lady Gringham's brows furrowed with concern.

"I am terribly worried about leaving you before your companion is well," Lady Gringham said, reaching for Louisa's hands. "Perhaps I should check on her myself."

"I just did. Mrs. Fitzpatrick is much recovered today. I'm quite certain she will be able to join us for supper, and by tomorrow we shall continue on to Scotland."

Harry's lips formed a tight line as if he was trying to contain a comment. Louisa wondered what he was bothered about now. Perhaps he was only trying to keep from blurting out that her companion wasn't real.

Lady Gringham pulled away with a frown. "Of course, my dear," she muttered slowly. "Good luck with Lord Ainsley. I do hope he is up to your rather high expectations."

Louisa pressed her lips together and gave the woman a brief nod. The nerve of that woman. Was it truly high expectations that she might want a man who would respect her and her opinions? A man who might be companionable? While she'd always thought she wanted love, the reality of her situation had slapped her in the face with Emma's engagement.

Twenty-five, unmarried, and no prospects.

"Safe travels," Harry said as the couple walked out to the drive. Once the door shut, he turned to Louisa with a deep scowl and added, "You do realize you gave your companion a new name."

"I beg your pardon?"

"It was Mrs. Fitzhugh, not Mrs. Fitzpatrick."

"No." Louisa slapped her hand over her mouth. She could not have made such a blunder. This would only drive Lady Gringham's suspicion even more.

This plan was a dreadful notion. If Louisa had only stopped to discuss her scheme with either of her sisters, they would have talked her out of it. But no, she had impetuously run off without thinking something through. It wasn't like her to act so rashly. She was the one who thought things through, made thorough plans, lists to remember details. But she had done none of that before leaving Tessa's home.

"Now that they are on their way, it is time we talked," Harry commanded as he clasped her elbow and led her toward his study.

Her courage failed her. "Perhaps I should return to town. Coming here was a mistake."

"I am quite certain it was a mistake, but one you have committed to so now you will tell me why you are here."

Louisa sat in the brown leather chair across the mahogany desk from him and then sighed. She couldn't just blurt out her idea. Seeing the look of irritation on his face, she had to say something.

"Very well," she started deliberately. "As you know, Tessa is happily married with a child on the way, and Emma is betrothed to Lord Bolton."

"Yes, you said as much last night." His lips turned down. "What does any of this have to do with you being in my home alone?"

She bit her lip and tried to think about how to broach the subject with him. Seeing how much he'd changed in the past few years, she doubted he would care about her predicament.

"Louisa?"

Louisa blinked, then looked away from the image of him leaning back in his seat. Certainly, she had perceived how handsome he was years ago, but since she'd arrived here, she couldn't seem to stop noticing everything about him. The way his gray waistcoat cut across his broad chest and the lovely way his trousers stretched over his bottom. His strong jaw and the straight line of his nose. And then there was his mouth. How had she never truly looked at his lips before now? Perfectly formed and made for kissing ladies senseless.

How had she not noticed any of this before now?

"Louisa?"

"Oh Harry, I've made a real mess of things," she admitted softly, staring down at her hands.

"How so?"

"While there was some talk after Blakely, it died down quickly due to his honorable behavior." She hesitated to tell him more.

He tilted his head and stared over at her. "What happened, Louisa?"

"Mr. Emerson started to court me a few months ago."

"Emerson? Even I know he's a scoundrel."

"I agree. But he didn't seem to understand that I wanted no part of his attentions. He believed when Tessa's husband received his inheritance, that I would have a larger dowry. After a fortnight of calling on me, he proposed."

"You damn well better have rejected him."

She gave him a weak smile. "And that is what caused the talk. Within two days the gossips were attacking my name for refusing yet another suitor. Some started calling me the *Selective Spinster*, which only brought to everyone's mind my sister's moniker of the *Cursed Countess*. Many people thought it quite humorous."

Harry blew out a long sigh. "And what does any of this have to do with me?"

"With everything that happened, it made me think about marriage and who could help me achieve that state." Perhaps she could still reach him with humor. She pulled the worn slip of paper from her pocket and held it up. With a timid smile, she said, "I still have this, you know. I could hold you to it."

She slid the note across the width of the desk as his scowl deepened. How could she think this would be a good idea? The old Harry would read the pact and laugh, knowing it was in jest. But with this Harry, she had no sense of how he would react. Second thoughts forced her to reach out and try to retrieve the paper, but he snatched the note from her.

"What is this?" he asked with furrowed brows.

"A promise we made to each other years ago." She cast him a broad smile, hoping he would see she wasn't serious.

As he opened the paper, his jaw tightened. "This is not legal in any sense of the word."

"Legal?" That was his thought process now? She took his attitude as a challenge, refusing to back down and tell him her real reason for being here. "Perhaps not, but it does clearly state that if I reached the age of twenty-five and you thirty, we would marry if we had not already done so. It is more a matter of honor than legalities."

She watched as his fists clenched tightly, and his lips pressed together as if holding back his rage.

"We were drunk," he bit out.

"Yes, I had imbibed a bit too much that afternoon. While you had barely touched your second brandy, so I doubt you were foxed. And if my alcohol-soaked memory serves me, you wrote the pact. I only signed it."

She still remembered that day like it happened yesterday. After lamenting her sister's upcoming engagement—and drinking far too much brandy—they'd struck their agreement. Both assuming they would be long married when the time came. When she'd found the paper before she departed town, she thought it might remind him of all the lovely times they'd shared, not infuriate him.

"I won't be thirty for a few months yet." He stared down at the paper again.

"But I turned twenty-five two months ago." She supposed the time had come to confess her motive.

Harry blew out a long sigh. "Did you do this on purpose?"

"Do what?"

"Attempt to compromise yourself?"

"Compromise…?" Louisa's mouth fell open. "How can you ask such a thing of me?"

"You arrived so conveniently before the Gringhams. No chaperone in tow. And when I requested you remain in your room last night, you defied me. You gave Lady Gringham an incorrect chaperone name. Then, you hurl a paper at me demanding marriage."

Stunned, she could only stare at him for a long moment with her mouth agape. How could her dearest friend believe such a thing? "You are truly mad, Harry," she whispered.

"Am I? You are the one who stated you needed my help."

"Yes, with marriage." Well, that didn't come out exactly as she'd hoped, but before she could clarify, he rose to his full height.

Leaning over the desk, he stared down at her until she looked away from his hard glare. "Do I need to remind you of all the complications between our families?"

Nothing that happened was his or her fault. Her ire rose as she jumped out of her seat, slapped her hands down on the desk, and leaned across until they were only a few inches apart. She could feel his heated breath on her cheek.

"I hardly think you need to remind me that *your* father murdered three of my sister's husbands *and* your wife before cowardly committing suicide to avoid the repercussions of his actions."

A low hiss escaped his mouth as they glared at each other for a long moment. Her gaze slid to his lips. Were they always so perfect for kissing? Louisa's heart pounded in her chest as she stared at him. It would only take a slight movement to reach his lips. With that thought, she jolted back as if burned from the scorching heat of his gaze.

What just happened?

She didn't desire Harry! If she hadn't wanted him when he was a light-hearted young man, she couldn't possibly desire him now. He was so different. Darker. Colder. Handsome. Intriguing.

No!

"Harry, I want to be married," she whispered, easing herself back into her seat as her anger dissipated. "I want children."

Why did everything she say come out wrong today?

"You came all this way to get me to marry you?" He slowly returned to his seat with a long sigh.

"I did not expect you to run into my arms and propose when I gave you that paper. Five years ago, if I had tossed that paper at you, you would have laughed and teased me until I gave you the real reason. What happened?"

"I inherited a dukedom with responsibilities. I do not have time for amusements any longer." He folded his arms over his chest and stared at her. "So, if you haven't come here to demand marriage of me, why are you here...alone?"

"As I said, I need your help, but you haven't returned a letter to me in years. I felt I had no choice but to come out here." She shrugged. "And who would I have coerced into coming with me? Tessa is with child and Emma is about to plan her life with Bolton."

"A friend?" he suggested. "A maid?"

"All my friends are married now. And we only have one maid for my mother, Emma, and me."

He closed his eyes, but she noticed the way his fists clenched and unclenched as if fighting with his anger. "Why didn't you marry Blakely two years ago when he proposed?"

She rose and paced the length of the room from the fireplace to her empty chair. "I don't know...yes, I do. I just couldn't...I mean, how could I? He was a lovely man. I should have been able to...but I couldn't. Could you imagine me with him? It just—"

"Louisa, you are babbling."

She stopped in the middle of the room and placed her hands on her hips, breathing hard. "He talked more about his damn horses than any other topic."

He cast her a ghost of a smile. "The man does love his horses."

She returned to her seat with a sigh. "I'm a spinster, Harry. Once Emma marries, it will be Mamma and me, living in the house slowly driving each other mad. I cannot live that way. I must marry."

"You have a major flaw in your plan."

Considering her lack of thoroughness, it was entirely possible.

"How exactly am I supposed to help you? My father was instrumental in the ruination of your family's name."

His hands continued to tighten into fists. Perhaps it wasn't just anger causing his emotional distress, she thought. Irritation. Her being here had brought back all the memories of the evils his father had wrought. Why would he wish to help her?

"I want you to find me a husband. Foolish of me, I know."

Harry looked up at the ceiling. "I am sorry, Louisa. But you ask too much of our past friendship."

Past friendship?

Now they couldn't even be friends? Her heart ached with sadness.

Of course, he was a duke and didn't want to help a plain woman, whose family reputation was questionable at best, find a husband. And being a duke, he certainly couldn't maintain a friendship with her. She rose and commenced pacing again, only so he wouldn't detect how her eyes welled with tears.

She'd been so wrong about coming here and asking him for assistance. Leaving seemed her only recourse now, but she was stuck until the snow was packed down enough for the coaches to get through again.

"Louisa—"

A slight rap on the door sounded. "What is it?"

"Your Grace," Jenkins said as he opened the door. "I am sorry to intrude, but Lady Charlotte insists you join her for tea."

Lady Charlotte? Who the devil was Lady Charlotte?

"Of course, we have finished here anyway," Harry responded with a glance at her. "Excuse me, Miss Drake."

Before she could get a word out of her speechless mouth, he strode from the room. Had Harry remarried? If so, why hadn't his wife joined them for supper last night? Louisa stood and then followed Jenkins out of the room.

"Jenkins, where is Lady Charlotte? I have not greeted her properly."

"In the nursery, miss."

"Of course," she replied. "Thank you."

Had he remarried and had a child already? Without even telling her? Without introducing her?

She clutched the balustrade for support. No! He couldn't be married already. Everything would be ruined. No wife would allow her husband to help a woman find a husband.

Determined to discover the truth, Louisa raced up the stairs to the third floor where the nursery was located. She could hear high-pitched giggles emanating from the room. Slowly, she peeked into the room and then covered her gaping mouth. Harry lay sprawled out on the floor of the room with a small dark-haired girl no older than three sitting on top of his chest.

It made no sense. While Louisa had only met the late duchess twice before her murder, there had been no talk of a child. Harry's father had never mentioned a granddaughter. But seeing the black hair on her, Louisa knew the girl would also have light caramel skin and likely brown eyes just like her mother.

"You have a daughter," she whispered in awe.

The little girl turned and looked at her with a frown. "Papa, who's that?"

Harry lifted his head from the floor and scowled at her. "Louisa, what are you doing up here?"

The little girl scrambled off her father and stood to stare at Louisa. "Who are you?"

Louisa suppressed a smile at the little girl's brashness. Seeing her stand, Louisa realized the girl was either tall for her age or closer to four than she'd initially thought. "A friend of your father's."

Big brown eyes with long dark lashes dominated Charlotte's small face. "Papa, may she join us for tea?"

Harry sat up, brushed his fingers through his hair, and leveled Louisa a dark look. "I'm certain she has other things to do, poppet."

Oh, no. He was not about to scare Louisa off. She smiled down at the little girl. "I would be most pleased to join you for tea, Lady…"

He rose to his feet and waved her in. "Miss Drake, this is my daughter, Charlotte."

"Lady Charlotte, it is a great pleasure to meet you," Louisa said with an exaggerated curtsy to her.

"Miss Drake," Charlotte replied with a deep curtsy to her. "It is a pleasure." She turned back to her father. "Is that right, Papa? Nurse makes me practice."

"You did it perfectly," he replied, smiling down at Charlotte.

A daughter. Another thing he had kept from her.

"Miss Drake, sit here," Charlotte said, pointing to a child size chair.

"Thank you." Louisa took the seat as Harry attempted to sit in the chair across from her.

"This never works," he grumbled, moving the chair out of the way to sit on the floor. He stretched his long limbs under the table. His leg brushed against hers as he tried to find the best way to sit at a table much too small for him.

She ignored the rush of gooseflesh his movement caused. She must be desperate for a husband if Harry caused such reactions.

Charlotte giggled as her father tried to sit. Her smile touched Louisa's heart. She wanted a husband who had no issue joining his daughter for tea even if his body was too large to fit at the table and the teacups too small. Determination filled her as she glanced over at him. He gave her a half-smile and a shake of his head. His russet colored hair was longer than she'd ever seen on him and made him far more handsome. Or maybe it was the beard he had not yet shaved. She rather liked it on him.

"Now, who will pour?" Harry asked.

"Miss Drake."

"Ah, but the guest should never be asked to pour the tea," Louisa said firmly to Charlotte. "The hostess must oblige her guests."

"Oh," the little girl said with a pout. "Nurse says I spill."

"Nonsense," Louisa said with a smile. "Even if you spill some, we will clean it up straight away."

Charlotte stared at the small teapot. "Very well." She concentrated as she picked up the teapot and poured a little into Louisa's cup. "I did it!"

"Yes, you did," Louisa replied. "Now you must pour some for your father and then yourself."

Charlotte pressed her lips together, and her dark brows furrowed as she carefully poured some tea into Harry's cup. The expression of concentration on her face reminded Louisa of Harry. Other than her mother's Indian coloring, the girl had Harry's strong jaw and bright smile.

"Very good, Charlotte," Harry said after she had completed pouring.

"But I spilled," she said, pointing to the spot.

Louisa placed her napkin on the damp stain to soak up the tea. "I will tell you a secret," Louisa said, leaning in closer to Charlotte. "I still spill a little tea every time I pour."

"You do?" Charlotte asked with a tone of amazement.

"Yes, she does," Harry added with a smile to his daughter.

Charlotte giggled again. "Biscuit, Miss Drake?"

"Thank you, Lady Charlotte." Louisa picked up the small biscuit and took a bite. "These are excellent." She then sipped her tepid tea.

"Oh, no!" Charlotte exclaimed. "I forgot to ask what you put in your tea."

"She drinks it plain. No sugar, no milk, and no lemon. Very odd, don't you think?" Harry smiled at Charlotte.

"Very odd," Charlotte parroted her father before pouring a healthy amount of milk into her teacup.

He remembered how she drank her tea. Louisa thought that particularly odd. "Now, you must make conversation, Lady Charlotte."

Charlotte looked over at her as if attempting to decide on an appropriate question. "Where did you come from?"

"Where did you come from, Miss Drake?" Harry corrected her.

"London."

The little girl's brown eyes widened.

Louisa smiled and continued, "London is a very busy and noisy town. It's not like here where you can go outside and have all this greenery around you. In town, people stay up very late and then call on their friends in the afternoon before going to balls in the evening."

Charlotte sighed wistfully. "I wanna go to London. There're elephants in London. Nurse says Mamma rode an elephant."

"Your mother was raised in India, where there are plenty of elephants, poppet. There are not many in England."

"There is one elephant I am aware of," Louisa said then looked over at Harry. "You must take her to see Chunee."

"Miss Drake," Harry said in a low tone. "I do not believe my daughter is of an age to go to London."

Charlotte's eyes watered. "I wanna see an elephant."

Harry tilted his head and stared at Louisa as if to say, "*See what you've done.*"

"I am sure when you are a little older, your father will take you to town, and you can see Chunee then," Louisa said softly.

"I wanna go now!"

"Charlotte," Harry scolded in a fatherly tone. "We will go, but not today. Even Miss Drake is stuck here because of the snow."

"That is very true," Louisa said. "The time to go to London is in the spring when the weather is warmer, and your father can take you riding in Hyde Park." She smiled sweetly at Harry.

He narrowed his eyes on her before glancing over at his daughter. "Perhaps we shall go this spring, Charlotte. If you learn everything Nurse wants you to know."

The little girl smiled, not sensing the tension between them. "I will! I promise!"

"I have no doubt of that, Charlotte," Harry said but still frowned at Louisa. "Nurse has returned, and Miss Drake and I have much to discuss."

"We do?" Louisa said innocently. "I thought we had finished with our discussion."

He tilted his head at her. "Oh, no, we have much more to speak of now." He scrambled back to his feet before leaning over and kissing his daughter on the forehead.

"What do you say to Miss Drake, Charlotte," her nurse prompted.

"Thank you for coming to tea, Miss Drake." Charlotte glanced over at her nurse, who nodded her approval.

"Thank you for inviting me for tea, Lady Charlotte." Louisa gave the three-year-old a quick curtsy and then smiled as the little girl did the same. Harry clasped Louisa's arm and led her out the room. "Are we going somewhere, Your Grace?"

"Back to my study."

"I believe we have already discussed everything, and I am rather tired. I shall retire to my bedchamber for a rest. Good day, Your Grace." She twisted her arm out of his firm grip and raced to her room. As she closed the door behind her, she leaned against it with a long sigh.

That little girl needed a mother.

Chapter 4

Harry paced his study as aggravation simmered in him. How dare she come back into his life and create such chaos? His being here suited him just fine. Until *she* arrived, Charlotte had no notion of going to town or seeing elephants, at least none that he heard of before today. He enjoyed his quiet life away from everyone.

It had taken him years to get over Louisa. Even after what happened with Sabita in India, he'd always thought how ashamed Louisa would have been of his actions. But he'd pushed those feelings aside to focus on his wife and daughter. For a year it worked, until upon his return from India, he saw Louisa again at his father's home.

He had deliberately arrived late for the small dinner party that night two years ago. His father had befriended Mrs. Drake and her daughters when they had first arrived in London. Harry had known they would be attending the dinner party, but he hadn't known they were the only guests Father had invited. Seeing Louisa at the long table had brought back feelings he'd tried to forget.

If he'd paid more attention to his wife, and not the woman he could never have, maybe, just maybe, Sabita would still be alive. He might have noticed how oddly his father acted that night. How strange that a duke would pour wine for Harry and Sabita with three footmen in the room.

Instead of watching his father, he'd been gazing at Louisa out of the corner of his eyes.

Now his mind thought of nothing but her again. In one day, Louisa Drake had turned his life upside down.

With her here less than one day, those feelings were returning, and he couldn't allow that to happen.

He should have known the brash woman would follow him up to the nursery. Now she knew about Charlotte. Now everyone might know. He could not bear to see the pain on his daughter's face when she saw the scorn of the ton for nothing more than being half-Indian. Those gossipy women in town were all dreadful people, which was part of the reason he had chosen to live at his estate in the North.

He had to keep Charlotte safe from them. And he'd been doing an excellent job of it.

Until Louisa came to call.

"Damnation!"

She had done more than turn his life out of order. She had brought back sensations in him that he had buried. Lust was at the top of the list. He couldn't take Louisa to his bed as much as he might wish it. She deserved a better man.

"Damn her!"

"What are you damning me for now?"

He turned and found her at the threshold of his study. Once again, tendrils of hair had slipped out of her chignon, framing her heart-shaped face in hues of red, gold, and brown. The breath left his lungs in a rush.

"Why do you think I was speaking of you?"

Her light laugh suffused the room and swirled around him until gooseflesh rose on his arms. *Damn her!*

"Who else would you be using such indelicate language on?" She stepped into the room and took a seat near the door as if to make a quick escape should she require. "And it's hardly the first time you have cursed me. Do you remember when we caught Lord Ridgely having...well...*in flagrante delicto*," she paused, her cheeks turning pink, "with a woman who was not Lady Ridgely? If I remember you blamed that all on me for wanting to discuss the economic effects the war had had on England in the back of the gardens."

"I thought you wished to rest." He stood near the fireplace staring at the flickering flames.

"I daresay we did not finish our conversation after all."

"Oh?" He moved to a seat closer to her. "And what part did we forget?"

"I wish to learn why you are so unwilling to assist me, Harry. You know me better than any man. And as a man yourself, you know which of the currently available gentlemen would make a good husband for me."

A husband. She wanted him to find her a husband. He couldn't do it. The more time he spent with her, those too familiar feelings came back to him. And he couldn't allow that to happen. He muttered a curse under his breath.

"I did hear you."

"I beg your pardon," he muttered.

"Now, back to my plan. All you need to do is come to town for the Season. Introduce me to some eligible gentlemen with whom you think I will be compatible. If I find one I agree with, then if needed, you might exert a little ducal influence on the man."

Exert a little ducal influence? "Louisa, I haven't been part of Society in years. I'm certain when the Season starts you will find the perfect man."

Her face fell as she shook her head. "Harry, I am twenty-five years old. This year marks my seventh Season. The men out there desire younger ladies without any disgrace attached to their name."

The last thing he needed was Louisa Drake reminding him of what his father had done to them all. Many people had wondered if the late duke had been mad to kill those people and then take his own life. His sister had told Harry there was some speculation making the rounds that he might also be insane for burying himself out here for so long.

"You are not the only one whose name has suffered," he said in a biting tone.

"You are right." Closing her eyes for a long moment, she finally said, "But you are a man. And a duke at that. No real harm has come to your name."

More guilt knifed him in the belly. It was his father's fault, not his. Seeing Louisa's pained face across from him, he couldn't help but think he had some blame in the matter. He should have noticed the changes in his father before he left for India.

"Louisa, I do not have the connections any longer," he said, hating how she blinked quickly as if hiding tears.

She slowly rose and looked over at him, but not with tears in her eyes. Those blue orbs shone with the fire of anger. "You are the Duke of Worthington. If you return to town, you will be back in the bosom of Society in a day. You will have contacts, friends, and marriage-minded mamas seeking you out."

"No."

"But you must," she insisted.

"Why must I?" he retorted in an angry tone.

She paused briefly before saying, "You need an heir. And Charlotte needs a mother." Her full lips turned upward, and her blue eyes sparkled. "And I can find you a wife."

"Absolutely not!"

She took a step close to him. "Yes, and you shall find me a husband. Who better than I to find you a lady who you will come to love?"

"You truly have lost your mind, Louisa Drake."

"See," she said with a bright smile. "You do know me so well. Find me a man who will tolerate my madness."

"I am not sure one exists," he muttered, shaking his head. Once again, she had turned everything upside down.

He leaned against the fireplace mantel as frustration swept across his body. The idea of matching her with a husband did not sit well with him, but the thought of her finding him a wife was abhorrent. There was no point in continuing this conversation. Nothing would drag him back to those miserable, small-minded people.

"I have no intention of returning to London."

"Harry, you have a daughter. If she does not socialize with your peers, she will never be ready when the time comes to enter Society."

Harry cringed. Not arriving in Society until sixteen, Louisa had never fit in with the fine people of town, which was a part of what had drawn him to her.

"There is no need for her to be part of that group," he retorted, even knowing she might be right. At some point, Charlotte would want a Season.

Louisa rose and walked the room. "You are being terribly selfish, Harry. She needs friends. She needs a mother."

"No."

"You need an heir," she said, turning to face him.

"Enough," he rasped. "I am not returning to London. I am not marrying again. And under no circumstances will I take Charlotte to town."

Her sapphire eyes sparkled with anger as she glowered at him silently.

He pointed at her and said, "And you will not speak of Charlotte to anyone."

"You are being foolish, Harry," she said with a hint of anger in her voice. "What do you propose to do, wait until she is eighteen before you allow her to visit town? Think of the talk then. Very few will believe she is your true daughter and not just a by-blow you are trying to pawn off on some fool man."

He started to protest, but the words wouldn't form. Was she right? No, she could not be correct for that would make him an utter cad in everyone's eyes, especially his daughter.

"I understand your reasons for keeping Charlotte isolated. I might not agree with them, but if that is your wish, I will not speak of her to anyone."

He released a frustrated sigh, angry with himself for even thinking Louisa would do such a thing. "I promised Charlotte I would take her out into the snow. Good afternoon, Miss Drake."

He strode from the room and didn't stop until he reached his bedchamber.

"Damn her!"

Everything Louisa had stated was correct. Charlotte did need friends. At Northwood Park, all she had were adults. There were no other children near her age. And if he was truthful with himself, she did need a mother, and he did need an heir.

Harry closed his eyes against the painful memories. He could not marry again.

Louisa stared out the window as Harry pulled the child's sled up the small incline. She could hear Charlotte's giggles and shrieks as he turned around and then ran down the hill, pulling her with him. Leaning her head against the cold glass, Louisa sighed, wishing he'd invited her to join them.

As Harry raced down the incline, he reminded her of the younger, carefree man she'd known. A happy smile on his handsome face, laughing at his daughter's reaction. It was the first time she'd heard him laugh since arriving. Until that moment, she hadn't realized how much she missed his easy laugh.

Something was wrong with Harry.

The change in him went far beyond the standard transformation as a man took responsibility for his estates and family. She supposed after the anguish of his father's attitude toward Harry's Indian wife, any man would be cautious introducing his daughter to Society. Still, his stance seemed extreme.

The right woman could help him. Surely she could help him find a proper lady. There had to be a way to come to a compromise with him about finding her a husband. She could not live alone with her mother. Louisa wanted to believe her mother only had the best of intentions for her, but she knew better. Mamma wanted Louisa married and out of the way of her scandalous relationship with Lord Hammond.

Louisa moved away from the window and picked up a book of poetry from the bookshelf. Sitting by the fire, she stared down at the pages but read nothing. Her mind wouldn't stop thinking about how to help Harry.

After nearly thirty minutes of contemplation, nothing had come to her. A clatter from the hall told her Harry and Charlotte had returned. The sound of small footsteps and giggling came closer.

"Charlotte, we need to get you changed." Harry's voice sounded as if the good humor of the afternoon remained in him.

"Miss Drake, where are you?" Charlotte called in a singsong voice.

"In the library," Louisa answered in a similar voice.

Charlotte raced into the room with Harry right behind her. She giggled and fell to the floor by the fire. "We went on the sled!"

"Charlotte, I need to take you up to the nursery," Harry tried again.

Ignoring Harry, Louisa replied, "I saw you from the window."

"You should've come outside," Charlotte said as Harry reached down to grab her and then tossed her over his shoulder. "Papa! I'm talking."

Louisa suppressed a giggle.

"You are always talking, poppet. You're wet and need to change before you get a chill."

Louisa glanced over at Harry and tried to ignore that strange feeling of breathlessness when he was near. "Indeed. Although, I must say I think you are wetter than she is. I'll take her upstairs while you change into something dry."

"Yay! I want Miss Drake to take me."

His steely eyes glared down at Louisa. "As you wish."

"Come along, Charlotte," Louisa said as Harry put her down. She held out her hand for the little girl. "Now you will have to show me where the nursery is again. I fear I may get lost in this big house."

Charlotte led her away with a giggle. "It's this way, Miss Drake."

The sensation of Charlotte's small hand in hers warmed Louisa's heart. She followed the girl up to the nursery, where she helped the nurse change Charlotte's dress.

"Papa said tomorrow we'd build snowmen," Charlotte said as Louisa pushed a wool dress over her. "Will you play with us?"

Louisa blinked. At this point, she didn't even know if she would still be here tomorrow. She and Harry hadn't discussed how long she would stay yet. "If I am still here, I would love to play with you."

"Yay!"

"All right, Lady Charlotte," Nurse said. "It's time for you to let Miss Drake get dressed for supper."

Louisa nodded, even though supper wouldn't be for several hours yet. No doubt, Nurse wanted her charge to settle down for a while.

"Yes, it takes a long time to dress."

"Will you come back before supper?"

Unable to say no to such an adorable face, Louisa nodded. "I will if Nurse allows it."

"Please," Charlotte whined to her nurse.

"As long as you sit with me and work on your letters," Nurse said. "I will!"

"Excellent, then I shall return at six," Louisa added before heading for the door. Once in the hall, she glanced around, not sure what to do with herself. It was too early to dress for supper, but after the glare Harry gave her, Louisa had no wish to seek him out. Perhaps she should ask for a tray in her room. But she didn't want that either.

She walked into her bedchamber and glanced out the window. The snow had melted some during the daylight. With dusk settling upon them, she assumed everything would freeze again overnight. If this continued, she might be here until spring.

Not knowing when Harry would ask her to leave, she had limited time to convince him that he must return to town. Appealing to his emotions for his daughter hadn't worked this morning. Logic. She must think of the most logical reason why he should come to London.

An heir.

All her focus had to be on convincing him that he must produce an heir. He only had a sister, and a bastard half-brother, neither of whom could inherit if Harry failed to have a son. She could find him a lady who could give him what he needed most.

With a plan in place, she rang for her maid to help her dress.

Harry wandered through the salon and library. He wasn't searching her out. But the last time he'd seen Louisa, she was taking

Charlotte up to the nursery. Perhaps she still needed more time to dress before dining.

After walking back to her bedchamber, he knocked on the door. "Miss Drake, are you there?"

Silence. Except for the childish laughter coming from the nursery. She couldn't possibly be up there still. It was nearly seven. Nurse would want Charlotte to be off to bed soon.

He walked toward the nursery with a grimace. As he approached, he heard Louisa's voice imitating a high-pitched mouse voice as she read Charlotte's favorite book. He slowed his step and peeked into the room. His heart twisted at the sight of his daughter on Louisa's lap, giggling as Louisa read to her.

Backing out of the room, he retreated to his study and a large brandy. He had to get her out of his house before he went mad.

"Damn her," he muttered.

"Cursing me again, are we?"

Harry turned, and the breath left his lungs. She wore a simple blue gown with a white lace fichu at the neckline. Her dress yesterday was far more fitting a formal dinner, and yet, she looked even more beautiful tonight. Anger swept over him. She should not be in his home without a chaperone.

Or in his home at all.

"Apparently, I am," he replied coldly.

She acknowledged that with a quick nod. "I must apologize if I am late. I'd promised to read Charlotte a story."

Harry closed his eyes for a long moment to let the irritation go. Louisa would be gone soon enough. He could be civil. "And knowing my daughter, one story turned into three."

Louisa smiled. "Five."

"She is quite a determined little girl." He returned to the table in the corner and poured her a glass of sherry.

"She has an excellent verbal aptitude for a three-year-old, Harry."

Of course, she did. She only spoke with adults. Another reason Louisa would tell him to take Charlotte to London. He pushed away the guilt, rationalizing that remaining here kept her safe from the prying eyes of the ton. "Yes, but she is nearly four. Still, Nurse says she is very advanced. She is already learning her letters and numbers."

"I'm not surprised, given her father," Louisa said with a smile.

"Nurse says Charlotte will be reading in no time."

"Is there time for this?" she asked, taking the glass of sherry from his outstretched hand.

"Yes."

"It looked as if you were enjoying yourself outside today."

He returned to sipping his brandy, feeling a bit abashed for not inviting her to join them. "Yes."

"It's been a long time since I was out in the snow like that." She gave him a wistful smile. "Almost six years ago."

"The frost fair," they said together.

Harry turned away from her as memories flooded him of that day. He'd come upon her and her sister, Emma on the ice, skating. Emma took a tumble and hurt her ankle, so he carried her home.

Louisa commented as if recalling the same event, "Emma called you her hero."

All he'd wanted to be that day was Louisa's hero. Not that it mattered any longer. He had his responsibilities. And the guilt his father left him.

Chapter 5

The sound of Charlotte's giggles filled the vast snowy field like music. Another few inches had fallen overnight, blanketing the area with white. Louisa couldn't help but giggle too as Harry attempted to roll a snowball to form the base for a snowman. The ball was now half as tall as Harry. She trudged through the snow to where he and Charlotte played.

"Do you need some assistance?"

"Miss Drake!" Charlotte shrieked and then raced over to her. "Yay!"

Louisa glanced over and noticed the way Harry only gave her a brief nod.

"Charlotte, come back and help me roll this middle section," he said, ignoring Louisa.

Charlotte clasped her hand with Louisa's and pulled her toward Harry. Charlotte's giggles lightened her mood slightly. After last night's stilted conversation at supper and then over chess, Louisa assumed today wouldn't be much better. And so far, it hadn't been.

But his daughter's laughter was contagious. When she was near the stiffness disappeared, and Harry seemed like his former self.

"You will never get a middle and head on him," Louisa said to him.

"I will. Find some sticks for the arms and something for eyes and a mouth." Harry stopped with the bottom section and then started rolling more snow for the middle section. Charlotte found two sticks for arms while Louisa looked around for something to use as eyes.

"We need to find some small round stones for the eyes," she said to Charlotte. "Or maybe some pieces of coal."

"There're stones near the pond!"

Before Louisa could stop her, Charlotte ran off toward the large pond in front of the home. Louisa chased after the youngster to ensure her safety. "Charlotte, do be careful. We might not find the stones because of the snow."

"Yes, Miss Drake," Charlotte called out. She stopped by the edge of the pond, which had a thin film of ice over the surface.

"Do not go near that water," Louisa commanded.

"But there are two stones right there," Charlotte replied, pointing at the water. "I can reach them."

"No!" Louisa caught the little girl's arm and yanked her away from the edge. "I will get them."

She glanced into the water and noticed the two small rocks that Charlotte had spied. They were only in a foot of water with a thin layer of ice on top. Louisa crouched down by the edge and leaned over to reach the pebbles. They were slighter farther away than she'd thought. She stretched her arm out to grab them. Her feet slipped out from under her, sending her splashing into the icy water.

"Louisa!" Harry shouted.

"Miss Drake!" Charlotte screamed.

She scrambled to get out of the water. Strong hands pulled her out and into a warm embrace. Frigid water trickled down her face from the brim of her hat. She let her head rest on Harry's chest until her teeth started to chatter. "Dear G—God, that is c—c—cold water."

"We need to get you inside," he said, rubbing her arms with his gloved hands.

"Are you all right, Miss Drake?" Charlotte asked before fat tears rolled down her red cheeks. "I'm sorry."

"Charlotte, I am unhurt, only c—cold and wet." Louisa held out her right hand. "Here are your snowman's eyes. I will let you two finish him off while I go change."

Harry looked down at her, shaking his head with concern or irritation. "Charlotte, before we continue, we must get Miss Drake into the house."

"Yes, Papa." Charlotte took hold of Louisa's hand. "Come along, Miss Drake."

They walked back to the house quickly. Jenkins opened the door and then hid a look of disdain. "Miss Drake, are you well?"

"I—I—I," she couldn't form a single word with her teeth chattering.

"Jenkins, alert Lily that Miss Drake needs her assistance this minute," Harry commanded. "Miss Drake, I will carry you upstairs and help you until your maid arrives."

"Y—You d—d—don't need to c—carry me," she protested, feeling rather foolish for slipping. "I—I'm always tripping over my b—big feet."

He swung her up into his arms for the second time in three days. At this point, she did not care to protest. He was warmth. She snuggled in closer to his heat and listened to the sound of his heart beating in his chest. A hint of leather and cinnamon swirled around her, enticing her with the fragrance.

"Now I owe you two scoldings," he grumbled as he attempted to open the door. "Three days here and you have walked through a blizzard and fallen into an icy pond."

"I'll do it, Papa." Charlotte swung the door open, allowing Harry to enter the room.

"You don't need to worry about me." Her heart warmed by his

care.

"You are in my home. While you are here, you are my concern." His voice softened before speaking to his daughter, "Charlotte, go into my bedchamber and bring back the bottle of brown liquid on the table near my bed. Do hurry, poppet." Slowly, he lowered Louisa to her feet. "We have to get you out of these clothes before you get frostbite."

"Lily will b—be up in a moment," Louisa managed to get out. The chill returned with the absence of his heat.

"We are not waiting for her." He unbuttoned her cloak and removed it from her. After tossing it over a chair, he said, "Turn around."

"Harry, this is very improper."

"Says the woman who is the epitome of improper behavior." He turned her around and attacked the laces on her dress. "We have a three-year-old chaperone."

"Papa, is this it?" Charlotte asked, holding up an almost empty decanter of brandy with two hands.

"Yes, now carefully pour Miss Drake a glass."

As Charlotte concentrated on pouring the brandy, Harry slipped the wet dress off Louisa's shoulders. She shivered as the warm air of the fire hit her bare arms.

"The decanter is too heavy for her," Louisa said as Charlotte attempted to pour.

"She's a big girl, and the decanter is almost empty," Harry replied.

Charlotte beamed over at her father as she emptied the contents into the glass. "I did it, Papa!"

"I am here, Your Grace," Lily said as she raced into the room. "Oh, Your Grace, you must leave. I will undress her."

"Come along, Charlotte. We will build your snowman now."

Charlotte shook her head. "I want to stay with Miss Drake."

"We have a snowman to finish."

"I want to stay with Miss Drake!"

"She can stay if she would like," Louisa said with a slight smile.

"As you wish," he said stiffly before leaving the room.

"Do you want a hot bath, miss?" Lily asked as she unlaced Louisa's stays.

"No, thank you. Just some warm clothes and that brandy would be fine."

Charlotte had poured the small water glass almost to the top. Carefully, she brought the drink over to Louisa.

"Thank you, Charlotte." Louisa slowly sipped the heady liquid as Lily instructed Charlotte to pull out a wool gown for her. Finally, her teeth had stopped chattering, and warmth seeped into her bones again.

Lily stoked the fire before gathering her wet clothes. "Do you need anything else, miss?"

"No, thank you, Lily." She glanced over at Charlotte who sat in a chair across from her. "Charlotte, you need to get out of your wet things, too. Afterward, I will read you a story."

Charlotte bounced out of the chair and then started removing all her wet outdoor clothing. "I'll get a book from Nurse."

She returned a few minutes later wearing a dry dress and carrying a storybook. She scrambled up into Louisa's lap and settled in. Louisa sipped her drink, enjoying the warm sensation of the brandy and the child on her lap. As she read the fairytale, Charlotte's breathing became steady, and slowly, her eyes closed. Louisa sat there, unable to move without disturbing the child. The sweet smell of soap surrounded the little girl. Unable to keep her own eyes open, she rested her head in the crook of the chair and let sleep take her.

"Come along, Charlotte."

The sound of Harry's whisper forced Louisa's eyes open. "What are you doing?" she asked softly.

He lifted a groaning Charlotte into his arms. "I'm taking Charlotte back to the nursery to eat."

"What time is it?" she asked, noticing that darkness had already fallen.

"Five. Shall I have a tray brought up?"

She paused, remembering last evening's detached conversations. But the idea of being in her room alone held even less appeal. "No, I would prefer to come down…unless you have already eaten?"

"I have not," he whispered. "Come down, and we will dine together."

"I'll be down in a few minutes." Louisa slowly rose and noticed her half-full brandy glass still sitting on the table by the chair. She took a few more sips as she attempted to straighten the wrinkles from her dress. Then a few more sips as she adjusted her hair again. By the time she was ready to leave her bedchamber, the rest of the brandy was warming her belly and making her a little dizzy.

She walked into the salon to find Harry pouring two glasses of sherry. He handed one to her. The sherry tasted very sweet after the smoky brandy, but it didn't stop her. "Will supper be announced soon? I did not eat much today and well…"

"A little hungry?"

"A lady never lets her true appetite be known," Louisa aped her mother voice. Then she smiled and added, "But yes, I am famished." And a little dizzy, but he didn't need to know that.

Jenkins announced supper before she could finish any more sherry.

Louisa took Harry's arm as he led her to the dining room. Feeling the effect of far too much brandy on an empty stomach, she wanted to put her head down on his shoulder. Instead, forcing herself to keep her head upright, she strolled into the room with dignity. At least she hoped she had some poise. She wasn't entirely sure. She didn't trip, and that was something, especially for her.

Once seated, a footman placed a bowl of soup in front of her. She giggled.

"Is everything to your liking, Miss Drake?" Harry asked before moving a spoonful of soup to his mouth.

"Please tell me this is not all there is tonight?"

Harry's brows furrowed. "Would that be a problem?"

"No, but it would explain your weight loss." She looked him over from head to chest. "You are very lean now. You used to have a bit more weight on you."

"There is much more exercise in the country."

"Hmm," she muttered. Her heart pounded as she stared at Harry, wondering what he might look like without a shirt, or any other clothing. Heat inflamed her entire face. She had categorically had too much to drink. "I rather think it suits you."

"You didn't drink that entire glass of brandy, did you?" he asked, casting her an odd look.

Louisa chortled as she picked up her water glass. "Of sourse— course I didn't drink it all."

"Of course not," he repeated with a shake of his head.

"I am sorry I ruined your time with Charlotte building a snowman today."

"We shall do it another time."

When she wasn't here to ruin their time together, he must have meant. She sipped her water, hoping to clear her head. The footman removed the soup bowl and brought out the main course consisting of lamb, potatoes, and carrots. "Your cook has outdone herself tonight, Your Grace."

"Thank you, Miss Drake."

By the time they had finished, Louisa had no idea what they had even discussed. She thought it had something to do with the crops on the estate but couldn't be positive. Somehow, she had made it through supper without Harry realizing she was slightly inebriated.

They walked back to the salon, and he poured her a snifter of brandy. "I fear it is not as much as Charlotte would pour."

"This is more than enough, thank you." She took the glass from him and sipped it slowly. The room seemed to spin a little as she placed the glass on the table.

The large room seemed rather intimate with just the two of them, and the door shut for warmth and privacy. Harry sat on the brocade chair across from her. How had the man become more attractive? She decided to blame it on the beard that he still sported. She wanted to touch it, feel it against her cheek.

"Will you be staying until Twelfth Night, then?" he asked quietly.

Hearing the odd tone of his voice, she replied, "No. I should return home."

He released a long sigh, of relief, no doubt. Now he wouldn't be stuck with her in his home. Louisa wondered how the younger Harry would have reacted. Most likely, he would have been happy for the company and insisted she stay.

"How did you travel without telling your mother where you were going? I highly doubt she would have approved of you visiting me."

"I suppose you could say I ran away." She shrugged and took another sip of brandy. "I left and never told anyone where I was heading."

"Your mother has no idea where you are or when you are returning? Good God, Louisa, she and your sisters must be sick with worry over you."

She doubted they even missed her. The idea of remaining here sounded ideal. No mother fussing over Emma's wedding plans.

No sister telling her about the baby growing inside her. Blessed peace. Except, there was no peace with this rather odd attraction she felt for her friend. And then there was his unusual coldness toward her. It was so unlike him.

Still, returning home seemed her only option.

When she remained silent, he asked, "Are you all right, Louisa?"

"Yes, why do you ask?"

"You haven't replied." His molded lips turned upwards. "Have you had too much to drink tonight?"

Staring at his mouth, she realized how much she wanted to feel those lips against hers again. She had never wanted the younger Harry to kiss her, but she wanted this Harry to kiss her. And press her against the hard length of his body. This wasn't like her in the least. She shouldn't want a man who so obviously wanted nothing to do with her any longer.

"No, just many things on my mind."

"Such as?"

"Wondering why my dearest friend refuses to help me find a husband?"

Harry wasn't sure he knew her at all any longer. The Louisa he'd known thought out her actions in a logical manner. Her only reckless activities involved meeting him on a terrace or in a garden alone to talk.

"You should never have come out here, Louisa."

"Where should I have gone then...to Ainsley?"

He barely contained a growl at the thought of her with Ainsley. "No, of course not. Why can't Tessa find you a husband? No one believes she's cursed now. And everyone knows who murdered her late husbands."

She rose and then stared down at him with anger in her glassy eyes. "Tessa is the reason I cannot find a husband."

"How so?"

"Your father's death letter only confirmed that she wasn't cursed or a murderess," Louisa continued her outburst. "It did nothing about the fact that she'd continued to marry men who were of increasing rank. They blamed her for that, not your father."

Harry rose to stand in front of her, his anger rising with this never-ending quarrel. "She only married those men because my father recommended them to her to increase her position in Society."

"No one cares about that," she replied, throwing her hands up in frustration. "Who is going to blame a duke when you can blame the daughter of a banker? After all," she mimicked a disdainful voice of quality, "perhaps those men got what they deserved for not marrying someone from 'good' Society."

He flinched, knowing she was likely correct. But being mere inches from her was doing terrible things to his mind and body. Her eyes were blazing in anger. Her chest raised and lowered in uneven bouts. And while she'd clearly had too much to drink, she wouldn't back down.

Why couldn't she realize he was the wrong person to help her for so many reasons?

"I am not coming to town to help you," he finally said.

"Then you shall have to marry me in five months when you turn thirty."

"I cannot marry you." He leaned closer, breathing in the heady scent of lilac mixed with brandy. Her tongue swiped across her full lower lip, distracting him to no end.

A kiss.

He couldn't.

Kiss her. You wanted to for years.

He really shouldn't. But his head moved even closer to hers. Toward her lips. Rosy, full and ready to be kissed. Her pink tongue slid across her lower lip, tempting him even more. For years, he'd imagined what she would taste like…sweet like sugar with maybe a hint of tanginess from the brandy. She would be an overwhelming sensation he'd remember all his life.

Her eyes widened, and her mouth gaped as if realizing his intention.

He couldn't do this. Kissing Louisa would only make her believe there was a chance he would marry her. He lifted his head abruptly as if he'd been burned from getting too close to a flame.

"Leave, Louisa," he commanded, pointing to the door.

"Leave?" She sounded confused.

"Yes." Before he made a mistake that they both would regret.

"Oh, I'll go," she replied tartly. "But don't think for one moment that this is over."

It was over between them when he left for India. The day his life changed forever.

❦

"Wake up, Papa!"

"Stop bouncing, and I might open my eyes." Could it be morning already? He rubbed his eyes with the heel of his hands.

Charlotte sat perfectly still until he opened his eyes. "Why did you let her go?"

"Who?"

"Miss Drake! She said goodbye a few minutes ago. Why didn't you stop her? I like her. She seemed sad. She had tea with me. And she read to me. And she found the eyes for our snowman. Can I call her mamma?"

Harry sat up in bed and stared down at his loquacious daughter.

Far too many questions after being up half the night berating himself for almost kissing Louisa. Did his daughter just ask if she could call Louisa mamma? He shook his head to clear the fog. One question at a time.

"What do you mean she left?"

"She said her Mamma missed her."

Highly unlikely.

"She said she'd walk to town. I don't think she should, Papa. It's cold out."

"Charlotte, where are you?" Nurse called out from the corridor.

"She's in here."

"Papa!"

Harry moved his daughter out of the way and then scrambled out of bed. The nerve of her leaving without so much as a by your leave. "Go back with Nurse, poppet. I will fetch Miss Drake."

"You will bring her home?"

Harry sighed. "If she wants to return to London, there is nothing I can do. But I will lend her my carriage at least, so she is comfortable."

Charlotte's lower lip stuck out. "I want her to come home. I want her to read to me again."

"I know, Charlotte." Knowing he would never be able to leave his daughter if he didn't give her something, he said, "Perhaps in the spring we can go to town and see the elephant."

"And see Miss Drake?"

Harry closed his eyes and shook his head. His darling, determined daughter would never stop now. "Yes, we will call on Miss Drake."

She jumped up and down, clapping her hands. "Yay! I will tell Nurse."

"April is four months away, poppet."

"Oh." Charlotte ran off to tell Nurse her news. Thankfully

forgetting to ask more about whether Louisa would be her new mother. The last thing he wanted to do was disappoint his daughter, but there was no chance he could marry Louisa or anyone.

Harry dressed quickly before running down the stairs. Seeing Jenkins, he asked, "Why didn't you provide a carriage for Miss Drake?"

"I did try, Your Grace. She refused."

"Then you should have informed me." There were days he wanted to let his butler go, but he had been with the family for years.

Jenkins reached for a missive on the salver. "She left this for you."

Harry reached for the letter and moved to the salon for privacy.

Your Grace,

You have until May 30th, 1820, the occasion of your thirtieth birthday, to find me a suitable husband or marry me yourself.

Should you refuse to do either, I shall be forced to show the pact we signed to the ton's biggest gossips.

L.

Harry let out a curse before hurling the note into the fireplace. He should be pleased. She was gone. Out of his life. He'd pushed her away for her own good.

So why did he feel so bloody irritated?

Chapter 6

Three days later, a hackney pulled up in front of her mother's home on the outskirts of Mayfair. Not a large house, but enough for Mamma, Emma, and her. Dread slowed her pace to the door.

She still had no idea what to tell her mother.

On the way to Northwood Park, Louisa had concentrated on how to ask Harry for what she wanted. She'd assumed, quite incorrectly so, that on the return trip she would invent an excellent excuse for her mother. Instead, all she'd done was scrutinize every conversation with the frustrating duke. His attitude toward her continued to puzzle her.

They had never quarreled as much in all the past seven years combined. Nor had she ever felt such tension between them. A part of her felt guilty for leaving Harry when it was apparent that he needed a friend. But with the odd desire for him, it was for the best that she had departed before she'd made an impulsive mistake.

Like, kiss him.

Which was exactly what she'd almost done. No, this was for the best. If she had stayed, kissing him might have been the least of what happened.

Davis opened the door as she ascended the brick steps. "Oh, Miss Drake, we have all been so worried for you. Your mother will be pleased to have you home safely."

"Thank you, Davis." She walked into the house and sighed. "Is my mother at home?"

"Yes, miss."

"Louisa," her mother bellowed sharply from the top step. "You have finally decided to return?"

Another door upstairs banged shut and then Emma was standing there too. "Louisa!"

Both rushed down the stairs. Emma pulled Louisa into the salon as their mother followed behind. Mamma sat on the floral divan as Emma and Louisa sat across from her.

"I will call for tea," Emma said, glancing at them both.

For a long moment, Louisa could only sit and look at them both. She felt terrible for making them worry. "I am sorry, Mamma. I should not have left as I did on Christmas. It was very thoughtless of me."

"Emma, I need to speak to your sister alone. You may return when we are finished."

"Mamma, I am about to be married. Surely there is nothing you cannot say in front of me," her sister complained.

"Leave us," Mamma ordered, pointing her finger at the door.

"Yes, ma'am."

Once her sister left, her mother crossed her arms over her puffed out chest. "Exactly where, and with whom, have you been?"

"What did you tell everyone?"

"I said you went to see my aunt in Scotland. What else was I supposed to say when you left on Christmas Day with some story about finding a husband? You could have ruined us all!"

Louisa knew there was no point in lying to her mother. "I went to see Harry."

"Harry?" Her mother paused with a frown. "You mean Worthington! How could you do such a disastrous thing, Louisa?

That family wants nothing to do with us, and I feel the same. His insane father all but ruined us." Her mother pulled out a handkerchief and twisted it in her hands. "Why would you go to see him?"

"He was always a friend to me, Mamma. And I needed his help."

"You didn't think he would offer to marry you, did you?"

"Of course not." She'd never really considered the idea, not even when they made that foolish deal. Years ago, he'd hinted that he desired her, but she'd always disregarded his innuendos as nothing more than his rakish behavior. Because who would desire the plain Drake sister?

"Did that blackguard do anything improper?" When Louisa only stared at her in confusion, her mother added, "Do we need to worry about a child from this?"

"No, he is a gentleman."

"Well, that is one blessing." She waved her handkerchief at Louisa. "Still, you mustn't let anyone know you went to see him, including Emma. If Lady Bolton ever discovered this, she might force her son to break their engagement. Think of the scandal then! After your refusal to marry Blakely and Emerson, a rejection by Bolton would be the end of us all."

All her mother ever cared about was getting her daughters married with no scandals attached to their name—no easy task when Mamma held the one secret that would scandalize everyone.

Her mother went to the door and called a sulking Emma back into the room.

"How is Tessa feeling?" Louisa asked as the footman brought tea in for them.

"She is now past the dreadful morning sickness," Emma said before falling into a chair. "I do not think I would like to be with child."

Her mother shook her head. "If you wish to marry, Emma, you should get used to the idea of childbearing. Your betrothed is a viscount and will expect an heir and a spare."

Emma sipped her tea and then asked, "Did you really go to Scotland?"

Louisa slid a glance over at her mother, who sent her a warning look. "Yes, I did. I thought Aunt Greyson might help me find a suitable husband."

Emma laughed. "Aunt Greyson can barely see or hear any longer. How could she help?"

"She has always had the respect of the *ton*." Louisa hated lying to her sister. "I thought she might have some words of advice."

"Did she?" Emma asked.

"No." She might have been better off paying a call on her aunt than visiting the reclusive duke. But she needed to change the subject before she confessed everything to her sister. "How are the wedding plans going?"

"Slowly. Bolton insists his mother must agree to a date. Lady Bolton has yet to give any response."

Louisa tilted her head and stared at her younger sister. "She must be trying to determine the best date for the maximum number of people to attend."

"I suppose you're right."

Louisa hoped Emma was right, and the reason wasn't due to Lady Bolton hoping Emma would call off the wedding. Louisa had never like Lady Bolton. The viscountess always seemed a bit too concerned with Society and keeping her family name impeccable. Louisa wondered if the viscountess had even been aware of her son's decision to offer for Emma until it was too late. Louisa rather doubted Lady Bolton would have approved the engagement.

A fortnight had passed since Louisa left Northwood Park and still, all Harry could think of was her. She never seemed to leave his mind. If he wasn't thinking of her, then Charlotte was asking about her. Or worse, he dreamed of her. Erotic dreams that left him hard and unsatisfied.

This had to stop. Somehow, he had to find a way of eliminating her from his thoughts.

He stared down at the ledger on his desk, not seeing the digits in front of him. His steward spoke of the number of lambs predicted this spring, but Harry could only wonder what Louisa would think. Would she agree with Mr. Leeds or believe his estimate inaccurate? Would she recommend something different?

"In conclusion, Your Grace, I do believe we should continue to increase our production of rye."

"Yes, of course." When had Leeds started discussing rye?

Mr. Leeds rose and stared down at the ledger. "Your Grace, if I may, are you well?

Hardly. "Just distracted today. I apologize."

Mr. Leeds shook his almost bald head. "I understand, sir. You have much to worry over with your estates. Will you go to town this year?"

"I have not decided yet," Harry lied. He couldn't return to town and face those dreadful people.

"Very good, Your Grace. Would you like me to leave the ledgers for you to review?"

Harry pushed the leather-bound book across the desk. "No, I have looked at the numbers and everything seems to be in order."

"Good afternoon, then." Leeds bowed and departed for his home.

Staring out at the grass finally peeking through the melting snow, he wondered again if she'd arrived home safely. He had no way of knowing since she had stopped writing to him, and the uncertainty of her predicament pricked his conscience.

Ever since she'd departed, he wondered if he'd done the right thing. Should he have agreed to find her a husband?

Bloody hell, no!

His conscience wouldn't let him offer for her as it would do nothing but bring up the past for them both. The gossip both families might have to endure would be endless. She deserved better—not a man whose father's mad actions completely ruined their family name.

And not a man who failed his own wife.

Staying away from her, from town, seemed the only course.

She deserved a gentleman who would understand her. A man who was unburdened by the shame of his actions and those of his father's. And as usual, every time he had that thought darkness seeped into his soul, covering him like a shroud.

In many ways, he was as guilty as his father.

Thrusting the frustrating thoughts away, he poured a brandy and then sank into a chair. But as soon as he sat, his thoughts returned to Louisa. He completely understood her reasoning for wanting a husband. A spinster was nothing but a burden and something her family could ill afford.

While Tessa had a decent inheritance from her last husband and her current husband had money from his grandmother, she now had a child on the way. Her husband was trying to build his law practice, but it takes time for a solicitor to land well-paying clients. Money could be tight for a while.

Emma would marry Bolton. Harry almost smiled, thinking about how Louisa would vex Bolton. She had twice the brains as the viscount, and Harry could only imagine the quarrels that would happen if she lived with them.

That only left her mother with whom she could live, and that would drive her mad.

Dammit, there was no easy solution to this mess.

Louisa's situation was his fault. He was the duke now and responsible for the family name. If not for his father's interference with Tessa's marriages, Louisa would be able to have any man she wanted. There was no other choice in this matter. He should do the right thing by her.

He should want the best for her.

Every day was a day closer to his thirtieth birthday and her informing the gossipmongers of their pact. He wasn't entirely positive she would make good on her threat, but he had his daughter to think of now. If Louisa did release the details of their deal, Charlotte's name might be brought into the mess. With her mixed blood, any talk would only confirm her status as an outcast. He had to determine the best course of action.

Time was running out.

As January gave way to February, Louisa felt as if the gloominess of the weather had seeped into her very soul. Or perhaps her mood could be blamed on the death of King George III three days ago, which had brought the entire country into mourning. She'd scarcely left the house since arriving home from Northwood Park. No matter how hard she tried, her thoughts kept returning to her short time with Harry.

Over the past few weeks, her anger at him gave way to pity. If he ever discovered she felt sorry for his situation, he would be furious with her. He had changed since the death of his wife. Louisa wanted desperately to help him but was at a loss as to how. While she'd hoped he might agree to marry again, he must have had loved his wife deeply to feel the impact of her passing still.

He just needed to quit Northwood Park. Being back in town and amongst friends would help him see that no one blamed him for his father's actions, least of all her. A diversion from his mourning might help him discover that he could love again.

Now she sounded like a hopeless dreamer.

She doubted the appalling threat in the note she left would make any difference. He likely assumed she would never show their deal to anyone, which would be correct. The hope had been that he would believe her threat long enough to decide to come to town. But he could continue to molder in the North, and there wasn't much she could do about it. A repeat visit to Northwood Park was highly unlikely at this point.

Returning to London now, only to find the entire town draped in black, would be particularly unpleasant for him. But he would have to attend the King's service. Not even a duke would forgo a king's funeral without an extraordinary reason. Her shoulders sagged. He had to go to Windsor, but there was nothing that said he had to then come to town.

But he might. And if he did arrive and decide to help her find a husband, he would need a list of her requirements. Finally feeling like she had a task to perform, she moved to her writing desk by the window. So…what did she want in a husband? She pulled out paper and ink to prepare her list.

For the longest time, she could only stare at the blank paper.

Louisa spent the next few weeks refining her requirements for a husband. After waking early this morning, she spent time reviewing her requirements again. Harry might be here any day, therefore she needed to be prepared, and her list was woefully inadequate. An hour later and with still nothing new to add, she went down to the morning room for breakfast.

Emma sat at the morning table, drinking her strong coffee and smiled over at her. "Good morning, Louisa."

"Good morning." Not loving the strong coffee Emma drank, Louisa chose tea to go along with her ham and eggs.

"I've heard most of the gentlemen have returned from Windsor," Emma chatted.

"Yes, I suppose they have." Louisa felt a sting of disappointment. He wasn't coming to town.

"Hopefully things will get back to normal, and before long the coronation will occur. Being engaged and mostly likely married to Bolton by then, I should be able to attend."

Louisa smiled at her sister's enthusiasm. "It may take a few months to coordinate such an event. And the poor man has been ill since he ascended, which may delay the ceremony even more."

"I suppose you're right," she replied before sipping her coffee. "Lord Huntley arrived home yesterday, so Mamma wishes to pay a call on Lady Huntley to hear all the news from Windsor. Will you join us?"

"No. You can tell me all about it when you return."

"Louisa, you should get out. Since you arrived home from Aunt Greyson's, you have been moping about the house."

Louisa shrugged. "I suppose I have. I feel as if this might be my last Season, Emma. If I don't find a husband…."

"Then you shall come live with Bolton and me."

Louisa tried not to roll her eyes at the thought of living with the dimwitted viscount. "Thank you."

By afternoon, her mother and sister departed to glean all the news from the funeral while Louisa retired to her bedchamber to read but couldn't concentrate on the treatise in front of her. With a deep sigh, she walked to the desk and glanced down at the list.

From a good family
Intelligent
A good father
Handsome

Almost three weeks and that was the best she had come up with, and after rereading her list, she crossed out handsome. She wasn't eighteen any longer, and never had she been any great beauty.

Frustrated with the entire process, she crumbled the paper and threw it toward the fireplace. There seemed little point in the list since Emma had told her most of the gentlemen had already returned. Harry had not arrived home.

The house was dreadfully quiet with her mother and sister departed. When the knocker banged on the front door, Louisa started. Hearing voices, she assumed her mother and sister had returned early. Light footsteps sounded on the steps.

"Louisa, may I come in?"

"Of course."

Tessa entered the room wearing her black bombazine. "Good afternoon. Mother and Emma are out paying calls, so here I am." With only another four or so months to go, Tessa's rounded belly suited her perfectly. After two years of marriage, everyone had thought it might never happen.

"Do you wish to go downstairs where we can be more comfortable?"

Tessa laughed and took the chair by the fireplace. "No, this room is warm, and the salon is cold." Staring down at her black gown, she said with a sigh, "I will be glad to be out of these dratted mourning rags."

"Three more weeks until we can move to half-mourning." Not that Louisa was wearing black since she stayed at home today. Gray wool for a cold, dreary day would suffice.

Louisa rose from her small writing desk and joined her sister by the fire. Glancing down, she noticed the crumpled list that hadn't quite made it into the fire. Her sister spotted it too and reached down to pick up the paper.

"Secret letters, Louisa?"

"Please don't read it," Louisa begged as she tried to grab it from Tessa's hands.

"Hush, when have we had secrets?" Tessa's brows furrowed as she opened the wrinkled paper. "What is this?"

There was no point in denying it. She and Tessa had grown up sharing confidences. "It's a list of what I want in a husband."

Tessa scanned the shortened list with her lips pressed together as if suppressing a laugh. "This is it? If this was all you wanted in a husband, you should have found a gentleman your first Season."

"I suppose so." Perhaps her expectations were too high as Lady Gringham had said, which if true, Louisa should have a long list of requirements, not only three.

"The real question is, why do you need such a list?"

Heat crossed her cheeks. "I just do."

"Does it have anything to do with why you left my home on Christmas Day, stating you were going to find a husband?"

Louisa shrugged and then reluctantly nodded. "I decided to ask Harry to help me find a husband."

"Worthington?"

Hearing the censure in Tessa's voice, Louisa grabbed the paper out of her sister's hands and tossed it into the fire. "It is none of your concern."

"Anything that involves that family concerns me. His father murdered my husbands."

"Yes, his *father*. The same man who killed Harry's wife. He is as much a victim as you."

Tessa slowly shook her head and pressed her lips together. "I understand that, Louisa. But you must know how dangerous it is to your reputation to associate with him. Many think he may have gone a little mad after what happened with his wife. Burying himself at Northwood Park for so long hasn't helped the gossip either. And think of Emma. With her engagement to Bolton, she must not have any ill will connected to her."

"I realize that, but he knows me better than anyone. Even you."

Tessa's face relaxed as she released a breath. "Emma's engagement sparked this rashness in you, didn't it?"

Louisa nodded. "It occurred to me that if I do not find a suitable husband this Season, I will either have to live with Mamma, Emma, or you. I couldn't do that to either of you. And the idea of living in this house with Mamma might drive me to Bedlam."

Tessa chuckled. "I can understand that. But Worthington? I know you were close before he left for India. I even thought an engagement might happen, but you haven't corresponded with him in a few years now."

Her sister had thought she and Harry might marry? Wherever did she get such an idea? "I tried, but he was too busy with the estate in India. And after his return…."

"He didn't write after his wife died," Tessa finished the sentence.

"No." And after months of trying, Louisa had stopped writing.

"So, he wants a list of your requirements in a husband to help you. Then what?"

"Not exactly," Louisa started hesitantly. "He didn't completely agree to assist me. I assumed he would return to town after going to Windsor. So, with a certain amount of misplaced optimism, I thought I would create a list of what I want in a husband."

Tessa sent her a look of pity. "I will do everything in my power to help you find a respectable husband, Louisa. I am sure Lady Leicester will have many ideas."

"Thank you," she replied, knowing Tessa would not be much involved with the Season with a baby due in June. And Louisa wasn't certain she wanted Tessa's grandmother-in-law assisting with finding a husband.

They both stopped talking as the sound of footfalls pounded up the steps. "Emma," Louisa stated.

"She will need to check herself when she marries Lord Bolton," Tessa said with a scowl. "A lady never runs."

Without a knock, Emma hurled the door open and stared at them both. "You will never guess the news!"

"Oh, do tell," Louisa said in a slightly sarcastic tone. Emma was far more concerned with the gossip of the ton than Louisa ever would be.

Emma closed the door as if the gossip was far too good for the servants to hear before moving to the bed. "Worthington is opening the house for the Season. Lady Rockingham says he may even hold a ball once this dreadful mourning is completed."

Tessa tilted her head and stared over at Louisa.

She pressed a hand to her belly as it fluttered with anticipation. Harry had returned.

Chapter 7

"I thought you said you didn't believe he would return," Tessa commented as Emma sat on the bed.

"I didn't think he would."

"You knew!" Emma exclaimed. "And you didn't tell me! And how did you know he planned to attend the Season?"

Louisa shrugged. "As I said, I wasn't certain he would attend the Season." Which was still two months away. Perhaps he thought to find her a husband and retreat to Northwood Park before the Season began. Not that doing so would be easy with the country in mourning for the King. Or perhaps his arrival had nothing to do with her or her attempt at intimidation.

"Why is he here?" Emma asked, still excited about the news. "Do you think he will marry again?"

"He is a duke now, Emma," Tessa explained as she slid a glance at Louisa. "He must have an heir."

The thought that he might be here to marry touched a painful spot in Louisa's heart. He needed a mother for Charlotte. An heir. A wife.

It was what she wanted for him. Or least that was what she told herself.

"There is more." Emma's light blue eyes sparkled with excitement. "Someone thought they saw him enter the house with a little girl in tow. Whose child could that be?"

Louisa smiled wistfully. "He brought Charlotte with him."

Both sisters turned their heads and stared at Louisa. "Charlotte?" they asked in unison.

Now they wouldn't stop until she told them the truth. "His daughter."

"When did he have a daughter?" Tessa questioned. "We dined with him and his wife at the late Duke's home the night she died. No one mentioned a baby then."

"Harry hadn't told anyone because of the duke's reaction to his wife. He went up to Northwood Park to mourn and took Charlotte with him. Oh, you should see her. She is beautiful."

"How do you know what she looks like?" Emma inquired innocently.

"Yes, Louisa, how would you know that?" Tessa arched a brow in question.

"He sent a sketch of her."

"Louisa! You were not corresponding with an unmarried man, were you? That would be scandalous, indeed." Emma stood and then retied her bonnet. "I must go to tell Susan about this news."

"Please don't mention his daughter, Emma. He is a private man." Louisa hoped her younger sister would listen to her for once.

"Louisa, everyone will know by tomorrow anyway." Emma raced from the room with a slam of the door.

"So, where is this drawing? I would love to see his daughter," Tessa said as she rubbed her belly. "Feel this."

Louisa placed her hand on her sister's belly and laughed as what felt like a tiny foot kicked her. "Oh Tessa, that is the most amazing thing. Does it hurt?"

"No." Tessa smiled. "It's quite lovely. Now, where is that sketch?"

"I don't have a drawing, Tessa," she slowly admitted as heat crossed her cheeks.

"You went to him, didn't you?"

Louisa nodded.

Tessa clapped her hand over her mouth. "Does Mamma know?"

"Yes, and please don't look at me that way. Nothing happened." Except for one moment when she thought she might kiss him, or he might kiss her. Why would he kiss her when he was so furious with her for being there? Instead of kissing her, he had demanded that she leave.

"I…I cannot believe you did something so scandalous."

She glossed over the details of what happened at Northwood Park, by only saying she went to ask him to find her a husband. She wasn't about to admit to her sister that she'd thought about kissing Harry. "I tried to convince him to return to town. Then he would find that no one blames him for what happened."

A light rapped sounded on the door. "Miss Drake, you have a letter."

After the footman gave her the note, Louisa glanced and noticed the strong, neat script. She broke the seal and scanned the letter as she worried her lip.

"Is everything all right?" Tessa asked.

"It's from Harry. He states he will call on me tomorrow to see my list of requirements in a husband."

"Why is that distressing you?"

"You saw my list!"

Harry knocked on the door of the Drakes' home. Perhaps he should have given her more time before demanding the list from her. Since he had no intention of staying in London longer than necessary, he needed her requirements today. The sooner he found this man for her, the better.

The door opened to reveal a footman in shabby livery. "Yes?"

Harry gave him his card. "I am here to see Miss Drake."

"Of course, Your Grace. Please come in." The footman opened the door fully and then led him into the salon. "Tea?"

"Yes. Miss Drake is at home, is she not? She should be expecting me."

"Yes." The footman bowed to him and then left the room.

"Your Grace," Louisa said with a curtsy a few minutes later. Her maid trailed behind and sat in the chair nearest the door. "I heard yesterday that you had opened the house early."

Harry rose and bowed stiffly to her. "Yes. I had to attend the funeral, so I decided to come to town early."

Louisa moved away from her maid toward the conversation seating by the fireplace. Walking by him, she arched a daring brow, smirked, and asked, "So, have you come to find me a husband or to propose?"

Ignoring her taunt, he stared over at her. Her chestnut hair was pulled up, but light tendrils lay across her forehead and framed her face. He hated seeing her in her mourning rags. Black was not her color, making her skin look pallid. No, sapphire was her color. The brilliant color brought out her sparkling eyes.

She finally sat in the chair across from him, allowing him to return to his seat.

"You shaved," she finally said with a slight laugh. "I almost didn't recognize you."

"The funeral," he reminded her.

"Of course. You couldn't attend a formal occasion looking so dreadfully unkempt." She fell silent as if searching for something to say.

Making conversation with him was not a difficulty Louisa typically had, at least not years ago. Just as at Northwood Park, the air around them swirled with tension. A part of him hated the stiffness between them. The other part of him knew it was for the best to keep a distance.

A light rap announced the refreshments. A footman brought tea to the table between them. "Anything else you require, Miss Drake?"

"No." Louisa poured the tea. She handed him a cup of tea with milk and a touch of sugar just as he liked. "How is Charlotte?"

"She is well. She turned four a fortnight ago and believes she is all grown up now."

"I heard you brought her with you."

"People are talking about her already?"

She shook her head. "Not in that manner, Harry, only that you were seen entering the home with a little girl in tow. No one was aware you even had a child, which is the curiosity, not her heritage."

"I see."

"Have you brought her to see Chunee yet?"

"I planned to take her next week for that outing."

"Do you think you will be able to make her wait that long?" she asked, reaching for her tea.

"It is a wonderful bribe to make her do things she would prefer not to, such as go to bed." He couldn't take his gaze off her delicate fingers as they wrapped around the teacup as if to warm them.

She laughed. "So, it is in your best interest to keep her from seeing the elephant for as long as possible."

"Exactly." Harry placed his teacup down. Hearing her laugh warmed his heart, and that would never do. Distance was the plan. After another sip of tea, he pulled out the paper from his pocket. He needed to get right to the point and leave. "Based on what I know of you, I created a list."

"But I never told you what I desired in a husband."

"Louisa, I do have an idea of what you need in a husband."

She narrowed her eyes on him. "How is that when you have not written to me in years?"

"I doubt you have changed much."

She reached over and snatched the list from him. After scanning the page, she looked up with a frown. "I'm afraid I may have been mistaken about your ability to perform this task."

Taken aback, he asked, "How so?"

"Of the five men on this list, the only decent man is Lord Collingwood, and I have never been introduced to him. Reddinford married Miss Harris last fall. Winfried married Miss Lowe over a year ago. And you should have talked to Mr. Kingsley about Hoover."

Damn her for finding fault with almost all of the men. Maybe he should have reviewed the list with his brother. As the owner of one of the most exclusive gaming hells in St. James, Simon knew these people and kept up with their situations. "What about Stanton? He's the second son of an earl."

"I do believe he may be in love with another." She sighed and gave him back the paper. "This will never do, Harry." Louisa rose and then moved away from him, leaving a light fragrance of lilac behind. "We need to discuss what we want in a spouse. I shall call for more tea and some biscuits. This might take a while."

What they each wanted in a spouse? He had no intention of marrying again.

Charlotte needs a mother.

No, Charlotte was doing just fine with Nurse and next year he would find an excellent governess for her.

After speaking with a footman, she returned to the floral wingback chair next to him. "Let's begin with what I prefer in a husband."

She tapped her index finger against her lips in thought.

Damn her for drawing his gaze there. What the bloody hell was wrong with him? He seemed unable to stop the draw, the temptation. He shook his head and returned his wandering mind to the topic at hand. The sooner she gave him her requirements, the faster he could leave.

"You need a man who is near your age," he commented. "After your sister's marriages, I would have thought that would be first on your list."

"Yes, exactly." She paused before for adding, "Perhaps you should write these down."

"I will remember them."

"As you wish, then yes, I want a man closer to my age. I should think no older than thirty-five."

He glanced over at her as she looked down at her hands. She must have learned from her sister's mistakes. Until Tessa married Raynerson, her youngest husband had been twenty years her senior. "No more than thirty-five. And from a good family."

She sent him a look of annoyance. "I should think that obvious."

"No more than thirty-five and good Society. Titled?"

Her brown brows furrowed creating a slight line in her forehead as she thought about that question. "No, that matters not to me."

"Indeed? Your mother might object to a mere mister."

"My mother is not marrying the man I am."

"Go on."

"I would prefer he be of tolerable looks. I should hate the idea of...." Her cheeks reddened as her voice trailed off.

"Of not finding him attractive in the marriage bed? Very understandable." The idea of her making love with anyone forced his hand to fist until it ached.

She nodded as if unable to say another word on the subject. Hiding her embarrassment, she sipped her tea. As she placed her cup down, she added, "He must—"

"Tolerate your smart mouth? After all, you do tend to give your opinions rather freely."

"I can control my tongue."

"You have never been able to with me." He'd missed her smile the past few years. Her laugh, the way she would tilt her head and look at him. But he had to keep his mind on the present course. Find her a husband to assuage his conscience and then return to Northwood Park to live a quiet life.

"What else?"

"Well, before you interrupted me, I was about to say the man must have some intelligence to him. I should hate to feel I married a dimwitted fool."

"Of course." Harry already knew most of these requirements. His only issue was that he must reacquaint himself with Society life, which entailed returning to White's to learn who was still unmarried and looking for a wife.

"And a good father," she added. "I prefer a man who doesn't only see their children before supper each day. He should teach them to ride and to be gentlemen. Speaking of riding, have you started to teach Charlotte yet?"

"Not yet. She is still rather young for such things. Next year, I shall buy her a pony for her birthday."

She smiled over at him in approval. "Good."

"I believe I know what you are looking for. I shall gather a more extensive list, and you can let me know to whom you would like an introduction." He rose to take his leave.

"You are not leaving yet," she said with a shake of her head. "We have not discussed what you are looking for in a wife."

"Louisa," he replied, staring down at her. "I am not looking for a wife."

"Harry, you must have an heir. We both know your cousin is not the right man. He will gamble away everything your family has and then some."

He glanced away from her, not yet ready to admit she was correct on that matter. "I will handle that."

"Charlotte needs—"

"Enough, Louisa. I am her father, and I know what Charlotte needs. I am not marrying again."

"Why?" she whispered in an aching tone.

"I…I just cannot." He strode across the room, and as he reached the door, he remembered his manners. "Good afternoon, Miss Drake."

By the time he returned home, Charlotte had discovered he'd paid a call on Louisa.

"Papa, you said we could both go," Charlotte said in a demanding voice. "I want to see Miss Drake."

Harry sighed and looked up at the ceiling. Were all children so difficult or just his little girl? He couldn't explain to his daughter what seeing Louisa did to him. Charlotte only thought of her as a friend. But he had promised her they would call on Louisa.

"Charlotte, I needed to speak to her about adult things. We will pay a call on her in a few days." And with any luck, his daughter would forget that promise and forget Louisa. Charlotte was far too taken with her.

"Thank you, Papa," Charlotte replied, then jumped into his arms. "I love you."

"I love you too, poppet." He kissed her forehead and then said, "You play up here with Nurse while I finish my correspondence."

"All right." She tumbled out of his arms and picked up her doll.

"I will see you at supper tonight." He had promised her that she could join him in the dining room for supper when he had no guests. Tonight, she would get to show him all the manners Nurse had taught her.

He walked back down to the study and pulled out the estate books. While he trusted his stewards, he always verified the numbers. After an hour, his eyes had blurred from staring at the numbers but thinking about something, or rather someone, else. With the country in mourning, he had no idea how to introduce Louisa to the men she didn't know. The balls and soirees wouldn't start until the end of April, and he wanted to be back at Northwood Park by then.

Frustration swept over him. Why did he agree to this foolish plan? It was highly unlikely that Louisa would have gone through with her threat to show the gossips their pact. He banged his fist on the wood desk. She needed to marry. Once she was married, he would be able to forget about her.

But right now, he needed a diversion from this incessant thinking about her.

"Jenkins," he called out. "Have a groom saddle Hercules. I am going for a ride." And he prayed the park would be quieter now since it was near half three.

A short while later, he entered Hyde Park to clear his head. A few ladies gawked as if they didn't recognize him. Lady Leicester not only noticed him but stopped him.

"Where are you off to, Worthington? When an old lady like me waves, you do more than slow down."

Harry reined in next to her carriage. "Good day, Countess. Is it not a bit chilly for an open carriage?"

"No, it is perfect. Like you, I prefer the north too." The older woman must be over seventy and yet seemed filled with youthful energy. "Hmm, with you back in town, this Season might be interesting after all."

"I'm only here for a few weeks. I doubt I'll still be in town by the time the Season starts." At least not if all goes according to plan.

"No?" She eyed him up and down. "Then perhaps an intimate dinner party. I believe that would be acceptable once we get to half-mourning."

Damn. "There is no need to make a fuss, Countess."

"But I love nothing more than creating a fuss," she said with a smug grin before tapping her driver with her umbrella. "Drive on, Henry."

Lady Leicester was a notorious troublemaker. He didn't know what she was up to, but he had a terrible feeling it involved him. He urged Hercules to a gallop before departing for home.

Louisa opened the invitation to Lady Leicester's dinner party. After checking with her mother, Louisa sent off the affirmative reply. While still weeks away, it was the first invitation they had received since the King's death. Perhaps at the dinner, she would find a candidate or two to give to Harry. She shook her head. Lady Leicester was Tessa's husband's grandmother. It would most likely be just family and an acquaintance or two of the Countess.

Nothing to be excited over.

Once Emma and her mother left for shopping, the house quieted. She attempted to read but couldn't concentrate on anything. The invitation reminded her that she had only one goal this Season. She wondered if Harry would be successful in finding a husband for her. A man who might come to love her.

There she was getting all romantic again. Love didn't matter. At least, not to her any longer. She had to be practical and logical in her search for a husband.

Davis's cough brought her out of her wallowing.

"Yes, Davis?"

"The Duke of Worthington and Lady Charlotte, miss."

Louisa placed the book on the table and rose, straightening her skirts as she stood.

Charlotte walked in, holding her father's hand. The little girl curtsied. Before Louisa could even say good afternoon, Charlotte shot across the room and into her arms.

"I've missed you so much, Miss Drake."

Louisa closed her eyes to keep the tears at bay. "I have missed you, too."

"You didn't quite get that greeting right, Charlotte," Harry said with a chuckle. "What happened to 'Good afternoon, Miss Drake'?"

Louisa glared over at him as she held Charlotte tight. "You cannot expect a four-year-old to control her emotions."

"It was her wish to do it correctly to show you how she's grown up."

"Well, anyone can see how grown up she is now." Louisa slowly put Charlotte down on the divan with her. "After all, she is four."

"Miss Drake, we're going to see the elephant next week."

Louisa smiled at Charlotte's enthusiasm. "I heard."

"You're coming too," she added with a smile.

"Am I?"

She slid a glance to Harry whose face had turned down. Apparently, not his idea.

"Of course, you must join us, Miss Drake," he muttered in a reluctant tone.

"We shall have to see, Charlotte." Louisa paused as the footman set the tea down on the table. "Have you been practicing your tea pouring?"

"Yes, Nurse lets me now." She bounced a little on the divan as if she had too much energy to contain.

Louisa poured them each their tea. "Charlotte, all ladies sit very still when having tea."

Her bouncing immediately stopped. "Yes, Miss Drake. Will you come and read to me again?"

"I'm sorry, Charlotte, but that would not be appropriate." Louisa hated to see the downcast look on the little girl's face. Almost as much as she hated seeing the irritation lining Harry's face.

A commotion at the front door could only mean one thing. Mother and Emma were home early from shopping. Her mother opened the door with a look of shock, which she quickly replaced with a gracious smile.

"Your Grace," she said with a quick curtsy. "How good to see you again."

Harry rose with a bow and said, "It is lovely to see you too, ma'am. And you, Miss Emma."

Emma walked into the room with a smile. "And who is this?" she asked, nodding toward Charlotte.

Louisa took the teacup from Charlotte. "Mind your manners, Lady Charlotte."

Charlotte rose and then curtsied to them. "Good afternoon."

"Mrs. Drake, Miss Emma, this is my daughter, Charlotte."

"It is a pleasure to meet you, Lady Charlotte," Emma said sweetly. "What a lovely dress you are wearing today."

"Thank you, Miss Emma." Charlotte beamed over at Emma.

Her mother slowly sank in the nearest chair. "Your Grace, you have a beautiful little girl."

"Thank you. Charlotte, we have taken enough of Miss Drake's time today." Harry held out his hand. "Come along."

"Miss Drake, will you still come to see Chunee with us?" Charlotte asked Louisa.

She should say no, but she could not refuse Charlotte's big brown eyes. "Yes, just let me know which day next week," she replied, looking up at Harry.

"I will send a note," Harry replied in a reserved tone. "Good day, ladies."

As soon as the door shut behind Harry and Charlotte, her mother said, "He has called on you twice since he returned, Louisa. You must put a stop to it. Think of what people will say."

"What if I don't care what people say, Mamma?"

Emma stared at her with wide eyes.

Her mother continued, "You must think of your sister, if not yourself. Duke or not, there is too much scandal attached to his family name. Lord Bolton comes from an excellent family. If word of the duke's visits reaches his mother's ears, he might break off the engagement."

"Mamma, I will not tell a dear friend of mine that he cannot call on me because of something his father did," Louisa stated flatly.

"Besides," Emma added. "Bolton would never break our engagement. We love each other."

At least Emma had love. Something Louisa doubted she would ever have if she even married.

Chapter 8

Harry stared at the flickering firelight as he sipped a small glass of brandy. He couldn't get the image out of his head of Charlotte sitting next to Louisa at tea today. His daughter had been somewhat disruptive since they arrived in town. More demanding than usual and getting angry at every little thing. But the minute she was in Louisa's company, his daughter behaved like a proper little girl.

She needs a mother. Louisa's words haunted him. *You need an heir.*

Why was that damned woman always right? As much as he didn't want a woman in his life, after everything that happened, Charlotte did need a mother. And Louisa was correct that his cousin would be a completely unsuitable duke. It was up to him to do the right thing for his daughter and the family name.

Perhaps getting Louisa settled with a husband and him with a wife would help absolve him of the guilt that plagued him these past two years. She would have a good man and children. Hopefully, she would fall in love with the man because he knew, as much as she might deny it, that she wanted to love her husband. She'd always tried to hide her romantic tendencies, but he'd seen them in a few of the books she occasionally read.

He forced the heart-crushing sensations away from his mind as he sipped the brandy. Doing the right thing was what his father had taught him. No matter how much it might hurt.

"Your Grace," Jenkins said from the threshold. "Mr. Kingsley is here."

Simon strolled in and helped himself to a brandy. "About time you returned to town."

"I was in mourning."

"You were hiding," he said, taking the seat next to him. "I'm just not sure from what…or whom."

While he'd known about his brother for over ten years, he and Simon had never been close. But Harry wanted that to change. Simon couldn't help being born on the wrong side of the blanket, any more than Charlotte could help to be half-Indian. "So, why are you here?"

"I came to have a brandy with my brother. I figured now that you have returned it would be a little easier to get to know you better. That was your request when you returned from India."

Harry chuckled as he glanced over at his brother who looked so different from him. With the dark looks of his Italian opera singer mother and the strong features of his English forbearers, he was an odd combination.

His sister and Simon were the only two who had known about Charlotte when he arrived from India. As a mother, Daphne instinctually knew to protect his daughter like her own children. She also agreed that their father shouldn't learn of Charlotte until he accepted Sabita. As for Simon, the duke hadn't formally recognized his bastard son at that time so there was no need to worry that a conversation about Charlotte might occur. Harry had wanted someone in his family to meet her in case anything happened to him.

"So, Hell a little slow with the mourning?" Harry asked with a smile. He'd only been to Simon's gaming hell once, but he'd been impressed by every part of it.

Simon nodded. "Horribly so."

"Gambling should pick up in another fortnight. Half-mourning will begin in early March."

"Let's hope so, or I'll be coming to you for assistance," he replied with a laugh. "Now then, what has you so down in the mouth?"

Harry couldn't remember the last time he had a friend to talk to, except for Louisa. Maybe Simon could be that person who was missing from his life. His sister tended to lecture. "I'm considering marriage."

Simon held up his glass in salute. "Congratulations. Who is the lucky lady?"

"I haven't chosen one yet."

Simon sipped his brandy and then chuckled as he placed the snifter on the table. "I suppose as duke, you walk into a ballroom and point to an unmarried lady. She then falls prostrate at your feet in gratitude that you chose her as your duchess."

"Not quite." And there was one woman who would never fall prostrate at his feet. Nor would he want her to. "Besides, there are many things to consider before marrying."

"Such as?"

"She must come from a good family, for one."

"I suppose she must have good eyes and teeth," Simon added with a low chuckle.

Harry frowned at his brother. "This is serious business, Simon. The choice of a wife determines the connections your children will have and their selection of a wife or husband."

Simon tilted his head and arched a black brow at him. "Shouldn't marriage be about love?"

Harry's head fell back against the chair as he laughed. "Not in Society, dear boy. It's all about connections, or if the peer needs money, who has the largest dowry."

"Thank God I'm a bastard then."

"I suppose it does come with certain advantages."

"If you haven't chosen this paragon of Society, how will you decide?" Simon asked, sounding genuinely interested.

Harry didn't want to wait another two months until the Season officially began. Louisa had offered to help him. The idea of Louisa helping him find a wife left a bitter taste in his mouth. But if he was the best person to find her a husband, maybe she was the best person to find him a wife.

Everything inside him rejected the idea of a wife. He'd lost the right to happiness. His father had taken it away from him. And Harry had done the same thing by forcing Sabita to England. She had begged him not to leave India, but he had compelled her to return with him. Only to have her murdered within a fortnight of arriving.

But responsibility came first. He would marry a proper lady, whether he wanted to or not.

"Are you well, Harry?"

Harry blinked and glanced over at his brother. "Pardon, just thinking."

"I had asked how you would find a wife."

"I suppose I will have to attend the Season." Or have Louisa find him a wife.

"Excellent. I do believe I shall attend a few balls this year too. Drum up some business as they say. I will need to make up for this current dry period." Simon rose and looked down at him with a slight furrow to his dark brows. "Are you certain you are well?"

"I will be." Once he found a mother for Charlotte and retreated to Northwood Park. He had to do this for his daughter. Charlotte needed a mother. Love didn't matter any longer. Marriage needed to be a business arrangement and nothing more.

Louisa paced her bedchamber, unable to sit still. It was as if she knew something would happen today. But what? Harry would not pay a call on her again. It had been three days since she'd seen him with Charlotte. In a few days, they would both come to call on her to attend the menagerie and view the elephant.

A walk was what she needed to purge this excess energy. After pulling out her cloak, she called for a footman to accompany her. The walk to Hyde Park stretched her legs and focused her mind on finding a husband. As she walked, she glanced around but mostly noticed either couples or groups of ladies. Not an eligible man in sight. Strolling toward the Serpentine, she heard a familiar giggle followed by the excited cry of Charlotte.

"Miss Drake!"

Oh Lord, how was she to focus on bachelors when Harry was walking directly toward her with his delightful daughter in tow? Her breath quickened as Harry turned to face her.

"Lady Charlotte, how lovely to see you," Louisa said to the little girl.

"Papa took me to the park!"

"Your Grace," Louisa said with a curtsy.

"Miss Drake," Harry replied with a stiff bow. "It's a pleasure to see you again."

"Yes," she said, unsure what to say next. Based on his rigid stance and slight frown, she doubted seeing her was any kind of pleasure for him.

"Miss Drake, we're to see the elephant in four more days!" Charlotte gleefully filled the awkward silence between the adults.

She smiled down at the little girl. "Yes, that is right."

Two ladies approached whispering to each other as they came near. "Your Grace," they said in unison before adding, "Miss Drake."

"Lady Anne, Miss Emerson, lovely to see you again," Louisa said with a smile.

Harry said with a quick bow. "Ladies, this is my daughter, Charlotte."

"I see," Lady Anne replied with a slight sneer. "Come along, Miss Emerson, we must continue our walk."

Louisa wanted to shake some sense into them both. How dare they give Charlotte the cut like that. Thankfully the little girl hadn't noticed the slight, unlike her father. She glanced over at Harry. His jaw clenched, he glared at the backs of the women as they strolled away.

"Charlotte, go look for some fish in the water. John will go with you." Louisa nodded at her footman, who smiled at the young girl.

"Come along, Lady Charlotte," John said with a grin. "Let us see how many fish we can count."

Once they were out of earshot, Louisa whispered, "I am so sorry, Harry."

"It only confirms everything that I have said about these ladies." They slowly followed John and Charlotte toward the water. "I should have known a walk was a bad idea."

Her anger at the ladies and him turned to sarcasm. "Oh yes, far better to hide her away and allow no one to meet your adorable little girl."

"This is not your business. We're leaving now."

"Don't you dare go running back to Northwood Park," she whispered harshly. "Just because those two b—witches cannot see what a darling Charlotte is, doesn't mean that all the ladies will react the same."

"We both know that is the typical reaction."

"Perhaps, but you cannot know that for certain. Hiding Charlotte away only confirms to them that you are ashamed of her."

His eyes grew dark as his fists clenched by his side. "I am not ashamed of Charlotte."

"Of course not," Louisa said softly. "Then bring her everywhere you wish. She did not observe their slight. If you react to the prejudices of a few ignorant ladies, Charlotte will start to notice. Before you realize, she will begin to think there is something different about her."

"So, you are suggesting that I ignore the comments...or lack of greetings."

"Yes. At four, Charlotte won't notice or care. As she gets older, you and your duchess will be her pillar. She will look to you for guidance in dealing with people of their ilk. You can teach her how to be graceful and at times..." She searched for the right word.

"Sharp-tongued?" he offered.

She shrugged. "Perhaps. There will be times she, as the daughter of a duke, will need to lead the way in Society. And sometimes give a cut direct to those who would besmirch her."

"Your Grace," a man called out.

Louisa turned to see Lord Collingwood sauntering toward them. "Well, this may be the perfect time for an introduction."

Harry glanced between the two of them and then released a long sigh. "As you wish. Just be forewarned, Collingwood tends to be a little shy with ladies. But he is a good man."

"Your Grace, it is so good to see you in town again," Lord Collingwood said as he approached.

"Thank you, Collingwood." Looking over at Louisa, he added, "Miss Drake, may I introduce Lord Collingwood?"

Louisa nodded with a smile.

"Miss Drake, lovely to make your acquaintance." He gave her a quick bow.

Louisa curtsied to the viscount. "It is a pleasure, my lord."

Collingwood cleared his throat as he returned his attention to

Harry. "We didn't have much time to speak while at Windsor."

Collingwood and Harry chatted for a few minutes, mostly about the King's funeral, which gave Louisa time to examine him. The man was slightly shorter than Harry but about the same build. His blond hair was almost light brown and starting to thin on top. Overall, not terrible, she decided. The fine wool of his black jacket and trousers bespoke his position in Society.

"I do apologize for taking up so much of your time," Collingwood said with a look to Louisa. "It was dreadfully rude of me."

"Not at all," Louisa replied. "Like you, I hadn't seen His Grace in such a long time, that I had to stop my walk to welcome him back to town."

"I must take my leave now. Good afternoon to you both."

Harry waited until the viscount was out of hearing distance before asking, "What do you think?"

"Hard to tell much at all. Collingwood spent most of the time conversing with you and ignoring me. Perhaps he will ask me to dance when Lady Leicester holds her annual ball to open the Season."

"I will see that he does."

A slow smile lifted her lips. That would mean Harry intended to stay at least until the Season started. They stopped and watched as Charlotte counted a few fish until she became bored and raced back toward them.

"We need to continue our walk, poppet," Harry said to his daughter.

"Can Miss Drake come along too?"

"No, sweetheart, I must return home now," Louisa replied but hated seeing the look of disappointment in the little girl's brown eyes. "But I shall see you again in—"

"Four days!" Charlotte interrupted as she clapped her hands.

As Louisa returned home, she concentrated on Lord Collingwood. The shyness Harry had spoken of wasn't apparent to her. Collingwood seemed to have no difficulty speaking with her after finishing with Harry, which was not unusual. Men tended to gravitate to the higher-ranking peers, whether for words of advice or just the respect of associating with them.

Still, even from their limited conversation, she felt something lacking in him. Unable to determine the cause of her uncertainty, she would have to wait until she had another time to speak with him. Louisa shrugged. Until the Season opened, there would be no balls and therefore, no opportunity to dance with him. Without either, conversation with an unmarried man was limited.

Except, she always seemed to find a way with Harry.

Harry awoke on Friday to the resonance of Charlotte's excited shrieks sounding from the hall. He braced for impact as she ran into his room and jumped on his bed.

"Papa, it's Friday!"

"So it is, poppet." He smiled as she bounced on the bed. "What is so special about today?"

"We're going to see Chunee!"

He couldn't help but laugh at her enthusiasm. Her brown eyes were bright, with the eagerness of a child. "Well then, I suppose you should go eat with Nurse while I dress."

"Then we will leave?"

"We cannot leave until just before eleven since that is the time I told Miss Drake we would collect her."

She bounced off the bed and raced back up to the nursery.

Harry tossed the coverlet off him, and the grabbed his dressing gown. After ringing for his valet, he glanced out at the light snow that had fallen during the night. The white layer coated the city, giving the streets a pristine appearance until people spoiled the beauty.

"Good morning, Your Grace," his valet said as he walked into the room with a tray of tea.

"Good morning, Andrews." While his valet readied his clothing, Harry sipped a cup of tea.

"I understand today is the day Lady Charlotte finally gets to see Chunee."

Harry laughed. "Has she been driving the staff mad with her desire to see the elephant?"

"Of course not, Your Grace. The staff adores Lady Charlotte," Andrews replied with a genuine smile.

After eating his breakfast and reading *The Times*, Harry finished some correspondence with his steward at Worth Hall. At some point, he would need to take a few days and visit the ducal manor. One more thing he had neglected over the past two years. Even though it was his childhood home, he much preferred the rustic charm of Northwood Park.

"Please may we leave now, Papa?" she asked, racing into his study.

"I called for the coach. As soon as it is ready, we shall depart."

Charlotte went to the window to watch for the coach. Within a few minutes, she shouted, "The coach is here!"

No need for a butler when there was an eager child in the house. "Very well, we shall be off."

Once they arrived at the Drake home, he left Charlotte in the carriage while he escorted Louisa and her maid out.

"How excited is she?" Louisa asked as they stepped outside.

He shook his head in reply.

"Driving you mad?"

"I believe she has driven even the servants insane with her anticipation. I do hope the poor elephant lives up to her expectations." Harry took her hand and assisted her into the carriage.

"Good morning, Miss Drake," Charlotte said politely, concealing her excitement.

"Good morning, Charlotte."

Harry took the seat next to Charlotte for propriety's sake when all he wanted to do was sit next to Louisa, inhale the light scent of her lilac soap and dream of stripping her naked. What the bloody hell was wrong with him? He could never have her. And his daughter was in the carriage with them. A wife was precisely what he needed to take his mind off Louisa.

"Are you well, Your Grace?" Louisa asked with a smile. "You seem to be lost in thought."

"Pardon me, Miss Drake. I was thinking about some business."

"Of course, I understand you have much on your mind."

The woman had no idea of the thoughts that plagued him. He'd hoped to have a private conversation at some point during their outing so that he could inform her of his decision regarding a wife. Hopefully, she would find him, someone, quickly.

The drive to The Exeter Exchange seemed endless with the stifled conversation. Perhaps it was Charlotte's presence that caused them both to struggle with a topic appropriate for her tender ears. Harry stared over at Louisa. With her bonnet on, her hair seemed to stay in place today. Finally, they arrived where the menagerie was located. Harry assisted Louisa out of the carriage and then pulled Charlotte into his arms.

"You must stay with either Miss Drake or me. You mustn't wander off, poppet."

"Yes, Papa."

He let her down to walk but took her small hand in his large one.

Once inside, her eyes widened, and her mouth gaped.

"There are so many animals!"

Louisa laughed as she saw the expression on Charlotte's face. "Did you not know there were others?"

Charlotte shook her head. "No." She pointed and said, "There's a monkey! And a camel!"

They stopped and watched the two monkeys chasing each other in the cage. Their antics had Charlotte giggling.

"Good afternoon, Your Grace. Miss Drake."

Harry turned to see Mrs. Mary Gardiner stroll by with her daughter in tow. She had married a friend of his from Eton only to become a widow after three years of marriage. "Good afternoon, Mrs. Gardiner."

"What a beautiful little girl. Is this your daughter?" she asked with a genuine smile.

"Yes, this is Charlotte." Harry appreciated Mrs. Gardiner's sincerity. After the reaction of the ladies in the park, he wasn't certain anyone in town would treat Charlotte with kindness.

"And this is my daughter, Elizabeth."

The two girls appeared to be near the same age and immediately started chattering to each other about the animals. Louisa took a step back as if to give him more room with Mrs. Gardiner. He frowned over at Louisa. She should be next to him, not feet away like a servant.

They walked up to the cage where Chunee was kept, passing the lions and tigers with barely a notice. Louisa stayed in her spot as if unable to move.

"I read he is over seven hundred pounds," Mrs. Gardiner said as they approached the elephant. "I also heard you might want to watch your hat, Your Grace."

Harry took a few steps closer to the cage and turned toward

Charlotte. "Now why is that, I wonder?"

Just then, he felt his hat lift off his head. Charlotte's eyes grew as large as saucers and Louisa let out a husky laugh. His gaze moved to Louisa, who immediately stopped laughing.

"He took your hat, Papa!"

The hat came back down on his head. It was all he could do to contain his laughter. "Charlotte, an elephant cannot take a hat off a person's head."

"He did, Papa! He did it with his trunk!"

Harry moved away from the elephant before he lost his hat for good. He picked up his daughter and moved a little closer to Chunee. The elephant stuck his trunk out to sniff Charlotte, causing a riot of giggles to erupt from the little girl.

"We should move on and allow others to see Chunee," Mrs. Gardiner stated, holding her hand out for Elizabeth.

"Yes, of course." Harry walked toward the lions.

As the afternoon progressed, he couldn't help but notice Louisa's reticence. It was utterly unlike her. And he didn't like it.

Chapter 9

"I heard a rumor that you went to The Exeter 'Change yesterday with a certain duke," Tessa said, sipping her tea in their mother's salon.

Louisa nodded. "Yes, I had promised Charlotte I would attend with them. Not to worry, our maid was with us."

"Indeed? I heard Mamma had insisted Emma accompany you as a proper chaperone."

"Emma had plans with Susan. Besides, she had no desire to be amongst the dirty animals. And it turned out that there was no need for a proper chaperone."

Louisa picked up a biscuit with a sigh, remembering how disappointment had gripped her as she watched Harry with Mary Gardiner. Mary appeared to treat Charlotte no differently than her daughter. And Harry had smiled at her. Something he rarely did with Louisa these days.

"Oh?"

"Mary Gardiner and her daughter joined us."

"Oh." Tessa rubbed her rounded belly. "Any news on the husband search?"

Louisa told her about meeting Collingwood. "I don't know what is wrong with me, Tessa. I look at Collingwood, and there is no spark, no excitement…nothing."

Not that she could tell her sister how looking at Harry made her belly flutter and think dreadfully improper thoughts. Tessa might be upset to learn that Louisa found Harry attractive after what his father had done to her husbands.

"Then he is not the man for you. Trust me. After three marriages to the wrong man, you will know when the right one comes along."

"I am twenty-five years old. Surely, if such a man existed, I would have noticed by now."

"And how old was I when I met Jack?" Tessa reminded her.

"Twenty-five," Louisa replied flatly.

"Perhaps that is the fate of the Drake sisters. We don't meet our true love until we are five and twenty."

"Don't tell that bit of nonsense to Emma or she may have an apoplexy," Louisa said with a laugh.

Tessa laughed and then sobered. Hearing noises at the front door, they both quieted, listening for a moment. After hearing no new voices, Tessa asked, "Where are Mamma and Emma this afternoon?"

"Lady Huntley's again. It is Mamma's favorite place to hear the gossip of the day."

"Miss Drake, this just came," Davis said, holding a salver with a letter.

"Thank you, Davis." Louisa picked up the letter and noticed the seal, before slipping it into her pocket.

"Oh, just open it," Tessa said, pouring herself more tea. "Is it from him?"

Louisa nodded as she retrieved the note and broke the wax. As she read the letter, her stomach roiled in protest. This is what she'd wanted. She was supposed to want him to be happy…but this…this hurt so much. "Oh Lord," she muttered.

"What is it?" Tessa asked quickly.

"He wants me to find him a wife." As she scanned the

requirements for his bride, she almost laughed.

"Isn't that what you had suggested?"

Louisa waved the paper in front of her. "Yes, but this? This is madness. This…this is a list that I shall never be able to satisfy. Just listen to what he wants…she must be beautiful, of superior intelligence, taller than the average female, preferably darker hair because he's not partial to blondes, she must love children, have a kind heart for Charlotte, and preferably one who doesn't giggle."

Tessa's brows rose. "Indeed."

"Yes, indeed. Where exactly am I supposed to find such a paragon of beauty, intelligence, and heart?" Louisa's mind went to yesterday and Mrs. Gardiner. While not quite tall, in fact, quite a bit shorter than Louisa, Mary had most of these qualities. Her shoulders sagged with the thought. "He means Mary Gardiner," she whispered as pain stabbed her heart.

There was nothing terribly wrong with Mary Gardiner. She just wasn't exactly what Harry needed.

"I do not think he meant Mary Gardiner, Louisa." Tessa grabbed the letter and read through it. "No, I don't think that was his intention. Mary is my height. I believe the duke intended someone closer to your size."

Louisa rolled her eyes. "Hardly. When we first met, he would tease me over my height."

"He also said the woman should be of particular intelligence. Quite frankly, I've spoken with Mary before, and while of some intelligence, she doesn't quite match yours."

"Hah!"

"And he explicitly states the woman must love Charlotte. Well, how will he know for certain?" Tessa smiled over at her as she lifted her teacup. "You know how a lady will say anything to catch a duke."

"Whatever are you trying to get at, Tessa?"

"The man wants a very exacting lady." Her sister sipped her tea and then placed the teacup down.

"I highly doubt he has one iota of an idea of what he wants in a wife."

"I'm quite certain he does," Tessa remarked with a smug grin. "I'm just not sure he realizes it yet."

"And who does he want?"

"You."

Louisa laughed until her belly hurt. "Being with child has addled your mind, Tessa."

Tessa slapped her hand on the arm of the chair. "I am not addled-minded. I saw the way he used to look at you, Louisa. He wanted you."

"Of course, he did. He was a rake. Harry has always been my best friend. And at Northwood Park, he told me quite distinctly that he could never marry me because of all that is between our families."

"Which is why I believe he doesn't even realize he wrote down all your attributes. I married my late husbands to help you and Emma be able to marry for love."

Her sister was making no sense today. Harry made it clear that he had no interest in marrying her. "You forget, he wants a beautiful wife. I am the plain Drake sister. You and Emma are the beautiful ones. And I do tend to giggle."

"You are beautiful, Louisa. You tend to giggle when drinking, and I think he must be used to that." Tessa smiled over at her. "Do you love him?"

"I've always loved Harry, but not in the manner you mean."

"Are you certain?" Tessa shifted in her chair. "I want you to find a man you love and one who loves you in return."

"If that is the case, then you should know that Harry does not love me in that way. He loved his first wife so deeply that he spent two years mourning her. And he only returned to town because I threatened him."

"You what?"

Louisa released a long sigh and then explained everything that had happened between them while at Northwood Park from the marriage pact to their constant quarreling. Nothing would ever be the same, as evident by his attitude toward Mary Gardiner. Harry had smiled and laughed when she was near. Unlike his constant scowl when Louisa was close.

Tessa tapped her fingers against her lips with a shake of her head. "No, you're wrong about him. He is pushing you away. But why?"

The idea that Harry would push her away hurt more than Louisa wanted to admit. Worse, ever since that almost kiss, she couldn't help but wonder what it would feel like if Harry kissed her. She wanted to know.

"There is only one thing to do," Emma said, striding into the room with a fierce look upon her young face.

"How did you get in without us hearing you?" Louisa asked, looking over at her younger sister. "And where is Mamma?"

"Davis opened the door for me when the post arrived. And Mamma went shopping with Lady Huntley. You two never tell me anything. Therefore I decided to eavesdrop." Emma strolled toward the chairs where they sat. After pouring herself tea, she added, "The duke wants you, Louisa. He's pushing you away because he feels guilty over the death of his wife."

Louisa's jaw went slack. "How would you know this?"

Emma laughed as she picked up her teacup. "Haven't either of you read any of the novels by Mrs. Henrietta Lewis?"

Louisa glanced over at Tessa who shrugged.

"She writes the most marvelous books of romance. They are full of adventure and passion." Emma shook her head with her lips in a frown. "I will make sure you each have one to read. Any matter, this is very similar to a story where Miss Brooks finds herself in love with Captain Harris. He fought alongside Wellington at Waterloo. But when he returns from battle, he discovers his wife and son are dead from some mysterious fever. He is distraught—"

"What does any of this have to do with Harry pushing me away?" Louisa interrupted, exasperated by the story.

Emma's blond brows furrowed into a scowl. "Captain Harris didn't believe he could fall in love again after such a horrific loss. So, he pushes Miss Brooks away time after time, but she doesn't give up on him. Eventually, he realizes that he loves her. They marry and live happily ever after."

Louisa could only stare at Emma. "So, I'm just supposed to not give up on Harry?"

"Oh no," Emma said emphatically. "You must pursue him."

"Pursue Harry." Louisa couldn't understand just how her sister had completely lost her mind. The man said he wanted Louisa to find him a wife. He didn't ask for that wife to be her.

"Yes," Tessa added with a nod. "Emma, I do believe you are right."

Emma gave Louisa a triumphant smile. "See?"

"No, I do not see!" Emma was only twenty-one. Louisa could excuse her ignorance of all the facts. But Tessa? Her older sister. The same woman whose name was ruined by Harry's father. How could Tessa think pursuing Harry would be good for any of them?

"Louisa, whether you love him or not, you do have feelings for the duke." Tessa rose and walked the room as she rubbed her rounded belly. "You will never know for certain if you do love him unless you put yourself in front of him at every opportunity."

"Just as Miss Brooks did with Captain Harris," Emma added.

Both her sisters had lost their minds. She could almost excuse

Tessa since she was with child, but her younger sister had the most to lose if Louisa chose to pursue Harry. Emma was telling her to chase Harry! This was the most ridiculous idea either of her sisters had ever had. She was not about to pursue her best friend.

She couldn't possibly.

He would be furious with her for attempting such a devious thing. Then again, it seemed he was always irate with her about something lately. Emma could not possibly be correct. No, he needed a perfect young lady to become his wife—not someone like her who had family secrets almost as dark as his own. If her family's secrets were ever revealed, it would ruin them all.

As Tessa left and Emma returned to her novel reading, Louisa stared at the fireplace. Her mind returned to his list of requirements. Was Tessa right that Louisa met every qualification he wrote requested? It didn't make sense. Except if she closed her eyes, she saw his face coming closer to hers, his eyes half-shut and his lips only an inch from hers.

Foolish thoughts, indeed.

If Harry had wanted to kiss her, he would have. If he wanted her as his wife, he would have paid a call on her and proposed.

Maybe the old Harry. But not this man who was so utterly different from his younger self. Could some of what Emma said be right? He was pushing her away out of guilt. If he felt guilty, then he might not have realized what he wrote in his list.

Could Harry want her?

There might be only one way to discover the truth. But it would involve flirting with him. While her sisters had learned how to flirt and be seductive at an early age, Louisa had kept her head in scholarly books. She had no idea how to entice a man.

Perhaps there were books on flirting.

Harry ascended the steps to Lady Leicester's home in Grosvenor Square. With the country finally into half-mourning, he had received a few invitations to dinner parties and even a poetry reading at Lady Gringham's salon. But tonight, he would have to fight his apprehension and re-enter Society. And face Louisa's sister.

The door opened as he approached, and the butler smiled at him.

"Good evening, Your Grace," the man said before Harry had even pulled a card out. "I am Stevens and if you should need anything at all, just let me know."

"Thank you, Stevens."

The butler helped him with his coat and then gave it to a footman. "Most of her ladyship's guests have arrived and are in the salon."

Instead of letting a footman show him the way, Stevens led him to the salon. Harry could hear the low tones of conversation and then a familiar husky laugh.

"His Grace, the Duke of Worthington," Stevens announced as he opened the door.

Harry took in the room and tried not to show his surprise. He'd expected no more than ten to twelve people, but there had to be near thirty in the room.

"Oh, do come in, Your Grace," Lady Leicester said and then gave him a quick curtsy. The rest of the room followed with either a curtsy or a bow. She ambled over to him. Taking his arm, she whispered, "If there is anyone you do not know, tell me, and I shall introduce you. I do hope you don't mind that I had to invite the Drake girls as one is married to my grandson."

"I don't mind at all. Nothing that happened was their fault."

"My thoughts exactly," she replied with a sharp nod.

"Miss Drake and I have been friends for years," he added as he spied her standing near her sister Emma.

Lady Leicester glanced over at Louisa. "Indeed, I had no idea. Do try to enjoy yourself tonight. I know how difficult it can be the first time out after mourning. Now you must excuse me, I must make a few minor changes to the seating arrangements."

Seeing Tessa and her husband speaking with Viscount Bideford, Harry walked toward them with a forced smile. He could do this. He hadn't spoken to her since her release from prison after his father hung himself, freeing her from all suspicion.

"Good evening, Bideford," he said before turning to Tessa and Raynerson. "Good evening, Raynerson, Mrs. Raynerson."

"Your Grace," they said in unison.

He released a long breath before saying, "Mrs. Raynerson, I do hope you will be able to see past my father's madness and realize I had no idea what he was about."

"Of course, Your Grace. I do not hold you to blame. You were in India for most of the time."

Not for the first husband. Perhaps he should have seen the signs then, but he'd been too involved in trying to court his dearest friend.

"My sister has always spoken favorably of you, Your Grace," she added with a smile.

"Thank you."

Not knowing what else to say to her, he bowed and walked away. Looking around the room, he realized that Lady Leicester must have been particular with the invitation list. He knew everyone in the room. As people came up to greet him, he lost sight of Louisa. At some point this evening, he needed to speak with her to see if she'd decided on a list for him.

After spending the past fortnight going to White's, he had a few more men on which he needed her opinion. He still thought Collingwood might be the best choice for her. The viscount was an even-tempered man who would indulge Louisa with her books and other interests. Harry had heard nothing about a gambling problem with him. Finally, Louisa returned to the salon with her sister.

"Excuse me, I must speak with someone," Harry said to the group that surrounded him. Walking toward Louisa, he forced the feeling of warmth that invaded his body away and concentrated only on what he'd come here for. "Good evening, Miss Drake, Miss Emma."

"Good evening, Your Grace," they said in unison. Emma excused herself to speak with a friend.

"Miss Drake, I do hope you are well."

"I am indeed. And you?"

"Very much so. I do have a few matters I need to discuss with you." His gaze moved to the bodice of her lavender gown.

Stop looking at her like a reprobate.

"As do I, Your Grace," she said, casually sipping her sherry as she looked about the room. "But we can hardly discuss this here."

"I agree. Take a walk in Hyde Park tomorrow morning. I shall meet you there," he whispered before giving her a bow and strolling away. He glanced back, and she smiled over at him with a nod.

Focus on the ladies in the room and not the one you can never have.

Heeding his conscience's advice, he strolled the room and slowly realized that the only unmarried ladies in attendance were Louisa and Emma.

"Dinner is served, my lady," Stevens announced to the room.

"Your Grace, you must walk me in," Lady Leicester said, at the threshold. "You are the guest of honor."

"Of course, Countess." Harry walked over and held his arm out for the lady. "Allow me."

They sauntered to the dining room as the others followed. After escorting Lady Leicester to the head of the table, he found his seat to her right. He couldn't help but watch Louisa enter the room accompanied by an elderly baron. A sliver of disappointment trickled through him as she took her seat at the opposite end of the table where he could only watch her from afar.

"Are you well, Your Grace?" the countess asked with a look of concern. "You seem a bit forlorn."

"Forlorn? I do hope not," he replied as a footman placed a bowl of cream soup in front of him. "Just a flickering thought about my sister. I haven't seen her for some time."

Lady Leicester glanced down the table toward Louisa. "Of course, that is all that is on your mind. I do hope you have decided to marry again. Society has become a bit dull. If you are ready to enter the marriage mart again, I can only imagine the excitement of all the mamas."

He sipped his potato soup and then nodded. "As a matter of fact, I have."

The conversation at the table quieted and then buzzed with whispers.

"Excellent news, indeed, Your Grace," she said with a sly smile. "And as I always try to hold the first official ball of the Season, it is certain to be a crush."

"Unless I am married and gone back to the North before then," he said with a smile to make her think he teased her. And tomorrow he intended to make sure Louisa understood his plan. Now, if he could only stop glancing down the table at her.

But as he did once again, she lifted her wine glass in salute with a smile at him. His heart pounded in his chest. That was the most flirtatious look she'd ever given him. Louisa flirting with him? His imagination was playing tricks on his mind now.

The next morning, Harry walked the length of the Serpentine and back, waiting for Louisa. It was nearly noon. She should have been here by now, unless she decided against meeting him. Thinking back on last evening, he realized that she hadn't answered him when he told her to meet him. Then again, he hadn't given her a chance. He'd moved away from her to prevent talk before she had the opportunity to reply. He'd assumed her nod was consent.

Or might she be avoiding him? There was the possibility that she found his list a bit rigid. But the next duchess needed to be perfect. After Sabita, he wanted no gossip regarding his next wife. He had to think of his daughter's future.

The March wind whipped around him. Pulling his overcoat tighter around him, he glanced farther out into the park, hoping to find her.

Harry patted the pocket of his waistcoat, which held the names of five more gentlemen that should be suitable for her. Hopefully, her list would be well thought out with ladies who would accept his daughter and find him to be agreeable. Turning around for one last look, he spotted her, and the breath rushed from his lungs.

"Where have you been?" Louisa asked in a hushed but annoyed tone. "I've been here for over an hour looking for you."

"I was here the entire time. Did I not say to meet near the Serpentine?"

"No, you did not." She glanced back at her footman, who had accompanied her. "I don't have much time now. I promised John we would leave by noon."

"Shall we sit?" he asked, pointing to a small bench near the water.

"Heavens, no. We must keep walking to make it look as if we just came upon each other, not that we planned to meet here."

Apparently, Louisa was only sensible about her reputation in town. He pulled out his paper with the names he'd discovered. "Very well, then. I did a little more investigation before creating this list."

She grabbed it from his hand and scanned it. "Brentwood is a dimwitted fool."

"I went to Eton with him, and he excelled."

"No, you attended with James. He passed away when you were in India. His brother Nigel has the title now."

Harry closed his eyes for a moment. *Damn.* Would he ever get this right? "You're correct. Nigel is a dimwitted fool. Still, there is no need to get testy about it."

"I am not testy! It is dreadfully cold."

He stifled a smile. "Of course not," he said in a condescending tone.

"Oh, do be quiet, Harry." She perused his list again. "I suppose Deering might be acceptable."

"You don't sound certain." They walked along the Serpentine a few more feet before she stopped.

"He is not the most...."

Attractive? How was he supposed to judge that?

"Well-mannered," she finally continued. "I sat near Deering at one of Lady Huntley's dinner parties. The man was speaking with his mouth full of food. I felt dreadful for poor Mrs. Montgomery. She sat next to him, and by the time dinner was finished, she had food spittle on her silk gown."

He blinked in surprise. "Very well, then. Walker?"

"Absolutely not!" She shivered. "That man is horrid. He was dreadful toward my sister when she came out of her last mourning."

Harry sighed. "Two more to scratch off your list, then."

Louisa picked up a small stone and skipped it across the water without looking at him. "What do you think about Ainsley?"

"Have you completely lost your mind?" The thought of her marrying one of his closest friends was beyond the pale.

"Why not? I realize he was a bit rakish in his day." Louisa paused as if trying to put him in a good light. She continued to walk along the lake as her footman trailed behind. "But surely he has matured by now."

"Louisa, I have been friends with Ainsley since we were children. He was my worst influence."

She shrugged. "Rumor has it that Ainsley is looking for a wife this Season because of the estate debts." She looked up at him from under her lashes with a sensual smile. "He is an earl from an excellent family. He won't mind my small dowry with the money he is to inherit from his uncle. And he is rather attractive."

Harry's hands tightened into fists. He would see her everywhere with Ainsley. A man who knew exactly how to make a woman think she was in love with him so that he could—

No!

Anyone but Ainsley. "No, Louisa. He is not the right man for you. God knows he won't be faithful to you."

She shrugged. "How many men are faithful?"

"Many."

"Yes, and many times it's the men Society least expects. The reformed rake, for one."

"And you think you could reform Ainsley?"

She shrugged again with a secret little smile that nearly drove him insane. Did she not realize how much of a reprobate Ainsley could be?

"I do believe the earl is not as much of a scoundrel as people like to say."

Harry stopped walking and closed his eyes, debating how much he could tell her without breaking a promise he'd made to his friend. "Louisa, please listen to me. I know things about him that no one else does. Things of which even he is not proud."

She glanced to the ground as her cheeks flushed. "Just as there are things that no one knows about my family, including you, that would ruin us all."

"What things?" He'd never heard of anything, except the business with his father and Tessa.

She gave him a delicate shrug before continuing to stroll. "Let us say, something that many members of the ton would love to learn about to ruin my family for good."

He had no idea what she was speaking of, which made no sense. They'd told each other everything. "Since when have we kept secrets from each other, Louisa?"

She abruptly stopped and turned to glare at him. "Indeed? Let me think...leaving for India without telling me. Then there was getting married while in India. Let us see, what else...oh, yes, a daughter!"

The heat of embarrassment and anger at the reminder of his transgressions crossed his face. "That was different," he said, knowing it was not.

She rolled her eyes. "I must take my leave now."

"We have yet to discuss your list for me."

Pulling out a paper from her reticule, she handed it to him. "I'm afraid I only have three names. Once the Season starts, I shall have a better idea of who is coming out this year." "A debutante? She will only be eighteen."

"Is that a problem, Your Grace? Age was not a requirement on your list."

"I will be thirty in a few months. Why would I want someone so young?" Harry looked down at her in confusion. "No, I need someone at least two and twenty."

"You are the most exasperating man I have ever known," she commented in an aggravated tone. "Review the list and let me know if you would like more information on them or an introduction."

"As you wish." She walked away from him, but the hauntingly familiar scent of lilac remained in the air and seemed to wrap around his heart like a vise.

Chapter 10

Louisa spent the next few weeks doing the exact opposite of what Emma suggested by avoiding Harry. If she didn't meet with him, she could not give him more names of prospective brides. While he'd said he would attend Lady Leicester's ball, she was positive if he had the chance, he would run back to Northwood Park.

He sent a message every few days asking if she would be attending some function so he could get an update on her search for his duchess. His letters had become increasingly terse. And every note reinforced the thought that he wanted to marry as quickly as possible to avoid the Season. With only a week until Lady Leicester's ball, Louisa had to evade him a little longer.

The Season would provide far more opportunities to test Emma's theory that he was pushing her away out of guilt. It was much harder to flirt at a poetry reading or musicale than a ballroom with dancing and gardens for private tête-à-têtes.

While she'd been thankful for a cold, forcing her to miss several functions, another week in this house might drive her insane.

Walking to the window of the salon, she glanced down onto Chandler Street. A few carriages rumbled down the street dispatching callers but none to this house. The spring day seemed to call her to get out of the house and go for a walk. Her shoulders sagged. A stroll in the park meant the chance of seeing Harry, which would never do.

A tall figure of a man riding a chestnut horse ambled down the street. Reaching the Drake home, he reined in and looked up toward the salon window. Louisa gasped and moved away from the glass. Had he seen her? Davis had orders to tell Harry she was not at home if he happened to call.

Hearing the loud thump of the knocker, she was certain Harry would not be placated with lies today. The sound of male voices approaching caused her heart to leap.

"Your Grace!" Davis said in his sternest voice, "You cannot go up there."

"I saw her standing at the window in the salon, Davis. She will see me today."

The low, harsh tone of his voice sent a shiver of apprehension down her spine. Perhaps it was time to test Emma's theory. She opened the door to the salon as he reached the last step. "Good afternoon, Your Grace."

"Miss Drake," he said with a nod before looking back at Davis. "She appears to be at home, Davis."

"Yes, Your Grace."

"Davis, do send some tea and biscuits in for the duke," Louisa said before returning to the salon. "That was dreadfully rude to Davis, Harry."

Harry followed her into the room but closed the door behind him. "Are you well, Louisa?"

"Perfectly now." She sat on the floral chair near the window. "And you?"

"I am well," he replied. "I have sent you several notes but have received no replies. I was worried—"

"That I wasn't focusing on finding you a wife?" she interrupted with a brow deliberately arched.

"That you might be ill."

"I did have a dreadful cold that kept me from a few functions."

He tilted his head and looked over at her with a questioning look. "Well, it is good to see you are well enough to attend a musicale tonight. I hear many people have already arrived for the Season, so it might be quite a crush."

"Oh, Mrs. Smyth's musicale?" She cast him a dejected look. "I fear we were not invited. Even after two years, some people still wish to blame my sister and her family for what happened."

"Indeed," he replied, walking by the fireplace before taking a seat near her. His gray eyes sparkled with irritation as he stared at her. "I'm quite certain I can send word to Mrs. Smyth about the oversight."

Of course, Mrs. Smyth would invite them all, including Tessa, if the Duke of Worthington requested. "Do not put yourself out on my account. Lady Leicester's ball is in a week. Once the Season officially begins, I have plenty of time to find you a wife."

"And you know I wished to return to Northwood Park before the Season."

She shrugged. "Perhaps, but you have no choice now."

He clenched his fists in apparent frustration. "Have you come up with any other names for me?"

Davis brought tea and biscuits in and placed the tray on the table in front of them. "Do you require anything else? A maid to chaperone perhaps?"

"No, Davis. His Grace is always a perfect gentleman." She bent over to pour the tea as the butler walked out. "Now, I have a few names for you, but I would prefer to verify their status first. Miss Jane Bigby might be a good candidate, but I am not well acquainted with her."

"At this point, I do not care. Just find me someone." He reached for the tea she held out for him.

As he grabbed the tea, she brushed a finger over his. Focusing on him, she searched his eyes for some reaction but did not see any change. What did she expect? It wasn't as if the brief contact would create such turmoil that he might drop his tea. She was a fool for listening to Emma. Her sister's head was filled with fluff from the nonsense she read.

Perhaps she needed a more direct manner. She stood, knowing as a gentleman, he would do the same. Walking across the room, she said, "Why such haste, Harry? The lady will be your wife. Finding someone who meets your every requirement will take time."

"You have had weeks, Louisa."

"Yes, but the mourning has put a damper on entertainment. Many people even restricted their daily calls." She stopped in front of him, staring at a brass button on his gray waistcoat. Remembering she was supposed to act flirtatious, she said, "I do believe you have a loose button."

She placed her hand on his chest and twisted the button until it loosened.

Hearing him suck in a breath, she smiled. He grabbed her wrist and held her hand away from him. Staring up at him, she noticed the hardness of his gray eyes seemed gone, replaced by a look that would burn the hardiest of spinsters.

"I apologize, Your Grace. I thought you would prefer I tell you than to lose a button."

He continued to look down at her and hold her wrist, unable to break the contact. For a long moment, they continued to stare at each other. She had a fleeting thought that he might try to kiss her. Oh, how she wanted him to kiss her. Her heart pounded in her chest.

Kiss me!

If she could only say the words aloud. But would Harry kiss her if she asked? Before she could find out, the sound of the front door opening broke them apart. Hearing her mother and sister's voices coming closer, they said nothing but returned to their seats and the tea waiting for them.

Louisa had no idea of what to say to him. As she listened to his swift breathing, she had to admit Emma might indeed be on to something.

"Shall I speak to Mrs. Smyth, then?" he finally asked.

Mrs. Smyth? Oh, yes, the musicale. Thankfully, her mother walked into the salon with Emma in tow. Mamma cast her a look of disapproval while Emma smiled over at her.

"Good afternoon, Your Grace," Mamma said with a tight smile.

Harry rose and bowed to them both. "Good afternoon, Mrs. Drake, Miss Emma."

"Mamma, His Grace was just asking if we should like to attend Mrs. Smyth's musicale this evening."

Her mother frowned. "I am afraid we have plans to attend an intimate supper at Lady Huntley's tonight. We were invited just this afternoon."

Harry gave a slight nod. "Of course. I did not wish you to miss out on Mrs. Smyth's evening of music, but since you are otherwise occupied, I shall take my leave now. I look forward to seeing you all at Lady Leicester's ball."

As soon as the front door closed, Mamma spoke, "I thought we had agreed that the duke should not make any more calls on us."

"Mamma, how am I supposed to tell a duke not call on me?" Louisa inhaled deeply to keep her anger from showing.

"I like the man," Emma added with a smile.

Her mother turned on Emma. "And will you like him if your fiancé's mother decides His Grace is not acceptable company? Bolton may be forced to throw you over."

Emma's gaze moved to her lap.

Louisa desperately wanted to tell them both that it might be for the best if Emma jilted Bolton. The man was far too controlled by his mother. He and Emma could never be happy while Lady Bolton was alive, but if her sister loved him, then Louisa could try to be supportive. "I highly doubt Lady Bolton would believe a duke to be unacceptable company."

"Indeed?" Her mother reached for her tea. "She cut the Duke of Cranston in the middle of Almack's."

Louisa pressed her lips together. Cranston's only offense was his immoral behavior, including taking a mistress into his own home. Not quite on par with an admitted murderer for a father. She would need to speak with Emma alone before continuing this plan of pursuing Harry.

When neither of her daughters had a retort, Mamma rose and looked at them both as she stood. "I thought as much. And the invitation to supper at Lady Huntley's is for me alone."

After Mamma left the room, Emma looked up at her with a smile. "What was His Grace doing here?"

"He came to call because I have not answered the notes he has sent."

"Perfect strategy."

Was it? Louisa had assumed Emma might feel she was ignoring her plan. "How so?"

"He came to call on you."

"I suppose he did." Louisa stared down at her hand, unsure if she should mention what she had done. "I touched his chest."

Emma's blue eyes widened. "You what?"

"I made an excuse that he had a loose button on his waistcoat." She refused to admit to her little sister how touching the brocade waistcoat had warmed her entire body. Or how she wanted to remove his jacket, waistcoat, and shirt to feel his skin under her hand.

"And did he react?"

Embarrassed by her thoughts, Louisa only nodded.

"How?" Emma pressed.

"His eyes…there was something different, unlike anything I had seen before. He sucked in a breath and could only stare at me."

Emma smiled. "Excellent."

"I'm not certain, Emma. You heard Mamma. What if Lady Bolton forces her son to break it off with you?"

"Bolton would never do such a thing. He loves me."

"I am certain he does, but his mother is very controlling. You've admitted as much." She wanted to shake Emma until she realized that Lady Bolton would never let Emma have a say in her son's life. Emma was only to be a trophy, brought out to shine at the balls on her husband's arm and then returned to the glass case and into the background.

"It will be different when we are married," she replied confidently. "Now, what are you going to wear to Lady Leicester's ball?"

"My ivory silk."

"No, you are not." Emma pressed her lips together and widened her eyes as if she had a big secret that she was unable to contain.

"What do you mean?"

"Tomorrow, you and I will go to Madame Beaulieu's shop for a fitting on your new sapphire silk gown."

Louisa shook her head. As much as she might have wanted a new gown for the ball, there was not enough time to make up something now. "It's far too late, Emma."

"Not when she has been working on the gown for over a week."

Louisa stared over at her sister. "How?"

"I might have told Madame that you were too ill with a cold to come yourself, but you wanted the blue silk. Since she already had your measurements, she worked her magic and created the most beautiful gown I have ever seen. I am sincerely envious."

"Why would you do such a thing?"

"Because you will be the next Duchess of Worthington. And as such, you must dress like a duchess. Since you don't care about fashion, it will be my duty to make certain you are dressed accordingly."

She was amazed by her scheming little sister. Louisa hadn't noticed how much she'd grown up in the past few years. While still slightly immature, Emma might be far more interesting than Louisa ever imagined.

Louisa stood in front of the mirror at Madame Beaulieu's shop as the madam herself with two assistants made a few minor adjustments. Frequently, Madame Beaulieu oversaw the pattern and fabric choice but left the fittings to her assistants. Regardless of how many women were attending her, Louisa couldn't take her eyes off the gorgeous blue silk gown. The gown had a typical high-waist with a laced V front satin panel and short cap sleeves. But it was the dark blue lace puff hem that Louisa fell in love with at first sight.

"Since you've barely said two words, I can only assume you like the gown," Emma said with a proud smile.

"It is the most beautiful gown I have ever worn." Louisa glanced over at her sister. "But how will Mamma pay for such a luxury?"

"Do not worry about that," Tessa said as she walked into the dressing room. "Oh my, it is more beautiful than you told me."

Louisa looked at them both. "You knew about this too?"

"Who do you think is paying for that gown?" Tessa sat down and smiled over at her.

"Thank you, Tessa. But it's too—"

"Too grand to wear to Lady Leicester's ball? I don't think so. Lady

Leicester, won't you come in and give us your opinion?"

"What is Lady Leicester doing here?" Louisa whispered.

"She is shopping with her grandson's wife." The older woman strolled through the curtain using her cane although Louisa suspected the countess had no real need for assistance walking.

Louisa felt as if she'd been ambushed in the dressing room of Madame Beaulieu's shop. She prayed Tessa had not told Lady Leicester about her plan to pursue Harry. The fewer people who knew, the better.

"And dear, you really must learn how to whisper, so others don't hear you," Lady Leicester added.

Louisa rolled her eyes. "Yes, Countess."

"Don't get petulant with me. I am here to help. Without my assistance, your sister would never have married my grandson." The older woman nodded at Emma, who jumped out of the chair for her. "Now, have a turn toward me."

This was worse than shopping with her mother. "Yes, ma'am."

She made a quarter turn toward the dowager countess. "What do you think?"

The countess rubbed her chin in contemplation. "The color is perfect for you, but if you are to catch a duke—"

So much for her pursuit of Harry being kept secret.

"—that neckline must be lowered."

What did the countess just say? A lower neckline? "This is perfectly low enough."

"Nonsense. Madame Beaulieu, if a lady of a lower standing wishes to win the affection of a duke, would you recommend that neckline?"

The dressmaker rose and looked at Louisa thoroughly. "A duke, eh?"

"Yes," the Countess replied.

"Do you remember what you did for the Duchess of Danvers

when she was still Miss Eliza Smith, a nobody from that little village…what was it called?"

The dressmaker grinned. "Ah yes, from Laceby. And I do indeed remember you suggested something to make the duke realize what he would miss if he let her go. Unfortunately, we don't have as much material to work with here."

Both Lady Leicester and the dressmaker stared at Louisa's bosom. Heat scorched her cheeks. She couldn't help it if she had less there than her sisters, especially Emma.

"Still, I believe a lower neckline might help," the countess commented. "And perhaps a little padding the stays."

Louisa's face heated with embarrassment. If only a hole could open in the earth and suck her down.

"Yes, do that so Worthington sees he might not be the only man interested in Miss Drake." The countess stood and stared at Louisa. "Do not think this will be easy, my dear. A duke is never easy to catch."

"Yes, ma'am." She had no idea what else to say.

"Very well, I shall take my leave. Tessa, do not forget to come for supper tomorrow. We need to discuss nurses for my great-grandchild."

"As you wish, my lady," Tessa replied, quickly taking the empty chair.

Louisa turned back toward the mirror as Madame Beaulieu attacked the trim of her neckline. "I thought the gown was perfect," Louisa muttered.

"It will be," the dressmaker replied. "I had no idea I was dressing a future duchess."

That was left to be seen. Louisa looked over at Tessa. "How could you have told her?"

Tessa laughed. "I didn't. His Grace mentioned at her dinner party that you and he had been friends for years. She happened to notice the looks he was giving you during dinner and mentioned it to me."

Louisa's mouth went dry. "He was giving me looks?"

"So she says. But I never know with her. Sometimes I believe she is half-mad."

Half-mad? Louisa was convinced the lady was completely mad.

Chapter 11

The night of Lady Leicester's party arrived far too quickly for Harry. Dread seeped into his soul as he climbed each step to her front door. He should have already found a bride and retired to the country. As the door opened, the sound of endless chatter filled his ears, deafening him.

"Welcome, Your Grace," the butler said as he allowed him inside.

He nodded. "Good evening."

Harry entered the spacious front hall where only a few people lingered as if waiting for someone. He hoped not him. Many nodded at him with a slight smile, but a few ignored his presence. Lady Leicester ambled toward him with a smug grin on her face.

"Good to see you, boy," she said as she took his arm to lead him into the salon. Only Lady Leicester would call a duke, *boy*.

"Thank you for the invitation, Countess."

He let her guide him into the salon and then stopped. Harry scanned the room for a familiar face. Spotting Louisa, his heart lightened. She looked beautiful tonight with a sapphire silk gown devoid of all the bows typical on most of her unmarried peers. She wore only a small pearl necklace and matching earbobs to complete the simple ensemble. But it was the neckline of the gown that took his breath away. He'd never seen her wear something so daring.

"Are you looking for someone special, Your Grace?" Lady Leicester asked innocently.

"Just a familiar face."

He stared down at her to see a twinkle of humor in her brown eyes.

"I do expect you on the dance floor for the first dance," she said. "After all, the party is in your honor."

Looking over at Louisa, he nodded. "Certainly."

"Do try to enjoy yourself tonight, Worthington."

"Thank you." Harry walked toward Louisa who was speaking to a lady he didn't know. "Good evening, ladies."

Both ladies curtsied to him. "Your Grace," Louisa said with a smile. "Miss Bigby, may I introduce His Grace, the Duke of Worthington."

"Miss Bigby, it is a pleasure." Harry bowed over the hand of the very young Miss Bigby. Did Louisa have no sense at all? Miss Bigby couldn't be more than eighteen.

"I was just telling her all about you, Your Grace," Louisa said with a mischievous smile.

"Were you now?" He turned to Miss Bigby. "All lies, I am quite certain."

The younger woman giggled and blushed.

He looked back at Louisa with a cocked brow. "I have been told by Lady Leicester that I must dance the first dance."

"Excellent," Louisa replied with a broad smile. "Miss Bigby would love to dance with you."

"I would," she said breathlessly.

Harry narrowed his eyes on Louisa. Dancing with Miss Bigby was not the plan when he walked over here. Dancing with Louisa was about the only way to speak with her properly. And he was positive Louisa knew that. "I would be delighted."

"Your Grace, is that not Lord Collingwood over there?" Louisa asked glancing at the man who just entered the room.

"I believe it is. After my dance with Miss Bigby, I shall endeavor to speak with him." Letting Collingwood or any man in the room dance with Louisa left him feeling irritated.

"Thank you, Your Grace."

"Miss Bigby, shall we?" he asked, holding out his arm to her. "The music is set to begin."

"Of course, Your Grace," she answered with a slight giggle.

He led her to the dance floor, mentally cursing Louisa for getting the upper hand. Miss Bigby's constant giggling was already driving him mad. As the dance started, he searched for Louisa to see if she had partnered with someone for the dance. Instead, he found her standing against a wall sipping her wine, staring at him with a self-satisfied smile. Thankfully, the dance was fast-paced, so he didn't have to attempt conversation with his giggling partner.

Once the set finished, he searched for the only woman he wished to speak with tonight. Only this time, Emma had her sister's attention. He grabbed a glass of wine and watched Louisa from afar.

"Well, at least you have excellent taste in women."

Harry turned at the sound of his brother. "I didn't expect to see you here tonight."

"Since our father's death, I am now a somewhat respectable bastard. It's interesting how inheriting a large sum of money from a duke will do that for you."

"Well, congratulations on gaining some respectability."

Simon laughed. "Now, back to those two ladies you were eyeing. I suppose, as the bastard, I must take your cast-off, so which one do you prefer?"

Harry frowned. "Hold your tongue. They are both ladies. Miss Louisa Drake to the left, is a dear friend of mine."

"A friend, is it?" Simon smirked. "I don't believe I have ever had a lady friend, except in the bedroom where they all are my friends.

And what about the angelic-looking one?"

"Miss Emma is engaged to Lord Bolton."

"She looks a little too innocent for my liking. The brunette has a passion in her manner that is hard to resist."

"Simon," Harry growled. "Do not think about it."

"I see how it is," Simon replied with a smirk. "I suppose I shall have to settle for a lonely widow tonight."

"Good luck."

Simon chuckled. "I don't need luck, brother. I had a fortune from my gaming hell before Father bestowed even more upon his 'poor' bastard."

Spying Collingwood, Harry said, "I must go speak with someone."

Harry left his brother and focused on Lord Collingwood. "Collingwood, might I have a word?"

Collingwood turned and nodded. "Of course. What do you need, Your Grace?"

"If you remember you met Miss Drake at the park a few weeks ago. It would be a favor to me if you would dance with her. She gets so few opportunities."

"I would be honored to dance with any friend of yours." Collingwood scanned the room.

They walked over to where Emma and Louisa stood. Louisa smiled at Harry and then Collingwood. "Your Grace, my lord," she said with a curtsy.

"Miss Drake," Collingwood said with a bow. "It is a pleasure to see you again."

"Emma, this is Lord Collingwood."

"A pleasure, my lord." Emma made her curtsy and then excused herself.

"Would you honor me with a dance, Miss Drake?" Collingwood

asked politely.

"Yes, that would be lovely."

While they went off to dance, Harry picked up a snifter of brandy and gulped it down. What the devil was wrong with him tonight? The idea of that man laying a hand on her, even with gloves on, touched a nerve with Harry. He stifled the urge to go over and cut in on Collingwood. That would never do. Louisa would be furious…with good reason.

Except, seeing her with Collingwood might drive him insane.

Louisa enjoyed her dance with Collingwood, who conversed with her about his family and his sister's new child. He was a handsome man with his blond hair and brown eyes, but she felt as if she were dancing with a brother. She supposed if she must settle, then Collingwood would be an acceptable choice. Her mother would be pleased that he was a viscount as that was the most important thing to her. But Louisa didn't wish to settle now that she had spent time with Harry again.

"I do hope you will honor me with one more dance before the night is through?"

She smiled at him. "Of course."

He left her with her mother, who beamed. "A viscount, Louisa! Very good."

"A very nice man, Mamma."

"The only thing that matters is that he has a title and enough income. Now catch this one."

Louisa shook her head as she walked away from her mother and spied the terrace. A few minutes alone would do her good to think. She slipped outside, hoping no one noticed her. Staring out at the gardens, she wondered what her life would be like in a year. Would she finally be married and perhaps with a child on the way? Or firmly on the shelf? At twenty-five, this was quite probably her last chance.

If things didn't work with Harry, Collingwood might be an acceptable solution. Everything she'd heard about the man was kind. The son of a viscount, his mother lived with him when she wasn't visiting her daughter's family. He should have enough income to satisfy her mother, although she honestly didn't know. So why did she feel so empty inside?

She felt a presence before the man spoke. *Please don't let it be Harry.* She needed space from him if she were to contemplate Collingwood. The light breeze carried the scent of leather and cinnamon, and she knew it was Harry. Her pulse quickened, and her breath seemed to steal away from her.

She could always sense when he was near.

He stood directly behind her now and then brought a glass of wine around her. She stared down at the gloved hand, which held the glass and said, "Thank you, Your Grace."

His low chuckle tightened her belly. "We are alone. I believe so you may call me Harry."

He moved away, and she felt an instant chill. After her sipping her wine, she said, "We shouldn't be out here alone, Harry."

"It is far from the first time we've been on this terrace alone. Besides, I want to hear about your dance with Collingwood." He casually leaned against the balustrade and then looked at her. "Was it enjoyable?"

"Yes, he is a very nice man. And your dance with Miss Bigby?"

"She did nothing but giggle most of the time." He sipped his wine. "It occurred to me while dancing with Miss Bigby that you and I have never danced. How is that possible?"

Louisa frowned in thought. He was right. In seven years, they had never danced together. "I suppose we were usually outside conversing."

"Miss Drake, you should not be out here alone with the Duke!"

Louisa turned at the sound of Jane Bigby's high-pitched voice. "Good evening again, Miss Bigby. I suppose you are right that the we shouldn't be here alone. But we are dear friends, and it is one of the few times we can speak with each other. We are in view of the windows, so there is nothing scandalous."

"Friends?" Jane gaped as if the concept of talking with a man other than for a marriage proposal was mad. "What do you speak to each other of?"

"Various topics from his estates to the politics of the day," Louisa responded while Harry rolled his eyes at her.

"But Miss Drake, you should not let a man be friends with you," Jane said seriously.

"Why ever not?"

"He will think you are…fast," she whispered with a glance back at Harry.

"On the contrary, Miss Bigby," Harry responded. "Conversing with Miss Drake makes me believe she doesn't need to use her beauty and wiles to capture a man when she has such an intelligent mind to entice him."

Miss Bigby's lips puckered in disdain. "But Mother says men don't like women who speak their mind or are more intelligent than they are."

"On the contrary, an outspoken, witty lady is very…intriguing," Harry said, staring at Louisa with a small smile. "But we must all go in now for Miss Drake has agreed to a dance."

"I do hope there might be one more dance in my future, Your Grace," Miss Bigby said with a flirtatious smile as her eyelashes fluttered at Harry.

Louisa felt her frustration rising. Why couldn't she act as coquettish as the younger lady?

"Ahh, but we would not wish to cause gossip, Miss Bigby. Good evening." Harry held out his arm for Louisa.

She accepted his arm with a smile. "You were rather rude to her, you know."

"I doubt she even noticed." He glanced down at her with one brow cocked. "You thought that young lady would be acceptable?"

"I am running out of choices, Harry," she whispered as they entered the ballroom. "You are extremely fastidious."

"A word I doubt Miss Bigby even knows."

"Stop," she said with a feigned swat to his arm. "And why are *we* dancing?"

"Because I want to dance, and you have yet to find a partner who meets my fastidious demands."

Louisa couldn't help but giggle. "I do apologize. I understand you do not like giggling ladies."

"I never minded your giggle." He stiffened as if realizing he'd made an error.

She went silent for a long moment. "What is the next dance?"

"I believe it is time for a waltz."

"A waltz?" she squeaked. "I might step on your feet or stumble."

"I shall take my chances," he retorted.

He gathered her near as they waited for the music to start. Damn him for choosing this dance for their first dance together. Having him near was overloading her senses. His heady scent surrounded her. She could feel the heat of his gloved hand on her upper back, which sent strange sensations to her belly. How had Harry become so dangerous to her senses?

She could barely catch her breath with him so near. Never had she been this close to him for such a length of time. But she wanted more. Who was she fooling? He didn't want her. The man was all but glaring at her right now. A duke as particular as he was about his future wife would never think of her as a possibility.

Unexpectedly, she felt like crying.

As the dance ended, she said, "Excuse me, I must find the ladies retiring room."

"Of course."

Louisa left the room as quickly as she could, but instead of finding the retiring room, she headed out to the gardens for some peace. She needed to be away from the allure of the one man she could never have without destroying her sister's future and even poor Charlotte's future. How could she think for one moment that she could be with Harry?

Damn her mother and Tessa for all they had done that caused Harry's father to kill Tessa's husbands. She supposed *caused* was too strong a word. All Tessa had wanted was for Louisa and Emma to find a good match.

Louisa walked back to the far end of the garden, hoping no one would be out this far on a chilly night. There was a lovely bench in the rear surrounded by rose bushes that wouldn't be in bloom for months. She sat down on the cold, wrought iron bench and wiped a tear away.

The Season had started, and now she was having second thoughts about trying to pursue Harry. She was a damned fool. Why would he want to be with her? She was the plain Drake sister. The two beautiful sisters had men.

Perhaps she should find him a wife in truth.

"Damn you, Harry." Why did he have to be so damned handsome?

"Is it your turn to curse me now?"

She started and then slowly looked up at the imposing man. "What...how...why did you follow me out here?"

"Well, I noticed you didn't quite make it to the retiring room. I decided to make certain you stayed safe. Why were you cursing me?" Harry moved to sit on the bench with her.

"You shouldn't be out here with me alone," she said, trying not to notice how the side of his muscular thigh touched hers or how much his presence seemed to warm her body.

"What happened to my impetuous Louisa who never cared what anyone thought of her?" He touched her chin to turn her head toward him.

Don't look in his eyes, she told herself. *Do not do it!* "It has been a difficult few years, Harry."

"I can't apologize enough for my father's actions."

Louisa shook her head. "It is far beyond just what your father did. My father had plenty of blame for our current situation, as does my mother."

"What exactly happened, Louisa?"

"I cannot speak of it. Not even to you."

He reached for her hand and squeezed gently. "You know I have always kept your secrets."

She nodded. Still, she had never told Harry. She'd never told anyone. When he departed for India, she had lost her confidante. With a deep breath, she started, "My mother decided Tessa needed a Season when she was eighteen. My father fought her on it due to the expense involved. But she insisted and my father..." she pressed her lips together to keep her tears at bay.

"My mother purchased the gowns for her and had arranged for a house in town. My father stole money from the bank in Cornwall, where he worked to pay for everything. Emma and I were visiting our aunt while all of this happened. When we returned, we were told he had died, and we were moving to London that very day. We were never even allowed to visit his gravesite, which of course didn't exist because he was in prison."

She shook her head and wiped a tear. "After his imprisonment, my mother came to London and began the story of how she was a widow of a London banker."

"Which should not have been enough to get her into Society," Harry commented.

"No, she used her connections to her uncle, Lord Greyson. And that is where my sister takes over by befriending your father."

"I see," he replied stiffly.

"Once your father noticed my sister, my mother was able to influence him to gain invitations to certain balls and parties. Once Tessa married Langley, we were all in Society. After Langley died, the small inheritance kept us from the poor house. Tessa paid some of our father's debt, and the rest went to maintaining our position in Society."

"When did you discover all this?"

"After your father died. Tessa finally admitted everything to me. Until that time, I still believed my father had died in Cornwall."

"I'm sorry, Louisa. Why didn't you write me?"

"You were mourning your wife and your father. I didn't wish to disturb you with my troubles. And you hadn't returned any of my letters of condolence, so I saw no point."

"I am dreadfully sorry for that," he whispered, staring out at the gardens. "Have you spoken to him?"

"Not in any detail. My father came for Christmas at Tessa's. A part of me is still angry with him for what he did. He shouldn't have allowed my mother to plan a Season for my sister when we didn't have the money."

"He loves his daughters and wanted only the best for them. Anything to make them happy."

"Well, that didn't work. My father went to prison. Tessa married three men she did not love because of the guilt she carried over our father. And now we're all living a lie." Every time she thought about what they all had done, her stomached roiled.

She glanced up into his eyes and was lost. Her gaze fell to his lips, which were full but not too full. Perfect for kissing. She could see the stubborn stubble on his chin where his valet didn't get close enough.

"Louisa, stop looking at me like that," he said in a low tone.

"I cannot seem to stop lately," she whispered.

He muttered something under his breath as Louisa brought her lips to his. It was nothing more than a quick kiss until he wrapped his arms around her. Turning her body towards his, she opened her mouth for him. He responded quickly, deepening the kiss. She trembled as his tongue brushed against hers, sending waves of desire through her. Skimming her hand over his cheek, she felt his strong jawline and then let her fingers touch his hair. He'd cut it before coming to town, and she missed the slightly longer length.

The world slipped away until they were alone, not in a garden where anyone might stumble upon them. She shivered as his large hands cupped her cheeks, caressing them as he continued the passionate assault on Louisa's senses. Never could she have imagined kissing her dearest friend would make her melt. But now she felt she could crumble to the ground if she let go of him.

He broke away and rested his forehead on hers, breathing hard. "We really must stop," he whispered.

Louisa closed her eyes as she attempted to get her breathing under control. "Of course. I must apologize."

"For what?"

"Kissing you."

"Louisa, I kissed you too. I owe you an apology." He moved away from her. "I shouldn't have kissed you. It will never happen again."

Oh, that was where he was wrong. They would kiss again. She

had to get her emotions under control before returning to the ball. Now that she knew he was not immune to her, she would never back down. But for now, Emma had insisted that Louisa had to try to make him jealous tonight.

"I must go back to the ballroom. I promised Collingwood another dance."

"Then, by all means, go. You wouldn't wish to keep Collingwood waiting," he grumbled, moving away from her.

"Do not be angry with me," she shot back. "Collingwood was your choice."

Before he could say another word, she jumped up and raced back to the house with a determined smile.

Chapter 12

Harry tossed the coverlet off and scrambled out of bed. There was no point in lazing about when he hadn't slept at all. Every time he closed his eyes, the image of Louisa's lips on his compelled his eyes to open to remove the picture from his mind.

After seven years, he'd finally kissed her. She may have kissed him first, but her innocent kiss scarcely counted. He had taken control and returned her soft kiss with seven years of pent up frustration.

Her sweet tongue had brushed against his, wreaking havoc with his restraint.

For years he'd assumed if he ever kissed her it wouldn't be enough...he would want more. He couldn't have been more wrong. More wasn't what he wanted, but what he *needed*. Needed to feel her body against his. Needed to taste every inch of her body and desperately needed to be deep inside her.

Whatever had possessed him to return her kiss? He was a bloody fool to succumb to the tears in her eyes. Only some semblance of sanity had forced him to break away from her tempting kisses.

A hint of anger still lingered in him with the thought that it had taken her seven years to accept a kiss from him. Seven years they could have been together. Now too much stood between them for any lasting happiness.

He'd hurt Sabita by forcing her to leave her family, among other things he could not think about. He refused to hurt Louisa. They could never be together when doing so would dredge up old gossip for all involved.

After putting on his trousers, he paced the room. The restless energy inside him wouldn't subside. How he wished he'd never returned to London. Never saw Louisa again.

For the past two years, he'd all but put her out of his mind, except for the fleeting thoughts of her smile that would drift into his consciousness. Or the wonder of what she was doing at the exact moment he thought of her. But no more.

A ride would ease his frustration today. He had to stop obsessing over Louisa. Surely a fast ride through Hyde Park at this early hour would help. After ordering Hercules saddled, he dressed and left the house without eating.

Turning into the park, he sighed with relief. At seven in the morning, the park was nearly empty. Most people were probably still sleeping off the excesses of the night at Lady Leicester's ball. But he wasn't here to think about last night. He was here to put the previous evening out of his mind. Urging Hercules to a gallop, he raced down the path until he noticed a rider coming toward him.

All he'd wanted was a little peace this morning. Now he would be forced by good manners to stop and talk to this man.

But as the rider came closer, Harry's scowl turned into a smile as he reined in. Simon slowed his horse and tilted his head with a grin.

"You're up early after a late night of amusements at Lady Leicester's ball," Simon commented.

"And I thought you were going to meet a lonely widow."

Simon laughed. "You know 'the best-laid schemes o' mice an' men' and all that."

Harry still wondered where Simon received an education that would have him reciting Robert Burns. While his mother had been an opera singer, Simon's stepfather was only a lowly baker. Perhaps his mother had been well educated. She'd been cultured enough to keep his father engaged for over a year.

"Do you still box?" The idea of a ride had been a good thought, but Harry needed more.

Simon's lips rose slowly. "I own a gaming hell. Of course, I visit the pugilist saloon with my man Riley at least once a week."

"Want a go at me?"

"A chance to punch my older and titled brother. Who could resist such an opportunity?"

"Excellent," Harry replied. "Shall we head to Bond Street, then?"

"At this hour?"

"Yes."

Simon nodded. "As you wish. Am I supposed to take it easy on you?"

"No," Harry replied, urging Hercules to a walk. "Just not the face. I don't want to scare my daughter."

"Or any of the unmarried ladies."

Harry cringed. "Please, not a word about that after last night."

"So, this is about relieving some frustration from the ball. Not to worry, then. I do know how to aggravate many people." Simon rode ahead with a chuckle.

Harry couldn't help but smile at his younger brother. Already, a feeling of lightness slipped over him after a few quick words with Simon. Once they arrived at Gentleman Jackson's Saloon, they stripped down to just their trousers and shirts.

"You two are in early," Jackson said as he entered from the rear of the establishment. "I do hope you both are here strictly for exercise."

"Of course," Harry replied, knowing Jackson's reputation for following strict rules.

"Excellent. I have an appointment with a lady who likes to box in private for exercise." Jackson picked up his hat and headed for the door. "Good morning, Your Grace, Mr. Kingsley."

"A woman who likes to box," Harry commented as Jackson departed. "How odd."

"Sounds like my kind of lady. Gloves?" Simon asked, pointing to a selection of boxing gloves.

"Yes." Simon preferred bare-knuckle boxing, but Harry only wanted to relieve a bit of frustration.

"Was it the blonde or the brunette who has you so bothered today?" Simon asked, holding up his fists to block a punch.

If Harry could have clenched his fists tighter, he would have, but the gloves where so thickly padded, he couldn't. How did his brother determine the source of the issue so quickly? "Louisa," he muttered, striking out but he hit nothing but air as Simon nimbly moved away.

"Your *dear* friend." Simon's fist snaked out and landed a hard punch to Harry's side.

"Yes," he bit out before finally getting a blow to Simon's midsection.

"If you're so bothered by her, why is she not the one you are courting?" Simon danced away from another attempt.

"I cannot." Harry groaned as his brother hit him again. "Dammit."

"Come on, Harry," Simon taunted. "Hit me. Think about how it felt to watch her dance with other men last night. How it would feel if you could only kiss her."

Harry's anger flowed over him like molten lava, firing his fists to action. He finally landed a punch that sent his younger brother reeling backward.

"That's more like it," Simon groaned before waving him back. "Come on."

Harry secured another shot to Simon's upper arm and then to his belly again. Simon hit back.

"I do wonder if any of the gentlemen kissed Miss Drake last night," Simon mocked.

Harry did his best to ignore the taunting from him. Instead, he focused on gaining the upper hand in this contest, but Simon's practiced moves were lithe and light.

"I should have focused my attention on her. She must be something special." Simon avoided a jab to his middle. "Perhaps, I am just what she needs."

The idea of any other man kissing her, much less his wicked brother, infuriated him. Forgetting their rules, he slammed his fist into his brother's jaw. "You're not going to touch her."

Simon fell back against the wall with a bloody grin. "Feel better yet? That last one was more than I expected from you."

Harry closed his eyes and nodded. "I apologize."

"Let us go get some breakfast and talk about what happened." Simon held out his hands for the attendant to remove his gloves. Another man gave him a cold cloth for his jaw.

Harry followed him, but the feeling of shame would not leave him. He'd allowed his brother to goad him into injuring him.

"We need sustenance," Simon said once they were both dressed. "And since you bested me, you must feed me."

"Something tells me I would never have won if you'd been serious."

Simon only shrugged.

By the time they arrived back at his home, Charlotte was on her way for a walk in the park with Nurse.

"Uncle Simon!" she shouted, seeing him jump off his horse. "We're going for a walk in the park. Will you come with us?"

Simon picked her up and kissed her cheek. "Sorry sweetling, your father and I just returned from the park."

"Please," she begged.

"Not today."

"What happened?" she asked, touching the mark on his jaw that had already started to turn purple.

"Your father punched me."

"Simon," Harry said in a low tone.

Charlotte laughed. "Uncle Simon, you're funny. Papa wouldn't hurt you."

Simon gently placed her back down on the step. "You go. Your papa and I must talk."

"All right. But I might see Miss Drake in the park."

Harry closed his eyes but could still feel Simon's penetrating stare on him.

"If you do, tell her your papa says good morning," Simon said with a smirk.

"I will." Charlotte took Nurse's hand to start their walk.

Harry opened his eyes to find Simon's sardonic gaze still focused on him. Now there would be no reprieve until his brother knew the truth.

"Good morning, Your Grace," Jenkins said as he opened the door for them. "Mr. Kingsley."

"Good morning, Jenkins. How are you today?" Simon replied in a booming voice purely meant to irritate the old butler.

"Simon," Harry warned. "The first rule of privilege is never to annoy the butler."

"I apologize, Jenkins. I am still new to this world." There was an undercurrent of humor to his voice.

"Of course, sir." Jenkins closed the door behind them. "Breakfast will be up in a moment."

Harry and Simon walked to the morning room and waited as the footmen carried trays of eggs, herring, ham, toast, pastries, tea, and coffee. Once all the food arrived, he dismissed the footmen.

Simon sipped his coffee and then grimaced. "I will send over a blend of my coffee. This is dreadful stuff."

They ate in silence for a few moments, but Harry knew the quiet wouldn't last. He adjusted his posture slightly. An ache at his midsection reminded him that he would likely feel quite sore tomorrow.

"All right, then," Simon started as he placed his coffee cup back on the table. "What happened last night?"

"Nothing happened." Except he kissed Louisa. Which turned out to be more amazing than his imagination could have envisioned.

Simon laughed. "Harry, while I haven't known you for long, I do know evasion when I see it."

"I danced with Louisa," he admitted slowly.

"And is there an issue with dancing with a friend?"

"No, in fact, we were both a little surprised by the thought that we had never danced together. What bothered me was watching her dance with the other gentlemen. It shouldn't have annoyed me, but it did. I'm supposed to find her a husband."

Simon jerked his head toward Harry. "I beg your pardon? I don't believe I heard that last bit right. I thought you said you were supposed to find Miss Drake a husband."

Harry nodded. "We agreed upon it when she visited me over Christmas."

"She visited you…with her mother?"

"No." Harry stared down at his plate. "She came alone. That is how Charlotte came to know her."

Simon covered his mouth as if trying to hide a smile. "Just so I understand, Miss Drake paid a visit to you over Christmas, alone. She did this to ask you to find her a husband. While there, she met Charlotte, who seems completely taken with her. And you agreed to find her a husband."

"Yes, that sums it up."

"The woman you love wants a husband, but not you?"

Harry glanced over at his brother. "I do not love her."

Liar. Damned conscience.

"I see," Simon commented. "And she doesn't love you?"

"No. We are strictly friends. Nothing more than that."

Simon shrugged as he ate a bite of eggs. "Very well. You don't love her. She doesn't love you. Then seeing her dance with other men shouldn't be a bother, now should it?"

"You are a very annoying younger brother."

"Thank you," Simon replied with a smirk. "I believe you have a decision to make, brother dear. Either marry the girl yourself or find her a husband and spend the rest of your life watching her from afar. Because no matter how much you deny it, the fact is, you are in love with her."

"It matters not," Harry admitted slowly. "She does not want to marry me."

"You're a duke. What girl wouldn't wish to marry you?"

"Louisa Drake."

Simon frowned as he scraped his chair back. "I hate to run, but I have a meeting at noon. Harry, are you certain she doesn't want to marry you?"

"Oh, she has made that obvious many times."

"I am sorry then."

No, it was for the best that she didn't want to marry him, but he didn't tell Simon that bit. As his brother left, Harry finished his coffee. Jenkins bought in a post that had just arrived. Harry ran his finger over the neat script of his name, wondering why Louisa would write to him.

He read the note, crumpled it up and hurled the offending missive into the fireplace. Louisa had the nerve to thank him for introducing her to Collingwood and told him how much she'd enjoyed dancing with Collingwood last night. Not one mention of their kiss. As if it never happened.

As it shouldn't have happened.

At least one of them had good sense. Harry walked to his study to send a quick reply thanking Louisa for the introduction to Miss Bigby, and while a sweet, young lady, she was not the type he was looking for in a duchess. And that he hoped Louisa would have someone to introduce him to at the Marchtons' ball tomorrow night.

Louisa walked to the salon after sending off a note to Harry. Emma had read the letter before Louisa sent it and agreed the tone should make him particularly jealous. A part of Louisa wished she didn't have to play these games with him. There had to be a way to make him realize what he wanted was right in front of him.

Maybe it was her fault for not seeing him in this manner years ago. If she had, he'd never have gone to India. Never would have fallen in love with Sabita.

Never had Charlotte.

What a dreadful thought! He needed that little girl, and she needed him. Louisa had never been one to believe in fate and love, until lately. But perhaps it was fate that sent him to India so that he could have Charlotte. Fate that made her not realize until now how perfect Harry was for her.

Fate?

Predestination was a ludicrous thought only for the romantics of the world.

Louisa set her shoulders, no more thinking about what might have been. He was here now and unmarried. And she had every intention of making the most of the situation.

As she strolled into the salon, she found her mother reading a letter with a deep scowl lining her face. "Is everything well, Mamma?"

"No, it is not."

"Oh?" She sat down across from her mother close to the fire. "What is wrong?"

"I have received a letter from Lady Huntley. She and Lady Gringham noticed you returning from the terrace last evening followed by Worthington only a minute later. Lady Gringham mentioned to Lady Huntley how you were at Northwood Park when she arrived. And that she never met your companion."

Her mother crumpled the note and stared at Louisa. "How could you be so foolish? And why did you not mention the most important fact that the Gringhams were at Northwood Park?"

Louisa closed her eyes for a long moment. "Mamma, the duke and I are strictly friends. He noticed me leave the ball and feared for my safety. We spoke for a few moments and then returned to the ball."

"When will you remember, it only matters what people imagine might have happened?" Mamma dabbed at her eyes with a handkerchief. "What will Lord Bolton do when he hears this awful news?"

Louisa doubted Lord Bolton would do anything. But Lady Bolton would need to be appeased. The Boltons were an ancient family, tracing their roots back to the conquest. Lady Bolton had been the daughter of an earl of a similar lineage.

"Mamma, send a note back to Lady Huntley and explain that His Grace thought I looked ill and came outside to ascertain that I was well. And let it be known that my companion was ill with a fever when we stopped at Northwood Park, which is why Lady Gringham never met her."

"Oh Louisa, you make this seem so easy." Her mother twisted her handkerchief in her hands. "But you know how gossip takes on a life of its own. I fear this may bring shame down upon us."

More shame than a dead father being released from prison? She would never forgive her mother for that lie. Nor would she forgive him for stealing money from the bank he worked at in Cornwall merely to give Tessa a Season.

"Only if we let it." Louisa sighed as she stared at the fireplace.

"Mrs. Drake, Lady Bolton is here," a footman announced.

Her mother's eyes widened. "Oh dear, send her in. Louisa, you should leave."

"It might help if I stayed," Louisa commented. "After all, I was the reason for the gossip and should have the ability to defend myself."

"Well said, Miss Drake." A large woman dressed in black bombazine entered the room with a huff. Her graying hair was up in elaborate curls that would better suit a woman of much younger years. "Mrs. Drake, I do believe your daughter should explain her case to me."

"Lady Bolton," Louisa said with a curtsy. "Welcome to our home."

Her mother blathered on welcoming Lady Bolton and then ordering tea. Lady Bolton eased her large frame into the chair Louisa's mother had vacated. The poor chair protested with a loud creak as the viscountess sat. "Dreadful day outside. At least you have a warm fire for me."

After ordering the tea, her mother returned to the room and sat on the sofa away from them both as if an outsider in her salon. "It is lovely to see you again."

Lady Bolton turned her lip up. "I believe you already know why I am here. I have made no pretense that my George is marrying beneath himself. It wasn't bad enough that you had the issue of your eldest daughter's husbands, but now your second daughter was observed returning from the gardens during Lady Leicester's ball followed quickly behind by the son of the man who killed your eldest daughter's husbands. It is preposterous!"

"My lady," Louisa started gently. "I have to agree that it is preposterous. Who would believe such an outlandish story? I went out for a breath of air on the terrace because I felt faint. The gracious duke, who by the by, is nothing like his father, noticed I had left and followed me outside to make certain I stayed safe. He has always been quite the gentleman. There was nothing more to the story than that. I fear I may be ruined for attempting not to faint in the middle of a ballroom."

Lady Bolton stared at her long and hard. "I am not sure why, but I do believe you, Miss Drake."

"It's the absurdity of the matter, my lady. Who would believe that the duke would be kind to one of the Drakes after all that has happened? But he is the epitome of compassion. The duke was most sympathetic to my companion Mrs. Fitzhugh when she fell ill while traveling. His Grace allowed us to stay with him for three days until she was well enough to travel again. Is he not just the kindest of men?"

"I see," Lady Bolton replied before pursing her lips. "I suppose it is far too impossible to believe he had an interest in *you*."

Louisa clenched her jaw to keep from retorting to the bitter lady. "I suppose you are correct, my lady. I am all but a spinster."

"Very well, the matter is settled in my mind. Now, where is Miss Emma this morning?" Lady Bolton asked in a cold tone. "She should have greeted her future mother-in-law."

"She had a headache this morning and returned to her bed," Mamma replied quickly before adding, "Would you like me to fetch her?"

Lady Bolton shook her head. "I shall be gone before she dresses."

"Lady Bolton, if I may, have you and your son decided on a date for the wedding?" Mamma asked softly.

"There is no hurry, Mrs. Drake. I should think you would want them to become better acquainted."

"Yes, of course, but Emma is quite eager to become—"

"A bride," Louisa interjected before her mother said something to insult the viscountess.

"Yes, a bride," Mamma repeated, nodding her head.

"Before the Season is over, I suppose," Lady Bolton said with a resigned sigh before standing. "I shall take my leave now."

"You don't wish to stay for tea?" Mamma begged.

"No, thank you, Mrs. Drake." She started to walk across the room before stopping and looking back at Louisa. "And please control your daughter's behavior before she causes a scandal from which you cannot recover."

"Of course, ma'am," Mamma said with a glare to Louisa. "Lord Collingwood danced two sets with her last evening. I am quite certain she will be far more circumspect now."

Louisa barely contained her eye roll.

Once Lady Bolton departed, her mother turned on her. "You are not to see or dance with the duke again. I will not risk your sister's marriage over your folly with that man. I forbid it."

"Forbid it?" Louisa asked incredulously. "I am five and twenty, Mamma. I will see my friend Harry and even dance with him should he ask."

Louisa stormed out of the room and decided to check on Emma. As Louisa strode through the hall, a footman closed the door with a post in his hand.

"Miss, this just came for you."

She took the note from his outstretched hand and smiled, seeing the handwriting. "Thank you, John."

Racing upstairs to Emma, Louisa wondered what he might have to say this morning. Perhaps her attempts to make him jealous worked.

"How are you, dear?" Louisa quietly asked as she peeked inside Emma's darkened room.

"Much better now. I think the coffee and toast helped." Emma sat up and looked over at her. "Didn't you send him the note yet?"

"This is his reply."

"That was quick."

"Indeed." Louisa pushed open the curtains before returning to the bed. "I think that is a very good sign."

"Open it already."

Louisa broke the seal and scanned the message. Her shoulders sagged as she pressed her lips together and blinked to keep from crying.

"What is wrong?" Emma asked, reaching out for Louisa's hand.

"He was happy to hear that I enjoyed my dances with Collingwood last night. And Harry thanked me for introducing him to Miss Bigby. While she wasn't what he is looking for, he hopes I will have someone else to introduce him to tomorrow night."

"Let me see that." Emma grabbed the note out of Louisa's grip.

"Do you think he might be using the same tactic we are?"

Emma shook her head slowly. "I honestly do not know."

Not even their kiss had affected him the way it had her. She was a fool to think he might feel something for her other than friendship.

Chapter 13

Memories of a similar night flooded Harry's mind as he glanced about the ballroom of Lady Marchton's home. It was seven years ago that he met Louisa at the Marchtons' ball. But tonight, he couldn't seem to find her. Picking up a glass of champagne from a passing footman, he walked the room. He shouldn't look for her. The goal of the night was to gain introductions to several ladies and speak with Blakely.

The room sparkled from the candlelight catching the cuts on the gems worn by the ladies and creating a kaleidoscope of colors on the walls. Perhaps she wasn't in attendance tonight. *Focus on the other ladies, not Louisa,* he told himself sternly. Pausing to scan the room again, he heard the two blondes in front of him speaking softly.

But he is a duke," the taller lady insisted.

"He is mad," the petite woman insisted. "His father killed the man's wife."

"And then there is the issue with his daughter."

"A heathen for certain."

He clenched his fist around the stem of the champagne glass. He couldn't help but clear his throat loud enough that the two girls glanced back. A sensation akin to pleasure slid over him as they blushed violently and walked away. As he moved through the crush, a lady in front of him whirled around, and he had to catch her elbow to keep her from slamming into him.

His heart pounded as he stared down into her sapphire eyes. Wearing an ivory gown with lace trim, Louisa looked breathtaking.

"Your Grace," Louisa said with a quick curtsy. "I had no idea you were here yet. Not that I can see anyone except those in front of me. I have never seen such a crush."

He nodded. "Good evening, Miss Drake."

"There is someone I would like to introduce you to if I can find her again," she said with a quick laugh.

"Oh?"

"Yes, Miss Turnbull."

Harry frowned. "Aren't the Turnbulls in trade?"

Louisa sighed. "I will never be able to marry you off."

"Marry me off?" Harry sipped his champagne. "You sound like a marriage-minded mama."

"I feel like one with a very difficult daughter who is too picky for her own good." Louisa glanced past him. "Oh, there she is!"

Harry took issue with being compared to a difficult daughter but turned as Louisa waved to Miss Turnbull. Watching the raven-haired woman gesture in return, a shiver of apprehension snaked down his back. Miss Turnbull had dark hair, and she appeared almost as tall as Louisa.

"Miss Turnbull, may I introduce His Grace, the Duke of Worthington?"

Miss Turnbull turned her attention to him, and Harry forced a smile.

"It is a pleasure, Miss Turnbull."

"Yes, it is," Miss Turnbull purred. "I have admired your fortitude in handling your father's death, Your Grace. It must be deeply disturbing to discover such dreadful things about your own father."

Was he supposed to thank her for that odd compliment? Perhaps the girl was nervous. His title had that effect on some people. Miss

Turnbull's brown eyes shifted back to Louisa as he remained silent. He supposed he should ask her for a dance.

"Miss Turnbull, I appear to be without a partner for the next set. Would you care to dance?"

Her smile a little too full, exposing a row of slightly crooked teeth. "I would, Your Grace."

"Miss Turnbull, do tell the duke what you were speaking of with me earlier," Louisa said with a grin. "About the possibility of locomotive uses."

Miss Turnbull's eyes widened in surprise. "I scarcely think the duke would like to hear of such things at a ball, Miss Drake."

"You underestimate him," Louisa said with a glance to him. "He loves to discuss topics of modern machinery and inventions, do you not, Your Grace?"

"Indeed," he replied, wondering why Miss Turnbull would prefer to hide her intelligence. "I do believe our dance is about to begin."

He held out his arm to her and escorted her to the dance floor. The entire dance, Miss Turnbull kept the conversation on the events of the day and the latest *on-dit*. Perhaps she didn't want any of the other dancers to overhear a dialogue on industry and acquire a reputation as a bluestocking.

As the dance ended, she pointed to where her parents stood, watching them approach.

"Miss Turnbull, I would love to hear your thoughts on the use of steam engines locomotives."

She laughed in a tinny tone. "Oh, Your Grace, only Miss Drake would wish to hear about such a thing at a ball."

"Miss Drake and I enjoy discussions on subjects other than the weather and gossip, even at balls."

She blanched before recovering quickly. "Then perhaps you should like to call on me tomorrow, and we shall discuss any topic you prefer."

Any topic he preferred? Louisa usually broached a subject of interest to them both. He had the feeling that Miss Turnbull was no bluestocking. But, could he settle for such a lady? And one from trade?

"Your Grace?" she asked expectantly.

"Of course." His lack of attention had now forced him to call on the chit tomorrow.

Harry left her with her proud parents, who gushed over him. Seeing Blakely, he threaded through the crowd until he reached the viscount.

"Worthington, how are you?" Blakely asked.

"Very well, but I was wondering if you had a moment to speak in private."

Blakely's brows furrowed in question. "Of course."

"Come out to the gardens."

They walked toward the back of the gardens where others hadn't reached yet. The crescent moon did little to light the way. Blakely pulled out a cheroot and offered him one, which Harry declined.

Harry wondered the best way to approach the question without blurting it out impolitely. "How have you been?"

Blakely blew out the smoke and laughed. "I have been well."

"Excellent." There was nothing else to talk about with the man, except one topic. "May I ask a delicate question?"

"If you must," Blakely replied with a slight frown.

"I know at one point you had asked for Miss Drake's hand." He paused for a moment having second thoughts. But this was the right thing to do. He knew far more about Blakely than Collingwood. "Well, she is a fine lady and a dear friend. I was wondering if you would ever reconsider."

"Reconsider? Your Grace, *she* rejected me."

"Yes, but I believe she regrets that decision and would be receptive to a courtship now." At least, Harry hoped she would. Blakely might bore her with horses, but he would be an excellent husband, loyal and stable, and she deserved that, and so much more.

Blakely shook his head. "After having time to consider things, I do believe Miss Drake made a sensible conclusion. We would not have suited. She's a bit high-spirited for me."

"High-spirited?"

"You know, always speaking her mind about things. And a bit of a bluestocking, if you ask me."

"Of course, she is knowledgeable," Harry replied slowly. Blakely's description of Louisa was precisely what made her so unique amongst the ladies of quality. Perhaps the viscount, like so many gentlemen, didn't wish to marry a woman who might be a partner instead of an ornament.

"And in truth, I find my heart has completely recovered from that chapter and moved on to another."

"Oh, I apologize then."

Blakely nodded with a smile. "I should return to the ballroom."

"Good luck with your new lady." The smell of the cheroot remained as Blakely strolled away.

"How could you!"

Harry cringed at the angry tone of Louisa's voice from the other side of the hedge. She was never meant to hear what Blakely had said about her. Before he could apologize for the viscount's comments, she strode down the path. Following behind her, he whispered just loud enough that she might hear, "Slow down."

Ignoring him, she continued until she tripped over something, landing on the grass with a muttered curse. Harry swiftly assisted her to a bench.

"Are you hurt?"

She yanked her elbow out of his grip. "Hurt? Of course, I am hurt. How could you think for one moment that I would reconsider Blakely?"

Harry sighed. "I meant, physically."

"No." She glanced down at her grass-stained skirt with a sigh.

"I am sorry you had to hear what he said about you. I deliberately removed him to the back of the gardens so that no one would overhear."

"You think I am hurt by what he said?" The acid in her voice contradicted the sadness in her blue eyes.

Confused by her tone, he said, "Of course."

She stayed silent for a moment either to gather her thoughts or her wounded feelings. "What Blakely said about me is nothing but the truth. And nothing I am ashamed of or would ever change. He was correct. We would have been a dreadful match. What I am offended by is your lack of sense on the matter."

"My lack of sense?"

"I told you in December why I did not marry him."

His anger slowly burned. "I am doing my best to find you a gentleman of good standing. You didn't seem terribly excited about Collingwood, and in my opinion, Blakely is a far better man. Higher standing in Society and far wealthier."

She rose from the bench and walked toward the brick wall separating the Marchtons' gardens from another family of lesser consequence. "I suppose you are right," she whispered. "I should settle for any man who will take me at this point in my life."

"Louisa, you are far from desperate." Guilt flooded him. How was he supposed to find her a husband when she was everything he'd wanted in a wife but now could not have?

"Am I not? Look at me," she demanded. "I have grass stains on my gown, and my hair is falling from its coiffure. What man would want me?"

He shouldn't have looked over at her. Seeing her in such disarray made his heart pound. Her ivory gown did indeed have a rather large stain near her right knee, her hair had once again started to fall out of its upswept style, and all he wanted to do was kiss her.

No!

Kissing her was out of the question.

And yet, his legs seemed to have a mind of their own, forcing him to walk closer to her. He tipped her chin up with his thumb. Her pink lips gaped slightly.

"There are many men who would want you, Louisa Drake." He lowered his lips to hers for a gentle kiss before whispering, "Far too many men."

He kissed her again, harder this time. As she slowly responded, her arms wrapped around his neck, pressing her slim frame against him. He backed her against the brick wall until she was caught between him and the wall. This was what he wanted, no matter how much his conscience railed against it.

The injustice of his plight troubled his mind night and day. The one woman he wanted more than any other was the one he could not have. What he did in India was unforgivable. But kissing Louisa made him want to believe in miracles. She could forgive him. She could love him.

With a groan, she pressed her hands to his chest to push him away. Harry stared down at her and realized his fantasy would never become a reality. The sadness in her eyes was now replaced with sparkling anger.

Louisa stared up at Harry in confusion. How could she be hurt and angry with him one moment and then kissing him madly the next? She needed some distance from him. But she also required some assistance. She couldn't return to the ball with grass stains, her hair mussed, and her lips swollen from passionate kisses.

"I would be obliged if you could ask my sister to call for the carriage. I will meet her at the front of the house."

"I will escort you home," he replied. "It is my fault you are in this condition."

"No, please ask Emma."

He nodded. "How will you get to the front of the house?"

"There is a small walkway between the houses with a gate. I shall come around that way."

"As you wish."

As he walked away, Louisa touched her lips in wonder. He'd kissed her again. This kiss more passionate than the last. For a moment, she'd wondered if jealousy over her desire for a husband had caused his reaction. But her senses returned, and she understood Harry most likely was trying to keep her quiet so that no one would hear them.

With a quick look down the path, she headed for the front of the house through the small alleyway that the servants used. She waited in the darkness of the alley for her sister and their coach. Hopefully, Emma would be able to steal away without drawing Mamma's attention. Hearing the low rumble of a coach, she glanced around the corner of the house. Her shoulders sagged in disappointment noticing the fine black landeau slow to a stop. A fat drop of rain hit her head, followed by another as she waited. If Emma didn't hurry, Louisa would be soaked.

"Come along, Louisa," Harry said with an umbrella over his head as the rain increased. "Hopefully, the umbrella will shield you not only from the rain but the overly observant eyes of the gossips."

"I asked you to get my sister." Louisa scrambled into the carriage quickly followed by Harry, who then pulled the curtains over the large windows.

"She was dancing with her fiancé," he replied, taking the seat next to her. "I did jot a message for her and left it with her friend, Miss Lancaster."

"Oh, what a dreadful mess I've made. Mamma will be furious that I left the ball without dancing."

A long silence filled the carriage as they headed home. Louisa wondered if Harry regretted that kiss in the gardens.

Finally, he spoke, "I must apologize for my actions this evening. I should never have asked Blakely to reconsider you without consulting you first."

Louisa noted that he had not apologized for kissing her. "Thank you. How did you find Miss Turnbull?"

"Pleasant enough, I suppose."

She'd convinced herself the issue of her family in trade would be an impediment, which is why she introduced them. It kept up her part of their deal without him realizing every woman she presented him to was not what he was looking for in a wife.

"That is hardly a ringing endorsement of the lady. What was wrong with this one? She was as close to everything as you had requested. Of course, you must wait to see how she would do with Charlotte, but I think she has a kind heart."

"Hardly everything I wanted, Louisa," he grumbled.

"What do you mean? She has height, intelligence, dark hair, a friendly demeanor, not the best of families, but they are generally accepted. She even attended Miss Simmons School for Young Ladies, which I hear is very exclusive. I believe your sister attended the same school."

"That is certainly not all that I asked for in a wife." He shifted in his seat as if uncomfortable with the conversation, his leg bumping into hers.

"You wrote she must be beautiful, of superior intelligence, taller than the average female, preferably darker hair, she must love children, have a kind heart for Charlotte and preferably one who doesn't giggle."

He chuckled. "I asked for more than that."

"That is what you wrote to me."

"That's impossible," he replied in a low voice.

"Why?"

"Because that is…" his voice trailed off in the darkness of the carriage.

"Is…?"

"Nothing."

The carriage stopped in front of her mother's home. Harry opened the door and held out his hand to help her down. Even with gloves on their hands, a shock raced up her arms, thrilling her with the sensation. She could only hope he had felt the same.

"Good evening, Your Grace," she said with a curtsy as Davis opened the door with a frown.

"Good evening, Miss Drake," Harry said with a nod.

"Miss Drake, where is your mother?" Davis asked, closing the door behind them.

"I took a fall in the garden, and the duke escorted me home. Emma and Mamma decided to remain rather than leave early."

And tomorrow she would, no doubt, face the wrath of her mother.

As the carriage rolled away from Louisa's home, Harry pressed his hands to his temples. The shock of Louisa's description of what he wanted in a wife wouldn't leave his mind. He could not have written that to her. Not to Louisa.

Damnation!

What if she had grasped what he hadn't even realized until she spoke the words? His list described her.

She was exactly what he wanted physically and mentally. He'd never stopped loving her, but he could not have her now. The only solution was to find her a gentleman straightaway.

And he must stop kissing her.

Perhaps he should offer to increase her dowry to attract more suitors, but her mother would never allow that because of how it would look to the gossips. There was Collingwood, but something niggled Harry with regards to the viscount. He couldn't put his finger on what it was, but he had to find someone else for her.

The other solution was simple. Harry must marry someone quickly and return to Northwood Park to forget Louisa. Mary Gardiner wasn't such a poor choice. She'd proven her ability to have children. That was something. He hadn't entirely determined her intelligence yet. While she'd participated in their conversation, he had noticed how her gaze roamed the room while they spoke.

Until he'd met Louisa, he resisted the notion of a bluestocking, but now it would be an asset for a duchess. It would help ensure his children's minds were engaged. The world was changing, while slowly up to now, he felt there were enormous inventions on the horizon that would change the world forever. He and Louisa had discussed how these changes might impact the future of the aristocracy. His children would need the sense to look at options other than farming to retain the duchy.

Miss Turnbull might be that woman, but until he spoke with her more, he would never know. His stomach unexpectedly roiled in protest. None of the ladies Louisa had introduced him to made him think about marriage. Nor did Mary Gardiner enflame his senses like Louisa. No one had ever affected him as she had. But he could not marry Louisa Drake.

Chapter 14

Louisa wanted to skip the poetry reading tonight but knew her mother would be furious if she did not attend. With her advanced age, it was anticipated Louisa would attend every event possible. Harry would likely be there, expecting her to have someone else to introduce him to, but she needed to find a lady who wouldn't make him think she was deliberately making a blunder of their pact.

She also needed to discover what he thought of Miss Turnbull. There was a rumor circulating that he paid a call on her yesterday. Whilst Miss Turnbull might not wish to display her intelligence at a ball, with a caller in the privacy of her home, she could be more open.

Harry enjoyed intellectual ladies, and she might be what he wanted in a wife. Louisa prayed she hadn't overplayed her hand. Hopefully, the issue of Miss Turnbull's parents in trade would keep him from thinking of her as an acceptable lady.

"Come along, Louisa. We must leave now," Emma said before staring at her in an assessing manner. "Are you well?"

"Well enough, I suppose." Louisa sighed before picking up her shawl and then followed her sister to the hall. Thankfully, the incident with her leaving the Marchtons' ball blew over quickly when Emma told Mamma that Louisa had departed the ball to return home because she was ill. Louisa smiled thinking about what a little schemer her younger sister had become.

"Will Bolton be in attendance tonight?"

"Yes," her sister replied with a sigh. "I do wish he and his ⟨...⟩ would decide on a date. The anticipation is driving me mad. Pe⟨...⟩ keep asking me when the wedding will take place. I feel like a fo⟨...⟩ saying we haven't set a date yet."

She hoped her sister realized just how much of a hold Lady Bolton had over her son. Louisa feared it might cause issues with their marriage. "Emma, have you asked Bolton about the date when you have been away from his mother?"

"We are seldom away from his mother. She seems to be everywhere we go."

"Perhaps you should mention that to him while dancing," Louisa murmured as they entered the carriage.

"I will, at the next ball."

Thankfully Mamma decided she had a headache tonight. Or as Louisa knew, her mother had an assignation with Lord **Hammond** while they were out. She had explicitly told Louisa not to return before ten.

Upon arriving at the Gringhams' home, Collingwood found her immediately. "Good evening, Miss Drake."

"Good evening, my lord."

He insisted on finding them seats for the reading. Louisa glanced around the room. What the devil was Harry doing standing next to Mary Gardiner? Louisa looked away from him as she pressed a hand to her aching belly. They appeared to be involved in a serious discussion. The sight of them standing so close was like a knife twisting in her stomach.

"Miss Drake, would you like some lemonade?" Collingwood asked as if eager to please her.

"A glass of wine would be lovely."

"Wine?"

"Yes, wine," she replied, trying not to show irritation at his ᶜ drink. Collingwood wandered off to the

..e taken aback by your request," Emma said with
.. "You'd best let him know how you do like your
..d brandy…and port."

.dush. Oh, look here comes Bolton…with his mother, of
course."

"I had hoped that for just one night we might be alone without
her chaperoning her son."

"Oh, but you are one of those Daring Drake sisters who might
influence her son in some immoral manner," Louisa said with a
smirk.

Emma chuckled. "Perhaps you and Tessa are daring, but I
decided long ago to not follow in your footsteps. I have every
intention of gaining a husband and a title in only the most proper of
ways."

Louisa stepped away as Lady Bolton approached, not wanting the
dowager to find any fault with Emma due to her. Glancing over at
Harry, she hated to admit how jealousy had overcome her seeing
Mrs. Gardiner and Harry together here and at the menagerie. It was
illogical.

Mary, while a widow, was not Harry's type. Before marrying, she
had been the classic young miss out for a rich husband with no cares,
except which new gown to wear. But watching Harry chuckle at
something Mary said, made Louisa's heart twist in ways she hadn't
thought possible. He seemed taken with Mary in a way Louisa hadn't
seen with any other woman.

And it was tearing her apart.

She should want the best for Harry. Mary was a good woman
from a better family than hers. And Mary seemed to genuinely like
Charlotte. Louisa stole another glance at Harry, who laughed again

at something Mary said.

Oh dear Lord, was Tessa correct? Louisa spied him again and knew it was true. She was in love with Harry.

"Here is your wine," Collingwood said as he returned. "I did tell the footman you would prefer the smallest glass."

"Thank you."

Damn him. Louisa wanted a large glass of wine followed by a snifter or two of brandy—anything to ease the pain of seeing Harry and Mary Gardiner together.

The poetry reading tortured her soul as the poet spoke of love, jealousy, and heartache. She pressed her lips together to keep from crying. It was not like her to be a jealous person. Or maybe she'd never had a reason to be envious before now.

Emma and Bolton whispered to each other with smitten smiles on their faces. Mary sat next to Harry, intimately close. While she couldn't see them, she knew Tessa and Jack were a few rows behind them, most likely telling each other how they couldn't wait for their child to be born.

Collingwood was a nice man but sitting next to him did nothing to her senses. He smelled, well…nice, not spicy, leathery, and wholly enticing like Harry. At one point during the reading, Collingwood's thigh accidentally touched hers, and again, she felt nothing. Not one spark of desire.

Was this to be her lot in life?

She could not live like that after Harry's kiss. Not when she craved another kiss from him. Craved seemed like too weak of a word. Desire. Want.

Need.

She needed another kiss from him. While she had jested about being a Daring Drake sister to Emma, the most daring thing she'd ever done was visit Harry in Northumbria, or walk alone in the gardens with him, or kiss him. Her ability to be daring always revolved around him.

When the poet finally finished, she politely clapped while all she wanted to do was throw something at him for torturing her. Emma and Bolton split off to speak with his mother and a friend. Thankfully Collingwood made his excuse to Louisa and departed their little group. She moved to the back of the room where a table was set with refreshments and light fare.

"Mary Gardiner must have lost her mind," Miss Comstock whispered to her mother.

"Indeed. I always had a high opinion of the lady until now."

Was there something she didn't know about Mary Gardiner? Usually, Louisa would ignore the gossips, but this topic held her interest. She pretended to be overly interested in the sliced ham closer to the Comstocks.

"I realize he is a duke, but why would she take a chance when there is every indication he may end up like his father?"

Louisa pressed a hand to her belly. A movement to her side caught her eye. Harry moved away from the table. She closed her eyes as the pain overwhelmed her. Had he heard those despicable ladies?

Hearing them continue, she finally turned and said, "I do hope you realize that the duke is a fine upstanding gentleman with not even a touch of madness. He stayed in the North to mourn his wife and keep his daughter away from small-minded individuals in town. I cannot blame him after overhearing you two speak of the man as if he belongs in Bedlam."

"Miss Drake!" Mrs. Comstock exclaimed in a whispered tone. "Your mother will hear of this exchange."

"I am certain she will. Good evening."

She spun around and strode away from them before either gape-mouthed lady could speak again. Glancing around, she realized Harry must have left the party. She must talk to him and make him understand only the pettiest members of the ton held those opinions of him.

Emma stood on the outside of a group conversation between Lord Danvers, Lady Bolton, and her son. Louisa's heart went out to her sister too. Bolton was a good man but dominated by his mother. Her sister moved away from the group as Louisa approached.

Tessa ambled over to her with a look of pity in her eyes. "Emma, I do hope you don't mind, but I would like Louisa to return home with me tonight. She and I haven't seen each other in a while and need to chat."

Emma scowled. "At this hour? And why can't I come, too?"

"I promised Mamma that you would return by eleven," Louisa said, curious why Tessa would wish to speak right now.

"You two always keep secrets from me," Emma commented with a pout before yawning. "It does not matter. I am tired."

"Thank you. I will go with Tessa and Jack. Let Mamma know I will be home late."

"Of course," Emma replied.

Louisa glanced back at Mrs. Gardiner, who now spoke with Collingwood. The ache in her heart overwhelmed her. Thinking back to the poet's words about giving up the woman he loved for her to have a better life, Louisa wondered if she must do this for both Emma and Harry. Emma would get the man she loved, and Harry would find a proper lady. Once Emma married, it would no longer matter. Louisa could pursue any man she wanted.

Except for the one man who would be married himself by then.

Once Tessa and Jack arrived at their house, Louisa and Tessa retired to the drawing room.

"What is wrong?" Tessa asked.

"How did you know?"

Tessa smiled over at her. "I couldn't help but notice how you kept glancing over at Worthington but looked as if you were about to cry even after that dreadful poet had finished."

Louisa told her sister what the Comstock ladies had said. "I need to see him, Tessa. Alone. Tonight."

"Have you lost your mind?"

Louisa bit down on her lower lip. It was not the answer she'd expected from her sister. "Tessa, I must see him privately. He must realize that not everyone thinks as Miss Comstock does."

"Louisa, you are asking me to let you see Worthington alone at night. You have no idea about the scandalous things that can happen to a young lady when she visits a man at night."

She tilted her head. "I spent three nights at Northwood Park and left in the same virtuous state I arrived in."

"Send him a note."

"I also need to know if Mary Gardener is a favorite and whether or not I need to continue to consider finding a wife for him." And then there was Miss Turnbull to discuss.

"Which you can do in a note," Tessa insisted as she stared at Louisa. "There is more, isn't there?"

Louisa sighed and told her sister the other matter on her mind. "The looks I have seen on Lady Bolton's face have me concerned for Emma. Mamma insists I stop speaking with Harry because Lady Bolton will not be happy about any connection between our family and his."

Tessa frowned. "Are you going to stop your search for a wife for him, then?"

"Of course not," Louisa agreed reluctantly. "If Mary Gardiner is not the right lady for him. We will need to be more tactful."

"I hardly think visiting Worthington at his home at almost

midnight is being tactful."

"It may be my only chance," Louisa whispered.

Tessa looked away wistfully as if remembering something from her past. "Promise me you are not going to his home for a liaison."

After the way he gazed at Mary, an affair with Louisa was the last thing on his mind. "I hardly think he is interested in me. I must talk to him about our pact, but after Lady Bolton's visit, I must be careful that no one sees us. I am having difficulties finding anyone suitable for him."

"Because he wants you," Tessa said, smiling.

"No, he does not." He wanted Mary, not her.

"Let me speak to Jack."

Within thirty minutes, Louisa walked out the door with Jack. Once they were in the carriage, Jack said, "One hour, Louisa. Not a minute more."

"Yes, Jack."

"I shall wait right outside should you decide to leave early."

The carriage departed for Harry's home in Grosvenor Square. She prayed Harry had returned directly to his house. By the time she arrived, her nerves were taut. Noticing several windows still lit, it appeared he had not yet retired.

The door opened slowly to Jenkins' scowl. "Miss Drake? What are you doing here at this late hour?"

"I—I must speak with the duke immediately, Jenkins."

He shook his head as he opened the door for her. "Come in."

"Tell him it is imperative."

"When isn't it?" he grumbled as he walked down the hall.

Louisa inhaled, praying for calm.

"Come this way, Miss Drake," Jenkins grumbled from the end of the corridor.

Louisa followed him to Harry's study, where he sat by the fire sipping a brandy. She suddenly wished she'd had far more than one glass of wine tonight.

Harry rose and shook his head. "Close the door behind you as you leave, Jenkins."

Jenkins paused as if to question the request, but then said, "As you wish."

Once the door closed, he glared over at her with clenched fists. "What the bloody hell are you doing here at this hour?"

"Good evening to you, too," Louisa replied, stepping further into the room. "I do hope you enjoyed the poetry reading. Although, I do remember you once stating that you didn't enjoy poetry."

"Perhaps it depends on the company during the readings."

"Certainly, sitting near Mary Gardiner must have made the evening so much more pleasant." She had no idea what made her sound so spiteful. Seeing him tonight reminded her of the poet's words about giving up the one he loved. Louisa did not want to give up Harry.

"Indeed, as I'm sure Collingwood was excellent company."

"Yes, he was," she said tartly.

"You still haven't told me why you are here?"

"I wanted to discover how your call went with Miss Turnbull. Should I keep looking? Or is Mary Gardiner the top contender." She hated the biting sound of jealousy in her voice. Oh, God, it was envy.

"Miss Turnbull is not a contender."

She nodded. "I see."

"There was no need to come to my house when a note would have sufficed. Have you no sense?"

Louisa laughed harshly before moving to the small table where the brandy was stored. "No, apparently, I do not."

At least not where he was concerned. She poured the brandy and filled the snifter almost as much as Charlotte had the day she'd fallen into the pond. "I needed to speak with you regarding another topic."

"What now?" he demanded.

She swallowed a large gulp and then coughed. "Can we not be civil, Harry?"

"By all means." He waved at the chairs behind him. "Do sit down, Miss Drake. Shall I call for tea?"

Ignoring his sarcasm, she walked over to the large cherry desk that dominated the room and leaned against it. She needed as much distance as she could get from his handsome face. "I felt dreadful when I noticed that you overheard those horrible Comstock ladies."

"They were only saying aloud what everyone is thinking. It is not the first time I've overheard such venom."

Louisa's closed her eyes. "Oh, Harry, I'm so sorry. But please believe me that not everyone thinks the way they do."

"It matters not."

Hearing the forceful tone of his voice, Louisa worried that he would marry Mary Gardiner only to secure a wife and depart for Northwood Park. "Why not?"

"I shall be leaving soon enough. Then all those lovely ladies of good Society can forget they know me at all."

"Oh? Leaving so soon?"

"Mary Gardiner and I might suit after all," he replied flatly.

"Oh?" she whispered, staring over at him. She clutched the overhang of the desk for support. She couldn't let this happen. Mary Gardiner was not the right woman for him. What had Emma said? If all else fails, push him away. If he loved her, he would find a way to make a marriage work. Attempting Emma's plan might kill Louisa, but she decided to try.

"Good luck with Mary, then," she said in a light tone that belied her true feelings. "I also came to see you tonight because it has been brought to my attention that our friendship may impact Emma's possibility with Bolton."

Harry drained his brandy and then moved to pour himself another. "I suppose your mother thought our friendship far too scandalous?"

"Yes." Louisa told him of Lady Bolton's visit after Lady Gringham had noticed them return from the garden.

"I see."

"I have to protect my younger sister, Harry. She loves Bolton."

"I see," he said again before sipping his brandy calmly.

Why wasn't he reacting to her rejection of him? Emma's plan was not working. "That is all you can say? *I see?*"

"What more is there to say?" he asked in a dark tone.

"Tell me how it is unfair that two friends cannot meet on a terrace with nothing more than friendship on their mind." Louisa set her snifter down. When she looked up, he was in front of her.

"Who said there is nothing more on either of our minds?"

"Wh—What do you mean?"

He leaned in closer until she could smell the familiar scent of him, leather, cinnamon, and tonight brandy. "You never push me away when I kiss you, Louisa." He drew a finger down her jaw until it reached her lips. "Why is that?"

"Why, Harry, I do believe you are drunk."

He smiled in a feral way that sent shivers down her spine. "Not even close to being foxed, my dear."

"Then you must be mad," she whispered, unable to look away from those piercing gray eyes.

"Yes, madness this is." He skimmed her jaw with light kisses until she shivered. "Did you enjoy sitting next to Collingwood tonight? He seemed to hang on to your every word."

"Of course, he is a perfect gentleman."

"Unlike me?" Harry asked before his tongue grazed her earlobe.

She moaned softly. "It appeared you were paying particular attention to Mary tonight," she managed to say in a breathless tone.

"Did that bother you?" He pulled away and stared down at her. "Were you jealous that I was speaking with her instead of you?"

She couldn't look away from his searching gray eyes. Heat crossed her cheeks and down her neck. How could she tell him her true feelings when they were supposed to stay away from each other? But she had no desire to be apart from him.

"Oh, Harry," she barely whispered before his mouth was on hers. She clung to him, grateful for the support of the desk behind her. Her knees felt as if they would buckle as his tongue played with hers.

Wrapping her arms around his neck, she pressed her body against his, feeling the strength of his arms securing her to him. Rational thought slipped away with each swipe of his tongue on hers. Her senses were overwhelmed with the taste of brandy on his tongue, the scent of his spicy soap, and the strength of his body against hers. The room seemed so hot. All she wanted to do was rid herself of her clothing and feel his skin against her.

No man had ever made her so crazed with lust. It should have felt wrong to be this intimate with Harry, and yet it felt incredibly right. She could not get enough of him and never would.

"Louisa," he whispered as she reached for the buttons of his waistcoat. "We must stop."

"Please don't say a word," she said, skimming her hands over the garment. She desperately wanted to feel the heat of his skin under her hands. Glancing up at him, she saw the raw hunger in his gray eyes.

Quickly his mouth returned to hers as they both fought the passion between them. Louisa knew she was close to losing all control and not caring about the consequences. Why shouldn't she have one chance with Harry? At least when she was an old spinster, she would have the memories of this night. Somehow, he had loosened the lacing on her dress and stays enough to pull the gown down over her breasts. He eased his large hand under the top of her stays and freed her breasts from their confinement.

When his mouth moved to one nipple, she thought her legs would give out. The sensation of his tongue brushing against the peak sent even more moisture between her legs. She moaned as he suckled her.

"Harry," she whispered as his hand slowly lifted the hem of her skirts. His fingers grazed her thigh until she felt him press a finger between her folds. She gasped at the contact.

Desire spiraled upward as he found that special spot. Never in the years, she'd known him had she felt anything but friendship for him. But now...now she wanted this Harry, the madly passionate man in her arms.

A loud commotion at the front door split them apart in an instant. The cool air against Louisa's breasts brought her back to reality. Louisa gasped as she realized how close she'd come to giving herself to him.

"Where the bloody hell is she?" a booming male from the front hall shouted.

"Oh God, it's Raynerson," Louisa whispered.

"Turn around quickly," Harry said before setting her stays and gown in order. "Jenkins will stall him. Fix your hair."

She looked in the mirror and paused. Her face was flush, her lips swollen from heated kisses and her hair in shambles from Harry's hands. While he donned his waistcoat and jacket, she pushed her hair back into place before sitting down in the chair by the fireplace.

Harry picked up her brandy from the desk and took the seat next to her, hoping it would appear to her brother-in-law as if nothing untoward had happened in this room. Of course, if he had to stand, Raynerson would be blind not to notice the painful erection pressing against his breeches.

Dammit, what had he done? If not for the interruption, he might have made love to her against the desk. Then he would have been forced to marry her and ruin her life for good. God, he was a fool around her.

The door to the study hurled opened with such force that it hit the wall.

"Jack?" Louisa said in mock surprise. "What are you doing here so soon? You had said you would give me an hour."

"My wife should have a better concept of what can happen in an hour when a man and women are alone in a room."

"Or forty-five minutes to be exact," Louisa commented, glancing at the mantel clock.

"Raynerson, good evening," Harry said with a nod. "Help yourself to a brandy if you wish. Although it would have been pleasant if you had given us enough time to finish our conversation before barging into my home."

"Conversation?" Jack said, suspiciously glancing about the room.

"Yes, as I told you and Tessa, I needed to speak with His Grace alone about some personal business." Louisa rose and looked over at Harry. "I suppose you now realize that we must be more circumspect due to Emma and Bolton. Most people cannot fathom how a man and woman could be such good friends without something scandalous going on between them."

"Of course," he said without emotion.

"We mustn't meet on the terrace or gardens during balls. I took a risk even coming here tonight. We should only speak when accompanied by others."

"I do understand, Miss Drake." He stared at her eyes now welling with tears and wanted to throw Raynerson out of his house and hold her, tell her everything would be fine. Even though he knew nothing was fine or good without her. And he could never have her the way he wanted. "Good evening."

He watched as she followed her brother-in-law out of his study. "Like bloody hell I understand," he whispered before gulping down the rest of his brandy. "I don't understand a damned thing."

How could he have done such a foolish thing?

She deserved someone so much better than him. A man who would think of her reputation and that of her family, not a man who could destroy her name just by association. And not a reprobate who came far too close to taking her on top of his desk. He knew they shouldn't see each other again. He had to keep her away.

Marrying Louisa would ruin her life with the association of his family name. As he'd destroyed Sabita's life.

And he would never allow that to happen.

Chapter 15

Harry sipped his brandy as the sun rose in the sky, lighting his study in pink hues. After Louisa left last night, he hadn't moved except to refill his snifter. What the bloody hell was wrong with him? After spending all night in his cups, he'd understood that there was only one option. He had to leave her alone. Not see her beautiful face any longer. Forget this idea to have her find him a wife. Louisa was right. The best thing to do was stay away from each other.

There were any number of unmarried ladies from which to choose. Even Simon had said Harry could have any lady he wanted, and the woman's family would be thrilled. He rather doubted most families would be elated to have a possibly insane duke marry one of their daughters. But some men would not care as long as their daughter became a duchess.

"Where the bloody hell is he?" a feminine voice sounded from the front hall.

"My lady, let me introduce you," Jenkins said as the door to the study opened.

"I believe my brother knows who I am, Jenkins." Daphne sailed in the room and then stopped short. "You look like shit, brother dear."

"And you still have a mouth like a sailor, Daphne. How does your husband deal with that?"

Daphne laughed before taking a seat near him. "He loves it when

I curse...at least in the bedroom."

Harry shook his head. "I did not need to hear that, Daph."

"So, long night or starting early?"

"Why are you here?"

"I believe you know why I am here," she replied, softening her voice. "This must stop, Harry."

Damn. Was his sister here to scold him now? "To what are you referring?"

"Do you think we don't hear gossip in Dorchester? I've heard the rumors that you are sneaking about with Miss Drake. Lady Gringham made a point of writing to inform me of the disturbing news that everyone believes Miss Drake is your mistress."

"She is not my mistress." Goddamn Lady Gringham! He should have let her freeze to death.

"It must stop, Harry." Daphne sighed as she looked over at him with a touch of pity in her eyes.

"Miss Drake is a dear friend, nothing more." A dear friend he'd almost made love to last night.

"After all that has happened between our families, it is for the best to have nothing to do with any of those Drake girls."

"I understand." He knew precisely how the gossipmongers worked to tear down people. If he wanted Louisa to find a gentleman, her reputation needed to be impeccable. *If.* He *must* want that for her. Her sister needed Louisa to be the perfect lady with no mars on her name.

Daphne frowned as she waited for the footman to deliver the tea for her. Once he departed, she continued, "Understanding is not the same as doing something about it."

"She already has," he rasped.

"Oh," his sister whispered before sipping her tea. "That explains drinking at eight in the morning."

"I suppose it does."

Silence filled the room as Daphne sipped her tea, and Harry became lost in his thoughts. He genuinely wanted the best for Louisa, and the best wasn't him. If he were a better man, Harry would encourage her progress with Collingwood. The viscount was a good man who would take care of her and wouldn't disgrace her name.

"How is Charlotte?" Daphne finally asked.

"She will be bounding down the stairs any minute."

Daphne looked him over with a frown. "Then perhaps you should switch to tea and get your priorities in order."

His older sister was right as usual. "Pour me some tea."

He raked his fingers through his short hair before putting his waistcoat and jacket back on. "Better?"

"You're still foxed. I see it in your eyes."

Perhaps he needed to act far more like his sister. Daphne had done the proper thing, the responsible thing, and married the earl Father had picked for her. She'd had her heir and spare. Other than the occasional curse muttered—and always in private—she was a lady of quality.

"Where are Radley and the boys?" he asked and then picked up a piece of toast that had been delivered with the tea.

"They will come down in a fortnight. I am going to stay here until they arrive. I hate being in the house alone."

"Of course." He looked over and noticed her nibbling on the dry toast, which didn't make sense because she only ate dry toast when.... "Are you with child again?"

Daphne paused in her eating and stared at him. "How did you know?"

"The dry toast. You only eat it that way when you are carrying. How exactly did this happen?"

She tilted her head and stared over at him with gray eyes so much like his own. "The usual manner, Harry. Do I need to explain that to you?"

"I thought you and Radley were distant."

She blushed. "We had been. Then a few months ago, we had a terrible quarrel. For a while, I thought we might live apart. But once we got through it, we made up and then we made up some more and haven't seemed to stop making up for all the time lost."

"Well, congratulations, Daphne. I hope you are happy."

"I am," she replied with a secret smile. "More than I have been in the past ten years."

Harry smiled tightly. At least one of them was content. The sound of running steps announced Charlotte before she even entered the room.

"Good morning, Papa!" His little ball of energy raced into the room and climbed up on his lap. "You don't smell good," she whispered.

Daphne laughed before covering her mouth with her hand.

"Aunt Radley!" Charlotte scrambled off his lap and onto her aunt's lap. "I'm so glad you're here. You can meet Miss Drake! We shall all go back to see the elephant."

Harry looked up at the ceiling, ignoring his sister's prying stare. "Charlotte, we are not going back to the menagerie. We have already discussed this matter."

"Then Aunt Radley can go to the park with us. Miss Drake loves to walk," Charlotte added.

"Charlotte, return to the nursery while your father and I talk. I will come up in a few minutes, and we will have tea together," Daphne said, still staring at him.

Charlotte clapped her hands. "Thank you, Aunt Radley."

As soon as the door shut, Daphne started in again. "Have you lost your bloody mind, Harry?"

"Many people believe so," he said in a dry tone. "Charlotte met Louisa when she came out to Northwood Park around the new year. That is when the Gringhams arrived too. She only stayed for three nights, but she made a big impact on Charlotte. When we came to town, Miss Drake accompanied us to The Exchange."

"And the park?"

"We have seen her there, too."

"Of course." She pressed her fingers to her temples. "I arrived just in time."

"How so?"

"To save you from yourself. You do realize that Miss Drake is only chasing you for the title and fortune?"

Harry fisted his hands. "Have you ever met Louisa Drake?"

"Of course, I have. Why?"

"Then you would know that she is not the type of woman to trap a man into marriage. She doesn't care about my title or the fortune that goes with it."

Daphne released a long sigh. "Oh, Harry, you are so naïve. That is all she is after. Her eldest sister made a point to befriend our father to gain his trust and climb up into Polite Society. When she failed to land him as a husband, she married her way from baron to earl. Obviously, they left duchess to Louisa who could twist you around her little finger to get what she wants."

"Enough!" He shot out of his chair and stared down at her. "Louisa Drake is not like her mother or her sister. She doesn't care if she marries into a title or not. All she wants is a man who will love her."

"She wants you," Daphne whispered.

"She is going to marry Collingwood," he stated, collapsing back into his chair.

"Collingwood? Why would he be interested in her?"

Sometimes his sister drove him mad. And this was one of those times. "Louisa Drake is a fascinating person. She is beautiful and intriguing. What man wouldn't be interested in her?"

"That is not what I meant," she muttered with a shake of her head. "Collingwood is low on funds. His father spent a fortune on horses but had a terrible eye for horseflesh. He lost huge amounts by buying overpriced horses, which couldn't win a race. I heard Collingwood sold the estate in Suffolk to pay back what he could but wasn't enough. Rumors are he is still in for at least ten thousand, and some say closer to twenty."

"Collingwood needs funds?" He should have known that. But still, the viscount had danced with her twice and called on her once. Collingwood should know she didn't have money, as everything her family lived on was from Tessa's late husband or Lord Hammond's kindest to his mistress.

Harry didn't think Collingwood was the type of man who would go after Tessa's money. Perhaps he was intrigued by Louisa. Harry's stomach roiled with too much drink and a slow ache pressing into his heart.

He had to find her another man. A better man than Collingwood…or himself.

After four days of not seeing Harry, Louisa didn't want to get up in the morning. She missed Harry dreadfully, but she'd been foregoing the few social events scheduled so she wouldn't see him after what happened in his study. She didn't know how she could ever face him again after what they had done that night.

How could she?

How could she see him without wanting him to do what they had done and more?

"Louisa, you must get up today," Emma said as she raced into the room. "Lord Collingwood sent a note stating he would like to take you to the park for a walk and Mamma replied that you would go with him. You only have an hour to eat and dress before he arrives."

Louisa threw the covers over her head. "I am not going."

"Oh, yes you are, young lady," her mother's voice sounded from the hall. "Get up this minute and be ready by one. And you will attend Lady Huntley's ball tomorrow night."

Louisa wanted to scream but knew it would do no good. Her mother wouldn't listen to her. She only saw a viscount calling on her plain daughter, which meant finally marrying her off.

"Come along, Louisa," Emma said softly. "Before the dragon returns."

Louisa flipped the covers off her head and stared at her younger sister. "I have never heard you be so mean, Emma."

Emma closed the door and then returned to Louisa's bed with a long sigh. "She is driving me mad over this wedding. She is pressuring me to tell Bolton that we must set a date now."

"Is that what has her ire up this morning?"

"I believe she wanted to discuss something important with Lord Hammond, but he sent a note stating he was occupied today."

Louisa didn't want to hear any more about Lord Hammond and her mother. Or hear any more about her pressuring Emma to wed Bolton. "Emma, if you don't wish to marry Bolton, then you should not marry him. It is your life. Tessa sacrificed so much so that we would be able to marry for love."

Emma blinked in confusion. "I do want to marry Bolton, Louisa. I am weary of Mamma trying to force the wedding sooner than Lady Bolton wishes. I need to be considerate of my future mother-in-law's desires."

Louisa drew her sister into a tight hug. "Mamma suggested I stay away from Harry. She fears Lady Bolton will influence her son to toss you over."

"Nonsense," Emma said with a laugh. "Bolton loves me. While he always considers his mother's opinion, he would never toss me over. You will pursue Harry and win his heart."

"I hope you are right." But at this point, she had no plan on how to win his heart or any other part of him.

"We need to get you dressed," Emma said, pulling away from her. After searching the linen press, she pulled out a dark blue striped walking dress. "This is perfect."

"Why are you pushing me toward Collingwood today?"

Emma giggled. "It's a beautiful day, and as such, you should be seen in the park with a man at your side. How else will you make the duke jealous?"

Louisa tossed the coverlet off her. Emma helped her dress and put up her hair. She had no wish to tell Emma that she'd already told Harry they could not see each other because of her.

"Perfect," Emma said, placing the last pin in Louisa's hair. "I suppose if all else fails, I could become a ladies' maid."

"And mother would have an apoplexy fit," Louisa replied with a laugh. "What time is it?"

"Half twelve."

"I need to eat something, or my belly will be complaining throughout the walk." She trudged downstairs and thankfully found tea and toast with strawberry jam set out for her. She finished quickly then brushed the crumbs off her skirt as a knock hammered the door.

She greeted him in the receiving salon. "Lord Collingwood, how lovely to see you today."

He rose slowly and gave her a bow. "I do hope you don't mind a walk today. The weather is quite fine, and I know you enjoy walking in the park."

"Thank you. Taking some air is just what I need today." He was a handsome enough man. So why didn't he make her feel as Harry did when he looked at her? No matter what Emma said, Louisa didn't quite believe Bolton would disobey his mother if she ordered him to break off the engagement. Louisa needed to be prepared to give up her obsession with Harry.

They walked to the park. Her maid trailed slightly behind so they could talk but was escorted. Louisa discussed some of the recent books she'd read, and he did the same. At least they had that in common, she thought.

"I read an interesting article yesterday about the progress of the steam locomotive. If someone can figure out a better design for the rails, I believe it will be a useful machine."

"Hmm," Collingwood said as if barely listening to her.

They headed toward the path near the Serpentine when she looked up and saw him. And Mary Gardiner. She could barely breathe as they approached. Harry tipped his hat to them, but Mary stopped him from passing by.

"Good afternoon, Lord Collingwood. Miss Drake," she said with a quick curtsy. "I do hope you are enjoying your walk."

Louisa slid a glance at Harry just as he did the same. She immediately moved her gaze back to Mary. "Yes, it is a lovely day."

"Miss Drake, I had hoped to see you," Harry said. "I must speak with you rather urgently. Collingwood, would you mind seeing Mrs. Gardiner home? I will escort Miss Drake home."

Collingwood looked back and forth at them before saying, "If that is acceptable with you, Miss Drake?"

"Of course it is," Harry interjected before she could say a word.

"Miss Drake?" Collingwood pressed.

She wasn't about to make a scene in the middle of the park. "Of course."

She blinked and watched as Collingwood held out his arm for
Mary, who glanced back at Harry with a frown. Louisa couldn't
blame Mary for being vexed. Harry had acted very highhanded.

"You are...are...insufferable," she sputtered as he led her back
toward her home.

"Hush." He led her away to a small copse of trees.

The man was impossible! And very handsome today. No, she
should not think of Harry in that manner. But he was striking in his
walking clothes. The stark white cravat tied in a barrel knot matched
the simplicity of his black wool greatcoat. And all she wanted to do
was strip every stitch of clothing off him.

"Are you all right, miss?" her maid asked in a worried tone.
"Should I get assistance?"

"The duke is a gentleman, Mary." Louisa glared up at him. "Or at
least he used to be," she whispered.

"I need to speak with you about something."

"You should have sent a note."

He moved her behind a tree to prying eyes from seeing them.
"No, it could not be written where anyone might read it."

"What is it, Harry?" She refused to meet his intent gaze. She
refused to let the sensation of his nearness overwhelm her. Or the
familiar hint of leather and cinnamon. Or the memories of what they
had done.

"My sister says Collingwood is low on funds. I thought you
should know that before you get too far into this courtship."

"Then why would he be courting me? I have nothing to bring to
a marriage." Louisa sighed. "When I rejected Emerson's proposal,
he made certain everyone knew my pittance of a dowry."

"I don't know why. I only wanted to warn you about his financial
position."

"I heard he has four thousand a year. That should be more than enough."

Harry shook his head. "I heard he's in for over ten thousand and growing every month."

"Ten thousand?" Louisa whispered. That was a considerable sum, indeed. "I must return home now."

She moved away from him, impatient to gain some much-needed distance from his tantalizing scent.

"I promised Collingwood that I would see you home," he said as he caught up with her.

"You mustn't. Think of how it would look."

"Since when have you cared about what others would think?"

"Since my sister's happiness was involved." Louisa wiped a tear away. Angry with herself for even imagining he might have feelings for her, she whispered, "Damn you, Harry."

"Between you and my sister, I have heard enough of ladies cursing for years."

"How is Lady Radley?" His sister had never done more than greet her at balls, but Louisa supposed she should be polite. At least this question would get their conversation off marriage to the wrong man.

"She is with child again," he replied flatly. "She also believes you are chasing me to gain my title and fortune."

"Oh." Louisa walked toward the path in silence, hurt by the fact that Lady Radley had such a low opinion of a woman she barely knew but also annoyed by the fact that he told her. "And what do you believe?"

He stopped walking and looked down at her. "Do you really need to ask that question? I defended you to her, in case you needed to know that, too."

"As well you should," she added sharply. "I told you from the beginning that I was not trying to trap you into marriage."

"You were the one who came to my home alone…twice," he retorted.

"Which a man of honor would not mention," she snapped before walking down the street again.

He pulled her arm to halt her steps. "Are you questioning my honor now?"

"If I had a desire to trap you, then I would have let Raynerson find us in the compromising position *you* put me in. Good afternoon, Your Grace."

"Loui—Miss Drake, please wait."

"I am a block from my home and have my maid with me," she cried, before increasing the pace of her stride.

Thankfully, he didn't follow her as she raced home. Once inside, she ignored her mother's calls to speak with her. Instead, she sought solace in her lonely bedchamber. She pressed a hand to her stomach as she paced her room. Why did he have to turn her emotions upside down? Why did he have to be a blasted duke? Why did their family names have to be forever linked in scandal?

Why was pursuing him so challenging?

Off all the questions, the last was the one that she could answer. She wasn't making any progress with him because she felt guilty that Emma could lose Bolton. Because after their passionate encounter, Harry should have paid a call and asked for her hand. But he hadn't. Not even a word about what happened had passed his lips.

It was time to trust Emma's intuition about her fiancé. Bolton had surprised everyone by joining them at Christmas and offering for her. Louisa doubted Lady Bolton had had an inkling of her son's intentions.

She understood that the issues between their families could never be easily resolved. But what happened with his father and her sister shouldn't matter if they loved each other.

And that was the real issue. Harry had loved his late wife. And while he might desire Louisa, he did not love her.

But that wasn't about to stop her. It was time to forget her mother's warnings and listen to her sister. Louisa's determination upped a notch higher. It was time to focus on his desire for her.

Chapter 16

H arry escorted his sister up the steps to Lady Huntley's home on Berkeley Square. Once inside the house, he scanned the crowded room for her. Knowing her mother was good friends with Lady Huntley, he was certain Louisa would be here. Not that he should look for her, but he couldn't seem to stop himself. Would she even speak with him after that episode walking home from the park yesterday?

"Isn't that Mrs. Gardiner?" Daphne asked, pointing to the young widow standing by the refreshment table speaking with Collingwood.

"Yes, it is." And what was Collingwood doing with her? They inclined their heads close, as if whispering intimate things to each other. But it was the smile on his face and the slight blush lighting Mary Gardiner's cheeks that sent a cold chill down Harry's back.

"We must go speak to her. I haven't seen her in ages."

"I had no idea you two were even acquainted, much less such close friends."

"Well, we are hardly close, Harry, but we must be polite." Daphne led him over to the couple who both seemed a bit put out by the intrusion.

Harry noticed the way Collingwood took a step away from the widow. As Daphne and Mrs. Gardiner chatted, he glanced over at Collingwood who appeared unable to say more than two words until

Louisa came near.

"Ah, Miss Drake, how lovely to see you tonight," Collingwood said as Louisa approached the group slowly.

"Miss Drake," Harry said with a quick bow. "You do remember my sister, Lady Radley, do you not?"

"Of course," Louisa said with a curtsy.

"Yes, Miss Drake," Daphne said with a stiff nod. "Please excuse me. I see a dear friend of mine."

Harry clenched his jaw. "Please excuse my sister. She is never quite herself when she is with child."

"Oh, how lovely, Your Grace," Mary said in a light tone.

"Yes, lovely," Louisa muttered.

"Miss Drake, may I have the next dance?" Collingwood asked after a glance at Harry.

"Of course, my lord," she replied with far too much enthusiasm for Harry.

Watching Mary slide a glance toward Collingwood, Harry wondered why they kept looking at each other. "Mrs. Gardiner, may I have the next dance?"

Her smile drooped before she said, "Yes, you may." Her gaze eased back to Collingwood.

Collingwood held out his arm to Louisa. "Shall we?"

Louisa smiled at him. "I do hope I did not bore you yesterday with my conversation on steam locomotives. I find the topic fascinating and truly believe that someday we shall be carried by locomotives and not horse and carriage."

Harry couldn't help but smile as he and Mary followed them to the dance floor. Louisa's intelligence intrigued him in so many ways. It went beyond book learning. She seemed to take what she read and examine the ideas.

"Oh, no, Miss Drake, it was quite...well, interesting,"

Collingwood babbled. "Although I highly doubt people will ever ride in such dangerous contraptions. Goods perhaps, but not people."

The man had no idea of her intelligence. Collingwood would never appreciate the fact that she could speak of more than clothing and gossip. Perhaps Collingwood wasn't the man for her after all.

Harry glanced down at Mrs. Gardiner. His sole purpose in asking for a dance was to stay close to Collingwood and Louisa. They lined up across from each other, and he noticed again how Mary's eyes sought out Collingwood. What were they about tonight?

As the music started, he watched them both now quite suspicious of their glances. He danced around Louisa, inhaling the light scent of lilacs surrounding her. They separated and were back to their partners. Perhaps dancing in the line so close to her had been a mistake. Every time she came near, desire flooded him, making him think thoughts, he should not be having for her.

Once the set finished, he bowed to Mrs. Gardiner and excused himself. He needed a moment away from Louisa and this crowd. The night had turned rainy. Instead of retiring outside, he moved through the crush to Lord Huntley's study. The dark room was just what he needed for a bit of privacy and maybe a glass of brandy. A small fire still burned in the room lending just enough light to find the drink.

He had come in here to think about prospective brides. Closing his eyes, the image of Louisa in that pale green gown invaded his mind. The dress cut across her chest, displaying a hint of her luscious rounded breasts. The same breasts he had lovingly caressed and suckled. God, he was a cad. He could still smell the light lilac perfume she wore.

A feminine gasp forced his eyes open. Louisa stood near his chair, her hand over her mouth. "What are you doing in here?"

"What are you doing here, Louisa?"

"I—I was getting a breath of air. You know how I get at balls.

The overwhelming smells and the crowds…"

"I know exactly how you feel." He should rise since she still stood by his chair. But this blasted erection would not ease. It had only become harder since he opened his eyes and noticed her. "There is brandy on the corner table."

"Would you pour me a glass?"

Damn. Damn. Damn.

"Of course," he replied tightly. He rose and turned away from Louisa, hoping by the time he reached the brandy, his shaft would be a little more compliant. Glancing back, he found her standing by the fireplace and with the flames behind her. In an instant, he was rock hard and desperate to have her.

The lilac aroma returned as he stepped closer to her. Her eyes darted around the room as if attempting not to look at him. His heart pounded in his chest as he handed the snifter to her. Finally, she looked up at him with those beautiful sapphire eyes.

"Are you unwell, Harry? You have a different look to your face."

"No, I am not well." Did he say that aloud? To her? Good God, now she would question him. "Too much to drink," he muttered.

"I don't think that is it. What is wrong?" She sipped her brandy, and then her gaze shifted down, and she noticed precisely what was wrong. "Harry?"

He pulled her into his arms, pressed his hardness against her. "This is what you do to me. Every time you are near, I want you. And I know I can't have you. It's driving me mad."

He brought his lips down on hers, harder than he should as if punishing her for his damned desire. This madness was his fault. He was supposed to push her way, but he could not seem to stay away from her. She was the reason he came to town. It had always been this way for him with her.

Send her away.

But he didn't want to send her anywhere except to a bedroom where he could slowly make love to her all night.

Hearing her light moans, he pulled away only to drop light kisses on her jaw until he reached her ear. His tongue traced the shell of her ear until she was nearly panting. Her hand slid down his chest, down his belly, reaching his trouser covered cock. She discovered the outline of him as he tried to keep some control.

"Is there anything I can do for you tonight?" she whispered as her palm rounded the top of him.

He nearly came then and there in Huntley's study with his trousers still on. He felt like an adolescent with his first woman. He wanted desperately to tell her yes. She could strip him naked and put her mouth on him. But he couldn't. This was Louisa. He had to remember that.

Before he could tell her no, she had reached for the fall of his trousers and found the buttons there.

"No, Louisa. You cannot do that."

She stared up into his eyes and smiled. "You touched me in a most intimate place. It is only fair that I touch you."

Damn, she had found him. Her soft hand circled him, stroking him lightly, agonizing him with pent up desire. He kissed her again as her fingers continued to tease him. A part of him wanted this to last. He didn't want to lose the sensation of her gentle strokes on him. But each caress brought him closer to the edge. He wanted Louisa Drake in his arms, naked.

He clasped his hand on hers, showing her how to rub her thumb around the tip of him, spreading the bead of liquid that had already eased out. Feeling the moisture brought thoughts of being deep inside her, giving her as much pleasure as she was giving him. The edge was there in sight. He couldn't control it much longer. He pulled his handkerchief out just as he exploded in her hand.

"Louisa," he moaned as waves of incredible pleasure coursed through him. He pulled her close and rested his forehead on hers as he tried to catch his breath.

He moved her hand away and wiped her clean before kissing the palm of her hand. The hand that had given him such pleasure. He wanted to return the sensation to her. But she pulled away.

"I must return. I fear we may have already been missed." She moved away from him. "Please don't come back into the room for a while."

"Not yet," he whispered.

"I must. We cannot be seen together." She glanced away, but he noticed the pain in her eyes. "For Emma."

"Of course," he said, watching her leave him once again. The door closed behind him, and he collapsed back into the chair. The fire had all but died out. He buttoned his trousers and wished once more that he'd had the chance to give her as much pleasure as she'd given him.

But that would only cause more issues for them both. Harry would be forced to marry her and subject Louisa to his poor reputation. Her sister might lose her fiancé. The gossip would cause her and her family even more harm. He couldn't live with himself if he brought pain to her.

They should stay away from each other.

He wasn't sure how he could do that after what she'd done in this room tonight.

He finished another brandy and then another before being interrupted by an amorous couple. As he rose, he felt a bit off kilter and knew he'd had too much to drink on an empty stomach.

Dear God! What had she done? And at a ball! Louisa doubted this was what Emma had meant when she told her to be flirtatious and make Harry jealous. Her sister would be shocked if she discovered what Louisa and Harry had been doing in Lord Huntley's study. But she had decided to use the one weapon she had against Harry's defenses. She smiled to herself. It must have worked.

Louisa walked back into the ballroom with unsteady limbs. As she turned a corner, she ran into a hard body.

"Excuse me," she said, looking up to see the face of Lord Ainsley.

"Well, if it isn't Miss Drake," he drawled with a feral smile. "I believe the same Miss Drake, who was supposed to spend a week with me in Scotland. With my mother, if I'm not mistaken. I do wonder what happened to scare you off. A rendezvous with a duke, perhaps?"

Her heart pounded in her chest as she tried to think of something to say to him. How could he know about her being at Northwood Park? "I must apologize, my lord. I fear some gossip has made the rounds. I am not quite certain how it started."

He tilted his head back and laughed. "I know exactly how it started. Dance with me, Miss Drake."

"I mustn't." The man was a notorious rake with his deep dimples and green eyes. It was rumored that he had even ruined Clarissa Carter and then refused to marry her.

"Oh, but you must. I should hate to spread gossip that you did indeed spend some time in Scotland with me, and me alone."

"Bastard," she hissed while he led her to the dance floor as a slow waltz started to play. He pulled her far too close with a smile. She had to admit he was a handsome man, but it was his smile that was truly devastating. "How did you find out? Lady Gringham?"

"That is my secret."

"What are you about, Ainsley?"

"I get what I want, Miss Drake."

"No one gets everything they want, my lord. Besides what you want could have nothing to do with me."

He shrugged nonchalantly. He swept Louisa across the floor in rhythm to the music. "I am not certain you have heard, but I have decided it is time to settle down and find a wife."

"I have heard that bit of news. What has caused the change in attitude? I thought you were a confirmed rake."

"A rake, yes. Confirmed?" He smiled down at her again. "An earl must marry at some point, as you well know. Carry on the family name and all that."

"I suppose so." Why did she suddenly feel nervous around him? It was not as if they had never met. He was a friend of Harry's.

"And at five and twenty, you must be ready to marry too? I'm sure you have had a bit of fun and now want to find a husband." His hand on her back attempted to press her even closer. "Perhaps even some fun with a certain duke just out of mourning. But who am I to judge?"

"My lord, I do believe you are mistaken. And I find your insinuations rather insulting."

"I don't believe I am mistaken, Miss Drake. But I fear you mistake my intentions."

"How so?"

"I said I have decided to marry. I never said you were the object of my decision."

Her mouth gaped slightly.

"Not that you aren't a beautiful woman," he continued hurriedly. "But since I am to marry, I think it only right that my dearest friend should also wed."

Louisa tilted her head in confusion as she stared at the man. "Whatever are you talking about, my lord?"

"Harry. It is far past time you two marry."

She couldn't have been more surprised if the devil himself had walked into the room. She almost stumbled, but he caught her close. "I don't understand, sir."

"Harry has loved you for years. It's time you stopped being so blasted picky and accepted him." Ainsley's green eyes flashed with humor. "After all, if I am to be chained in marriage, so should he."

"I do believe you are mistaken, my lord. His Grace loved his late wife. Never me."

Ainsley pulled her closer and whispered in her ear, "Always you, Miss Drake. I shall call on you tomorrow to discuss our plan."

Our plan? She had no scheme with him.

As the music ended, he escorted her off the dance floor, but not before she noticed Harry glaring at her as he sipped his drink. Her mother rushed to her side.

"Lord Ainsley? Oh my, Louisa! An earl!"

"A rake, Mamma."

"A rake whose uncle is worth a fortune and won't release the money until either he dies, or the earl marries."

What plan had Ainsley conceived that would help her with Harry? Perhaps her sister had an idea. She found Emma speaking with Bolton. Once again, the man's mother stood next to her son as if terrified to leave her with a Daring Drake sister. But Emma smiled at her viscount as if he was the only man in the room. Louisa's belly clenched. She could not ruin her sister's chance with Bolton.

"Good evening, Lord Bolton," she said with a smile. "Lady Bolton," she added a nod and quick curtsy.

"Good evening, Miss Drake," the viscount replied.

"Miss Drake." His mother gave a disapproving nod before strolling away.

"Have you two danced yet?"

Emma tilted her head and stared at her as if she had horns on her head. "Not yet."

"Perhaps we should dance now," Bolton replied, smiling down at Emma.

"May I have this dance?"

Louisa turned to find Harry staring down at her with a scowl lining his face. "I thought you were going to wait a few minutes more?"

"There was a line for the privacy of Lord Huntley's study." He held out his arm for her before leaning in closer. "What the bloody hell were you doing with Ainsley?"

"Harry," she admonished him in whispered tones. "He knows about me visiting you and using his name as an excuse for the Gringhams."

"Ainsley is a rogue."

"He is in town to find a wife." She decided not to tell him much about her conversation with his friend until after she listened to Ainsley's idea.

"Well, it won't be you." He pulled her a bit too close as the waltz was about to begin.

"Why not?" Harry seemed not to mind if she married Collingwood. At least Ainsley would be a far more interesting husband. "Is an earl too high for me to reach?"

"Not Ainsley."

"You are irrational."

"Yes, I am," he whispered. "Dear God, Louisa, you touched me…intimately. Completely inappropriately."

"I was there."

"And I loved it," he said, leaning far too close to her ear.

"Stop this nonsense!" Her cheeks flamed with embarrassment.

"I want to pleasure you, Louisa."

She felt as if her knees were about to give out. How she kept dancing without stumbling, she had no idea. "You must stop, Your

Grace. People might hear you."

"As long as you hear me, I don't care."

"I do believe you are completely and utterly foxed," she added, praying this dance would end quickly.

"Just drunk on you."

Oh, dear God, she might faint. "You must stop, Your Grace. People are starting to stare."

"Let them."

Not even logic was working on him tonight. As soon as this dance ended, Louisa would deliver him directly to his sister. Lady Radley could take care of him. But this had to be the longest set ever. At one point, he pulled her up against his body, and she could feel his manhood hardening again. If she was not careful, she would end up in bed with him.

A part of her wanted that most desperately.

Finally, the dance ended, and Lady Radley approached. "Lady Radley, thank God," she said softly. "I do believe your brother is feeling a tad under the weather."

"Yes, Miss Drake," Lady Radley said with a disapproving frown. "I think you are correct."

"Daphne, have you met Miss Drake?" Harry said with a slight slur to his words.

"Come along, Harry. You need to go home now." Lady Radley led him away as Louisa watched, half-wishing she could be the one to escort him home.

"Miss Drake, may I have the next dance?"

She sighed and turned to find Collingwood behind her. "Of course, but I do believe the musicians are on break right now."

"That is all right. We can talk for a few minutes. We get so little time to speak with each other. I feel I must confess something."

"Oh?" How had she become so popular tonight? Usually, she

might dance once or twice but rarely three times.

He looked chagrined as he said, "I only danced with you at Lady Leicester's ball because Worthington requested it."

"I assumed as much, my lord."

"But after that dance, I found myself enchanted," he said softly with a smile that didn't quite reach his eyes. "I could not get enough of you or your spirit."

"I see."

Collingwood laughed. "I don't think you do. While I did as Worthington requested, I found myself intrigued by you, Miss Drake."

"Oh?"

"Yes, I believe that Worthington's request was the best thing that ever happened to me."

"How so, my lord?"

He smiled down at her. "Because I found you."

"Oh." *Oh, dear God.* After what happened in the study, she could never accept Collingwood as a husband. She couldn't imagine doing to him what she'd done to Harry. It felt natural with Harry. The idea of touching Collingwood's shaft was rather abhorrent to her.

And she wasn't ready to give up on Harry yet. He seemed too close to the edge tonight. Jealous. Not of Collingwood but of her dancing with Ainsley.

"This is our dance, Miss Drake." Collingwood held out his hand for her as the musicians took their seats.

She chose to ignore her feelings for now and focus on Collingwood. She couldn't help but wonder why he would be courting her when the subject of her meager dowry was well known in Society. "How do you manage with your estates, my lord?"

"Quite well, but I only have the one in Hertfordshire. My late father had a thought to breed racehorses. After some careful consideration, I've decided it is not a worthwhile endeavor."

"Oh?" Well, that coincided with what Harry had told her. Except, she had been certain Collingwood had an estate in Suffolk as well as Hertfordshire. Perhaps it had not been entailed, allowing him to sell it and pay off his father's debts. "What will you focus on now?"

"Back to farming. It has always kept the estate with a steady income. I've already increased the number of sheep and plan to bring in a few more tenants. I need to build houses for them first."

Louisa nodded. "I see. It sounds like you have everything in order."

"Almost."

Except for the most crucial aspect of wealth…diversification. The large estates needed vast amounts of income to sustain them. Farming alone might not be enough to keep the estate solvent, but Louisa doubted Collingwood would like to hear her opinion on the matter.

Once the musicians ended, Collingwood led her toward her mother. "I just need to focus on a wife now." He bowed over her hand. "Good evening, Miss Drake."

"Good evening, my lord." The man had directly hinted that he needed a wife.

"Well done, Louisa," her mother said with a smile. "You now have an earl and a viscount interested."

And a duke she wanted the most, who her mother would deem completely unacceptable.

Chapter 17

Harry left the ball while his sister said her goodbyes. He had no intention of sharing the carriage with her only to be forced to listen to her convey her displeasure with his behavior tonight. After hailing a hackney, he headed to an area of town he rarely frequented any longer.

Once the hackney slowed to a stop, he jumped out and paid the man. Harry walked to the door of the gaming hell and knocked on the door of the old church. He slid his card into the slot and waited to be ushered inside. A large man with a long scar across his cheek opened the door.

"Your Grace," the man said. "Welcome to Hell."

He did love the simplicity of the name of Simon's gaming hell. "I'm here to see Kingsley."

The scar-faced man scowled. "Why would a gent like you want to see King?"

"Does it matter? I have asked to see Kingsley."

"Yes, Your Grace. I apologize." He started walking down the hall. "This way, Your Grace."

The man knocked on the door and then slowly opened it enough to say, "King, the Duke of Worthington wants a word."

A low chuckle sounded from behind the door. "Let my brother in, Hood."

Hood opened the door. "Excuse me, Your Grace. I had no idea

you were a relation."

Harry entered the large office filled with books and papers. Simon sat behind the large oak desk, leaning back with his hands behind his head.

"Well, well. Isn't this a surprise. I thought if you ever needed to speak with me, I would be summoned to the grand ducal home."

Harry shook his head. "Indeed? I will remember that the next time. Pour me a brandy."

"Not even a please," Simon said with a low chuckle. "If I were to guess, I'd say you've already had a few."

Harry sat down with a sigh. "Simon, just pour me a goddamn drink."

"As you wish." His brother poured brandy into two crystal snifters before handing one to Harry. "What is wrong?"

"I don't even know where to begin. I've made such a mess of things." Harry sipped his brandy surprised by the excellent quality. Then again, nothing about this place seemed in line with some of the gaming hells he'd been in before.

His brother had turned an abandoned church into a gaming hell and then bought the rectory for his office and living quarters. Simon made his fortune by catering to the upper crust reprobates who wanted only the best, and the idea of gambling in a church appealed to their sordid tastes.

"Miss Drake again, I presume." Simon sat down behind the desk and studied him. "How have you made a mess of things now?"

"Tonight, she happened to notice my rather large desire for her."

Simon chortled. "Did she go running off afraid of the big bad cock?"

"I wish she had."

"You didn't—"

"No," Harry interrupted. "She took matters into her own hand."

"Her own hand as in…?"

"Exactly."

Simon sipped his brandy, but Harry could see the laughter in his sapphire eyes. Harry knew this was a bad idea. Why would one of London's most infamous rogues take his problem seriously?

"I should go," Harry said as he stood and then placed his brandy down on the desk.

"Sit down, Harry. I'm sorry if I found this rather humorous, but honestly, I don't see what the trouble is. So she discovered you lust for her."

"She is supposed to be my friend, Simon."

"Maybe she wants to be more than friends."

"She has never wanted to be anything more than friends." Throughout several drinks, he finally told his brother everything about his relationship with Louisa.

"A friend does not do what she did tonight, Harry."

Harry wasn't sure what to think about her actions tonight. Each kiss they shared in the past fortnight had only become more passionate. When he almost made love to her on the desk in his study, he'd thought she must be too innocent to know what he was doing. But tonight, she had been more seductress than a friend.

This was not the time for her to finally see him as more than a confidante. And yet, the thought of her fingers wrapped around him wouldn't leave his mind. Perhaps he was going as mad as his father, for all he wanted was Louisa Drake.

"Harry?"

He blinked and focused on their conversation again. "Now Ainsley has come to town. He danced with her tonight."

"Well, isn't Ainsley a better candidate than Collingwood? He is an earl."

"He's a rake!"

"Rakes can change, Harry. You did."

"I was never as bad as Ainsley. Father wouldn't allow it."

Simon chuckled. "Yes, our dear sainted father who never strayed from the moral path. Of course, that doesn't explain my existence, now does it?"

"Shut up, Simon. Collingwood is a good man. I should be encouraging her to marry him."

Simon shook his head before taking another sip of brandy. "You mean he's a safe man. While Ainsley might have enough charm to make her fall in love with him."

"That is not it at all." How had Simon figured that out before he had? Harry closed his eyes and saw her dancing with Ainsley again. He saw how his friend looked at her with longing. How she smiled up at him and appeared to like the attention he gave her.

"Marry her, Harry. She may not have the best family, but you love her, and that's more than most men get in life." Simon sighed. "Or women for that matter."

"She doesn't wish to marry me."

"What's the real reason you won't marry her? Because I am quite sure you can damn well convince her to marry you."

"I couldn't." Harry stared down into his snifter of brandy. "I shouldn't."

"Whyever not?" Simon asked.

"After what Father did by murdering her sister's husbands, I cannot. The gossip would be dreadful for everyone involved, especially her youngest sister."

"And?"

"And I won't do anything to hurt Louisa…or her family." He added that last bit as more of an afterthought.

"How was any of that mess your fault?" Simon pressed before pouring them both more brandy.

Harry looked down into the dark recesses of his brandy, half-wishing the liquid would swallow him. "I should have been there. I might have seen the changes in him, Simon."

Simon stared at him for a long moment. "But there's more, isn't there?"

Harry banged the snifter on the desk with such force the twisted stem broke. "Yes. After what I did to my wife, I don't deserve a woman as sweet as Louisa. I don't deserve anyone. And when I thought I could make it up to Sabita by bringing her here, a fortnight after we arrived, she was poisoned by my father."

"What did you do, Harry?" Simon asked in a low tone.

Harry closed his eyes, trying to forget those days. Instead, he pictured the hurt in Sabita's brown eyes. "I cannot talk about it."

Simon released a long breath. "What happened here was your father's fault, not yours. You could not have known how he would react."

"I should have known," he shouted as he rose from his seat and paced the room. "I knew how he treated his workers over there. I did my best to improve their conditions without causing Father to notice the expenditures. He hated them just because they were different. Their skin a shade darker than ours. That is why I convinced him to sell the damned place."

"But you kept your daughter safe, Harry," Simon said softly. "You did that by not telling your father about her. You kept her safe and gave her a new life."

"A new life where people ridicule her because her skin isn't pale enough. I must get out of town for a few days," he said. "I need to think things through."

"Are you certain now is the best time with both Collingwood and Ainsley chasing the woman you love?"

"Louisa is not a fool. She will see past Ainsley's charm. Besides, he knows better than to cross me."

"Perhaps, but she might not see past Collingwood's safety," Simon muttered in a low tone as Harry reached the door.

"Where did you run off to last night?" Daphne asked Harry as he entered the salon the next morning. "I needed to speak with you."

"I went to see Simon," he said, sitting in the chair next to her. "And I do not want to hear one word about my behavior last night."

"Very well, but why would you go to see him?" Disdain dripped from her voice. "He's a bastard."

"He is our brother, Daphne. He could not help being born on the wrong side of the blanket."

"I don't have to like it," she said with a huff. "Father should have had better taste than an opera singer."

"I need to go to Worth Hall for a few days, maybe a week. Would you mind if I left Charlotte here?"

"Of course, you can leave Charlotte with me. But what do you need to go out there for?" she asked. "And you cannot go until after my party."

"I need to speak with the steward. Some numbers are not adding up." Harry rubbed his face. "What party?"

"On Friday, I thought we would host a small soiree here. Just fifty or so people. We'll have some musicians for dancing, and maybe a room set up for gaming. Invite Kingsley if you wish. I will try to be a better person and accept Father's bastard."

"Why are you holding it here and not at your home?"

"Radley was delayed another week. Besides this house is larger and accommodates more people."

"You just said it would be a small party." Harry waved a hand at her. "Do as you like, but I will be leaving Saturday morning then."

"Excellent." She rose with a smile on her face. "I must go prepare the guest list."

Louisa sat in the salon, reading a book on architecture. If only she'd been born a man. She could have done such great things. Although, perhaps not architecture since her drawing abilities were feeble at best. Instead, she was a woman with no clear path in front of her. As a woman, the possibilities were limited, indeed. Marriage was the most sought-after profession for a lady. But what other choices did she have? A governess position, perhaps?

She almost laughed aloud. If she ever applied for a position, her mother would have an apoplexy.

"Lord Ainsley," Davis announced before letting the earl in the room.

Ainsley swept into the room and bowed. "Good afternoon, Mrs. Drake, Miss Drake, Miss Emma."

"Lord Ainsley, how lovely to see you," Mamma twittered. "And you came to call on such a dreadful day. The rain hasn't stopped all day." She stood and walked to the door. "I will make certain there is tea for you."

"Miss Drake," he said with a slight smile to her. "How have you been?"

"Please sit down, my lord. I am quite well. Thank you."

Seeing the book on her lap, he asked, "What are you reading?"

Her mother swept back into the room and grabbed the book from Louisa. "Just some nonsense on architecture, my lord. Dreadfully dull stuff."

"On the contrary, Mrs. Drake. A woman who fills her mind with nonsense will speak of nothing else. While a woman who reads to enlighten herself will brighten the entire room with her knowledge."

Emma sighed. "Oh."

"Thank you, my lord," Louisa said, feeling a flash of heat cross her cheek. What was he about giving such compliments?

"Are you also artistically inclined, Miss Drake?" he asked as Mamma poured tea.

Louisa shook her head. "I fear I have never had any such talent. Emma is the artist of the family. Her sketches are so lovely."

"I share your lack of talent, then, Miss Drake." He sipped his tea before continuing. "You will be at Lady Radley's soiree on Friday, will you not?"

Louisa glanced about at Emma and her mother, who shrugged. "I don't believe we shall be able to attend."

"Indeed, that is a shame as I had hoped for another dance with you."

Emma let out a small sigh. "I do so wish we could attend."

"Perhaps your invitation was lost in the post," Ainsley replied with a smile toward Louisa. "After all, how could the Drakes not be invited? It would be a dreadfully dull party without the sight of you, Miss Drake."

"Thank you," Louisa muttered. He'd said he wanted to talk to her about something to do with Harry. She doubted Ainsley could not speak of it where her Mother and sister would overhear.

"I should be off, then," he said as he rose. "Miss Drake, I had hoped we might take a stroll in the park tomorrow, weather permitting."

"Of course, you may," Mamma replied for her with a smile.

Louisa nodded. "Yes, I would like that very much."

He gave them a quick bow before departing.

With no callers for over an hour, Louisa was about ready to return to her bedchamber to read in peace when Davis opened the door to the salon.

"Mr. Kingsley," Davis announced.

Mamma turned toward Louisa and whispered, "Why would Mr.

Kingsley calling on us?"

"I have no idea."

Simon Kingsley sauntered into the room with a smile on his face. Louisa wondered why Harry's brother would be calling on either of them. He was worse than Ainsley, who at least was a gentleman.

"I must apologize for arriving unannounced when we have not been formally introduced," Mr. Kingsley said. "I am on an errand for my half-sister, Lady Radley."

"Tea?" her mother asked.

"Thank you, no. I called to make certain you received the invitation from my sister. There was some mistake, and a few people did not receive them. She wanted to be certain you knew you were invited. The soiree is on Friday."

"Oh," Mamma whispered. "Thank you, sir. But I doubt we will be able to attend. I'm certain you understand."

Louisa wanted the ground to swallow her up and take her away from this awkward scene. It was blatantly apparent that Lady Radley hadn't made an error. If Harry wanted Louisa there, he would have called himself. But for some reason, both Ainsley and Mr. Kingsley wanted her at this party, and she wondered why.

"Of course we can attend, Mamma," Louisa interjected, desperately wanting to know what Mr. Kingsley was about. "We have no other plans for the evening. Is it to be at the Radleys' home?"

Mr. Kingsley gave her an approving smile. "No, the duke's home."

"But, Louisa, I am quite certain you have forgotten about that invitation from—"

"No, Mamma," she interrupted brusquely. "There were no other invitations for Friday."

Mr. Kingsley bowed but not before sliding a long glance at Emma, who immediately looked away. *Oh, bloody hell no*, Louisa thought then relaxed as Emma shot the man a look of fear and disgust.

"I shall accompany you all," he said as he walked to the door. "Expect me at eight."

Once he had departed, Mamma turned to her with a glare. "You know we cannot attend Lady Radley's ball. We were not invited!"

Louisa nodded slowly. "I believe we just were, Mamma."

"It's at Worthington's home," she started again.

"Please let us attend," Emma said prettily. "It will remind me of my come-out ball the late duke let us have there. Truly the highlight of my short, ruined Season. Besides, Lord Bolton is sure to be invited. Therefore, we must attend if only to prove to his mother that the sister of a duke accepts us."

Louisa stifled a giggle. Emma knew how to play her mother.

"Oh, very well," her mother said with an exasperated sigh. "But we shan't stay long."

"As you wish, Mamma," Emma said with a wink to Louisa before inclining her head toward the door. "I believe I shall go decide what to wear for the soiree."

"I will join you, Emma," Louisa added.

Reaching her room, Emma stopped. "What was that about, Louisa?"

"I wish I knew." She walked across the room and flopped on the bed.

"Why all the attention? Have I suddenly become beautiful? It makes no sense."

Emma fell onto her bed with a laugh. "Oh, Louisa, you are beautiful. You have a different type of beauty than Tessa and me. Your beauty is subtle, but any man with intelligence can see it."

"Thank you, Emma." Louisa joined Emma on the bed and stared up at the white ceiling.

"Do you think Ainsley is interested in you?"

"No." Louisa knew Ainsley was only trying to help her.

"Are you certain? There was a look in his eyes, but I couldn't ascertain if it was interest or something else entirely. I will say Mr. Kingsley didn't look at you in the same manner." She shuddered. "Oh, but I do not like that man."

"Kingsley?"

"Yes, there is something frightening about him. Almost as if…as if he sees you naked. Didn't you feel that?"

"Not at all." She sat up and looked over at her very innocent sister.

"Well, I did, and I don't like it."

"I'm not sure I like any of this," Louisa added, wondering why her life had suddenly turned upside down.

Chapter 18

The next day dawned sunny and finally warmer. She waited with anticipation for Ainsley to collect her for their walk. Finally, she would learn what scheme he had for Harry and her. And she would be gone for Collingwood's almost daily call at three.

Collingwood's calls had changed the past few days, but not for the better. As if he were going through the motions of courting but wasn't interested in it, or rather, her. He spoke of her beauty and wit while giving her the latest *on-dit*, which did not appeal to her at all. It was as if he had not even tried to get to know her. And every time he left, her mother remarked about how nice he looked or made some other such nonsensical comment.

When the knock hammered the door, she started. Her heart pounded not by the excitement of a possible suitor, but with the idea that several people believed she and Harry should marry, Ainsley included. After a quick greeting, they left the house toward Hyde Park with the footman trailing behind.

"It is a beautiful day, is it not, Miss Drake?"

"Very." Impatient to hear what he had to say, she added, "But I don't believe you decided to take a walk with me to discuss the weather."

He chuckled. "I see what Harry adores about you. He does like people to be direct." Sliding a glance back at the footman, he said, "I think the one thing that may draw Harry out of his current low spirits is jealousy."

"I tried with Collingwood, to no avail." Louisa sighed. They reached the park and walked toward the Serpentine, nodding at people as they strolled.

"I am not Collingwood," Ainsley with a grin.

"I suppose you are not." Louisa was intrigued by the earl and his plan. "What do you propose?"

"Is that not little Lady Charlotte with Lady Radley?" He pointed toward the pair watching the ducks on the water. "It would be rude not to greet them."

"Why, my lord, I believe you are correct. We cannot have people saying that we gave the cut to the duke's daughter and his sister in the middle of the park."

He smiled fully exposing deep dimples in both cheeks. "Gracious, no."

As they approached, Charlotte caught sight of them and shrieked, "Miss Drake!"

Lady Radley rose from her crouched position with a scowl until she noticed Ainsley escorting Louisa. "Good afternoon, Ainsley...Miss Drake."

Charlotte raced to her and hugged her tightly. "I've missed you!"

"I've missed you too, Charlotte."

The little girl pulled away long enough to Ainsley. "Uncle Ainsley!"

Ainsley picked her up and swung her around until she giggled uncontrollably. "Lady Charlotte, you have grown so big. Soon I won't be able to do this."

Louisa wondered when Charlotte would have met him. While he and Harry were friends, she had never considered Charlotte would know him, apparently quite well. Uncle Ainsley, indeed.

"Charlotte, come along," Lady Radley said. "I must get you back to Nurse."

"But Uncle Ainsley and Miss Drake are here now," Charlotte complained.

"Now, Charlotte," Harry's sister replied in a stern voice.

"Will you come and visit again soon?" Charlotte looked up at Louisa with pleading brown eyes.

"As soon as I can, darling girl. Now listen to your aunt."

Once Lady Radley and Charlotte had departed, Louisa turned to Ainsley. "Do you think Lady Radley will mention seeing us together in the park?"

Ainsley laughed. "Not until Charlotte tells her father how she saw you at the park with a handsome gentleman."

When Friday arrived, she hadn't expected any callers since most men would realize that it took a great deal of time for a lady to get ready for a party. By half-past two, Louisa doubted any gentlemen would call today. But as the hall clock rang three times, she heard the bang of the knocker and knew Collingwood had come to call.

"Lord Collingwood, Miss Drake," Davis announced.

"Good afternoon, Miss Drake," he said, glancing about the room. "Is your mother not at home?"

"She and Emma are preparing for the party tonight."

He looked over at the clock on the mantel and said, "I do apologize. I should let you go, but I feel I must speak with you now or lose my courage."

Dammit, he was not supposed to do this today...or any day. She remained silent, hoping his courage would wane.

"Miss Drake, I...I want to let you know how strong my feelings are for you," he said, staring at the carpet and not her. "I feel we should suit, and it is well past time for me to marry. I am quite certain at your age you must feel the same."

Lovely. Remind the spinster of her age.

"Anyway, I believe I should make an acceptable husband. I have the estate and title, of course. But now I need a wife." He bent down on one knee. "Would you please accept my hand, Miss Drake?"

Louisa stared at him in shock. Why she was shocked, she had no idea. The man had hinted at a proposal a few times. Perhaps it was the lack of emotion in his tone—not one word of love, only how they would suit, which Louisa now doubted.

Collingwood smiled as he rose slowly to his feet. "I understand if you need more time."

"I just feel it is rather sudden, my lord." And her heart wouldn't let her say yes. "Would you mind if I took a few days to think this through?"

She needed to formulate a rejection that would not cause her reputation or Emma's any harm.

"Of course not, my dear. I do hope you will give me a decision in a week. I should like it very much if we were married quickly. No more than a fortnight would be perfect."

"I see," she whispered. "Please don't let my mother know you have asked for my hand. She will try to influence me."

He smiled kindly down at her. "I understand perfectly." He kissed her hand. "Please save a dance for me."

"I will."

Collingwood bowed and left the room with a disheartened look. Louisa plopped into the chair and covered her mouth with her hand. She had one week. It wasn't enough time.

Recovering from the unwelcome proposal, she climbed the stairs to dress. Her mother opened the door to her room and peered out.

"Was that Collingwood?"

"Yes."

"Oh," she said with a hint of a smile. "Did he have anything of importance to speak with you about?"

Louisa did her best to hide her surprise at the question. "Nothing more than the usual."

"Oh." Her mother's lips drooped into a frown. "You should get dressed, so we are not late."

"Louisa, come help me dress," Emma said from her bedroom threshold. "Mary is helping Mamma."

"Of course."

"What is wrong, Louisa?" Emma took her hands and led her to the bed. "You look so pale."

"Can you please keep a secret from everyone, including Tessa and Mamma?"

"Of course, I can."

"Collingwood proposed," she whispered. "I didn't know what to do, Emma. He had hinted at a proposal, but I did not think he would do anything until closer to the end of the Season. Now he wants to be married in a fortnight."

"In a fortnight? Why the rush?"

Louisa shook her head. "I have no idea."

"What did you say?"

"That I needed time to think. Collingwood told me to take a week to give him an answer." Louisa felt the tears burning down her cheeks. "I don't love him."

"You love Worthington," Emma whispered before wiping the tears from Louisa's cheeks. "It's obvious to anyone who sees you two together."

She pressed her lips together as she nodded. "I do love Harry, Emma. But he doesn't love me enough to marry me. He will never get over his wife's death."

"But does he know you love him?"

"I believe so…of course, he does." Why else would she have let him take such liberties? Why else would she have helped ease his lust? He must know.

"Have you told him?" Emma asked as she sat down beside her.

"No, I cannot just blurt out that I love him."

"Unless you wish to be married to Collingwood, I would suggest you do just that."

Tell Harry that she loved him. Would that make any difference? She didn't think it would...but what if telling him did ease his guilt? Maybe he was uncertain of her feelings for him, and that held him from speaking of marriage.

"If I do tell Harry how I feel, and he wishes to marry me, Bolton might toss you over."

Emma laughed softly. "Bolton would never do such a thing. He loves me."

"Are you completely certain, Emma? If Bolton rejects you, it will be my fault. I could never live with the guilt of that."

"I am certain." She squeezed Louisa's hands. "Tell Worthington how you feel. Tonight."

"Tonight? There will be a hundred people there. I cannot just sneak off to speak with him alone."

Emma fell back on the bed, laughing. "Do you know how many times I have seen you sneak off with him?"

"You have never said a word about that."

"I'm your sister."

"Oh, Emma." She hugged her sister tightly. "I love you."

"I know. Now get ready to tell Worthington those exact words." She pulled away from Louisa. "Oh my Lord, you'll be a duchess!"

Not that she thought her title would matter to her mother if it came at the expense of Emma's future. "Let's not put the cart before the horse. I am not certain how he will react when I tell him."

"I was told you wanted to see me."

Harry glanced over at Ainsley as he sauntered into the study. Breathe. Don't attack him. "Bloody hell, Ainsley! What are you about with Miss Drake?"

"Is there a problem?" he asked in an innocent tone.

Harry wanted to strangle his friend. "You are at her home several days a week, and if not, you are walking in the park with her."

"As is Collingwood," he replied, taking the seat across from Harry. "It is the usual practice in courting a lady."

"You are not courting Miss Drake."

Ainsley arched a light brown brow in question. "Indeed? It is time for me to find a wife. I don't want some silly girl who will drive me mad with persistent chatter. I enjoy the fact that Miss Drake has a brain and isn't afraid to show it."

"Not her," Harry rasped. "You can have any woman you want, but her."

Ainsley's lips rose into a smug grin. "Is that right?"

"Yes."

Ainsley tilted his head at the glass in Harry's hand. "Drowning your sorrows?"

Harry sipped his brandy with a shake of his head. "I am not drowning my sorrows. Just trying to get drunk enough to be able to feign pleasure at having all these people in my home."

"Or enough for the courage to face Miss Drake."

"She was not invited. This is Daphne's party, not mine, and my sister would prefer that none of the Drakes enter this house."

Ainsley shook his head.

"It's better this way," Harry muttered. He would not think about her tonight. Not bloody likely. She was always in his thoughts.

"Of course," Ainsley said with sarcasm lining his voice.

"It is."

"Absolutely."

Harry glared over at the man who had been his wicked influence when they were younger.

"Are we done? I should like to get a dance with Miss Drake before the other handsome men have a chance." Ainsley rose before Harry could reply.

"I already told you she was not invited."

"Something tells me she might attend."

Harry had never wanted to wipe the smug grin off Ainsley more than he did at this moment. "Should she, by some odd chance, actually attend, you will leave her alone."

Ainsley smiled as he looked down at Harry. "Why would I do that? Perhaps she deserves an earl and not that idiot Collingwood."

Harry sighed. There was one way to keep Ainsley away from Louisa. "Five thousand."

"Five thousand? What are you talking about, Harry?"

"Stay away from Louisa, and I will give you the money. Think about it, Ainsley. You can pay down the death debts you owe. You won't need to marry for a while."

"You would pay me to keep me away from her?" he asked incredulously. "Would you rather see her with Collingwood?"

Harry slammed down his drink. "No, she deserves better than either of you."

"Then you'd better be willing to give Collingwood the same amount because he appears damned determined to have her. But quite honestly, I'm not sure it will be enough, at least for me. I find Miss Drake greatly intriguing."

Harry shot out of his seat as Ainsley rushed from the room with a low chuckle. Damn him! Ainsley wasn't supposed to find Louisa intriguing. Only Harry found her captivating.

What if Ainsley wasn't jesting? He had been paying particular attention to her. Harry had to know.

He strode out of his study and searched the crush of people for Ainsley who had disappeared into the crowd. Scanning the room, he glanced over to the threshold and noticed Simon standing next to Louisa, Emma, and their mother. The breath swept out of him as he saw Louisa in her blue silk gown. The lace sleeves covered her slim arms but must leave her chilled.

What the bloody hell was she doing here?

Daphne would kill him, assuming he had given her the invitation, but he could tell by the self-assured smile on Simon's face that this was all his idea. Why? Why would his brother deliberately try to vex him? Because that was Simon.

"What are they doing here?" Daphne whispered angrily in his ear.

"I believe you should ask Simon."

"I hate that bastard."

"He is truly an annoying little brother."

"Yes, he is. Just like you always are." Daphne strolled away with a tight smile on her face to greet her new guests.

Harry leaned against the wall and watched her from afar, feeling a bit like a voyeur. Was this to be his lot in life, watching another man escort her to various events? He wasn't convinced he could do that without going mad.

Marry her.

His insecurity had fostered doubts about what she would say when she found out what he'd done in India. How poorly he had treated Sabita.

Marry her.

The sound of Simon's voice echoed in his mind. If he failed Louisa…he didn't want to think how much that would hurt. The overwhelming doubts hammered at his head. Pressing his fingers to his temples, he realized there was only one thing to do.

Louisa had spotted Harry earlier but now couldn't find him anywhere in the crowd. She had even checked his study to see if he might, by chance, be avoiding her. But he was nowhere to be found. Disappointment surged in her as she made her way back to the ballroom only to discover Collingwood waiting for her.

"Good evening, Miss Drake," he said with a quick bow.

"Good evening, my lord. Are you having an enjoyable time?"

He smiled kindly at her. "I would have a most enjoyable time if you were to dance with me."

"Of course, it would be a pleasure." Not really, but she might catch sight of Harry while they danced. Where the bloody hell was he?

Collingwood led her to the dance floor as a reel started. At least that would limit conversation, she thought.

As the dance started, he asked, "Have you had time to think about the question I asked you?"

"I have not, my lord. It has been quite hectic with all the rigors of preparing for the ball."

"Of course. I apologize if I seem overeager."

"It is to be expected, my lord."

"Please call me Robert."

Until that moment, she realized she didn't know his Christian name. "It is not appropriate in public, my lord."

"As you wish." He frowned as they danced away from each other. She scanned the room for Harry until the dance brought her back to Collingwood.

Thankfully, the set was two quick reels, which ended quickly, allowing her to continue her search for Harry. Perhaps Kingsley might know where his brother happened off. She searched for Kingsley, but he was speaking in hushed tones with his half-sister.

As Lady Radley moved away, Louisa walked toward the man, but as she approached, he strode through the crush as if eager to be away from her.

"Miss Drake?"

Louisa turned at the sound of Lord Ainsley's voice. "Lord Ainsley, good evening."

"Good evening, Miss Drake. Are you enjoying yourself tonight?"

"Very much so," she lied. Until she spoke to Harry, she would be miserable. And since she'd seen no sign of him, she assumed she would be miserable all evening long.

He smiled at her. "Why do I feel you are lying? Might I persuade you to dance?"

"That would be lovely, indeed, my lord. Have you seen His Grace tonight? I had hoped to speak with him for a moment."

Ainsley shrugged with a little smile. "I had an interview with him in his study before you arrived. He seemed a tad out of sorts with the idea of me calling on you every day."

"That is good."

"I thought so too, until I heard a few moments ago that he left the party."

Chapter 19

Two days passed without a word from Harry. Louisa sat in the salon, staring at the book on her lap, wondering where he might have gone. And why hadn't he told her where he was going. She wasn't sure she could wait for him to return from wherever he'd wandered off. She had to find him and tell him how she felt. He deserved to know that she loved him.

She set off to his home to ask Jenkins where Harry had disappeared. As she climbed the steps, the door opened, and Lady Radley walked out, holding Charlotte's hand.

"Miss Drake!" Charlotte squealed with excitement. "Did you come to walk with us in Hyde Park?"

"Miss Drake," Lady Radley said with a nod. "You must excuse us. We were just off for a stroll."

"Of course," Louisa replied, noting the tight grip the woman held on Charlotte. "I am sorry, Charlotte. I only stopped by to pay a call on your father."

"He's not at home," Lady Radley said coldly, pulling on Charlotte's arm. "Come along, Charlotte."

The little girl started to pout.

"Charlotte," Louisa urged. "Go along with your aunt."

"All right," Charlotte said with a petulant sigh.

Louisa turned to Harry's sister. "Lady Radley, do you know when the duke might be at home?"

"He did not say." Lady Radley assisted Charlotte into the carriage for the drive to the park. "Good day, Miss Drake."

Louisa stood there with her mouth agape as the carriage rolled away. She had always known that Lady Radley disliked her, but the woman was insufferable today. With a determined stride, Louisa headed for the door where Jenkins stood watching her.

"Jenkins, can you please tell me where His Grace has gone?"

For once, the older man's face softened. "I am sorry, miss. I cannot." He leaned slightly closer and whispered, "Lady Radley has informed all the servants that they will be let go if we should give out any information on the duke's whereabouts to anyone."

Her shoulders sagged under the weight of disappointment. "Thank you, Jenkins. You have been most kind."

"It is a fine day to go to Hell, is not, Miss Drake? There is always a great deal to learn there."

She smiled at the butler, surprised he would disobey Lady Radley. "Thank you, Jenkins."

As she walked home, she wondered how she could meet with Simon Kingsley. His gaming hell was in a decent section of town but one that even she would never dare go to alone. She supposed her only option was to write to him and pray he replied quickly.

Entering the house, she thought of a way to accomplish her mission without writing. "Emma, is Mamma at home?"

Emma looked up from her sketch of roses in a vase. "No, she and Lady Huntley went to pay a call on Mrs. Amberley."

"Did she take the carriage?"

"No, they went in Lady Huntley's. Why all the questions, Louisa?" Emma put her pencil down and tilted her head.

"I need your help with something," Louisa whispered. "But we must do this in secret and tell no one where we are going."

Her sister sat up straight, her eyes twinkling with excitement.

"Where are we going?"

"To Hell," Louisa whispered.

"To where?"

"A gaming hell owned by Mr. Kingsley. It is imperative that I speak with him today."

Emma's face scrunched. "I do not like that man, Louisa."

Louisa knelt by her sister and clasped her hands. "I understand, Emma. I need to go with someone. I shall do all the talking. You can stand in the back by the door. Please do this for me. Normally, I would ask Tessa but with her being with ch—"

"I will do it!" Emma rose and then smiled. "I never thought you would include me in any of your adventures. I still long to know where you went on Christmas Day. I am quite certain you didn't go to aunt's house as Mamma told everyone."

"Do this for me, and I will tell you all about my trip on the drive back home."

"Very well. I shall call for the carriage." Emma started toward the door and then stopped. "But Louisa, what if the driver tells Mamma where we went?"

"Once I have my answer from Mr. Kingsley, it won't matter." Because she had no intention of being here to listen to Mamma's screeching.

Louisa went upstairs and threw a small amount of clothing into a valise. With Emma now on her side, Louisa felt confident that nothing could go wrong. She raced back downstairs to where Emma stood with her bonnet in her hand.

"Why do you need a valise?"

"I just do. Now, please hurry," Louisa said with a bright smile. Hopefully, in an hour, she would be on her way to find Harry.

Once they had situated themselves in the carriage, Emma asked softly, "Does this have anything to do with the duke?"

Louisa nodded. "I am taking your advice, Emma. You told me to tell him how I felt. I cannot do that if I have no idea where he is."

Emma's eyes lit. "You mean to run off to him."

"Yes, but you mustn't let Mamma learn the truth. If she discovers I ran off to find Harry again, she will have my head."

"Again? Is that where you went at Christmas?"

"I did," she whispered.

"Oh my God, does Mamma know?"

"I told her when I returned." Seeing the shock on her sister's face, she quickly added, "But you do know that Harry is a gentleman and nothing untoward happened."

Emma's mouth gaped. "Just being in the same house without a chaperone is scandalous, even if nothing happened between you both."

"I realized that. As did Mamma, which is why she made up that story of me going to our aunt's house."

Emma giggled softly. "I cannot believe what an adventure you have had, sister. I am quite envious as I have had none."

"You are still young. I am sure you have plenty of time for you to have adventures."

The carriage rolled to a stop. Louisa glanced up at the old church as she stepped down from the coach. It certainly didn't look like a gaming hell to her. She wrapped her arm around her sister and walked to the front door. After knocking, a small opening appeared in the middle of the door.

"I hardly think we shall fit through that," Emma whispered with a nervous giggle.

"Put your card in the opening," a deep voice sounded from behind the oak door.

Louisa fished out a card from her reticule and slid it through the opening. "I am only here to see Mr. Kingsley if you please."

They were quickly ushered inside what must have been the vestibule of the old church. Behind the large, carved wood doors, the gaming beckoned those with the urge. Louisa assumed the silence in the room beyond was due to the time of day.

A giant of a man with a shock of red hair stared down at them with a scowl. "Why do you wish to speak to King?"

"It is a private matter, sir," Louisa replied primly.

"Remain here. I will let him know you are here." The man skulked off down the hall until he disappeared into a room.

"We should not be here, Louisa," Emma said with a trembling voice.

"Oh, yes, we should." Yanking Emma's arm, Louisa said, "Come along."

"Where are we going?"

Louisa smiled impishly. "We are following that man."

"Oh, this is not good," Emma whispered.

"Shh, just remember this is an adventure."

They reached the man's location as he started to close the door to a room. Seeing them approach, he shook his head. "King is occupied at the moment. Give him ten minutes, and then you can see him."

Emma slipped passed the man, pulling Louisa with her. "You're right. We are having an adventure, and I'm going to embrace it."

They both halted as soon as they stepped in the room. Louisa looked over at the desk to find Mr. Kingsley with a woman on his lap in the throes of ecstasy.

"You vile man," Emma said, slamming the door behind her.

"Miss Drake, what an inopportune time to pay a visit," he said, as the woman slipped off his lap and adjusted her gown with a scowl. He buttoned his trousers and then rose to escort the woman out of his office.

"What are you doing here?" Mr. Kingsley asked Louisa after closing the door behind them. "And you brought your sister into your folly, too?"

"Leave Emma out of this," she retorted. "If you are angry then be so at me, not her. She is innocent in this."

The man looked at Emma intently. "Of course, the angel is innocent."

"Do not call me that," Emma said tightly.

"Hush, dear." Louisa approached the desk Mr. Kingsley had taken refuge behind. "I am only here for one thing, and then we shall leave you in peace."

He smiled in almost a feral manner. "I do like you, Miss Drake. Ever so direct in your speech. Go on then, what is your question?"

"I need to know where Worthington went, and I believe you know." She crossed her arms over her chest.

Mr. Kingsley leaned back in his chair in a position that reminded her of Harry. The man must look far more like his mother than the late duke as there was little physical resemblance. Except, those hard eyes reminded her of Harry the few times she'd seen him truly angry. And their mannerisms were remarkably similar.

"Why would you believe I know where the duke is?"

She leaned forward and stared at him. "Because Jenkins told me you would know."

"Bloody butler! He should know better." Mr. Kingsley held her gaze. "Why do you want to know?"

"I need to tell him something." She finally broke away from his stare. "Something of great importance."

He crossed his arms over his chest and stared at her with those piercing blue eyes. She could have sworn his gaze would steal her soul away. No wonder Emma disliked the man.

"Do you love him, Miss Drake?"

Louisa closed her eyes and nodded. "Most desperately, Mr. Kingsley. I fear he may not love me in the same manner, though."

"I see."

"Will you help me?" she pleaded.

He paused for a long moment, deliberately Louisa assumed to agitate her. "He is at Worth Hall. Send your sister home in your family carriage. I shall provide you with a comfortable coach for the trip. It is unmarked, so no one will know I lent it to you." A slow smile lifted his lips. "And do tell my brother that I assisted you. I am starting to enjoy vexing him."

"Thank you, Mr. Kingsley." She turned toward Emma, who stood near the door staring at Mr. Kingsley with a touch of panic in her eyes. "Emma, will that suit you?"

"Yes, I will tell Mamma you decided to stay with Tessa for a few days."

Louisa ran to her sister and embraced her. "Thank you!"

"Come along, Miss Drake," Mr. Kingsley said to Emma. "I shall escort you home."

"There is no need, Mr. Kingsley." Emma opened the door and raced down the hall.

"I don't believe she likes me," Mr. Kingsley said with a low laugh. "Smart girl." He turned toward Louisa. "Do you have a valise, or will you need clothing?"

"I have a valise in the carriage." She did wonder for a moment how he would procure clothing for her if she hadn't brought hers. No, she decided. She did not want to think about that.

"I shall order my best coach for you and have my cook pack you some cold food. It is only a few hours' drive, so you should be there around nightfall."

"Thank you again."

Within a few minutes, she was packed into the carriage with some food and heading out of London. Having not eaten all day, she dug into the basket and discovered a ham sandwich, an apple, and a jug of wine. In no time, she had a full stomach and sleepiness overcame her.

Harry arrived back at the estate just after ten. After spending the day with Mr. Fernwood, his estate steward, they had stopped for dinner at a tavern in Worth. He entered the house through the side door closer to the stables. Passing a footman in the hall, he requested a bath then went to his bedchamber.

Three days had passed since he left London during the height of his sister's soiree. All to get away from Louisa and somehow stop thinking about her. He'd hardly been successful, although, today was slightly better. He'd only thought of her half the day instead of the entire day.

The footmen filled the copper tub in the adjacent bathing room. His body ached from all the riding he'd done since he arrived. A few weeks in town and he'd become soft already. The hot water would ease his body, and brandy might ease his mind. He poured a snifter and then slipped into the tub.

A long sigh escaped him as the warmth soothed his tired muscles. Perhaps he should stay another week or two to get Louisa completely out of his mind. Then he might be able to return to town and focus on finding an appropriate wife. He shook his head as his hand tightened around the crystal brandy snifter.

He swallowed down the drink and placed the glass on the nearby stool. After washing, he grabbed the towel and dried himself.

"Your Grace, might I have a quick word?"

"Come in, Andrews." His valet arrived a day after Harry left.

The door opened, and a short man with very little hair entered the room. "Begging your pardon, Your Grace. I only just found out you had returned. Do you need my assistance?"

"I ate in the village and believe I will retire after my bath. Mr. Fernwood has worn me out today."

"As you wish," Andrews said and then cleared his throat. "Excuse me, sir, but Cook was wondering how long your guest would be staying with us and if she should expect more company. She should like to know if she needs to order more food."

Harry stopped drying his hair and stared over at Lewis. "My guest? I was not informed I had a guest."

"She arrived near on seven, sir. Mrs. White wasn't certain the lady should be allowed to stay, but she arrived in a large barouche and marched right inside."

"Her name?" Dread filled him. He didn't need Andrews to tell him her name. There was only one woman who would travel alone to see him.

"Miss Drake."

Damnation! "Tell Cook that Miss Drake will be leaving in the morning." He could not have her here if he were to forget about her.

"Of course, Your Grace."

"Andrews?"

"Yes?"

"Where is Miss Drake now?"

"First door on the left in the east wing, Your Grace."

"Thank you," he bit out. *Damn her!* He left for a few days of peace to get away from her, and she followed him. Who the bloody hell told her where he was? Daphne would never let Louisa know where he'd gone. Charlotte didn't know. Jenkins knew better.

He pulled on a pair of buff trousers and grabbed his dressing gown before striding down the hall in his bare feet. This obsession had to stop. Being here without her had made him believe it was possible to live his life without her. His life would be different without her…dreadfully boring. But he could manage. He had to.

Maybe having it out with her would finally get her out of his mind.

He pushed the door open and walked into the room. It took his eyes a moment to adjust to the dim light of the fire. He'd expected to find Louisa wide-awake, waiting for him. He closed the door and leaned back against it as he discovered her fast asleep in one of his bedchambers. Seeing her sleeping form with a hand tucked under her cheek and a bare shoulder sticking out from the coverlet, every sane thought disappeared.

Slowly, he slid down the length of the door until he sat on the floor against the hard wood. He was a fool to believe he could live without her. She kept him stable and made him feel insane all at the same time. How could he ever have thought he could forget her? His life was nothing without her.

He was nothing without her.

For a few moments, he could only stare at her as she slept. Chestnut hair had come loose from her plait and fell across her face. His fingers itched to brush the tendrils off her cheeks to see her better.

Dear God, he was mad.

Three days away from her and with one look, he was utterly disoriented…again. He tucked his legs up and let his head rest on his knees. What the bloody hell was he going to do? She bewitched him. If he closed his eyes, he saw her face, her sparkling blue eyes, her pert nose with freckles and her perfect body.

He wanted to do the right thing for her. Influence her to marry a man who would help her reputation, not possibly tear it to shreds.

She'd turned his life upside down from the first time he'd seen her. It always came back to Louisa. She was the only one who ever made him feel this way.

A part of him didn't want to feel this way any longer. He wanted to be a better man and let her go…but he never seemed to be able to do that. He couldn't let her go…ever again.

"Damn you, Louisa," he whispered.

Soft hands caressed his head. "Why are you cursing me again?" she asked in a soft tone.

He looked up into her face and knew he was never leaving this room tonight. "Why are you here? I left to get you out of my mind, and now here you are alone in one of my bedchambers."

"Not quite alone, I believe you are here too," she retorted with an impish grin.

He wanted to put his hands around her neck and strangle her…or kiss her senseless. "Louisa, I can't do this any longer."

She pulled back slightly with a frown. "Do what?"

"Pretend that I can resist you. Pretend that I don't want to drag you to that bed and make love to you all night."

"Yes," she whispered.

"Yes, what?"

"Drag me to the bed and make love to me, Harry. You are not the only one trying to pretend. Do you think I don't feel this excitement every time we are close? You asked me why I am here. It's because I can't stay away from you. Even when you're not with me, I cannot get you out of my mind."

He lunged forward to kneel before her and then kissed her before she said any more. Her lips softened and slowly opened for him. He felt as if he were drowning and she the only one who could save him.

"I can't stop thinking of you either," he whispered before trailing kisses down her neck. "I tried to get you out of my mind, but it never worked. Every day I've worked myself to the bone, so I would be too tired to think of you. And every night, there you were, invading my dreams again."

She smiled slowly. "You dreamed of me?"

"Hmm," he said, moving his lips toward her earlobe. "I dream of doing unspeakable things to you, my darling. Indecent things. Wild things."

"Please," she whispered.

"Please what?"

"Do indecent things to me, Harry."

A low laugh escaped him. "I have every intention of doing just that."

Chapter 20

L ouisa stared at Harry and saw the passion in his light gray eyes. Before she could ponder the wisdom of her decision, his lips returned to hers, and all thoughts vanished. Needing to be closer, she wrapped her arms around his neck. He rose slowly, taking her with him, as he deepened his kiss.

He broke away from her and gazed down at her. "If we move to that bed, there will be no stopping what happens, Louisa. You either stop me now or…"

She took his hand and led him to the bed. "We are not stopping now."

"I thought you didn't want me," he whispered before sliding the night rail off her shoulders. "You only wanted to be friends."

"That was years ago, you fool."

"Louisa," he whispered, pushing the night rail over her hips. "You are so beautiful." He pressed her to his hard body and kissed her again.

She clung to his dressing gown as his tongue caressed hers. She'd never felt beautiful compared to her sisters, but those thoughts no longer mattered because Harry made her feel adored with every kiss, every touch. Her hands slipped under the burgundy silk fabric of his dressing gown and skimmed the hard warmth of his chest. When her fingers brushed across his nipples, he groaned softly. The heat of his hands against her back sent waves of desire flooding through her body.

"Harry, I want to touch you again."

He rested his forehead against hers. His breathing was almost as ragged as her own. "Not now, my love. I want to make this perfect for you. If you touch me, I will be done for."

She pushed the dressing gown off his shoulders, finally allowing her to see his chest. Hard muscles covered by light brown hairs that formed a thin line disappearing into his trousers. She traced the contours of his chest and stomach until she reached his trousers. Sliding a glance up at him, she unbuttoned the offending breeches and slid them over his hips. She giggled lightly.

"No drawers, Your Grace?"

"I was in too much of a rush to have it out with you," he murmured before nuzzling her neck. "This is not what I intended when I left my bedchamber."

Her hands paused on his chest. "You entered my room at night and did not think this would happen?"

"Expect? No. Desperately hope it would? Yes."

He kicked off his trousers and then laid her back against the soft mattress. Covering her with his warm body, she felt the hard thickness pressing between them and couldn't help but lift her hips slightly toward him. She could not believe how bold she was with him. It was as if her body was not under her control any longer.

"Louisa, please don't do that. You are driving me mad."

Spreading kisses down her neck, he didn't stop until he found a hard peak. He plucked and flicked her nipple with his mouth and tongue, making it impossible for her not to wriggle her hips. She wanted him to touch her, sear her with his passion.

He moved to the other nipple and lavished just as much attention until she was moaning in frustration. "Tell me what you want, Louisa."

"I don't know." But her body knew. "Touch me, Harry."

He smiled against her stomach and kissed a path down until he reached her legs. "Open for me, love."

Louisa relaxed her legs and let them slip apart. His index finger trailed between her private hairs and then split her folds. She started as his thumb found her nub, but she almost jumped when his tongue replaced it. The idea of his tongue brushing against her so intimately was madness. The sensation was pure wickedness. Arching her back, she tried desperately to get even closer to him.

She'd wanted this since he re-entered her life. With his touch, she felt alive, safe…loved. Emotions she only realized when he was near.

She moaned as he slipped a finger inside her wetness.

A second finger soon joined the first, sliding in and out of her. She felt as if her entire body was afire. Nothing had ever felt this incredible until suddenly she cried out as her climax shook her whole body.

"Oh God," she groaned. "Harry."

He kissed her softly, and she tasted herself on his lips. She could still barely get a good breath in her lungs, but he had returned his attention to her breast. Unable to deny him the same pleasure, she slid her hand between until she felt his hard shaft.

"Louisa, I am about to burst. If you touch me, it will all be over before I've even had the chance to enjoy you." He clasped both her hands and pinned them above her head. Staring down at her, he whispered, "I am sorry, love, but this may hurt."

"I know." She felt his cock pressing against her to gain entrance.

Louisa knew Harry would never consciously hurt her. She inhaled deeply and tried to relax her muscles. As she did, he slipped in further before stopping. She felt him pull out and then pushed himself in all the way. After the horror stories she'd overheard in the ladies retiring room, she'd expected far more than the slight sensation of pain, which dissipated rather quickly.

An odd sense of fullness quickly replaced the sting of her lost virginity. The experience of Harry deep inside her was a sensation she rather enjoyed. Was this all to it then? Her mother had never told her what happened after the man impaled her as Mamma liked to say.

"You've gone very quiet," he whispered as he lifted his head to look down at her.

She smiled shyly. "Is that all there is to it, then?"

He laughed. "No, but I thought you might need a minute or two to come to terms with me being inside you."

"But my curiosity is getting the best of me." She stroked his brown hair back away from his face. "I need to know what happens next."

Harry groaned softly as her hips moved slightly. He was already so close to the edge he was not certain he would be able to do much for her now. "Wrap your legs around my hips," he said before nipping her shoulder. He released her wrists from above her head as her legs curled around his hips, bringing him deeper inside her softness.

Hearing her gasp, he asked, "Are you well?"

"Yes, that felt…" her voice trailed off as if she had no words to describe the sensation.

"Just wait." He prayed he could make her see how wonderful this could be for them both. Slowly, he slid out of her and smiled at her groan of impatience. He slipped back in and noticed how her hips instinctively arched toward him.

He repeated the motion without leaving her altogether and loved how she reacted with such abandon. "Yes, love," he whispered as her hips met his lunges. "Just like that."

He felt her inner muscles press against his hard cock, and he was lost in ecstasy. Her body quaked and trembled as he lunged one last time inside before releasing his seed in a wave of passion. He let his body fall onto her warm softness as he returned to normalcy. Nothing with Louisa was ever normal. He should be condemning himself for taking her virtue. Instead, he couldn't wait to make love to her again.

He lifted off her and looked down at her face. Smiling up at him, she caressed his right cheek. He kissed her softly as he moved off her and then brought her close to him. She wrapped her arm around his chest and rested her head on his shoulder.

For once, he prayed she wouldn't speak just yet. He needed time to process what happened between them and determine what to do next. Oh, he knew what to do next, but exactly how to marry her with the least amount of talk was the issue.

"You are very quiet," she whispered.

"I suppose I have no idea what to say or do just yet. I hadn't counted on making love to my dearest friend." He skimmed a finger down her arm.

"I had thought it might be uncomfortable for us," she commented as if speaking of a dance and not what had just happened between them.

"Oh? Uncomfortable, how?"

She lifted her head and stared at him with a mischievous grin. "Why, Your Grace, I have seen you without your clothing. I should be most scandalized."

He smiled. "You don't seem appallingly shocked."

"That's the odd thing indeed. I rather like seeing you naked." She pressed a kiss to his chest before moving to a nipple. She flicked the flat nipple with her tongue until he groaned.

"Stop," he rasped. "I need a few minutes more. Besides, aren't you sore?"

She shrugged. "Not much at all."

Only Louisa could have her virginity taken and still be ready for more. "It was not as easy with Sabita." He shook his head. "I must apologize. I should not be speaking of her while you are in my arms."

"You never speak of her," she replied. "I always assumed you must have loved her deeply to be so affected by her passing."

How did he explain this to her without looking like the cad he'd been? "I came to care for her."

"That's a very staid answer." She reached up and kissed the tip of his nose. "What aren't you telling me?"

"I cannot, Louisa." Harry looked away from her. "You would think me a scoundrel."

"I already know you were a scoundrel, Harry."

The time had come to admit the truth to her. He prayed she'd understand what he'd done, even if he still couldn't accept his actions. "I met her after I arrived at the estate. Her father was the steward on the plantation, and the family lived in a small house on the lands. She was barely eighteen and still unmarried, which is rather late in Indian culture. I knew she was an innocent, but she took to following me about the estate."

"Oh," Louisa said in a soft knowing voice.

"One night, I was dreadfully homesick after reading one of your letters. I missed you so much, Louisa. I couldn't get you out of my mind."

"What did you do?"

"Drank too much brandy and went for a walk where I found her bathing in the pond, naked." He stared at the ceiling, unable to look at her and see the disgust in her eyes.

"And you made love to her."

"Yes," he whispered. "It was horrible. Sabita made such a fuss about the pain that her father caught us."

"Is that it? Many men have done as you did, Harry."

"I refused to marry her," he admitted slowly. "I was callous about the issue, brutally so, and blamed her. She was so young, and I treated her like a harlot. It wasn't until her father told me his daughter was with child that I finally agreed to marry her."

"I guarantee your father would have told you not to marry her or accept that Charlotte was your child. You did the right thing."

"She was a good mother." Emotion stuck in his throat as he pictured her dying in their bed. "I thought it would be better for them both to get away from the poverty and illnesses of her homeland. I forced her to leave her family and move thousands of miles away. I didn't even offer to have them come with us. Then she arrived here, in a foreign culture, with no friends, no family—save Charlotte and me—and in the span of a fortnight is killed. Murdered by my own father."

She tightened her grip around him. "I'm so sorry, Harry."

"I failed them both," he mumbled. "I am as much to blame as my father for her death. By bringing her here, I inadvertently caused my darling Charlotte to lose her mother."

A warm hand brushed away a tear he hadn't realized had fallen.

"It is not your fault, Harry. You did what any man would do who cared about his family. England is far safer than India, especially for women. Bringing them here should have given them opportunities they might not have there. And it will, for Charlotte. Your father is to blame, not you."

It still felt like his fault. He'd spent two years trying to get past his guilt and the feelings of hatred toward his father.

"Do you blame Tessa?" she uttered so softly he almost didn't hear her.

Harry released a long breath. "I did for months, but slowly, I came to realize that she was not truly at fault. My father loved her but in a very odd manner. If he loved her as much as he professed in his suicide letter, he should have married her and not tried to marry her off to various men to increase her station first."

"He was very concerned about his position in Society," she reminded him. "For many people, it would have been scandalous for him to marry the daughter of a London banker. Or in truth a banker from Cornwall who was in prison."

"*He* was the duke. He could do as he liked. He already had an heir, so it should not have mattered." Just as he would marry Louisa no matter the objections from her mother, his sister or anyone else, she would be his.

"He didn't look at it in that manner."

"I don't want to talk about my father when I have a beautiful woman in my arms." He pulled her on top of him and kissed her softly. "I can think of far better things to do."

"Oh? Again?" She smiled, flirtatiously at him. "It could not possibly get any better than what happened earlier."

He laughed softly. "Better and better. I want you to tell me what you want me to do, and how you want me to do it. Never be afraid to speak your mind in the bedroom."

She glanced down at him and then laughed. "Have I ever been afraid of speaking my mind?"

"Point taken."

"What about what you want me to do? Will you tell me how I can please you?"

"Absolutely." He moved his mouth along the line of her jaw until he reached her earlobe. Tracing the shell of her ear, he whispered, "I want you to touch me."

"As you wish." She slid off him and then skimmed her hand down his chest, deliberately stopping to circle his nipple. "Can I kiss you here?"

"Yes, please."

She flicked her tongue across his nipple until he groaned from the pleasure of it. Already his cock was hard and ready for her. As she kissed his chest, her hand reached for him. The soft touch stoked the desire burning in him to an inferno. He clasped her hand and showed how just the lightest touch on his sac send him moaning from the pleasure of it all.

"You are driving me mad, Louisa." He pulled her back on top of him. "Shall we try a different position?"

"There are more?" she asked with a hint of surprise.

"So many more."

"Teach me."

He'd always suspected she would be passionate in bed, but her lack of inhibitions aroused him even further. She showed no shyness at being naked with him, seeming to revel in their nudity.

I will show you everything," he said hoarsely as his cock pressed against her moist opening. He leaned forward and caught one perfect rosy nipple in his mouth.

She squirmed against him as he grazed his tongue over the tight bud. Her movements lined him up perfectly, and he lifted her hips enough to enter her. She gasped in surprise and giggled as he fell back on the pillows.

"It's up to you, love. Take as much or as little of me as you can handle."

Slowly she eased down on him until her eyes widened. "Oh my," she whispered.

"Too much?"

"No, so perfect."

He couldn't agree more. Being inside Louisa was more perfect than he dared to imagine over the past seven years. Slowly, she began the timeless rhythm as she became accustomed to his size. He couldn't help but stare at her face as emotions overcame her. Her eyes closed, and her mouth gaped open slightly as her moans of pleasure became more intense. He felt her inner muscles start to quiver and knew she was getting closer. He slid his hand between them and rubbed the sensitive spot in her folds, sending her over the top.

She tilted her head back as her body quaked. Her muscles tightened against him until he couldn't help but go over the peak with her. One last plunge and he exploded with the pleasure of making love to his dearest friend. The woman he loved more than he ever thought possible.

Chapter 21

Louisa awoke, feeling a thick muscular arm wrapped around her, clutching her breast. She sighed, enjoying the feeling of him holding her tightly against him. Last night had been the most incredible night of her life. Making love with Harry left her sated and fulfilled, unlike anything she had ever felt. And yet, she thought slowly, neither of them had admitted any lasting affection for the other.

Not that she could put the blame entirely on him. She had not professed her feelings, either. Perhaps there hadn't been that perfect time. Maybe he'd been too busy kissing her for her any rational thoughts to cross the haze of passion.

Or in truth, she was simply afraid to tell him.

"What are you thinking about?"

"What makes you believe I'm thinking about anything?" she replied.

He nipped her shoulder with his teeth. "You are always thinking about something."

"Perhaps I am just lying here, enjoying the warmth of your body and the feel of you next to me."

"Hmm, I like that." He paused. "I don't believe you, but I do like the sentiment."

Her stomach decided to announce its lack of nourishment with a loud grumble.

Harry laughed. "I believe we have three things to accomplish this morning."

"And what would that be?"

"The three Bs. Breakfast, bath, and bed."

She turned in his arms with a smile. "I rather like the thought of those Bs, especially the bath. I feel a bit…."

"Sticky?" he suggested with a quick kiss.

"Yes."

"Very well, bath or breakfast first?"

Louisa giggled as her stomach growled again. "I think we had best feed the beast."

He tossed her on her back and kissed her stomach. "I believe you are correct. There is something very wrong in there." He flung off the coverlet and then dressed in his trousers and dressing gown. "I will ring for breakfast in my room. When you are dressed, join me. I'm in the last room on the left."

She watched as he left the room and then put her night rail on. Glancing in the mirror, she was happy to see she didn't look that different, except she felt different. She now knew the secrets the matrons whispered about at balls when they thought no one could hear them. It made her feel as if she had joined an exclusive club, of which only married women could become a member.

Except, she wasn't married. And there had been no talk of marriage between them.

Her heart went cold.

Surely, in the heat of the moment, he had forgotten to speak of love and marriage. Hadn't he? But he would. He must!

Mustn't he?

She sat back down on the bed and wondered. There was nothing but honor on which to demand marriage. Harry was a gentleman and would be honor bound, wouldn't he? Her father could not mandate a marriage since he was supposed to be dead. Raynerson, as her brother-in-law, could act on her behalf, but that could put her sister's husband in danger. With a child on the way, Louisa could not allow him to do such a thing.

Where did that leave her?

Nowhere. She was entirely at Harry's mercy. This would never do! She'd always said she would never attempt to trap him into marriage, but she could not take the chance of being with child. For now, she would leave it be and let him bring up the subject. The chances of her being with child, after it took Tessa nearly two years, were very slim.

Her stomach rumbled again, forcing her to leave her pondering for another time. Cracking the door open, she peered both ways before running down the hall to his room. Hopefully, the servants would have brought up the food and left by now.

As she shut the door behind her, she leaned back against it and sighed. The man was far too handsome for her senses. Even with his back to her, she couldn't help but stare as he struggled to button his breeches. His muscular back flexed as he worked to cover himself.

"Stop staring at me like that or we will skip breakfast," he said with a low laugh before turning to face her.

Only that was far worse as now she could see his face and his chest. "I cannot seem to help myself."

He grabbed a linen shirt and pulled it over his head before rolling up the sleeves. "Better?"

She giggled. "Only because I am truly famished."

He shook his head with a grin. "Come over to the table. Breakfast should be here at any moment."

Louisa glanced around. "It's not here yet?"

"No," he said slowly. "Why?"

"The footman can't see me in your room dressed like this. Or in your room, period."

"I do believe they may have figured it out when I requested breakfast for two," he replied with a casual smile.

"No! This is dreadful!" She turned to open the door, but he was there before she could leave. His hand pressed the door firmly shut.

"My servants would never gossip about you being here to anyone. They work for a duke. That is about as high an honor as they might get."

She closed her eyes and nodded. "I suppose you are right," she whispered.

"Come sit down, Louisa." He led her to the small table by the window and held the chair for her. As he sat down, a knock sounded on the door. "Come in."

One footman opened the door as a second man walked in, carrying a tray laden with delicious smelling food. As the aroma drifted by Louisa pressed a hand to her belly, hoping it would keep quiet in front of the footmen. After placing the tray on the table, the man lifted the covers displaying an array of breakfast items from coddled eggs and ham to pastries.

"Do you need anything else, Your Grace?"

"No, this will do," he said, smiling over at her. "Now, what will she eat first?"

"The eggs." Louisa moved her plate in front of her and then grabbed a fork.

"When was the last time you ate?" he asked, pouring the coffee.

"Yesterday on the drive here. I was rather tired when I arrived, and you were not at home, so I went to sleep." She took a bite of eggs and sighed. "Delicious."

He continued to smile over at her as she devoured her food.

"Why do you keep smiling at me?" she asked before popping a bite of pastry into her mouth.

"I am still a little amazed that you are sitting across from me, in my bedchamber, wearing nothing but your night rail with your hair mussed and looking quite content."

"Is my hair that dreadful?" She combed it away from her face with her fingers.

"I will brush it for you while you bathe."

She felt heat cross her cheeks. "You cannot stay in the room when I bathe."

He tilted his head back and laughed soundly. "We just spent the last eight hours naked together, and now your modesty comes out. I will be in the room with you, brushing your hair."

Her mouth went dry with the idea of him brushing her hair while she bathed. She sipped her coffee and looked at him over the edge of her cup. "As you wish," she finally said.

"I do like it when you're agreeable."

"I'm never disagreeable."

His lips twitched. "Perhaps...but stubborn for certain."

She tilted her head and smiled. "I do believe it is determination, not stubbornness."

"You're headstrong."

"Resolute," she retorted.

"Impulsive."

"Only where you are concerned. After all, three times, I arrived without a chaperone at your home." Louisa stared at her plate. "There was not a tremendous amount of thought involved before making those decisions."

"But I am quite pleased that you did pay me a visit."

"You didn't seem pleased any of the times."

His smile made her heart pound in her chest. "I suppose, but I wouldn't be having breakfast with you now if you hadn't made that impulsive decision."

Harry took a bite of pastry and wondered if he'd ever been as happy as he was at this moment. And yet even as he thought it, a slice of guilt cut through him. How could he think to allow himself to be so happy after all that he'd done?

"Why are you suddenly so quiet?"

"No reason," he lied. "Just enjoying the moment."

She sent him a quizzical look. "If you happened to look content or even happy, I might agree. But you appear quite miserable." She reached over and clasped his hand. "You need to let go of your guilt."

"I can't seem to," he muttered, looking away from her.

"I understand."

"How can you possibly understand?" he asked in a rougher tone than he'd intended.

"I was there for Tessa. Before she learned of your father's actions, she had tremendous guilt for each of her husbands' deaths, believing she must be, at least in part, responsible. She felt she drove the first two back to their mistresses within a week of marriage. By the time she married Stanhope, she had prayed nothing would happen to him. He, unlike the other bastards, actually loved her. But she was afraid to let herself love him. Then a week after their marriage, he was dead too. She assumed she must have a curse over her head."

"But those deaths were not her fault," he said and then sighed. "I understand what you are saying, but there is more to it than just Sabita's death. I treated her so poorly. I would never have acted in such a manner with an Englishwoman. I tried to convince myself that she was less than an Englishwoman and deserved what happened to her."

"But you did eventually do the right thing, Harry. Many men of your rank would never have married an Indian woman."

He didn't want to talk about this or even think about this any longer. Thankfully, a knock on the adjoining room door interrupted their conversation. "Yes?"

"The bath is ready, Your Grace."

"Come along, love. Your bath awaits." He rose and then held out his hand to her.

She stood and then cupped his cheek. "The more you talk to me of your thoughts, the better you will feel. I helped Tessa, and I can help you."

He closed his eyes and pressed his head to her warm hand. She was the only woman he had ever felt so close to and never wanted that to end. "Thank you."

She reached up and kissed him softly. "Where is my bath? Did they put in it in the duchess's room?"

"Not quite." He led her to the door and then opened it wide. A small room made just for bathing awaited her.

"How luxurious," she said with a touch of awe as she walked into the room. "And a fireplace to keep the room warm. I am starting to like this house better than Northwood Park."

He came up behind her and wrapped his arms around her drawing her close to him. "Perhaps you didn't see the bathing room at Northwood Park," he whispered in her ear.

"I don't believe I did."

He bunched up her night rail and then slipped it over her head. "You had best get in while the water's warm." His cock stirred as she eased herself into the water with a contented sigh. He couldn't remember feeling this insatiable with any other woman. They had made love three times last night.

Instead of focusing only her naked wet body on a few feet away, he ran the brush through her messy tresses. She let out little moans that made his cock stiffen more. *Focus on her hair.*

"That feels lovely."

"Your hair is shorter than I thought."

She giggled lightly. "I sold some of it to a wig maker."

"You did what?"

"I needed a little extra money after I returned from Northwood Park, so I cut my hair and sold it." She shrugged. "Women do it all the time."

"Because you spent all your money on an impulse to pay me a visit," he reprimanded. "That was not the wisest of ideas."

She nodded slightly. "I believe we already decided I'm not the most logical around you. After all, I'm sitting in the bathtub with the most eligible duke of the realm. Perhaps not my best decision."

"Not quite sitting with me as I am out of the tub playing lady's maid," he retorted before leaning in to kiss her bare shoulder. "And personally, I think it was an excellent decision."

"This tub is quite large, and I can only assume it was built to hold more than one person."

"Perhaps," he said, plaiting her hair.

"You could join me while the water is warm."

Harry looked up at the ceiling and sighed. "I am trying to be a gentleman and let your body recover a bit."

"I don't remember complaining about being sore. Besides, I only said you could join me in the tub. I did not say anything about making love."

"If I join you in that tub, we will end up back in bed." Where he wanted to stay all day.

"I thought that was the last of the B's. We had breakfast, I am bathing, and the last was bed. I doubt either of us could be in your bed and just sleep."

"At this point, I rather doubt I'll ever get a good night sleep with you next to me." Against his better judgment, he pulled his shirt over his head and stood to remove his breeches. "Slide forward so I can climb in."

As she moved toward the front of the large copper tub, he climbed in behind her and then circled his arms around her, bringing her against his chest. She leaned back and let her cheek rest against him.

"When did you learn how to plait a lady's hair? Or is that an indelicate question?"

"My daughter loves for me to do her hair. Nurse taught me," he admitted. "And it is much easier to work on a woman who sits still than a four-year-old."

She giggled lightly. "Charlotte is a bundle of energy."

"Yes, I am afraid she may have inherited that from me." Harry caressed her cheek as she closed her eyes. "I do believe she likes you very much."

"The day I departed, I stopped by your home to find out where you had gone. I saw her for a moment then. Lady Radley was taking her to the park."

He frowned. "Daphne told you where I had gone?"

"Of course not. I don't believe your sister likes me at all."

He couldn't deny that, so he remained silent. "Then how did you discover I was here? Jenkins would never have told you."

"No, he would not speak of it." She smiled against his chest. "At least not directly. I might have been told that it was a good day to go to Hell."

He stiffened. "You should not have gone there, much less alone."

"Emma came with me. Your brother was quite lovely, Harry. He lent me his carriage."

Harry tilted his head back and stared at the white ceiling. "Simon should have told you to return to your home."

"If he did, I wouldn't be here right now."

As if to emphasize her point, she rubbed her back against his shaft, which immediately started to harden. "Not fair, love."

She turned around to face him and then smiled flirtatiously at him. "You are rather insatiable, are you not?"

"Around you, yes." He kissed her loving how quickly she responded to him. "I was trying to be a gentleman."

"You can be that later and show me the house. Right now, I want a scoundrel."

"As you wish, Miss Drake."

Chapter 22

They finally rose from their bed in the early afternoon. Louisa didn't want to consider what the servants must think of them. After a lovely dinner, Harry gave her a tour of the enormous home. Louisa figured that about twenty of her mother's home could fit inside this grand manor. They walked into the family salon, and Louisa was struck by the extravagance of the room. Gilt chairs, gilt frames, even a gilt family crest on the fireplace.

"It's very…very…"

"Indulgent?" he replied with a slight scowl.

"You don't like this place much, do you?" They continued down the hall to the music room, which was double the size of her mother's salon.

"No. This was my father's favorite home, mostly because it was the ducal estate. But I much prefer the intimacy of Northwood Park."

She nodded. "I agree. Northwood is smaller and feels more like a home and not a grand palace."

He smiled down at her. "True, but I do believe there is one room you will love here."

"The library! I remember you telling me about it years ago. Show me!"

"Yes, ma'am." He led her down the long marble corridor lined with large portraits of former dukes and duchesses.

She noticed one portrait and stopped. "Wait," she said, pointing to the picture. "Is that you?"

"Yes, when I was twenty. A year or two before we first met."

Louisa studied the portrait. Harry appeared quite a bit younger, even though only ten years had passed. Now, he had a maturity that made him look far more handsome than in his youth. The painting showed the rascal he'd been and not the gentleman he had become. "You look every bit the rake I know you were for a few years."

"If you remember, I was in my rakish days when I met you."

"True, but I don't remember hearing much about that after we met."

Harry looked away, knowing she was the reason for the change in his behavior. She had disapproved of his rakish manner. After meeting her, he had settled down until that awful night in India. "Come along. I want to show you the library."

"Yes, of course."

He'd forgotten about describing the library to her, and now he couldn't wait for her to see it. They approached the heavy door, but he stopped her from entering the room. "Close your eyes."

"Harry!"

"Close them, or I won't show you the room."

She muttered a low curse at him. "Very well."

He swung the door open and led her into the room.

"I smell leather," she said in a giddy voice. "Can I open my eyes now?"

"Yes."

He watched her blue eyes widen in awe as she looked around the room. The library consisted of two floors with books stacked from floor to ceiling. A circular staircase led up to the second level with just as many books.

"Oh my," she whispered. "How does anyone keep this

organized?"

"A few years ago, my father hired a man to catalog and organize every book. There are over five thousand books in this room—subjects ranging from Architecture to Zoology and hundreds of works of fiction and estate journals. I have not added to the collection yet. But I believe it may be time to start."

"No one would be able to read all these books." She walked up to one of the shelves and skimmed a finger down the leather binding. "This is simply amazing."

He sat down on a leather sofa and just watched as she pulled a book out to examine it.

"This is one book on gardening," she said, turning toward him and then pointed to a row of books. "There is an entire row on gardening."

"Well, the gardens here could use some assistance if you would like to read up on it. I never felt the gardens truly represented the house well."

She giggled as she picked up a book. "As duke, you should have a maze."

"Hmm, I like that idea. Read up on it then design one," he said with a wave of his hand. "Just make sure there is a beautiful statue in the center of the maze for people to find. Something Greek perhaps. And a nice long bench so that when I finally find you there, I can make love to you for hours with no one able to interrupt us."

She looked over at him and blushed. "That is too audacious by far. Making love in the out of doors."

Harry laughed. "Oh, I shall show you how daring it is, love. On a nice warm day with the sun on your bare skin. I have a feeling you will enjoy yourself immensely."

She shook her head and returned her gaze to the books. "First you need to build the maze, Harry."

"Well, you'd better find a book on mazes over there because I just gave you that task."

"I think I found one," she replied as she pulled a book from the shelf. "Oh my, Harry, look at this! There are sketches in here that someone did years ago." She sat down next to him and opened the book on her lap.

He took the sketches and nodded. "These are quite good, if I say so myself."

What?

"Father insisted I learn to sketch as part of my proper education. I had no desire to sketch fruit, so I asked my teacher if we could do architecture or gardens. Mr. Reynolds decided gardens were a more appropriate subject than houses." He had forgotten about the design for the maze until she brought it over to him.

"Why didn't your father have the maze built?"

"He didn't think it worthy of the ducal manor. He told me that when I inherited Northwood Park, I could put a maze in there."

She stared down at the design and traced her fingers through the pattern. "It is most difficult, which I believe would only add to the enjoyment. Think how much fun Charlotte would have trying to find the center. You might lose her in there for hours."

"Well, that might tire the girl out. I suppose I shall have to build it now." He clasped her hand in his and squeezed. "Thank you for finding this, Louisa."

She looked up at him with love in her eyes, and he was lost. He had to tell her how he felt about her. That he could not imagine his life without her in it. "Louisa—"

A sharp rap on the door interrupted him. "Your Grace, I have a letter for Miss Drake. It came express."

"Express," Louisa whispered with a frown.

"Bring it in." Harry squeezed her hand tighter. "Who knows you are even here?"

"Only Emma."

The footman brought in the missive as he felt her tremble under his hand. Harry grabbed the letter and handed it to her.

"Would you like me to leave you alone while you read it?" Harry asked as she broke the seal.

"No, please stay. It is from Emma. I do hope no one is ill. Or Tessa had an issue with the baby." She stared down at the unopened letter.

"You will worry yourself to death until you read it."

Louisa nodded, knowing he was right, but nothing good ever came express. Her hands shook as she slowly opened the letter.

Dear Louisa,

I do hope you will not mind that I opened the enclosed letter. I feared Mamma would attempt to read it and discover something untoward. I have no idea who sent it as the boy was a messenger and refused to inform Davis who had paid him.

I am dreadfully sorry.

Your dearest sister,
Emma

Louisa frowned wondering who had sent the second letter.

"What is it?"

"I am not certain. Some messenger boy delivered this without stating who had sent it." She opened the second letter and looked to the bottom for a signature, but there was none.

Miss Drake,

I only send this letter to you because I believe you deserve to know the truth about the gentlemen in your life. Lord Collingwood has proposed to you strictly because he is being paid to marry you. Whilst you may have heard he is having financial difficulties, I doubt he told you the full truth of the matter, as he did me.

Some people say he has four thousand a year, but in truth, he has less than half that amount. The income does nothing to resolve his remaining debts.

He informed me that someone was paying him five thousand to marry you. Regretfully, he did not disclose the name of the person. Although, I am quite certain you must already know the likely candidate.

I do apologize for causing you any distress.

Louisa stared at the paper, unable to comprehend what it all meant. Slowly, she pulled her hand out of his grip. Who had done this to her? There was only one man she knew with the means to make such a payment. But why? Why would Harry pay Collingwood?

But who else could it be?

While she knew Harry had asked Collingwood to dance with her the night of Lady Leicester's ball, she had never imagined Harry had played any other part in the matter. He had been the one to push Collingwood at her, telling her he was a good man for her. Anger flooded her as she concluded there was no one else who could have done such a thing.

"What is wrong? Is someone ill?" he asked.

She rose and then turned back to face him. "Did you do this?" she asked, waving the paper at him.

He tilted his head and stared at her with a scowl. "Do what?"

"Pay Collingwood to marry me," she cried.

He rose and looked down at her as anger darkened his face. "I never paid Collingwood to marry you. To my knowledge, he hasn't even screwed up the courage to propose."

"Well, he has," she retorted, crossing her arms over her chest.

"When?"

"Five days ago. The afternoon of your sister's party." Louisa's heart pounded as her anger took over her entire body. Her hands shook as she stared at his gray eyes. But there was something else in his face too. She had noticed it the moment he denied paying Collingwood.

Guilt.

"A man proposes to you, and then you run to another man's bed?"

"I ran to you, Harry. The man I thought was my dearest friend. The man I thought I…"

"Though you what?"

She was not about to tell him that she loved him right now. "I thought I could talk to about anything. But if you didn't pay Collingwood, why do you look so guilty? What did you do, Harry?"

"Nothing," he replied, turning away from her.

"I know you better than that. What did you do?"

He turned back around and faced her. "I told Ainsley to stay away from you."

"You did more than that, didn't you?"

"I offered him five thousand to stop courting you."

She covered her hand over her mouth as her eyes welled with tears.

"Don't you dare look at me like that," he shouted. "This was all your idea. You wanted to marry and foolishly thought I should marry too."

She heard the commotion of footsteps coming down the hall but could not stop her tirade. "Of course, it all makes sense now. I wasn't good enough for you or your friend. The only thing I was good enough to be was your mistress."

"That's not true, Louisa. I never said you weren't good enough for me! Christ, Louisa, I—"

The door hurled opened as a footman stared at them both. "I apologize, Your Grace."

"Get out!" Harry yelled.

"Your Grace, Mr. Smith's house is ablaze! It's very bad."

"Dammit!" He looked at her with anger, still burning in his eyes. "We will finish this when I return."

She refused even to acknowledge his command as her heart shattered into a million pieces. As he strode out the door, she knew that she would not be here when he returned. How could she stay? Her heart was broken. He'd betrayed her in mind and spirit. She found the young footman.

"Have my carriage readied."

"Miss?"

"I am returning to London. I need my carriage."

"Yes, ma'am."

Louisa wiped the tears off her cheeks and then ran upstairs to gather her things. As she packed, the housekeeper entered the room.

"Miss Drake, do you think this is wise?"

"Mrs. White, nothing I do is wise, but this was the most foolish thing I have ever done. I thought he loved me."

"Come along, let me pack your things." The housekeeper shooed her away from the bed. "You are not the first lady to make a fool of herself over a man."

"I realize that."

"Give the man time. I have known the duke since he was a toddler racing through this house. He is a very good man…better than his father, if you ask me."

"I would have to agree with you on that," she admitted, not knowing if the housekeeper had heard the entire truth about the late duke. "But I must return to town. My mother will worry."

"Of course." Mrs. White picked up the valise. "Come along. The carriage should be ready momentarily. I will have Cook prepare some food for the trip."

"Thank you, Mrs. White, but I couldn't eat anything."

As they reached the hall, Mrs. White said, "I do hope I shall see you again, Miss Drake. I believe you might be just what the young duke needs."

"It is highly unlikely now but thank you." Louisa walked out to the waiting carriage and then cried herself back to London.

Harry doused the smoldering timbers with one more bucket of water. The tenants and several servants from the house had all helped to put out the fire, but the stubborn blaze had destroyed the home and left Mrs. Smith with burns on her legs. The physician had done what he could to help her before leaving her in the capable hands of Mrs. Hill, who assisted the tenants with some minor healing.

"I think that is about it, Your Grace," Mr. Hill commented as he stared at the destruction.

"Yes," he replied, wiping a sooty hand across his weary brow. "I will look in on Mrs. Smith before I head back. Tomorrow I will have Mr. Fernwood stop by and get things started on rebuilding. There is still an empty home on the south side of the estate where the Smiths can stay until their house is rebuilt. Please make sure if they need anything to put it on my account in the village."

"Thank you, sir. I will be sure to tell them. I can't tell you how glad we were to see you here." Hill looked down at the ground. "Many lords of your station wouldn't have cared."

"You're my tenants, Mr. Hill. My responsibility. I apologize for not being here more."

"Sir, we all knew you were in mourning. Mr. Fernwood is a good man and kept everything in order."

"Goodnight, then." Harry sighed as he walked back to the estate. Guilt slid over him. Leaving the estate with only Mr. Fernwood for two years had been irresponsible. A duke had responsibilities, and he had neglected his far too long. He was bone tired and wanted nothing but a bath and bed, but knowing Louisa, she would be waiting for him to finish their row.

As he reached the house, the front door opened, and a footman greeted him. "Good evening, Your Grace. We've had bath water heating for you. I will get the lads to bring it up now."

"Thank you."

He dragged himself up to his bedchamber and warily opened the door, expecting to see Louisa. Finding the room empty, he prayed she was pouting in her room for now. He needed time to bathe and rest before facing her. The door was open to the bathing room, and he could hear the footmen filling the copper tub.

He removed his filthy clothes and then sank into the half-full tub. The footmen continued to fill it as he leaned back, closed his eyes, and let his muscles relax.

"Send up a tray of sandwiches," he requested.

"Of course, Your Grace."

"Did Miss Drake eat supper?" When no one answered, he opened his eyes to find the two footmen giving each other strange looks. "What is wrong?"

"Miss Drake departed for London not long after you left to assist with the fire, Your Grace."

"Dammit!" He'd told her they would finish their argument when he returned. How could she be that upset over their quarrel? She had to know he loved her.

But he hadn't told her, had he?

Dammit!

"That's enough water, boys. Pack a bag for me."

"Are you leaving tonight, sir?"

Harry released a long sigh. He'd most likely fall off his horse if he tried to ride tonight. "No, at first light."

That would get him there by noon. He'd pay a call on Louisa to finish their discussion and make sure she understood that no matter the scandal, no matter the talk, no matter what, she would be his wife within a fortnight.

But what if she refused?

She could not. There was a chance she might be carrying his child right now. She would have no choice but to marry him. Not that he wanted her to feel forced into marriage, he wanted her willing, knowing how much he loved her.

Why hadn't he told her last night?

Because he was a fool, no doubt about it. Instead of telling her how much he loved her, he'd foolishly spoken about his first wife. He was an idiot. But he would fix everything tomorrow, assuming she didn't do anything impulsive like accept Collingwood.

He finished cleaning the soot and grime off him determined to eat something and then sleep so he'd be ready to ride at dawn. After completing his bath, he walked into his room and opened the box on his bureau. He picked up the sapphire ring with diamonds on the band and smiled. Her eyes were not as dark as the gem, but still, it reminded him of her.

He placed the ring on the nightstand, so he would not forget it in the morning.

Chapter 23

"Good evening, Miss Drake," the ginger-haired man at the door of Hell, said with a bow.

"Good evening. Is Kingsley in his office…? I'm sorry, I don't know your name."

"Riley, ma'am," he replied with a hint of an Irish lilt. He escorted her down the hall to the old rectory.

Louisa knocked at the door and waited to be allowed entrance.

"Come in."

She opened the door hesitantly and found Kingsley studying something out a window that faced the gaming room. After sliding a glance toward her, his gaze returned to the window.

"You have returned sooner than I expected," he commented.

She remained silent not wishing to malign his brother, even if Harry deserved it. Hours in the carriage had strengthened her resolve. Leaving had been the right thing to do. He had tried to marry her off to another man and paid his friend to stay away from her. And after giving herself to him, he had not spoken one word of love or marriage.

He walked to the door and spoke to a man there before returning to her. "So, are congratulations due? Are you to be my half-sister-in-law? That's a mouthful."

"Hardly. After what he did, I never want to see him again." So much for not criticizing him. And telling Mr. Kingsley a complete lie. She doubted anything would stop the desire to see Harry again. She couldn't think about this now, or she would end up crying in front of his brother.

Mr. Kingsley poured two snifters of brandy and handed her one. "Sit and tell me what happened."

"I just want to return home," she said before sipping her brandy.

"Of course you do, which is why you had my driver come here instead of directly to your mother's house," he replied. "Sit. Talk."

Louisa sank into a chair and took another long sip of the heady liquid. Before she could stop herself, she told him almost everything. She wasn't about to admit that she had taken his brother to her bed. No one must learn of her greatest mistake.

Mr. Kingsley took a long draught of his brandy before saying. "So, you honestly believe my brother has no feelings for you at all?"

Lust. But she couldn't say that. She wiped away a tear that had fallen. "I doubt he does."

Mr. Kingsley smirked. "If you say so."

"You don't believe me?"

"Not at all." Mr. Kingsley took another sip, draining his snifter. "I am quite certain you did not come back in the same virtuous state you left here two days ago. And my brother would never do such a thing unless he loved you."

Her heart leapt with the thought until reality returned. "He wanted me to marry Collingwood. He offered Ainsley five thousand to stop courting me. Does that sound like a man in love?"

Mr. Kingsley laughed. "It does indeed."

She would never understand this man. "I must leave. Will you arrange a hackney for me?"

"No, you will go in the carriage."

"I mustn't. My mother might notice and know I wasn't at my sister's home."

Mr. Kingsley shook his head. "Your mother is at Lady Huntley's musicale with your younger sister."

"How would you know that?"

Mr. Kingsley leveled her a knowing look. "I keep track of what events are happening amongst the ton. And I do know your mother would never miss her dearest friend's musicale."

"Very well, thank you again for the use of your carriage." Louisa stood and then curtsied to him. She walked to the door but stopped at the sound of his low voice.

"Miss Drake, I look forward to the day I can call you my sister."

"Unless you marry Emma, I do not believe that day will ever come."

He laughed then sobered. "Miss Drake, why do you think he offered to pay Ainsley to stay away from you?"

She shrugged and departed for home.

The next day Louisa and Emma walked in Hyde Park, discussing some of what happened over the past three days. Louisa still felt weary since she'd done little but think of Harry even in the middle of the night. She'd tossed and turned until dawn when she finally rose and tried to think of something other than Harry to no avail. Nor had an answer to Mr. Kingsley's question come to her.

Why would Harry offer to pay Ainsley not to court her?

It made no sense. Ainsley was a better man than Collingwood. Ainsley was Harry's friend. When his inheritance came through, he would have more than enough money to sustain a family.

"Louisa, did you and Worthington…"

"What?"

"You know what I'm asking. Might you be with child?"

Louisa sighed. She had thought of little else last night. The scandal of her being with child would eclipse the deaths of Tessa's husbands and the duke's suicide. Lady Bolton would insist her son break the engagement. Louisa shook her head. Oh, what a mess she'd made of things.

"I won't know for some time, Emma."

"Oh, dear," she whispered before leaning closer. "What was it like? Did it hurt dreadfully?"

She smiled, thinking about how happy she'd been for that short time. "No, it didn't hurt much. A pinch and then…"

"What?" Emma asked eagerly.

"I don't think Mamma would approve of me speaking to you of such things."

"Mamma will never tell me what it is truly like. She told me that I must lay there and let Bolton do what he must."

"Mamma said that to you?" Louisa could not believe what a hypocrite her mother was when it came to such matters.

"Yes."

"Very well, it was the most amazing thing I have ever experienced, Emma." At least it was until the next afternoon when her world fell apart.

"Oh my," Emma whispered. "He was very big? I've heard some men are bigger than others."

"Emma!"

"Susan told me. She has four brothers and knows these things."

"Harry was…well…perfect," she admitted slowly. He was her weakness. The man who could anger her one second and touch her heart so deeply the next.

"Oh, my," Emma said again.

A carriage pulled to a stop near them. They stopped to see who had blocked their path. Lord Collingwood jumped down from the coach with a smile that didn't quite reach his eyes.

"Good morning, Miss Drake," he said with a nod toward her and then added, "Miss Emma," with a nod toward her sister. "Would you mind if I interrupt your walk with your sister? I need to speak to her for a moment."

"Of course not," Emma said with a worried look toward Louisa. "I will be right here."

Collingwood held out his arm toward Louisa who took it hesitantly. "I am so happy you have returned from visiting your sister."

Thank God for Emma's lie. "Yes, I haven't spent much time with Tessa lately, and it was lovely to have a few days with her before the baby arrives."

"Have you thought about my proposal? It's been almost a week."

"My lord, this is not the place for such a conversation."

"I need an answer now," he demanded.

Taken aback by his forceful demeanor, she answered truthfully, "I am sorry, then, my lord. I cannot accept your proposal as I find my heart has become lost to another."

"I see." Collingwood tightened his grip. "I will speak to your mother regarding this matter. Perhaps she can impart a little common sense."

"My mother has very little influence over me, sir." She softened her voice, realizing she might have hurt his feelings with her rejection. "I am certain you will find another woman to love."

"Love?" Collingwood laughed as he neared his carriage. "I do believe you have my feelings for you all wrong, Miss Drake. I do not love you."

"Oh?" A tingle of fear straightened her back. "Then why would you wish to mar...." her voice trailed off. The money, of course. She must be tired to have forgotten that so quickly.

Collingwood tapped the toe of his boot impatiently waiting for something. "Well? That is your answer, then?"

"Yes," she replied more firmly than she'd ever felt about any proposal. She would rather live off Tessa for the rest of her life than marry this man.

"Very well then," he spat.

Louisa watched as he abruptly turned and climbed into his carriage without a glance back at her. A sense of relief mixed with unease. If not Harry, someone must be paying him a fortune.

And she needed to discover who.

Chapter 24

Harry was delayed arriving home due to his steward's questions regarding the fire at the Smiths' house the previous night. When he finally returned to London, it was nearly four, and he was filthy from riding. As soon as he had bathed and dressed, he would call on Louisa to settle this mess. His valet entered the room to pull out the appropriate clothing.

"The burgundy jacket?" he asked as Harry worked on the buttons of his dust-covered breeches.

"Yes, that will be fine," he replied.

A scratch sounded at the door. "Your Grace, Mr. Kingsley is—"

"Here," Simon said, pushing past Jenkins. "Everyone out."

Jenkins and Andrew sent glances to Harry.

"You heard my brother," Harry commented.

"Yes, Your Grace," they replied in unison.

"Thank God you are home," Simon added as the door shut. "What the bloody hell happened at Worth?"

Harry continued to work the buttons on his breeches. "I do not believe that is any of your business."

Simon sank into the chair by the window with a sigh. "It is when a beautiful lady returns to my gaming hell in tears from a liaison with you. Then she relates a story of how you paid Ainsley to stop courting her. And that she believes you paid Collingwood to marry her. None of this makes any sense at all, Harry."

"I didn't pay Collingwood, Simon."

Simon stared up at him with an angry look. "And Ainsley?"

Harry gave up on the breeches and poured them both a whisky. After sitting on the end of the bed, he replied, "I offered Ainsley money to stop courting her. But he didn't accept the money. Too much damned pride."

"Why would you do such a thing?"

"He needed the money, so he wouldn't have to marry some unacceptable lady."

Simon shook his head. "But you tied it to his courtship of Miss Drake."

"Killing two birds." Harry sipped his whisky.

"No, it was completely thoughtless of you," Simon said in an irate tone. "If you didn't wish to marry her yourself, Ainsley would have been a far better match for her than Collingwood. But you were only thinking of yourself. You could not stomach the idea of seeing her with your friend, knowing that he was taking her to his bed while you were stuck with some plain-faced acceptable lady."

Harry bore the scolding from his younger brother as penance for his actions. But enough was enough. "You're right, Simon. I was a pigheaded fool for trying to bribe Ainsley."

"No, you were a pigheaded fool for not telling that beautiful lady how much you love her."

"Does she hate me?" he whispered, not wanting to know if she did.

Simon closed his eyes with a sigh. "I doubt she hates you, but she is not happy with you now. You will need to make this up to her."

"How can I do that?"

His brother glanced over at him with a smug grin. "I believe she might be willing to accept your apology if it came with the name of the person who was willing to pay Collingwood."

Harry rose and paced the room. "Except I have no idea who might have paid him off."

"Lady Bolton?"

"Why?"

Simon shrugged. "The viscountess loves her son and will do whatever is necessary to keep her good name. Associating your name with the Drakes will cause talk…again. If she keeps you and Miss Drake apart, then there is no gossip."

"Seems a rather extreme measure." Harry paced the room. "How can we find out for certain?"

"Whoever is paying him is keeping this extremely quiet. I've heard nothing of it until Miss Drake mentioned it to me. So, he or she is not telling anyone about the scheme."

Harry looked over at his brother. "Then how do we discover the culprit?"

"We break into his home and search it." Simon gave him a wicked smile. "A man like Collingwood would keep all written correspondence in case he needed to blackmail the person."

Harry blinked and absorbed what his brother said before laughing. "You suggest we just sneak into his home, while his servants are about and ransack his study?"

"Yes."

Harry let out a bark of laughter. "Simon, people do not break into houses of peers. It is truly bad form."

"Perhaps not peers, but I know a few people who will sneak into anyone's house for a price."

"We would have to be certain Collingwood wouldn't be in the house." Was he considering his brother's insane idea? "No, this is foolish. I will stick to my original plan and go to Louisa's home and apologize."

"She needs more than an apology."

"She will have my love and become my duchess."

Simon rose slowly. "And she will always have that sliver of doubt."

"She will get over that."

"And if you believe that, you're a bigger fool than I thought possible." Simon strode out the door.

Harry grabbed his whisky and swallowed it down in one long draught. His brother was wrong. He had to be. Harry had known Louisa for years. He knew her better than Simon.

Still, doubt remained. But there was only one way to discover who was right in this matter. "Andrews, get in here!" he shouted to his valet.

An hour later, Harry climbed out of his carriage in front of the Drake home on Chandler Street. He moved slowly toward the door. If he was wrong, then what? He couldn't live without Louisa. He had to make her understand why he paid Ainsley and that he had nothing to do with Collingwood.

He banged on the door with the silver head of his walking stick.

"Good evening, Your Grace," the butler said with a nod.

"I am here to see Miss Drake."

"I am sorry, Your Grace. Miss Drake is not at home."

"Please inform her that I am here," he demanded.

The butler stiffened. "Sir, she is not at home. For anyone."

Louisa wouldn't even see him. Emotions swirled in him from anger to disappointment to guilt. He had done this by not being honest with her. If he hadn't let the guilt of his actions over Ainsley show, she would have believed him when he said he hadn't paid Collingwood.

"Your Grace? Is there something else I might assist you with?"

"No."

He returned to the carriage and banged on the roof to gain the driver's attention. "Take me to Hell."

Louisa watched Harry leave from the window of her bedroom. Her finger traced the square windowpane. A part of her wanted to run down the stairs and jump into his carriage. But she could not. At some point, she would see him. She could force Davis to refuse him entry to the house, but her mother would insist she attend the next ball. That only gave her two days to determine how she would act. He might even try to cause a scene.

No. Harry would not do that. He hated being the subject of the gossipmongers' bitter talk.

But he might attempt to get her alone.

She could never be alone. Tessa or Emma would be with her at every moment. That would take care of the issue, until the next ball. Or the one after that. At some point, she would have to face him.

Her door swung open, and Emma strode into her room. "Why did you refuse him?"

Louisa closed her eyes. "This is not one of your penny novels, Emma."

"No, it is not. This is your future happiness at stake."

She had no illusions of her future now. She would live her life, watching her sisters with their husbands and their children. She would be the eccentric aunt who never married. The one, her nieces and nephews, would always wonder about. And she would love each one like the children she could never have.

"I can't do this," she whispered. She wanted a husband and children of her own. No, she only wanted Harry.

"What did you say?" Emma asked. "I didn't hear you."

"I need to know who paid Collingwood."

"And how do you propose we do that? I doubt asking him outright would work."

Louisa shook her head as she crossed the room to her bed. "I don't know."

"Whoever paid him will not be happy that he hasn't completed the task. Perhaps we attend Lady Holcombe's fancy dress ball. If we are disguised, we might be able to overhear a bit of conversation."

"I suppose we could try."

"You don't sound very convinced," Emma remarked.

"I highly doubt anyone would be careless enough to get into such a discussion at a ball. Masked or not." Disappointment slid over Louisa. She must discover who paid Collingwood. The more time away from Harry, the more she missed him. But the lingering doubt remained. He'd paid Ainsley, so it stood to reason that he would have compensated Collingwood. Except, her mind refused to allow that he'd paid the viscount.

Then why had he paid Ainsley? Kingsley question still reverberated in her mind. She'd told him that Harry paid Ainsley to stop his courtship. So why did he ask that question?

"Emma, why do you think he would have offered Ainsley five thousand to quit his courtship?"

Emma laughed, but her eyes grew widened. "It's just like one of Mrs. Lewis' stories again! Oh, what was the name of that one?"

"Emma, just answer the question." Louisa had lost patience with her sister's flair to compare her issues with Harry to some story of romance.

"Ainsley is the duke's friend. If you were to marry Lord Ainsley, then the duke would see you all the time. And quite honestly, Ainsley is a very handsome man. You might come to love him."

Her mouth gaped as she realized Emma was right again. Louisa's intellect was nothing compared to her sister's ability to figure out relationships. Harry would be miserable if he truly loved her and had to see her falling for Ainsley. Perhaps there was still hope.

However, it still didn't explain who paid Collingwood.

"We need to determine your costume," Emma said, opening the linen press. "We need something…special."

"Isolde," Louisa whispered.

Emma glanced back at her with an arched blond brow and a smile. "Isolde it is. Though many might mistake you for Guinevere."

Harry would not. He would expect her to dress as Caroline Herschel or Elizabeth Fulhame or even Joan of Arc. The last lady he would expect her dressing as was one of ancient legend. "Do I have anything that might work?"

Emma shook her head. "Not really. To be authentic, you would need handspun wool. It's doubtful that the Irish would have had much else back then."

"She was the daughter of the Queen of Ireland. Surely some muslin would work. How about the sage? We could rework it to lower the waistline. Add a few strands of pearls, a mask, and perhaps some curls in my hair."

Emma laughed. "Curls? In *your* hair? I shall never manage that."

Louisa missed Lily's touch with her hair. Harry's maid had been magical, putting curls in Louisa's hair that stayed the entire day. No one had ever matched Lily ability with Louisa's hair.

Emma pulled out the green muslin and stared at it. "I don't believe it would be that difficult. But we will need Mary's assistance. She's a far better seamstress than either of us."

"True." While Emma rang for Mary, Louisa prayed this would work. She had to avoid Harry until she knew for certain. Her shoulders sagged. *You should trust him.* Her damned conscience poked her. Deep down, she did trust him. She didn't actually believe he'd paid Collingwood, mostly because he'd admitted his part with Ainsley. But she had to discover who had.

After conferring with Mary, Emma sketched a few enhancements to give the gown an older look.

Two days later, Louisa stepped into the ballroom of Lady Holcombe's Berkeley Square home. Masked ladies and gentlemen filled the room, leaving Louisa awed by the costumes. She felt dowdy in her simple green low-waisted gown. Mary had managed to give her hair a bit of curl, but Louisa knew it would be straight by the time she left tonight.

Emma dressed as Anne Boleyn in red silk.

"You do realize Anne had dark hair, not blond," Louisa said as they followed their mother into the room.

"Hush. Isolde most likely had blond or red hair," Emma shot back. "Where is he?"

No need to ask which he that she was speaking of. For once, Emma wasn't thinking about her fiancé. Now that Louisa thought about it, her sister had barely said a word about Bolton in days.

"I don't see him yet," Louisa replied. "But it is a crush in here."

Spying a tall man with brown hair, Louisa assumed it was Harry dressed as King Arthur, but wasn't positive it was him. At least not until she noticed a man with black hair dressed as Lucifer speaking with him. Her heart pounded. She wondered if he'd spotted her yet.

They were both moving toward her position near the entrance to the room. But instead of stopping to speak to her, they continued out the door as if they hadn't even seen her. What was that about?

"Wasn't that the duke and his brother?" Emma whispered.

"I believe it was," she answered flatly.

"Where are they going?"

"I have no idea." She released a long sigh. Once again, she'd been thwarted in her quest.

"Why tonight, Simon?" Harry asked again as he followed Simon out of Lady Holcombe's home. "Louisa had to be in there."

"Because I happen to know that Collingwood is at the ball tonight. And that the back window to his house will be left unlocked."

"How do you know that?"

"Collingwood's butler is in rather deep at Hell. Dismissing the servants early and unlocking a window will greatly reduce what he owes me. And not force me to speak to his employer," he added with a wink.

Harry thought over Simon's plan and finally nodded his agreement. Once they reached the mews behind Collingwood's house, they stopped speaking and cautiously made their way down the alley. Harry counted the houses until he came to the fifth, which he was sure was Collingwood's home. They ducked into the shadows as a stableboy walked back from the house to the stables.

"Are you certain the window will be unlocked?"

"Yes," Simon whispered back.

Simon waved Harry closer as they crossed the small terrace to the back windows. He tried the first window to no avail.

Harry lifted the next window, and it slid upward with only a slight stickiness. Relief that at least one part of their plan had been successful. "Come along."

"Where is his study?" Simon whispered.

Harry stopped in the middle of the receiving salon and glanced over at his brother in the dim light of a half moon. "I thought you knew!"

His brother leveled him a quick grin. "Not one clue. Do you think he might keep any papers in here?"

"Not likely. We must find Collingwood's desk."

"Your study is the front of the house," Simon commented, peering into the corridor.

"I thought you said the servants were in bed early."

Simon grinned back at him. "The butler is a gambler. Never trust a gambler."

Harry shook his head but followed his brother into a small room with books and a large cherry desk. The only light in the room was from the embers glowing in the fireplace. He lit one candle on the desk to help him read a note if he found one. Large bookshelves lined one wall. Simon went to the shelves and searched while Harry checked the top of the desk.

Finding nothing but some correspondence from his estate steward, he reached for a drawer pull. The middle drawer of the desk opened but yielded nothing that would help. The side drawers were locked.

"Please tell me you know how to pick a lock," Harry whispered.

"Let me," Simon said quietly. He expertly picked the lock and opened the top drawer. Shuffling through papers, he shook his head. "Nothing here."

"Try the other drawer."

Simon worked his magic on the drawer and opened it slowly. After scanning one letter, he exhaled slowly.

"What?" Harry asked as apprehension trickled down his back. Seeing two letters in Simon's hand, he grabbed them. Harry felt frozen in place, unable to believe what he read.

"Is it as I fear?" Simon asked.

"No. Far worse."

Chapter 25

It was nearly midnight, and Harry hadn't returned to the ball. Louisa tried to focus on finding Collingwood, but her mind returned to Harry. Where had he been going with his brother? It made no sense. They both had dressed for the masked ball. Unless Mr. Kingsley had received word that Charlotte had taken ill. It seemed the only logical conclusion.

"Over there, talking with Cinderella," Emma said. "I think Cinderella is Mary Gardiner. Collingwood must be the man dressed as King Henry."

"You'd best watch yourself. He might try to lop off your head, Anne."

"Ha, ha," Emma replied.

"They are about to dance," Louisa said, frustrated by the entire night. "I do believe Bolton is looking for you. He does know it's supposed to be a masked ball, does he not?"

Emma sighed and gave him a little wave. "He refuses to come to a ball in disguise."

Lord Bolton found his fiancée and escorted Emma to the dance floor. Louisa stood against a pillar and watched the rest of the room. She supposed she must become accustomed to being a wallflower.

"Dance with me."

A familiar male voice forced her to look up. Hoping for Harry but finding Ainsley dressed as Robin Hood, she replied, "I'm not dancing tonight."

"Yes, you are," he replied with a smile. "Now. With me."

"How did you know it was me?" she asked.

"When Bolton danced with Anne Boleyn, it was perfectly obvious you were Guinevere."

"Isolde."

He shrugged and held out his arm to lead her to the dance floor. They joined in with the other dancers as the waltz began.

"Why are you dancing with me?" she asked. "I heard you recently came into five thousand."

Dimples creased his cheeks. "I would never accept a bribe from a friend. Even if he has everything wrong about you and me."

"So why the dance?"

"I would like you to go to the back of the gardens when this dance is over."

Back of the gardens? "Why?"

"I need to speak with you alone and must not be seen or overheard." He leaned in closer. "It's about Harry."

"What is it?" Worry line her voice. Did something happen to him? She wanted this waltz over immediately.

"After the dance. Now smile up at me like you and I are courting."

"But we are not."

"If circumstances had been slightly different, we might," he commented with an arched brow.

As the dance progressed, Louisa scanned the room for Harry. This set was taking far too long. "Can you not give me a hint of what you need to tell me?"

He'd moved them toward the terrace doors and then off the dance floor. "Go now, while people are watching the dancers. I will join you in a few minutes."

Louisa nodded and slipped out of the room and down the stairs. Torches lit the gardens, lending just enough light to see how many people were outside. Several people milled about, waiting for others or just getting a breath of air. The muffled sound of music filled the night. Finding a small bench in the rear of the gardens, she waited for Ainsley.

"Miss Drake, I need you to come with me and not ask any questions."

She glanced up to see Simon Kingsley with his hand outstretched. "Why?"

"That is a question, my dear. Just trust me."

"Trust the King of Hell? Oh, why not." She took his hand, and they escaped from the gardens to the mews. A plain black carriage awaited them. "Where are we going?"

"Not to worry."

"That wasn't an answer."

He smiled over at her. "I realize that, but I did say no questions."

He assisted her into the carriage and closed the door. She was alone in the carriage. "Kingsley!"

"Trust me…"

His voice faded as the horses walked down the alleyway. This was dreadful. Her sister and mother had no idea she had even left the ball. They would be worried sick! She wasn't confident where she was going.

But with Simon, and she suspected Ainsley, involved it must be to Harry's home.

She tapped her fingers on the seat until they finally arrived at the large, brick town home in Grosvenor Square. Twice the size of the other homes on the street, the house exuded ducal ownership. What was all the subterfuge about tonight? When the door to the carriage opened, she expected to see the driver, or even Jenkins standing there ready to assist her.

"I am very glad you came tonight," Harry said softly, extending his arm to her.

"Yes, well, your brother did not give me much choice in the matter," she retorted, taking his arm.

"I did try to call on you, but you were not at home."

She shrugged. "Did you expect a warm welcome?"

He released a low laugh as they walked inside. "Hardly."

"Good evening, Jenkins," she said with a nod.

The old butler gave her a nod. "Good evening, Miss Drake."

"I do hope you will note that I was invited tonight, Jenkins." She gave the butler a wink.

"Duly noted, Miss Drake."

Harry led her to the family salon on the first floor. Smaller and much more welcoming than the larger receiving room, she'd never been in here before now. Blue damask chairs sat near the fireplace for conversation while two cream sofas were meant for larger groups. He brought her to the chairs.

The safe option. Here they would be close but still separated by the short distance between the chairs. Louisa sat as a shiver raced across her body. Not an overly cool night, she wondered what brought about the nervous energy in her. She glanced at the table in front of them. He'd thought of everything. The table was laden with tea, brandy, cakes, biscuits, a variety of cheese, bread, and meats.

"What is this about, Harry?"

Harry followed her line of vision. "I assumed supper hadn't been called for yet, and you might be hungry."

He did know her too well, she thought. She hadn't eaten since breakfast.

"Thank you," she said, reaching for some bread and cheese. "But I doubt you dragged me out of the ball just to feed me."

He poured a brandy and looked over at her. She nodded. He handed her the snifter and poured one for himself.

"I wanted to apologize and clear the air for that mess at Worth. I shouldn't have become so defensive."

"Guilt is an ugly emotion," she whispered.

"Yes, I suppose you are right." He sipped his brandy. "I owe you an apology for Ainsley, too. It was bad form to try to buy off my friend. My only excuse is I was…"

"Was what?" she pressed when his voice trailed off.

"Bedeviled with jealousy," he admitted slowly. "I had never felt such hot rage until I saw you dance with him. And you allowed him to call on you."

Louisa pressed her lips together. She was not blameless in this quarrel. "Apology accepted on one condition."

"Oh?" He tilted his head and stared at her with a slight smile.

"Yes. You must accept my apology too." Louisa stared down at her brandy, unable to meet his eyes. "I'm sorry, Harry. I shouldn't have made accusations against you. I was angry about the note. Confused by what had happened the previous night. Unsure of your feelings for me and—"

Suddenly drawn up into his arms, he kissed senselessly, and she kissed him back, unable to finish her confession. When he slowly pulled away, he stared down at her. His gray eyes sparkling with, dare she think it, love?

"That was my fault, Louisa. Instead of focusing on the beautiful woman in my bed and professing my love to her, I admitted my guilt over my late wife."

Her heart swelled. "You love me?"

He smiled fully. "I have loved you since that first night on the terrace at the Marchtons' ball. Why do you think I'd stopped the foolish ways of my youth? I wanted to prove to you that I could be a better person."

She reached out and caressed his cheek. "I didn't love you then," she admitted. "I only wanted your friendship. When you returned from India, I noticed that you had changed, but it was too late. After your wife died, I wanted to comfort you…"

"But I never returned your letters," he finished.

Nodding, she continued, "I had thought to re-establish our friendship. When I arrived at Northwood Park, I realized you were not the same man I had known. And for some reason, I was attracted to the dark, cold man I'd found up north. After reuniting with you, I never wanted to find you a wife. I tried to match you with ladies I thought you would never wish to marry. I started chasing you so that you would notice me. But I'm a dreadful at flirting."

"Louisa," he said softly. "I always notice you."

Another thought flittered through her brain. No! She prayed she was wrong, but Harry was a man of honor. "It's after midnight. You are officially thirty. Is this all because of that damned deal we made? I would never hold you to it."

Harry shook his head. "That damned deal, as you call it, is what brought you to me in the dead of winter. It forced me to return to London. It was the pact that brought us back together. While it had nothing to do with tonight, I want you to hold me to our deal for the rest of our lives."

"Are you certain?"

He kissed her tenderly with a hint of the passion under the surface. "I love you, Louisa Drake. Deal or not. Will you be my duchess?"

"Emma," she whispered as her heart ached. "Lady Bolton may insist her son reject Emma. I cannot marry you if that might happen that to her. She loves him."

"Bolton is a fool if he tosses her over due to our marriage. The

Drakes will now be associated with the Duke of Worthington. A most prestigious family, even if there was at least one mad duke."

Louisa worried her lower lip. "She told me he loves her and would never reject her. But I'm not so certain."

"Then she will find a better man. We can make sure of that."

She knew Bolton wasn't the best man for Emma but had not pressed the issue. Emma loved the viscount and had assured Louisa numerous times that Bolton would never reject her. But Harry was right. If something happened, they could ensure she had a proper dowry and found a gentleman.

"Yes."

"Yes?" he asked.

"I will marry you." Louisa wrapped her arms around his neck. "I love you, Harry."

"Good because I'm taking you to my bed." He picked her up and carried her down the hall. "Goodnight, Jenkins."

"Goodnight, Your Grace, Miss Drake," the butler replied stiffly.

Louisa pressed her face into his chest with a giggle. "I believe we may have scandalized Jenkins."

"It won't be the last time that happens."

Spent, Harry pulled her close in the large bed and kissed her forehead. "You know," he whispered in her ear. "We could run off to Gretna Green and elope."

She slapped his chest lightly. "We will have enough scandal with marrying each other. A church or home wedding would be better. Just not a large wedding, if you please. I understand you are a duke and might wish to have a formal wedding...just not too many people."

Part of him wanted this elopement more than he wished to admit. He lifted his head and stared down at her. Marrying her now would only be easier on him. Her mother and sister would have no ability to talk Louisa out of marriage. "I suppose we do not need any additional gossip."

"Besides, your daughter deserves to see her father married," she reminded him.

"You are right," he admitted. "We shall have to face the gossip and objections together."

She smiled. "We can always retire to Northwood Park until the gossip fades from us to someone else. Perhaps Emma will reject Bolton and cause a scandal. Tessa had her turn. It's our turn now."

Harry laughed. "I highly doubt Miss Emma will ever have more than a slight bit of gossip attached to her name. Any man with half a brain will see that she would make a beautiful wife."

"True, but I want more than that for her."

"Give her time. She's young still."

"Bolton is never going to be the right man for her."

Staring into her eyes, he knew he had to tell her the truth. God, he hated causing her more pain.

"What is wrong, Harry?"

"Simon and I discovered who paid Collingwood."

"Who?"

He wanted to look away, but instead, he said it quickly as if that would lessen her pain. "Your mother."

Her mouth gaped as she sat up and stared down at him. "Mamma?"

He nodded. "We broke into Collingwood's study and found two letters detailing the offer of five thousand pounds to marry you."

"Five thousand?" Louisa's shoulders relaxed as she smiled at him. "It has to be a forgery, Harry. Mamma doesn't have that kind of money. She lives off what Tessa and Lord Hammond give her."

Harry eased off the bed and pulled his waistcoat off the floor where she'd tossed it. After handing the letters to her, he waited. Sitting naked on his bed with her hair down to her shoulders, she looked incredibly vulnerable as she stared at the handwriting on the letter.

"It's her handwriting," she muttered.

He waited for her to come to terms with the idea that her mother had attempted to bribe a man to take Louisa off her hands. Louisa covered her mouth with her hand as she read. Her lashes fluttered as if to keep the tears at bay. One lone tear fell down her cheek followed quickly by another. Returning to the bed, he brought her into his arms.

"Did you read the one from two days ago?" she whispered in an aching tone. Without waiting for an answer, she continued, "She was arranging my abduction by Collingwood to Gretna Green. She said she would invent a story that I went to visit Collingwood and his mother at his estate and that after a week we two decided to marry by special license. All Collingwood would need to do was take me back to Hertfordshire after marrying him at Gretna to make the story plausible. Oh my God, she even gave him the name of a man who would marry us without my permission!"

Tears tracked down her cheek to his chest as he held her. "Shh, darling. It's over now. You and I will marry, and she will never be able to hurt you again."

She nodded slowly. "Damn her, Harry. I used to blame everything that happened on my father. Now, I don't know what to think."

He wanted to take her pain away. See her smile. "Perhaps you should talk to your father. Write to him."

"I need to confront her." She wiped away her tears and looked up at him with a fire in her blue eyes. "I want her to understand that I know and will use it against her if she tries to interfere with our marriage."

Smiling, he reached out and caressed her cheek. "You are my little fighter."

"Tomorrow, we will see her together. I will let her know that we are marrying and about the letters." She moved back into his arms. "But right now, I want to be with the man I love."

Chapter 26

The next day, they pulled up to her mother's house. Louisa's hand trembled as she reached for Harry's assistance disembarking the carriage. She wondered if she could have faced this without him by her side. For the past seven years, she'd blamed her father for what had happened, until now.

"Come along. After we speak to your mother, I must get a special license."

"Very well." Louisa and Harry climbed the steps together.

Davis opened the door with a look of shock. "Miss Drake, you have returned...and with His Grace."

"Where is my mother?"

"In the salon with Mrs. Raynerson and Miss Emma."

Louisa blew out a breath. She'd hoped she would be able to speak to Mamma alone. She opened the door to the salon and plastered a smile on her face.

"I'm home."

Her mother rose slowly from her chair. "Louisa, where have you been? Emma said you went to Tessa's house last night, which I believed until Tessa arrived wishing to speak with you."

Louisa glanced over at Tessa who gave her a slight shrug as if to say, *you should have told me*. Time for the truth and the dressing-down she would receive.

"I was with Harry."

Tessa, Emma, and her mother finally noticed him standing behind her. "Your Grace," all three said with a curtsy.

"Good morning, Mrs. Drake, Mrs. Raynerson, and Miss Emma," he said flatly.

Mamma recovered first. "What do you mean you were with the duke?"

Louisa tilted her head and leveled her mother a smug smile. "I am certain you know exactly what I mean, Mamma."

Her mother gasped. Tessa smiled. Emma giggled.

Mamma's cheeks flushed. "That is most dreadful, Louisa! But I'm certain we can keep the talk to a minimum once you marry Collingwood."

"Mamma!" Louisa had no idea how she could feel shocked after all she'd learned, but the thought that her mother would still expect her to marry Collingwood was beyond the pale. "I'm afraid that is impossible now."

"You didn't elope with the duke? You couldn't have!"

Louisa laughed lightly. "No, we haven't wed…yet."

"Yet?" Tessa asked with an encouraging smile.

"Yes." Louisa pulled a piece of paper from her reticule and smiled over at Harry. "You see, today is the duke's thirtieth birthday. And seven years ago, we made a deal stating if I reached the age of twenty-five and him thirty, and we were both unmarried, we would wed each other."

Louisa let out an exaggerated sigh. "If I don't marry him, he will tell the gossipmongers that I refused to marry him. Imagine the gossip if it was known that I had rejected a viscount, a gentleman, and now a duke. Poor Emma would never be able to marry."

Tessa's lips twitched as she attempted to hold back inevitable laughter.

"Madam, I am arranging for a special license this afternoon,"

CHRISTIE KELLEY

Harry said to her mother. "We will marry in a fortnight to give your daughter time to have a gown made fitting a duchess."

Her mother's eyes widened and then fluttered as if she might faint. She sank back into a chair.

Emma broke the tension by saying, "Oh Louisa, I am so happy for you."

"You won't be when your engagement is broken because of this scandal." Her mother had found her voice again. Her mother picked up a fan and waved it in front of her face. "This is too much, Louisa. Look where your impulsiveness has gotten you now!"

"She landed a duke, Madam," Harry said bluntly. "Most mothers would be quite proud of that fact. Being that you wanted nothing more for your daughters than money and a title, I should think you would be quite pleased."

"I have never been so insulted in my own home. I must ask you to leave now."

Louisa smiled over at Harry with a wink. "He can leave, but it will not stop the marriage, Mamma."

He reached over and brought her hand to his lips. "I will call on you tomorrow. Let me know if you are staying with your sister." He turned and bowed to Tessa and her mother. "Good day, ladies."

Louisa watched him leave until the door closed behind him. She knew the real objections would start now. But her focus turned toward her oldest sister.

"Tessa, are you all right with this? I know any gossip will involve your name more than anyone else."

"I am happy for you, Louisa." Tessa smiled over at her. "I married those men to give you and Emma a chance to marry for love. I glad you found it."

"Think of what his father did," Mamma said in a low tone. "He ruined this family."

"And what did you do, Mamma? I know all about it, though I doubt you wish to wash your dirty linen in front of Tessa and Emma."

Tessa and Emma shared a shocked look.

"I only ever did what was best for my daughters," she retorted.

"Oh? Collingwood was the best for me?" Louisa shook her head slowly. "You were so certain your scheme would work."

Her mother straightened her spine. "Perhaps it's best if you both leave so Louisa and I may speak in private."

Tessa glanced between Louisa and Mamma and finally said, "As you wish. Louisa, you are more than welcome to stay with me should you prefer it."

Louisa nodded. "Thank you. I will have Mary pack my bags."

As soon as her sisters departed, her mother asked, "Just what is it you believe I have done, Louisa?"

Louisa sat in the chair across from her and then crossed her arms over her chest. "Where did you come up with the five thousand, Mamma?"

Her mother blanched before replying, "Five thousand? What are you talking about? Did Worthington put some mad idea into your head?"

"Why would you think Harry would say something? Collingwood courted me for weeks. Perhaps he mentioned something in passing."

"Collingwood? That fool. He needed the mon…"

"I believe the word is money, Mamma. Yes, Collingwood needed the five thousand that you promised him. Although, I am not sure how he assumed you would come about that amount of money." Louisa watched her mother's face contort as if trying to determine an excuse or lie.

"What are you accusing me of, Louisa?" Her mother finally demanded.

"I would just like to hear the truth from you. Why would you suggest Collingwood abduct me in the middle of Hyde Park, thereby ruining my reputation and putting Emma's marriage to Bolton at risk?"

Her mother rose and glared down at her. "If the fool had kept his mouth shut, everything would have been fine."

Louisa stood, allowing her to glare down at her mother. "Why, Mamma?"

"Emma loves Bolton. I could tell you were getting too close to Worthington. Lady Bolton would never allow our name to be associated with his again. I was trying to protect you and Emma."

"Protect me?" Louisa shouted. "Protect me from a man who loves me. A man who I love. I will marry Harry, Mamma."

"Louisa, think about what this will do to your sisters. Poor Emma might be rejected by a viscount. That will ruin her."

"Mamma, my marrying a duke will not ruin Emma's chances with Bolton or any other man. I fear word getting out that you planned your daughter's abduction, will have a far bigger impact on Emma's reputation."

"No one would believe you," she said with a hint of bravado.

Louisa pulled out the letters from her reticule. "No? I do believe most people will believe your letters."

"Please don't say a word," she whispered, looking suddenly vulnerable.

Louisa shook her head as a devious thought came to mind. "It is not me you have to worry about. It's Collingwood. I'd suggest you pay him some, if not all, of the money you promised him to keep him quiet."

"Hammond will be furious with me," Mamma mumbled, twisting her handkerchief.

Louisa's assumption about Hammond being involved with the

money was correct. "Yes, I expect he will. And I will be staying with Tessa until the wedding."

Harry faced his own grueling interrogation when he arrived home. After spending some time with Charlotte, Daphne finally arranged to catch him alone.

"Absolutely not, Harry."

"What now, Daphne?"

She sank into the chair across from his desk in the study. "Do you think I haven't heard the rumors that Miss Drake was here last night and that you intend to marry her?"

"It's not a rumor."

"What do you mean?" A scowl darkened her face.

"I have every intention of marrying Miss Drake. I have a special license already."

Daphne's mouth gaped. "How could you possibly have arranged that so quickly?"

Harry laughed. "I'm a duke. The archbishop was rather pleased to hear I would be marrying again."

"I cannot bear that family, Harry. Her mother wanted nothing but to better themselves at our expense. At least the eldest Drake sister didn't marry Father. But I won't stand for that middle sister to marry you just to better their social position. If not for them, our father would still be alive. For all we know, Tessa urged him to get the poison for her husbands so she could marry Father."

"Daphne, I know you loved our father. As did I. But you forget, he also murdered my wife in this very house. He was mad. Tessa had nothing to do with the murders and neither did Louisa."

"But—"

"Mrs. Drake did not want Louisa to marry me."

"What? Why?"

"Because she was more concerned with Emma marrying Bolton than Louisa's happiness." He explained what they knew about her mother's schemes to keep them apart.

"But why would you want to marry her?"

"Daphne, I love her." Harry poured two brandies and handed one to his sister. "I have loved her for years. I raced off to India to give her time to realize that she loved me. Instead, I married a woman I didn't truly love. At least not like I love Louisa."

"You went to India to get away from her?"

"Yes. I never told a soul that. I loved her from almost the first time we met." Harry sipped his brandy and let it warm his belly. He finally told her the entire story of their relationship. "I don't suppose you will ever understand, but I cannot live without her any longer. I won't live without her."

Daphne went silent and sipped her brandy. "I might understand more than you think. When I was nineteen, I met Lord Shipley. He was a rogue, to say the least, but the moment I saw him, I fell in love. We spoke of marriage but then..."

Harry vaguely remembered even though he'd been at Eton at the time. Shipley's brother had been there when the accident happened to make Tom the new earl. "The carriage accident."

Daphne nodded. "He was on his way to speak to his grandmother. He wanted her approval before speaking with Father. After that, I didn't care who I married so I accepted Radley." She looked over at him. "Please do not think ill of Radley. I have come to love him, perhaps not as strongly as Shipley, but we have a good marriage. I finally told him about Shipley. So, I do understand."

"But can you accept her?"

"For you, I suppose I must try. At least you know your daughter adores her." Daphne raised her glass. "Congratulations, Harry. Have you told Charlotte yet?"

"Told me what, Aunt Radley?" a small voice sounded from the threshold.

"What are you about, Charlotte?" Harry asked with a smile.

"Nurse brought me down to say goodnight. What are you going to tell me?" She scrambled up on Harry's lap.

"I am getting married. You will have a new mother."

Her eyes widened. "Who, Papa? Is it Miss Drake? Please say it is her!"

He kissed her forehead. "It is," he whispered in her ear.

Charlotte clapped her hands and bounced on his leg. "Yay!"

"Would you like to pay a call on Miss Drake with me tomorrow?"

"Yes!"

"Then off to bed, poppet. I love you." He kissed her cheek.

"I love you too." She gave him a wet kiss to the cheek. "Goodnight, Papa." She climbed off his lap. "Goodnight, Aunt Radley."

"Goodnight, dear," Daphne said, rubbing her slightly rounded belly. "I do so hope this is a girl."

"Me too, Daphne." And he hoped Louisa might already be with child. He wanted brothers and sisters for Charlotte. A large family filled with love for Louisa.

The fortnight passed in a blur to Louisa. She awoke on Friday praying nothing would go wrong today. She'd barely seen Harry the past ten days as Tessa had kept her busy with fittings for the gown and other assorted clothes she would need when married. Even though only family had been invited, Tessa insisted a new dress was required to marry a duke. Her stomach roiled, nervous with the thought of becoming a duchess.

Yesterday had been a trying day. Bolton broke off the engagement, stating Louisa's transgressions had tarnished Emma's reputation. Poor Emma had been heartbroken by his disloyalty. As much as Mamma thought they should sue Bolton for breach, Raynerson and Tessa talked her out of it, hinting it would only keep the family name embroiled in scandal even longer. Only Louisa knew her mother's desire to sue Bolton had to do with the money to pay Collingwood.

She wanted this wedding over, so she could start her new life. She and Harry had agreed only family would be invited to the wedding and after they would have a small family breakfast before departing for Worth Hall. After a fortnight there, given Harry's estate business was complete, they would return for the rest of the Season.

"Louisa, are you awake?" Emma asked from the hall.

"Yes, come in."

Emma's usual enthusiasm had waned with her jilting. "I came over early to help you dress."

"I would love that." Louisa tossed off the coverlet. She walked over to the ice blue silk the dressmaker completed in only a few days once she heard it was to be worn by a duchess. It was a simple design with no flounce or ribbons. Tessa had called it elegant enough for a duchess.

Emma remained relatively quiet as she helped Louisa dress into her underclothes. "I do wish I could fix your hair, but it's always so difficult."

"Emma, are you certain you still want us to marry?"

"Yes, I do. This has opened my eyes to just how dominated Bolton is by his mother. I could never marry him at this point."

"I shall do everything in my power to find you a good man," Louisa stated firmly.

A light rap on the door was followed by Tessa's announcement, "Louisa, there is a maid here who says Worthington sent her to do your hair. It's all very odd to me."

"I am here, miss. If Mrs. Raynerson would allow me inside your bedchamber," a voice called from the hall.

"Lily?"

"Yes, miss, that's me." She pushed passed Tessa with a scowl. "Go along then, Mrs. Raynerson. I shall have Miss Drake all set in no time."

"Louisa?" Tessa asked, staring at Lily with a confused look on her face.

"Lily assisted me when I was at Northwood Park." Louisa smiled over at the young woman. "She is the only person who has ever been able to get my hair to stay in place."

"All ladies out of the room so I can get her hair dressed." Lily waved Emma and Tessa out the door. "Phew, now show me your gown."

Louisa rose and then held up the gown to her body, allowing Lily to determine the best style for her hair. The brash maid spent the next hour arranging Louisa's hair to perfection and guaranteed it would stay put until the duke removed her hairpins tonight. Once her hair was done, Lily assisted her in the gown.

She heard voices downstairs and assumed a few people might have arrived early. But as her mother's loud voice came closer, Louisa suspected there was a problem already.

"You cannot go in there! You shouldn't even be here!" Mamma shouted.

"I will see my daughter on her wedding day," a low voice grumbled.

"Oh, no!" Louisa exclaimed as her father strode into the room, as best he could with a slight limp. "What are you doing here?"

Her father stopped and stared at her for a long moment. "Oh my, Louisa, whoever called you the plainest of the Drake sisters must have been blind."

He walked forward and attempted to take her hand in his, but she pulled it away. He acknowledged the slight with a nod. "I cannot believe you hooked a duke."

"Hooked a duke?" she repeated in disbelief. When Tessa finally admitted that their father was alive two years ago, she'd said he hadn't wanted to go along with Mamma's plan for Tessa to have a Season but eventually succumbed to her pressure. "Papa, I thought you were different. I thought you didn't care about such things."

"What father wouldn't want to see his daughter become a duchess?" He sank into a chair by the fire and held out his hands as if chilled by the weather.

Seeing his gnarled aged hands, Louisa forced herself to sit and hear his side of the story. He deserved that much. "What happened, Papa?"

He stared at the fire. "You know what a stubborn woman your mother is when she gets an idea in her head."

Louisa knew all too well. "Yes, but you are her husband and should have taken control."

A loud snort sounded from the threshold. "Because that would work so well with you."

Louisa and her father rose to face Harry.

"Your Grace, this is my father, Mr. Drake."

"Your Grace," her father said with a bow.

"It is a pleasure to meet you, Mr. Drake. Thank you for giving me your consent to marry your daughter."

"Of course."

"Wait," Louisa said, glancing between then both. "When could you possibly have given your approval?"

"His Grace sent an express explaining the situation but still desiring my approval, which I gave gladly."

Harry had still felt the need to get approval even though no father would deny a duke his daughter's hand. It touched her heart that he wanted to be proper when their relationship had never followed the conventions of Society.

"Would you like me to leave so you can continue your conversation?" Harry asked.

"You might as well stay. If not, I will only tell you what was said tonight." Louisa returned to her seat while Harry sat on the end of the bed.

Her father cleared his throat and continued, "As I was saying your mother is a bit headstrong. She convinced me that one Season for Tessa would end in an advantageous marriage, thereby providing you and Emma the same chance. While your mother had her Season at seventeen, I had no thought to the costs involved. Suddenly the bills started to come in for the lease, and the new clothing for everyone, including you and Emma since you might be invited to some small gatherings."

"Oh, Papa," Louisa cried. "You should have stopped it."

"I couldn't," he replied, staring into the fireplace. "Before the Season even began, I had creditors asking for their money. Now, I realize that most people ignore the bills until the marriage occurs, but I had no knowledge of this world."

"Ignoring bills is the norm for the quality," Harry commented with a shake of his head.

"True, but I wasn't one of them," her father added. "They believed I should pay immediately. I didn't know what to do, so I started taking money from the bank." He hung his head low. "I knew it was wrong but felt my life was out of control."

Louisa glanced over at Harry, who looked away. "I wish I had known."

"When they arrested me, your mother and sister thought it best to tell you and Emma that I had died. Your mother went to her uncle's home, and you know the rest of the story."

The only thing that had saved him from the noose had been Tessa swift marriage to Langley, and her payments to the bank. Louisa's eyes welled with tears. "I am dreadfully sorry for what happened, Papa."

"I know, sweetling. But no tears. It is your wedding day, and you should be happy."

Louisa looked at Harry, who was smiling at her. "I am. I'm marrying my dearest friend who I love more than I ever thought possible."

"Will you let me give you away?" her father asked softly. "I never had the chance with Tessa, but I would be honored to give you to such a gentleman."

She nodded. "I understand, but please give me a few minutes to think things over."

"Of course." Her father rose slowly from his chair. "I will wait downstairs and try my best not to torment your mother."

Harry bowed to her and started to leave with her father.

"Har—Your Grace, please stay for a moment."

He glanced at her father, who only shrugged. "Of course, Miss Drake."

Her father closed the door. "Five minutes," he said from the hall.

Louisa smiled at Harry. "I do believe we are being watched by my dead father." She walked into his arms and pressed her cheek to his chest. "I have missed you the past few days."

"I've missed you too." He pressed a kiss on her head. "You look beautiful, love. Like a duchess."

"Oh, I am going to be a dreadful duchess," she said with a shake of her head. "Mother tells everyone she is a widow of a London banker, yet, my dead father is most definitely alive. My sister is on husband number four after the deaths of the first three due to your father, who committed suicide. My youngest sister was just jilted by a viscount." She looked up at him with a watery smile. "Are you certain this is a good idea?"

Louisa suddenly clutched her stomach and ran to the basin expelling the tea and toast she'd eaten earlier.

Harry approached her silently and poured a glass of water.

She took a few slow sips, praying she could manage to keep it down.

He then pulled her up against him, caressing her cheek. "I do believe that may be an indication that yes, we must do this no matter our own insecurities."

"No," she said, slowly comprehending what he meant. "It cannot be. I am only a few days late. It is nerves."

"Perhaps, but I am not willing to take that chance." He turned her back in his arms and walked her to a chair. "Besides, I don't care about any of those reasons you gave me. The only thing that matters is you will be my wife, my love, and at some point, the mother of my children. I love you, Louisa. And as long as we love each other, the rest will work out."

"You must have the most dreadful luck to be stuck with the plain Drake sister," she said with a smile. "But this sister loves you more than she ever thought possible."

"What are you going to do about your father?" he asked in a hesitant tone.

"I wish I knew." She sighed. "I suppose it wouldn't hurt too much to let him give me away. I'd told Raynerson that he could give me away, but I'm sure he will understand. Everyone here is family. Oh my, what about your sister?"

"She will find out at some point. There's no better day than today."

"Assuming she doesn't make a scene during the ceremony."

"She would never set out to purposely ruin someone. And she will come to love you, Louisa."

"If you say so," she muttered unconvinced that his sister would ever be anything but cordial to her. And only because of Harry.

"We have used our allotted five minutes. Shall we go get married?"

"Only if you're certain."

"Louisa, what else can go wrong?"

Louisa shook her head. "How could you say that after everything that has happened?"

He smiled at her. "There is nothing else. Because even if something happens, we have each other and will get through it...for the rest of our lives."

Epilogue

Christmas 1820

Emma sat in the salon of Northwood Park after arriving home from church. Being Harry and Louisa's first Christmas, and she heavy with child, it had been decided that the family would spend it at Northwood Park. Since the wedding and her jilting by Bolton, Emma's life had been anything but pleasant. Even the few invitations to balls had only been to appease the duke or his sister.

Emma's life was over. She might as well don a spinster cap and be done with it.

But at least her sisters were happy. Much to Louisa's surprise, she was with child during her wedding ceremony. Unfortunately, just like Tessa, Louisa spent the first three months with dreadful morning sickness. Hopefully, she would have an easy delivery as Tessa had.

"Emma, would you hold Jane?" Tessa asked as she walked into the room, holding her six-month-old daughter.

"I will!" Charlotte shouted. "I'm almost five now, Aunt Raynerson!"

Tessa laughed. "Let Emma hold her first. You will get a lot of practice in a few weeks."

"But I love babies, Aunt Raynerson."

Tessa placed her daughter in Emma's arms. "I know you do, Charlotte. And you are very good with Jane, too. But let your Aunt

Emma hold her first."

"Yes, ma'am."

Emma looked down at Jane and smiled at her. She pressed her lips together to keep anyone from seeing her lip tremble. Covertly, Emma wiped a tear away. At this point, she knew she was bound for spinsterhood with her reputation and that of her family now on all the gossipmongers' tongues.

Louisa had tried to introduce her to a few fine gentlemen during the Season as she'd promised. Perhaps it had been too soon after Bolton's betrayal because not one suited Emma. Most of Society ignored her. A woman rejected by a gentleman of high standing was considered damaged goods.

But she had already decided her New Year's resolution. If she were bound to have this reputation after being jilted by Bolton, she was going to deserve it. She was tired of always being the "good" sister. After her adventures with Louisa, it was time Emma had a few escapades of her own.

"Happy Christmas," a deep voice sounded from the hall. Simon Kingsley entered the room with an armful of presents for everyone.

Her stomach clenched with the sight of the vile man. Emma still couldn't abide him. She would never forget how she walked into his office to see him with that woman on his lap.

"Happy Christmas, Miss Drake," he said as he walked by her with a smile.

"Happy Christmas, Mr. Kingsley." She promptly decided to ignore him for the rest of the day. Watching how happy her sisters were with their husbands was becoming most difficult, indeed.

A stab of envy struck her. She'd been the perfect sister. The one everyone said would end up as a viscountess or higher. She'd never done anything to damage her or her family's reputation, and what did that get her? Thrown over by a viscount and now her family's reputation was in question because of it.

Louisa had gone unescorted to at least two of Harry's homes. And yet, Louisa not only married a duke, but they had fallen madly in love with each other.

Maybe she should try a scandal. Or maybe a few. Odds were, she wouldn't fall in love, but perhaps she might have a little well-needed fun in her life.

Ruination.

That was what she needed. And as soon as the Season started, she had every intention of ruining herself for good.

Award winning author Christie Kelley writes Regency set historical romances from her home in Maryland. When not writing, she is usually in the garden, fixing something around the house and surrounded by her two sons and two Siberian cats.

Christie loves to hear from her readers.

Please visit her at:
www.christiekelley.com
www.facebook.com/ChristieKelleyAuthor/
www.twitter.com/christiekelley
https://allauthor.com/author/christiekelley/